WHITE WARRIOR

"Hoka hey!" yelled Smith. The warriors were using mostly spears, axes, and bow and arrows to save ammunition. When they neared the soldiers, Smith held his fire. The cavalry line fell back, confused and disorderly. The young men yelled and shot and dashed forward and back and forward and back again.

The soldiers ran, and the ones at the rear were digging rifle pits. Behind Smith, Calling Eagle made a little trill.

Smith stood up and faced the retreating soldiers. He still felt a little self-conscious about his damned pants. He shook his rifle in the air and at the top of his lungs roared, *"Hoka hey!* You bastards!" He threw an arm around his grandmother and hugged her. He thought, Look at those bastards run.

The Powder River

A NOVEL IN THE RIVERS WEST SERIES

By Winfred Blevins

BANTAM BOOKS

NEW YORK • TORONTO • LONDON • SYDNEY • AUCKLAND

THE POWDER RIVER

A Bantam Book / June 1990

ISBN 0-553-28583-1

Published simultaneously in the United States and Canada

Bantam Books are published by Bantam Books, a division of Bantam Doubleday Dell
Publishing Group, Inc. Its trademark, consisting of the words "Bantam Books" and
the portrayal of a rooster, is Registered in U.S. Patent and Trademark Office and in
other countries. Marca Registrada. Bantam Books, 666 Fifth Avenue, New York,
New York 10103.

PRINTED IN THE UNITED STATES OF AMERICA

OPM   0 9 8 7 6 5 4 3 2 1

This book is for Martha Stearn, as they all are

acknowledgments: My valued guides to the intriguing world of the Cheyenne people and the Plains Indians generally are Murphy Fox of Helena, Montana, and the Honorable Clyde M. Hall of the Shoshone-Bannock Tribe, Fort Hall, Idaho. My deepest gratitude to them both. A salute as well to Gustav Mahler, whose First Symphony was my constant companion as I wrote this book.

storyteller: I'm going to tell a story.
audience: Right!
storyteller: It's a lie.
audience: Right!
storyteller: But not everything in it is false.
audience: Right!
                    —*ritual opening to Sudanese stories*

storyteller: Under the earth I go.
                 On the oak leaf I stand.
                 I ride on the filly
                 That never was foaled,
                 And I carry the dead in my hand.
                    —*ritual opening to Celtic stories*

storyteller: Once upon a time . . .
                    —*ritual opening to American stories*

The Powder River

≈ PROLOGUE ≈

Elaine held her breath, as instructed, tucked her chin a little, and tried to look radiant. This is silly, she thought. I feel radiant already, so why make it artifice?

The photographer opened the shutter. Dr. and Mrs. Maclean, standing still for too long a moment, rigid, chests sucked up and breath sucked in, recorded their union for posterity. Really, thought Elaine, for Mother and my darned younger sister. Dora had already been married long enough to become a widow. They heard the shutter click shut.

Elaine looked up—far up—at her new husband, who was nearly a foot taller than she, and she was a tall woman. We're probably recording it for our posterity, too, she thought. What she intended to do as soon as she and Adam were alone tended to create posterity, so they said. It would be her first time, but surely not his first time, and she intended to make it memorable. For both of them.

It was foolish and it was reckless, this getting married today. They'd been planning to go away to Kansas City to be married sometime later in the month. But this photographer showed up, an artiste-looking fellow with a goatee, saying he wanted to record Indian life before it went away, and Adam and Elaine decided impulsively to take advantage.

Not that Adam liked having Indians photographed. He said the white people were intent on preserving Indians like plant specimens, oh-so-affectingly dried and dead.

Adam called the Reverend Asa McClintock and his wife in next to the newlyweds. They were the presiding minister and witness, respectively, and were dear friends, and must be part of the wedding pictures.

The artiste made small adjustments in the way they were standing, called for the big breath, asked them to hold it, and again made a record of the nuptials. The photographs were certainly an extravagance. They would take most of the little bit of savings Elaine and Adam had. But Mother and Dora, disappointed to discover via telegram that Elaine was married, would be mollified by the pictures.

Besides, Adam looked so gorgeous. Breathtaking, really. Nearly six-and-a-half feet tall, in the handsome Prince Albert coat in formal black he'd worn when he was graduated from medical school, his dark skin gleaming, and his long, black hair with reddish highlights falling dramatically to his shoulder blades. Just looking at her savage made her a little weak-kneed.

The photographer called for Adam's family to step in for a picture. His grandmother Calling Eagle stood next to him, and his mother Lisette next to Elaine. Elaine put a hand through Lisette's arm. She thought the three of them made a terrific-looking group of women. Even on short notice and in rotten circumstances, they managed some finery for this occasion. Elaine had her borrowed wedding dress. Lisette had found ermine tails to wrap her braids in, and both the Indian women wore dresses ornamented with elk teeth and moccasins covered with quillwork. Lisette was silky and slender, a sexy woman for fifty, and Calling Eagle looked tall and queenly, her braids hanging to her waist. Barbaric splendor.

Elaine's brown hair was even longer, to her bottom. Today she'd let it hang straight, parted in the middle, as teenage girls wore theirs. She was showing off a quarter century of brushing, a hundred strokes a day. She wore a borrowed wedding dress, Lucille McClintock's full-length affair of silk damask the color of jonquils, tucked a little at the waist. She knew very well she looked smashing. Young and virginal, too. Well, she was virginal.

Elaine looked up at Adam, his head there in the ether, and got all weak-kneed again. Elaine! she reprimanded herself with amusement. Cummings women are sensible women, dedicated women, serious women, champions of worthy causes. We do not melt when we gaze upon attractive males of the species.

We thought we didn't until today, she answered herself. He is a prize. How many Cheyenne men have been graduated from medical school? Probably my Adam alone.

She'd really thought she wouldn't get giddy over a good-looking man. At the advanced age of twenty-seven, she'd half accepted the idea of spinsterhood. She'd permitted Dr. Adam Smith Maclean, known to the world informally as Smith, to call on her out of her need for a friend, and as a public statement of racial policy. She hadn't expected to fall in love with him. And the truth was that, though she'd been intrigued by him from the first, and then enchanted, until today she hadn't felt this, well, this "first fine careless rapture!" she quoted to herself.

So go away, Miss Sensible, Miss Serious, it's the giddy girl's day to play. Time enough tomorrow to do something about the rotten conditions the Cheyennes are living in. Time enough then to worry about being a schoolmistress with practically no students. Married to a doctor with practically no patients.

She held her breath and tucked her chin as the photographer instructed.

Adam leaned down, and whispered in her ear. "I love you," he said, eyes gleaming.

She wanted to wrap herself around him shamelessly. "Houghmagandie," she breathed back in his ear, putting a Scots burr on it to tease him. It was his playful word for the deed that created posterity. According to him, it was his father's playful word for it, and a genuine Scottish expression—his father had been a pure Scot. Nothing so tickled Elaine as hearing a giant Cheyenne speak English with a Scots burr.

"I think that ought to do it, folks," called the goateed artiste.

Elaine looked at Mr. Goatee and gazed at Adam up there in the ether and took in her breath firmly and said, "No, one more."

She turned to face Adam and put his hands around her waist. She'd made up her mind that she would do this, even if it was a little . . . outrageous. She put her arms around his neck. If a girl can't be outrageous on her wedding day, when can she? "Now, Adam," she said with mock sternness, "you can't move when we're doing this. Certainly not your hands, but not even your head or even your lips."

His eyes were laughing.

She looked at the photographer. He nodded. She closed her eyes, lifted her face into the sky (ridiculous!), and kissed her brand-new husband full on the lips.

"Hold your breath," called the photographer.

≈ **BOOK ONE** ≈

≈ 1 ≈

Scratch-scratch-scratch!

Elaine flinched, and turned over toward Adam. His face was perfectly relaxed in sleep, and sweet—he hadn't heard a thing. She shook his arm. He didn't move.

Scratch-scratch-scratch!

Dammit. She resented the way he was sleeping anyway. She lay here awake and edgy, flat on her back, to tell God's truth feeling lonely as hell on her wedding night, and in her marriage bed, with the strange smell of sex in her nostrils. With her husband grandly asleep right next to her, oblivious. She had a sore crotch, nipples that her nightdress irritated, jumpy nerves, and you name it, and he slept like a lord through the whole thing.

She shook Adam again. Dr. Adam Smith Maclean was dead to the world.

She could guess how he would report their first amorous experience—playfully and happily as a kid with a new pony. He had toyed and teased and cavorted and just plain—hell, why not say it?—rutted. He played the joyful giant all the way. (Well, he was a damn barbarian, wasn't he?) Not that he hadn't been gentle and considerate and tender—he had, as much as he could. He'd been a little amused at her shynesses, too—he hadn't tried to hide the fact that he knew his way around this territory very well indeed. But in spite of his tenderness, and her own eagerness to please, well, it hurt, and smelled peculiar, and worse, made her feel self-conscious and a little shaky and in need of a lot of reassuring. But now she lay here out of sorts and lonely, and at the same time mad and jittery and making up her mind that she was going to be damned good at this business of lovemaking, and he slept the sleep of the satisfied.

Scratch-scratch-scratch!

Dammit, even Indians weren't polite enough to wait all night. A scratch on the door instead of a knock—that made them Indians, and surely the doctor's charges, not hers. The agency Indians had been wretched all summer with dysentery and malaria, and often they did ask Adam for white-man medicine to help out. So tonight would be just the first of thousands of nights that her married life would get interrupted by the sick. That was OK—she wanted to be used, to give the days of her life to something. So did Adam. That was part of what she loved about this crazy Indian.

OK, drastic measures. She put a foot against his back and started pushing, hard. Suddenly he sat up on the edge of the bed. She slipped out and got a robe to put over her nightdress. "Someone's here," she whispered. She saw that he was grinning at her in the dark—he was alert. He must have been trained at medical school to wake up like that, all of a sudden. He slipped on his nightshirt—he thought wearing clothes in bed a strange custom. He lit the bitch light, and she followed him through their bedroom door and through the other room to the front door. Adam moved his huge frame not sleepily but confidently, and Elaine thought that was another part of what she loved in him, his air of competence. She had to admit she loved his size, too. It felt marvelous to be enveloped by so much of him.

It was Adam's grandmother, Calling Eagle. Behind her was his mother, Lisette. The queenly Calling Eagle spoke softly in the Cheyenne langauge, too low and fast for Elaine's Cheyenne. Adam hesitated, asked something softly, got a vigorous nod and one strong word in reply, and the visitors stepped back into the dark.

Her husband turned to her. In the flickering light he looked thrown off balance. She reached to put her arms around him, but he grasped her hands with his.

He leaned against the door jamb. "They're going home," he murmured, emphasizing the last word a little. She had the most extraordinary sensation at that moment, a sharp smell of something burning, acrid and almost painful. Later she would tell Adam that she had smelled the future in that instant.

When he looked down at her, his eyes were full of pleading. "Now. But the agent has said he'll use the soldiers to drive them back."

She repeated it to herself, word by word. She felt the bizarre sensation she felt when she was told her father had died, the roots of her hair burning and freezing in patches. She knew she could stand it if she didn't reach to her hair with her hands and kept her feet wide apart and stable.

So she told herself slowly what the words meant: The northern Cheyenne tribe couldn't stand it anymore at this agency. They were heading for Powder River, more than fifteen hundred miles and Lord knows how many soldiers away. Tonight. On her wedding night. And, unbelievably, she was their teacher, her husband their doctor.

"Right now," Adam said forlornly.

"We'll never make it," she rasped softly.

All right, it was futile. All right, it was dumb. Smith started arguing with his new wife anyway.

"Goddammit," Smith barked, "do you think being Dr. and Mrs. Maclean will keep us from getting killed?"

She had her back to him, hands on the bureau, shoulders pushed up. God, he wanted to provoke her, to make her listen to reason.

She turned to him, touched his arm, and put her head against the outside of his shoulder.

He almost permitted himself a smile. Listen to reason, indeed. She'd never listened to reason—other people's reasons. Instead she'd gone to the Hampton Institute to teach Indian boys. Then traveled west to visit the Cheyenne and Arapaho Agency, then talked the church into sponsoring a day school there, then talked them past her unmarried state and inexperience so she could run it. She was wonderfully stubborn.

He was born a Cheyenne. She'd chosen to be here, and he loved her for it.

But he argued anyway. Feeling dumb, he held her stiffly and repeated the arguments he'd already used. The Cheyennes would be fugitives, at war with the United States. This was Indian territory, a hell of a distance from Powder River, way up in Wyoming and Montana Territories. Soldiers would fight them all the way, out of Fort Dodge and Fort Hays and Fort Laramie and Fort Robinson—hell, he didn't know all the forts they might come from. People would get killed, white people and red. And by God, Adam and Elaine Maclean would not be immune.

And then the simple, practical considerations. His job was to doctor, hers to teach—they'd be walking away not only from their paychecks but their duty.

Some of it he didn't tell her. He couldn't imagine her trekking across the country for weeks and months on a horse, her belongings on a pony drag, her privy the bushes, her bed—her marital bed—crowded into a tipi with Smith's family, her meals puny and full of dust, her life bitter as alkali and cold wind. He didn't say, either, that she was too precious to him, that he could not risk her life at the hazards of war.

God, but he loved her.

Christ, it was awful.

Elaine lifted her head off her husband's shoulder. If he thought Elaine Cummings would be intimidated, he had another think coming. We Cummings women, flinty New Englanders, ardent abolitionists and suffragists, do not quail at rough going.

She stepped away from Adam, looked up into his eyes, and told him in an unmistakable tone, "They're our people." She took a deep breath. Her husband was a good man, but in some ways not grown up. "You can't walk away. I won't walk away."

She let the words hang. She decided not to add what else she knew—that he secretly yearned to go on this adventure, and yearned for her to go with him. More important, he wanted to go home, to the Powder River country, and make his life there. *Home*. She turned to the bureau and started putting the rest of their few clothes into a canvas bag. He would see they had to go.

Smith saw the set of his wife's shoulders and slowly nodded. He turned and took down his Winchester from over their bed. He had lived this life—had been on the run, had taken scalps, had held a dying man in his arms—and she hadn't. He hoped she would stand up to it well, and not hate it too much. Inside, he had to admit, he could feel stirring a part of himself, a wild part he only half welcomed. It sang out, Let's fight like hell.

Elaine looked over her shoulder at him and took the canvas bag out to where the horses were waiting.

Dr. Maclean admired her. She was stronger than he was, wiser, and more devoted.

Half an hour later, past midnight in what was not yet Oklahoma, Smith made a last-minute check of his cabin for medical supplies. He'd packed his pocket surgical kit, cod liver oil, alcohol, chloroform, one tonic, one astringent, one emetic, laudanum, and some extract of smart weed for the dysentery—he didn't have any more quinine, and would just have to hope no one came down with malarial fever. These were all medicines he'd brought with him from the East. He'd be damned if he'd take agency stores and give the army an excuse to arrest him for theft. He didn't see anything else he could take, or needed, since his people mostly rejected his kind of medicine anyway.

He took a last look around the cabin. Elaine was outside, mounted, with Calling Eagle and Lisette, ready to go. Smith put in his copies of *Gray's Anatomy* and Hartshorn, and grabbed for *Apple-Blossoms*, the book of poems Elaine had published when she was at the Harvard Annex, the Harvard for women. It brought memories flooding into him, memories of Boston, and of meeting Elaine, and hearing her read her poems and discovering how much cultured people admired her.

My God, look what he'd almost left behind. His ivory balls. His old friend Peddler had taught him to juggle, and he'd found these three billiard balls in a pawnshop. They were perfect for his big hands. He used them for a kind of mesmeric relaxation. In fact, it was after a session with his ivory balls that he knew—simply knew, without question—that he must ask Elaine Cummings to marry him.

Smith took a last look around the room. Their bureau, the drawers hanging out, empty. The bitch light, its wick barely flickering—he blew it out. The chamber pot. The iron bedstead, their one luxury, its shuck mattress now stripped of sheets and blankets. He thought of the loving they had done on that bed just hours ago, and felt his loins stir.

He stepped outside, stuffed the last few belongings into his saddlebags. They had to leave the wagon, which wouldn't stand the rough country ahead. They had to leave the tent, which would have given them privacy but was Indian Bureau property. He looked at Elaine. She was perched on her sidesaddle. Though she was a good rider, the sidesaddle seemed . . .

Hell, what had he gotten her into? From Boston, the center of civilization, her family, and her way of life, to . . . what?

His life. He looked around at his mother and grandmother. The Cheyennes had spent Smith's whole life getting swamped by the white man. This red-white fighting had even killed his father. And his brother. Now he was throwing his wife into it. Christ, he was scared, and the fear tasted vile in his mouth.

He swung into his saddle and looked sideways at Elaine. She hung there on the side of her horse in her long skirt that hid the horns her legs used to do the work of riding. To Smith she looked like an old-fashioned daguerreotype of an ideal New England lady. He felt a skin-prickly rush of want for her.

Calling Eagle clucked, and they moved out.

≈ 2 ≈

Elaine looked at Little Wolf's face in the moonlight, and wondered what he was thinking. Was the chief having second thoughts about what he had done? It was a grave face, blighted by smallpox scars and lined by responsibilities.

Little Wolf was the Sweet Medicine chief, the carrier of the sacred bundle Sweet Medicine had brought to the Cheyennes, and so first among the four old-man chiefs of the Tsistsistas and the Suhtaio, the two strands of people who camped together and made up the Human Beings. One other of the forty-four was among the Cheyennes fleeing tonight, Morning Star, also called Dull Knife. Elaine thought he was the most beautiful man she'd ever seen. Elaine had worked with the two of them all summer, and thought them extraordinary men, devoted to their people and deserving of genuine respect.

Elaine, Smith, Lisette, and Calling Eagle waited for the people to come walking stealthily through the darkness. Calling Eagle had told them how Little Wolf and Morning Star threw the gauntlet in council yesterday afternoon, while Smith and Elaine were being wed. They told Miles, the agent, that the people had to go back home—the chiefs had repeated those words all summer. They reminded Miles of the promise made at Red Cloud Agency, that the people could come back north if they didn't like the southern lands. They spoke in a measured way, regretfully and firmly.

Miles said, also sadly, that if the Cheyennes tried to leave, the soldiers would drive them back to the agency. As a promise that they would not run off, the agent asked that they turn over ten young men as hostages.

14

Ten young men. They didn't have a hundred men of any age left. Silently appalled, Morning Star said he would speak to the people about it, and left to go to the camp. He knew he was walking out of that council for the last time.

Camp was temporarily in a valley among some sand hills in a corner of the reservation where the women could dig roots, for they had nothing to eat. Since the army was fearful that the Cheyennes would flee for their homeland, they had horse soldiers and cannon on both sides of the little valley, the far-shooting guns trained down on the quiet lodges, not lodges of fine buffalo hides but of pathetic, ragtag canvas.

After Morning Star walked out of the talk, Little Wolf made one further request of the agent. To the ears of the people it was a forlorn request: "I have long been a friend of the whites," he said. "The Great Father told us that he wished no more blood spilled, that we ought to be friends and fight no more. So I do not want any of the ground of the agency made bloody. Only soldiers do that. If you are going to send them after me, I wish you would first let me get a little distance away. Then if you want to fight, I will fight you and we can make the ground bloody on that far place."

The people hoped the agent would hear both the friendship and the soul-deep resolution in Little Wolf's words, would realize that the people knew they might die going home, and faced that prospect with an inner-smiling acceptance.

The choice was clear: stay in this bad country and die of disease, or strike out for home and live or die like human beings. It was an easy choice. Surely, they thought, if the agent Miles truly understood that, he would not send the soldiers after them—he would leave them alone. Surely. Was he not a man, with human feelings?

As he spoke those words to the agent, Little Wolf felt their uselessness. Miles was decent and sympathetic, but he didn't understand. He thought the people should adapt to the new life the white people had chosen for them, farming, school-going, learning new gods, feeding on white-man handouts. He thought they should just forsake their own way of life as a remnant of the past, the way a snake sheds its old skin. Accept life entirely on white terms.

Little Wolf hid his impatience. Miles had no idea that the Cheyenne people had to live as Cheyennes or not at all. He didn't know that their way of life had been brought to them from the powers by Sweet Medicine and Buffalo Calf Woman. He didn't see the importance of fidelity to the sacred arrows and the buffalo hat. So he didn't realize that once the holy ways were abandoned, the good life gone, pride and honor given up, a Cheyenne could find no joy in living. Little Wolf had to suppress his contempt for such a man.

The Sweet Medicine chief was glad the people felt these issues so profoundly—they made Little Wolf's eyes wet with pride. Now they chose to start acting like Tsistsistas and Suhtaio again. They would go to the Powder River country. Or toward it. We will walk north like Tsistsistas and Suhtaio—Human Beings, Little Wolf declared over and over, and if necessary die like Human Beings.

He added his motto: the only Indian never killed is the Indian never caught.

That night, as Little Wolf stood afoot beside the mounts of his friend Calling Eagle and her family, he waited with fear and admiration to see the first Human Beings starting on their journey.

He knew they had to sneak out of their camp. The soldiers and cannons were close, and ready. If they saw the people leaving, they would shoot. So the people would be walking quietly, even the children, and keeping to the moon shadows.

Back in camp, as Little Wolf had started out ahead, a young man played a song on a love flute, partly to cover the small noises of moccasins on earth and stone, and to make the night seem normal to the soldiers' ears. The chief thought of the northern Cheyennes creeping up this canyon, young and old, weak and strong, infirm and healthy, many bearing heavy loads. He loved them.

Little Wolf looked at his old friend Calling Eagle. He

wondered if Calling Eagle felt as he did at this probable catastrophe—exhilarated.

How had they come to such a state?

The thousand Tsistsistas-Suhtaio led by Little Wolf and Morning Star had come in to Red Cloud Agency a year and a half ago, in the spring of what the white men called 1877. As the soldiers intended, the Indians were starving.

These Cheyennes had been on the Red Cloud Agency the summer before, but they had gone hungry—the agent at Red Cloud never seemed to have the appropriations promised to the Cheyennes. In 1876 they left the agency for their summer hunt, and barely missed the Custer fight in June. All that summer and all that autumn Little Wolf and Morning Star's people got chased by the soldiers, just like the Lakotas and Cheyennes who did kill Yellow Hair. Because of the pursuit, they never got to make a proper buffalo hunt, so they spent the winter hungry. In the spring, they considered their empty bellies, and the white man's promises of food and a reservation in their country, the Powder River country. They came in to Red Cloud Agency.

That was when they discovered that they had stepped into the web of the *veho*, their word which meant both "spider" and "white man." General Crook, whom the Cheyennes fought and admired, argued hard for them to get an agency in Powder River country, but the Great White Father said no. He said these Cheyennes must join their southern relatives at the agency in Indian territory, far to the south.

Now the northern Cheyennes said no. They knew that country, and didn't like it. So the officials at Red Cloud Agency cut off their rations.

After a little starvation, the Cheyennes relented. They would go and see the new agency on the Canadian River, on the condition that if they didn't like it, they could come back. Blue-coated soldiers escorted them on the seventy-day journey to the south, and only three or four dozen Cheyennes slipped away and went back to their homeland, the Powder River country.

Right away the two old-man chiefs, Morning Star and Little Wolf, saw that the new agency was no good. The southern Cheyennes did not have enough appropriations to feed themselves, and the whites proposed to feed everyone, including nearly a thousand new Indians, without increasing the rations.

The old-man chiefs went immediately to the agent, Miles, and told him they were going back to Red Cloud Agency before the snow flew. Then the agent said, for the first time, that if the Cheyennes left, the soldiers would drive them back.

So, said Little Wolf, the promise that we could return if we didn't like the country of the Canadian River was only a dust devil, gone with the breath that spun the words. So, said Morning Star, the promise was only the bait that drew us into the web of the *veho*, pronounced "way-ho," the spider and white man.

During that winter the people were miserable with hunger. The next summer they began to die of malaria and dysentery, despondency and despair.

It was sick and dying that Smith found them in the summer of 1878. He had left his people's country in 1865, the year the War of the Rebellion ended, to go east to Dartmouth College. That had been the last wish of his father, Mac Maclean, a Scots trader who married Smith's Cheyenne mother and founded a trading post on the Yellowstone River.

Adam Smith Maclean, who was named after a Scots professor his grand uncle admired, had lived a life nearly as wild as any Cheyenne. True, he had sometimes gone to school in St. Louis. True, he had spent most of his nights at his family's trading post. But almost every one of his first twenty years he had hunted the buffalo with his mother's people and slept in his grandfather's lodge. He had danced the Cheyennes' dances and sung their songs. He'd dreamed of Cheyenne girls and courted them. In his last year in the West, the year following the massacre of the Cheyennes led by Black Kettle at Sand Creek, he had even gone on the warpath—shed white blood and taken white scalps.

Sometimes, during his teenage years, one or two young men of the tribe taunted Smith that he was no Cheyenne. His father was a *veho*. His mother was no true Cheyenne either, but the half-breed daughter of old Charbonneau and an Assiniboin woman who later married into the Cheyenne tribe. Some winters, they added, Smith and his brother Thomas disappeared downriver, all the way to St. Louis, and came back in the moon when the buffalo bulls are rutting with funny clothes and funny ways.

One of Smith's grandfathers (the white people would have said grand-*uncles*), a man who once had a strong vision, asked Smith closely about his dreams. Did Smith dream of enchanted buffalo or messenger magpies? Did the wind words of the grandfathers of the four directions sound in his dreams? Did he ever see painted horses or painted faces? Did he hear power in the sound of running water? Or did he dream of watches and telescopes and books, and the things he spoke of when he came back from St. Louis, railroads and steamboats and houses and especially his favorite subject, this science?

Smith answered honestly, and told the old man his dreams, which were a coat of all these colors, and more—castles with knights in armor he read of in books, stories of the men who investigated the stars and discovered that the earth circled the sun, and tales of coyote, the trickster of many shapes, and of Sweet Medicine and Buffalo Calf Woman, sometimes all in the same dream. In his recurring dream, he said, he felt himself swimming in the river among all the water creatures, not like a man holding his breath, but comfortable, a native there, quick and graceful in movement. He said he loved flowing water, and heard it constantly in his dreams.

The old man shook his head in puzzlement and put the pipe away. He didn't know water medicine, he said. Perhaps if the boy could find someone who did . . .

When Smith went to his buffalo robes in his own lodge, he felt uncertain what he was, *veho* or Cheyenne.

The next summer Smith and his brother and their Cheyenne comrades joined Red Cloud and Crazy Horse and the other Lakotas and made the white man pay for their blood lust at Sand Creek. And then he knew. When you fight with your people, the dust acrid in your eyes and mouth, the smell of gunpowder and dung and blood rank in your nostrils—when you shed your blood with theirs, and sometimes hold them while they die, and make the enemy die for hurting them—then you are one with them. When Smith went to Dartmouth, he knew he was a Cheyenne.

He reminded himself all through the thirteen long years of his schooling. He wanted to be a white-man doctor, so he put in his learning time at Dartmouth, and then at Boston Medical College, and rubbed shoulders with white people, and learned the ways of their drawing rooms, and sometimes dallied with their women. Occasionally white men spoke to remind him that in blood he was three-quarters white, and although his skin was dark, his reddish hair marked him a *veho*. But he always wore two objects to remind them, and himself, that he was a Cheyenne. Underneath his shirt he kept tied to the inside of his right biceps a gift from his mother Lisette, the shell of a mussel, traded to the Powder River country from the western ocean, cobalt outside, silver inside, and to Smith reeking of magic. And he wore a small deerskin pouch, its strings braided into his long, reddish hair, its contents small seeds given to him by his other mother, Annemarie. To wear this pouch he had to stay away from white-man barbers—he left his hair long, and free.

By these gestures he helped keep his home country as the place of his heart during his years of exile. Like any exile, he dreamed of the time he would be able to go home.

Go home to his mothers and the family trading post on Powder River, where the Little Powder flowed into it. Go home and help his people. That was the reason his father, who loved the Cheyennes, sent him east—to get some of the white man's knowledge to put to use on behalf of the Cheyennes, and all Indian people. Smith's gift to them would be the white man's power of healing.

He saw no contradiction in bringing a white-man gift to the Cheyennes. He believed what his father had believed: The Cheyennes would take from white culture what was best in it—principally the beauty of science—and leave what was repugnant. For white people were inferior to Cheyennes in many ways: they often killed one another, which Cheyennes did not tolerate. They admired men who acquired wealth—Cheyennes admired those who gave it away. They had a religion of doctrines which affected their lives but little—Cheyennes had a half-spoken but powerful sense of the sacred that pervaded their daily lives and directed their steps almost without their being aware of it.

Smith was eager to get home and graft his learning onto the tree of the Cheyenne way.

But when it was time to go home, Dr. Adam Smith Maclean got a sharp disappointment. The Cheyennes were not in Powder River country, where he had grown up, and where the family trading post now was, moved by his mothers from up the Yellowstone. The Cheyennes had been moved by force to Indian territory, fifteen hundred miles to the south. His mother Lisette was there, his father's second wife, where she had followed her new husband, Jim Sykes. His biological mother, Annemarie, ran the trading post in the north country. Some of his relatives were still in the north. All the rivers and mountains and prairies he remembered and loved from his childhood and youth were there. That was where he belonged, where the Cheyenne people belonged.

Nevertheless, he went to Kansas City by rail and to the Cheyenne and Arapaho Agency on the North Fork of the Canadian River in Indian territory by stage and horseback. He went because one of his mothers and his grandmother

were there, and because the Indian Bureau told him to go.
On the way he mourned. His family divided, his people
uprooted, the land he was attached to lost—it was the fate
the white man had brought to the Cheyennes.

And there, in a country he disliked, which had only
slow, muddy rivers, where the water and the air were
making his people sick and despair was killing them, he had
the great good luck of his life—he met Elaine Cummings.

Not for the first time. He had come across her two or
three times in Cambridge and Boston, at proper social
events, and admired her, and heard her spoken of admir-
ingly as a poetess. But he had not gotten to know her. With
the quirkiness of life that he always noticed and delighted
in, she was now the teacher at his people's agency, the
person who would bring knowledge to the Cheyenne and
Arapaho children. She had even created the job. Since
knowledge was what Smith believed his people needed, he
thought her the most important person at the agency.

Therefore he believed in Elaine Cummings. After two
months' acquaintance, he discovered that he was also in
love with her ass-over-tea-kettle.

During those two months, he saw that his people's
circumstances at the Canadian River agency were desperate. They were dying of dysentery, for they were not
accustomed to the water. They were dying of malaria, and
he had no quinine to give them. They were suffering from
the heat. They were starving.

So Smith went to the agent, Miles, a reasonable man,
and since he was a Quaker an honest man, and had a talk.
Smith didn't trust those damned councils anyway. Half the
interpreters mistranslated what the Indians said, and the
other half converted it into a kind of phony biblical poetry,
and there was nothing poetic about starvation, malaria, and
diarrhea. Smith told Miles bluntly what had to be done.
The people had to get out of the hot southern climate, and
they had to get back to water their innards were used to.
The agent agreed with Smith: It was essential.

That talk was why Smith did not expect the scratch on
his door in the dark hours on his wedding night. Now Miles

brandished his troops. And Smith sat his horse here in the predawn darkness, with his new wife, both of them fugitives.

Three hours ago they had been making love for the first time. Now they were running pell-mell through the dark across a prairie, headed home. Angry words tumbled wildly in Smith's mind, words about starving the hungry, words about marching people who could barely walk, words about fighting the U.S. Army empty-handed. He couldn't keep track of the words—they were making him crazy. He forced himself to study Elaine's face, let himself wonder how she was taking it. She smiled a wan smile at him.

Calling Eagle gestured with her quirt into the darkness.

Coming out of the little canyon—Smith could not believe what he saw. He looked at the silhouettes of his grandmother and his mother. They could not be as stunned as Smith was. They must have known. The people were coming in twos, threes, and fours—afoot, carrying what little they could on their backs. They had left the horse herd. They straggled far down the canyon, mere shadows, barely moving.

"They left all sixty lodges standing," Calling Eagle said softly.

Sixty lodges. My God, thought Smith. Suddenly he realized. Our marriage bed won't even be crowded into a tipi—it will be in the open, on the hard ground. He looked across at Elaine. Her face was set and somber. She realized. On top of everything, no shelter from the wind and rain and cold.

"Good Christ," Smith said in despair.

Elaine shook her head and pursed her lips against tears.

"My grandson was once a warrior," observed Calling Eagle. She smiled her mysterious smile at him, world-weary but at the same time full of love. His grandmother was the most intriguing person he had ever known, and the wisest. "Be a warrior once more."

Just then the sky erupted into flame. For a moment it

lit the sky and the earth and the four directions brighter than lightning. The people quailed, and knelt or stooped in fear, until they realized it was not the light of shell bursts. Then they rose and looked at each other and at the radiant sky.

"A falling star!" Smith hollered.

Smith heard low cries from the people in the canyon below: "*Ah-ho!*"

"*Ah-ho!*" echoed Little Wolf and Calling Eagle and Lisette in vigorous assent.

Calling Eagle turned to Elaine and then to Smith with eyes that had seen the griefs of more than seventy winters, and smiled enigmatically again. "The powers," she said in accented English, "send a sign for the helpless ones."

Smith heard in wonder. Hope flushed within him, and he squelched it.

Little Wolf smiled at everyone. It occurred to Smith that he hadn't seen the chief smile all summer. "We're going home," Little Wolf said. "I believe. We're going home."

≈ 3 ≈

Leading with the pipe and three good men, Morning Star went ahead. Then came the women and children and old people. Behind came the dog soldiers, in their proper place of rear guard to the people. A few were left at the village, to watch the soldiers' sentries, make sure they did not catch on to the trick being played—and if they did, kill them quickly. Among these were Little Finger Nail and Little Wolf's son Wooden Legs.

When the sun rose, the people would scatter, and meet at the end of the day at the appointed place, where the young men might be ready with the horses. Scattered, they would not offer so fine a target for Captain Rendle-brock and his soldiers. Little Wolf said the officer from the white-man tribe called Germany, who always had whiskey on his breath, was too eager to shoot Indians. If Rendle-brock found the people, he would find only two or three or four together, unarmed, and those would say they were on the plain only to look for roots to eat. Even an officer of the white man's army should understand the need to eat.

Little Wolf walked among the old men and women and the children struggling along, and his heart felt heavy with responsibility for them. He had thought of giving himself as a hostage to the agent, a hostage to sit in jail and rot and die of despair like the others. But he was the appointed bearer of the medicine bundle—he put his hand on it now under his shirt—and must not show despair, no matter how tired and hopeless he felt.

He fingered the scar beside his right eye, a habit he had when he was thinking. Sometimes he rubbed that one and the long, raking scar in his side at the same time. He never touched the scars on his face without thinking angrily

of where they came from—the smallpox that the white man
brought to the Indian. His face looked like a gopher village,
he thought bitterly, because of this white-man scourge. The
scars itched often and seldom let him forget.

He did not resent the seven scars from seven bullet
wounds gotten on the Powder River two years ago. That
day he gave as good as he got. He was glad the marks were
still red and angry—they were proclamations of honor.

So now Little Wolf and Morning Star were leading the
people home. Nearly a thousand Tsistsistas-Suhtaio had
come south, and on this September night only three
hundred were starting back to Powder River country. Most
of the rest were piled up at the burial place. Little Wolf
preferred not to think of the several dozen who were
staying in the lodges at the agency, afraid to leave for home.
Of the three hundred on the trek north, fewer than a
hundred were men of fighting age. Even to approach a
hundred, Little Wolf had to interpret fighting age liberally,
including all males thirteen and older, no matter how
infirm. Many of these were old enough only to be playing
with bows and arrows, or too old to wield weapons.

So Little Wolf knew he must avoid fights with the
soldiers—killing bluecoats would only bring more bluecoats. And Little Wolf must avoid, even more strictly, fights
with other whites. The *vehos* accepted fights with troops,
but they went crazy over fights with ranchers and towns-
people, even in self-defense. That made them set the
copper wires to talking and bring soldiers from everywhere
on the steel tracks and fight in a frenzy, not caring who they
killed, even infants and the aged or infirm.

Little Wolf needed more guns for the people and more
horses, but he would have to trade for them. If he stole
them, even though the whites had stolen his guns and
horses, the price in blood would be terrible. So the buffalo
robes the people had left, the beadwork that the women
had done, the parfleches they had made, and the
moccasins—these few items were the tribe's last resort.
Aa-i-i-ee, the traders would know the tribe was desperate,
and the trade prices would be high.

With it all, though, he would stick to his motto: The only Indian never killed is the Indian never caught.

He rubbed the scars on his face with both hands and pondered.

Wooden Legs and Little Finger Nail crawled on all fours, making sure they weren't silhouetted—black, moving shapes could be seen against the moonlit sand hills. They kept their elbows on the ground and eased over the hummock and into the gully below. Now they could move out more swiftly.

Good-bye, soldiers, thought Wooden Legs—be glad you will live to see the dawn.

Wooden Legs and Little Finger Nail had watched two sentries near the far-shooting cannons all night. The village lay below, apparently peaceful, the fires making the raggedy canvas tipis glow for a while, then at last dimming until only black tripod shapes marked the presence of the lodges.

Little Finger Nail and Wooden Legs' job had been to make sure the sentries only used their eyes, and not their ears. If they heard the people leaving the village empty, if they went to alert the soldier officers, they would have to be silenced. Instantly.

These two young dog soldiers understood the necessity for such a job. They had the wisdom to hold back if possible, and the audacity to act swiftly if necessary. Wooden Legs was a son of Little Wolf, the old-man chief, generally thought brave and maybe hotheaded. Little Finger Nail was a painter of beautiful pictures, a singer with a sweet voice, and a smart, bold man in a fight.

At first light the soldiers would find the camp abandoned and know they had been tricked. First light was soon enough. At just that time, when the soldiers were trying to figure out what had happened, Little Finger Nail and Wooden Legs and the other young men would run off the

pony herd. It would be funny, stealing the Cheyennes' own
horses from the arrogant white men. That is, it would be
funny if it was not so galling.

The two young warriors trotted lithely across the open
space toward the lodges. They were to meet their comrades
beyond, and movement here would look natural. Little
Finger Nail made a little cry, a phrase from one of his songs,
hoping that the soldiers would hear it.

Tonight Little Finger Nail had crept close to one of the
sentries, a beefy man with a walrus mustache of flaming
red. He liked to give Indian women jerked beef to open
their legs for him. He was said to be amiable, and even give
them a trinket or two he hadn't promised. He had offered
the woman Finger Nail loved, Singing Cloud, such a trade.

Until Cheyenne women had gotten here, they had
been chaste, many even belonging to the society of those
who had one man only. Now they were like the battered,
cast-off boots of soldiers.

Nail simmered to kill this one with the walrus mustache and the complacent expression. But not tonight. He
had promised his father. Besides, the people would soon be
out of easy range. And before long there would be fighting
enough even for the war-hungry son of a chief.

The old man was glad for the dawn light. He disliked
the nighttime. It seemed endless. He didn't mind dying so
much—he had lived a long time, and his time had been full,
and he was worn out. But at night he was afraid of death.
He wanted to die with the sun warm on his old, wrinkled
skin and the light shining through his closed lids onto his
resting eyes. If he was lucky, he'd even have a belly full of
buffalo meat. So he was glad when the sun rose and blessed
him a little.

The pony drag bumped, and made his achy hip hurt.
The old man lay on a litter stretched between poles behind
a pony ridden by his granddaughter Singing Cloud, one of

the handful of horses the Tsistsistas-Suhtaio had for now, until the young men stole their own herd. Singing Cloud had staked the pony by their lodge last evening, because the old man couldn't walk. During the night the poles had bumped over a lot of rocks Singing Cloud couldn't see. Now, in the daylight, his old bones wouldn't take such a bouncing. And he saw that she was coming out of the little valley into the sand hills. That was good—here he could see better. He still had strong eyes, and liked to see a horizon.

Perhaps it would have been better to die back there at the agency. He had hoped he would die there. When the two old-man chiefs told the people it was time to go home, he wished he was already dead. He would have to go, and his bones did not feel up to it. But he had to go—if he didn't, his granddaughter Singing Cloud would stay behind to care for him. He knew she must go north. She was the last blood of a long line of warriors. She was tall and erect, and moved around the cooking fire like a strong, athletic boy—the old man loved to watch her move. So she must live to bear warrior sons to a man like Little Finger Nail, the dog soldier, who was paying her attention. Or if she must die, it must be death in a dash for a true life, not a death by hunger, or by runny bowels.

So the old man headed north with his granddaughter. Somewhere in the journey, he knew, he would get too tired to go on. Then he would slip away during the night and hide well. His granddaughter, unable to find him, would have to go on toward Powder River. She would go to Little Finger Nail, and he would go back to the earth. It was worth it, to put up with the bumpings and pains, to help such a woman.

Half a night's walk behind Singing Cloud and her father, a small, young man named Twist stooped by the little stream, cupped his hands, and drank. Normally this creek would be dry this time of year, but the rainy summer kept a little lukewarm water dribbling down its sandy bed.

Twist was about to walk up out of this little valley in a moment and stand for a while and listen for sounds from the rear, the sounds of pursuing soldiers. Twist was helping the dog soldiers guard the people from the rear as they moved. To his shame, he was not yet a dog soldier himself, and he had to do the job on foot. The cursed *vehos* had the people's horses, and the people were scurrying away like crippled birds, earthbound when they should have been flying. Twist hated the white people for laying hands on his horses. He hated them for taking away the life of glory through the warpath, so that a brave young warrior like himself could not achieve honors, could not become a member of the dog soldiers.

But Twist and the other young men exulted in this flight from the agency. Now they would have the warpath, and they could achieve coups, so the Cheyenne women would look at them the way women look at men, in awe and pride.

He took another handful of water, rinsed his mouth, and spat it out. Foul water, warm, murky, and corrupted— not like the water in the Cheyennes' home country, where clear, gleaming creeks gushed out of the Big Horn Mountains, or farther to the west, out of the Yellowstone Mountains. He had heard the tall white-man doctor say it was the bad water here making the people sick, giving them what the white soldiers called "the shits." They smirked when they named it, and the people died.

For their contempt Twist intended to make them fill their pants from fear. Then he would splatter their blood and excrement across the dust and sand.

Sometimes Twist thought of spilling the white-man doctor's blood, too. He was arrogant, that doctor. He held himself better than other Human Beings. It was true the doctor had the right to count coup—the older men said the doctor had been a fierce fighter when the men went against the soldiers at the Platte Bridge. But now the doctor had given his mind and spirit to the whites, and was more a *veho* than any of them. That was his father coming out, another *veho*, that one. Otherwise, how could the doctor have married a *veho* woman?

Twist thought the doctor was no Cheyenne. He guessed the doctor and his *veho* woman were going to run off. When it looked like the soldiers were going to put a bunch of Indian blood on the ground, the way Twist judged it, the doctor and teacher would flee to the white-man troops, crying, "We're white people, don't shoot us! We're college-educated, don't shoot us!" When they did, Twist meant to see they did get shot. From behind.

Rain lay down just for a minute, lay down on a dry rivulet a hip-span wide and two fingers deep, filled with soft sand. She wasn't going to make a sound. She would let the tears run—she was tired, so tired—but she wasn't going to make a sound. She was too Cheyenne to make a noise that might give her friends away to an enemy.

Her companions, not far ahead, were completely defenseless. Led by two plucky women, Brave One and Enemy, they were all women and children, and they had fallen behind. None of them knew where the main group of the people was, only that they were ahead. Far ahead, and getting farther.

If the soldiers heard them, the women and children couldn't fight back and would get herded back to the agency, and their men would have to come back too, whipped.

Rain sat up and spread her blanket. She would rest a few minutes. That would make her feel better, stronger, and then she could catch up.

It came again, a moderate pull, longer this time. The tears ran, because Rain knew from listening to the older women what was coming, and she was alone to face her first time. If only she could catch up and get help.

She had never borne a child before. She wondered calmly if it would kill her. She looked around. If the soldiers came, she would have no hiding place and no protection, not here. She saw nothing around her but low buffalo grass and undulations of dirt and sand, nothing big enough to shield a human being. Well, maybe a hummock twenty steps away would hide her from sight in one direction, from where the sun was rising.

The pull came sharply this time, and longer. It felt like her insides were being firmly turned, as when she twisted a hide hard to wring the water out of it. After the pull she panted for breath.

So. Rain admitted it: she was not going to walk on. She would bring forth the baby here. That would put her hours behind even the laggards with Brave One and Enemy. And she would be even more defenseless. She had heard that at Sand Creek, where the bluecoats massacred Black Kettle's people, soldiers had bayoneted mothers' wombs and ripped the babies out.

The last hour she had felt by turns calm and racked with despair. When she despaired, she did not ask the powers for life for herself, or even for her child. She asked merely that she get the child out and lift it to the four directions, and hold it once to her small breast. She wanted to put her arms around her child, at least, before any soldier got to it. She wanted her child to breathe air and see the light, at least, to know that much of the world. When she despaired, that was all she hoped for.

The pain came again. This time it was pressure, intense pressure on her abdomen. When she was a little girl, a horse had stepped on her chest, and she had nearly passed out. Now it felt like a hoof planted on her gut, bearing down, all the horse's weight crushing her and her child.

As suddenly as it came, it lifted off, and all was peaceful again.

When she did not despair, when she was calm, she felt clear-sighted and easy enough. True, she was in danger. But she was too smart for the *vehos*. She would bring forth this child. She would hide as she needed to, and not permit the child to cry out. She would slip across the long miles

and rejoin the Human Beings. And perhaps her dead
husband, Red Hand, would somehow know there in the
Starry Path where he lived now, and would have a full
heart.

The pain came. It felt like a hand in her guts—she
yelled in her head that it was not the child's hand. The
fingers were grabbing, pulling, twisting. She felt sweat pop
out on her face, and she was sure the sweat was blood. She
gasped for air and got nothing. She gasped again, and
breathed, and the pain quit. She felt peaceful, and exhausted.

How much more, she wondered, how much more?
She lay back, fully stretched out, and turned her cheek to
the cool sand. How much more?

The pain came in a great wave this time. She mounted
the wave, riding higher and higher, still higher and still
higher, endlessly higher. She clutched her knees and
endured.

Sergeant Breitshof reined in. He had seen something.
He couldn't see it now, but Karlheinz Breitshof had been on
the plains a long time and wasn't going to be fooled.
Something had moved off to the right. And then maybe
not—these plains could fool a man. Sergeant Breitshof had
soldiered in this country for twelve years, and he had seen
lots of things that weren't there. The plains were too big
and too dry and the sun glared off them too strangely. You
saw ponds that weren't there, buffalo that weren't there,
everything. And you didn't see the goddamn redskins who
wanted to kill you.

Sergeant Breitshof had seen plenty of his comrades
killed, and he had no damn-fool romantic notions about
redskins.

He swung down off his horse, picketed the beast, took
his Springfield carbine, a trusty weapon left over from his
Civil War action, and started hoofing. Like most cavalry-

men, he hated being on foot. But on these goddamm short-grass plains you had to get down as far as you could and not skyline yourself for the savages.

He started walking to the northwest. He was a big man, big-framed and big-paunched, and did not walk easily. But he moved like a professional soldier, cautiously, easing from hummock to hummock, squatting, watching, making sure he knew about whatever was over there before it knew about him.

He caught himself thinking *it* for whatever savage he would find over there, and he liked that. He didn't hate Indians personally, individually, but he was clear about their being an inferior race. He couldn't tolerate the so-called idealistic Americans who didn't face that reality. Inferior race. A backwater of history, foul and rank. For the sake of humankind, which had advanced beyond them, they must be swept away.

The job of the soldier was to protect civilization—the state, the church, the family—against barbarians of every kind. Breitshof's grandfather had fought against the barbarians in Africa. He liked to think his ancestors had probably fought barbarians back to the Crusades, or even the Huns. His was a soldiering family. He had migrated to America from his native Saxony to go soldiering against slaveholders first, and then against savages.

Oh, some few of these Indian barbarians might adapt to civilization, like that tall, eccentric doctor at the agency. They were welcome to its benefits. But this bunch that was headed north, back to the blanket, they had thrown away their chance. They'd said they'd rather die than live like white men. That was fine with Karlheinz Breitshof.

He stopped and squatted down. He let his eyes play across the area where something had moved. He had learned to let his eyes roam, light and unfocused, instead of peering at some spot. Without looking down, he made a practiced reach into a blouse pocket, got out his Navy plug, opened his Barlow knife, and cut off a chaw. He didn't mean to move until he saw more.

For his part Sergeant Breitshof meant to help these

Indians die quickly. That would be merciful. He hated to see creatures suffering. But he had indulged in no false pity. He had seen too many of his comrades-at-arms die at the hands of these savages. Frederickson, especially, just this summer. Breitshof didn't call many men friend—they had to earn it—but Frederickson had been a friend, and a drunken Indian had knifed him over a woman.

Breitshof remembered the others. Davis, the boyish Welshman. Kelly—two Kellys, in fact. Morehead. Vanderkamp, the peculiar Dutchman. He didn't remember their Christian names, for he didn't hold with the American custom of calling people outside your family by their Christian names. He did remember their faces, though, and how they died, and how he had sworn to avenge them.

He thought he heard a gasp, or a little cry, almost like a plaintive birdcall. He waited. It didn't come again. He waited longer. He heard nothing, but he knew something was there. Someone.

Sergeant Breitshof moved forward in a crouch. Crouching was humiliating enough—he refused to crawl. He crept up onto a knoll of thin grass and squatted to look around.

And there she was, not twenty steps in front of him. An Indian woman, he supposed one of the Cheyennes who had run off, plopped out on a blanket in the sand. Her legs were spread wide, her knees were up, like she was rutting, but . . .

She cried out, or moaned, or . . .

Mein Gott, the sergeant saw. The woman was giving birth, actually giving birth. Right now. He could see the baby's head out of her. And she was stretched back, resting.

Breitshof shivered. Incredible. He felt his guts churn.

He felt a great urgency to have something to do with his hands. He got out a piece of cartridge paper and began the ritual of tying another cartridge for his ancient Springfield—powder, ball, stout string, two ties, twist the paper end tight and fold it back. He tied the cartridge automatically, barely looking at what he was doing, his eyes riveted on the woman. When he finished, he held the finished cartridge in his left hand, uncertain.

For the first time he noticed that she wore a white woman's dress, a kind of fancy one, actually, with a lace collar and buttons down the back. He felt a spasm of anger. The woman's buck would have stolen that dress, and likely raped and killed its rightful owner. Savages!

The woman hunched. She was not even a woman, really, just a girl. Her dark face drew into an expression of intensity—Breitshof had never seen anything so fierce, even in battle. She tensed all over and seemed to tremble, then shuddered violently.

The child lay on the blanket, free. From here Breitshof couldn't see what kind of child. It raised a cry, not like the mother's, yet infinitely plaintive.

Suddenly Breitshof felt that he must see. It was a raging fever, this need to see. He stood and walked up to the girl, towering over her and the infant.

The girl looked up at Breitshof and her face didn't change. She saw him, but showed no fear. It was as though huge enemies commonly appeared to her in impossible circumstances and did not surprise her. Her eyes closed, her face set once more, she shuddered again, and the woman gave forth something more, something bloody.

The child was a boy.

Breitshof really felt feverish now, crazy. His face flushed hot, and he wanted to bellow.

The woman picked up the umbilicus and bit it in half. Breitshof supposed she must have lost her knife. She picked up the little boy. She held the infant up to the west, the north, the east, the south, the sky above and the earth below—their damned pagan religion, Breitshof had heard. Then for the first time she acknowledged the stranger with her eyes. He saw that her face was very beautiful.

Karlheinz Breitshof stepped forward and squatted down beside them. Shaky, in disbelief at himself, he reached into a pocket, got a clean bandanna, and offered it to the woman. She pushed her skirts down, took the bandanna calmly, and began to wipe off the glistening child.

As Breitshof watched her, he was aware of being in a

bizarre state, abnormally lucid, somehow elevated, yet trembly. He hated it.

He still held the paper cartridge in his left hand. He put it into a cartridge box.

The woman seemed to study him for a moment, head cocked. Then she turned her back to him and pointed over her shoulder to the buttons.

So. She wanted to nurse the child and couldn't get the fancy white-woman dress undone. He chuckled without making a noise.

But the damned buttons wouldn't come. They were cloth-covered, and the button holes were little loops, and he couldn't get his fingers to work them. He tried several buttons, but his big, clumsy fingers wouldn't work any of them.

Karlheinz Breitshof touched the girl's shoulder and pushed her gently to the ground. She flinched, and then seemed to accept without uncertainty or fear. He got out his Barlow knife and with his other hand grasped the high front of the dress. Then he put the knife tip to the girl's throat, and neatly slit the dress down to the waist. Afterward he couldn't help giving her a kind of twisty smile.

Her small breasts exposed, she somehow seemed more naked than with her pelvis bared to the sky and bursting with child. She gave him a simple and indefinable look. She brought her son close and put a nipple in his mouth. The child sucked eagerly.

Breitshof looked again at the fine dress and its satiny material. He flared his nostrils in anger. Her eyes were lowered, on the child. The kid had a pinched-looking face and was covered with black hair.

Breitshof stood up. He brushed at his pants unnecessarily. He looked down at the mother and child. The mother looked up at him with beautiful, dark eyes, gravely, but he could not have said what her expression was.

The sergeant wheeled and started walking back toward his horse. He turned once and looked back at the woman and child. No, he'd not kill them. For some reason he'd lost the urge.

Adam gave her the news, and Elaine jerked her hand back from the fire—it was singeing the light hairs on her fingers. So. The soldiers would be here this afternoon. And presumably the people would have their first fight with the bluecoats. Well, first fight in Elaine's experience.

Adam sat down on his spread-out tarpaulin and started taking his rifle and revolver apart to clean them.

Elaine carefully turned the stick with her other hand, exposing a different side of the bread to the flames. So. All right, she would write that letter to her sister Dora now—she'd been planning to write it anyway. She reached for her ledger book and pencil. It was a silly thing to do, writing her sister, since she had no idea when the letter could be mailed, but it felt right. Adam understood, and had rigged a little tripod so she could cook while she wrote.

> in the Turkey Hills, Indian Nations
> September 13, 1878

Dear Dora:

   I write you in pencil because I must write under the most dramatic circumstances. On our wedding night Adam and I were forced to flee the reservation with our people, embarking on a journey of fifteen hundred miles back to our homeland. It is an adventure you cannot imagine! Even now we are holed up in some timbered hills, where we have a military advantage, waiting for the soldiers to come up. Everyone thinks they will not fight—who would deny a people the right to go home!—but we cannot be certain.

First a telegram informing you and mother without warning of my marriage, now a letter written on the eve of a possible battle! What a life you must think I live! (Adam says that if I lose this pencil, I'll have to write you with a lead bullet!)

Here she gave a brief summary of the Cheyennes' decision to go back to the Powder River country and an account of the first night's flight through the dark that made it seem like a child's adventure story.

I am confident that there is little danger of our being forced back to the reservation. Our country's Indian policy is more enlightened than it was even two years ago—we learned something from the Custer affair and its awful aftermath. I believe with Morning Star, one of our two principal chiefs (and a gorgeous man!), that the soldiers will not resort to force. And we will not go back. Our people were promised the choice of returning to their homeland, and that is what they want to do. Here is a case demonstrating the power of faith!

She decided not to emphasize further her view of that subject, lest she seem to protest too much. What Dora was eager to hear was the everyday part of Western living. Dora had even promised to turn Elaine's letters into some articles for magazines—they were said to be hungry for tales from the West and ravenous for authentic tales of Indian Life.

I am making a bread called bannack on a stick because we have no skillet. Adam's grandmother Calling Eagle showed me how. You mix flour with white ashes from the fire for leavening, add water to make dough, cut the mixture into strips, and wrap it barber-pole-style around a stick.

It would make an excellent campfire bread

for any of you back in civilized New England! The Cheyennes do not much care for bread, being unaccustomed to it. Adam, though raised without it, considers hot bread a rare treat and will complain only of the lack of molasses to sweeten it!

Two sticks of bannack are done now, the beans are hot, and I've opened a can of peaches for our family. You see we are about to have a feast! Canned peaches—such a treat! Fortunately, only Adam and I like them.

To everyone else the treat is buffalo. Our scouts found a few buffalo two days ago, and yesterday our people surrounded them and killed them all. You should have heard the shouts and seen the irrepressible smiles. Buffalo again! Since the great herds have been slaughtered for their hides—it's infuriating!—our people have eaten almost nothing but beef. Maybe that's part of the reason diarrhea has afflicted most of them, Adam says—their insides aren't used to beef.

So we're all celebrating, each family around its own little fire, many of us gorging ourselves. The occasion is compromised, though, by two matters. The first is those soldiers reported to be drawing up. The second is that several of our women and quite a few children are far behind us. The scouts found them only last night, straggling but coming along slowly. The scouts gave them some meat and encouraging words, and promised that the people would wait here in the Turkey Hills. Our thoughts are with them.

She took a deep breath, and let it out in a gush. Though many Cheyennes thought they would not have to fight, they had taken precautions: they had moved into this high ground last evening, a clump of timbered hills named Turkey Springs. It still had several springs, but the wild turkeys were gone, killed off. The soldiers were coming from the south, and gullies ran off to the north, offering sheltered spots away from the shooting for the women and children.

She set the stick on the cloth and slid the fresh-cooked bread off. She kept her mind carefully away from the thought of battle. She could see the soldiers in her mind, parading on their horses at Fort Reno, rank on rank of them, looking smart in their blue coats and Kossuth hats. She did not permit herself to think of these professional fighters against the ragtag bunch around her in these hills, a few dozen warriors, some old men and boys, lots of women and girls. Scores of modern Springfields—maybe even cannons—against a few, battered caplockers and lots of bows and arrows. Ridiculous. It wouldn't happen.

My husband, though, evidently feels no dread of anything. He has fought battles before— how bizarre it is to imagine him doing that! Killing people, and seeing his comrades killed!

He is inclined to manual and mechanical things, which seems strange for an Indian. If he had not come to industrial civilization, he could never have discovered some of his favorite pastimes. His favorite is juggling some ivory balls, which he will do to amuse others or for his own solace of mind. (He says he decided to ask me to marry him while juggling those balls!) I have also seen him spend half an afternoon repairing a child's toy, making it wind up and march once more. He was more pleased with his success than the little boy. I've helped him sew people's skin up, which made me queasy, but he delighted in the expertise of his work. And he declares that he loves to do surgery on people, even to remove limbs. He says the cutting and sawing and cauterizing and suturing—awful to imagine, all of them!—give him a marvelous feeling of power, benevolent power. My love once saved a man's life in Boston by amputating his arm below the

elbow, and spent weeks of excited experimenta-
tion helping an inventor come up with a mechanical hand that worked.

When he speaks about the adventures he had
in familiar Boston, it seems exotic, because he is
exotic. When he tells about the wild Virginia City
of the gold-rush days, or fighting with Red Cloud
and Crazy Horse against the army in Red Cloud's
War—or surviving the hazing at a snotty Eastern
school!—I feel as Desdemona felt about her dark-
skinned giant:

> 'I lov'd him for the dangers he had pass'd,
> And he loved me that I did pity them.'

She looked over at her juggler affectionately. He was
absorbed in the metal parts of his Winchester, cleaning and
oiling and making them gleam, checking and rechecking
the way they moved, getting the action perfectly smooth.

The center of Cheyenne life is the family.
Our people eschew order and discipline of the
group in favor of the sovereignty of the family.
Some of our families even stayed back at the
agency. If they decide to go a way other than the
group's, the leaders cannot make them change,
will not try means other than persuasion, and will
not judge their decision harshly. The chiefs are
leaders only through counsel and example, and
have no authority of force.

Our family is four—Adam and I and his
grandmother Calling Eagle and his mother Lisette. We would have been seven, but Calling
Eagle's son Red Hand died at the agency from the
malarial fever, and his wife Rain did not come
north with us. Lisette's husband Jim Sykes died
earlier of the same fever. We travel together, cook
and eat together, and sleep close to each other

under the stars (the people abandoned all their
tipis at the agency).

Calling Eagle is kind to me. She makes small,
nice gestures to me, like loaning me a mirror to
use for combing my hair and helping me take care
of my skin, which is terribly dried out by the sun
and wind.

Elaine began to wonder if she could send this letter to
her family. It painted too bleak a picture. She would recopy
it and censor it a little.

Calling Eagle's manner, though, is skeptical
and gruff. She likes to tease, too. In a woman of
her size—she's taller than many men—all this can
be intimidating. I think she suspects constantly
that I am about to go into a dither about the lack
of a roof or a chamber pot. Yesterday I hung back
instead of helping with the butchering of some
buffalo, which our people consider women's work,
so I am sure she thinks I will faint at the sight of
blood. You will laugh at that, since you always said
my callousness in skinning squirrels made you
stop eating meat! It's true, though, that the way
the women reveled in the skinning and cutting
took me aback. I am toughening my spirit for this
life! And my body!

Lisette, Adam's mother, who is even now
cutting strips of buffalo meat to dry on a rack, said
little to me in the weeks Adam and I were
courting, and still says little, for she is grieving for
her second husband. She is as attractive a woman
as you'll ever see at about fifty, and according to
Adam was quite the hellion as a young woman.
I'm sure her spirits will recover, a development
that will doubtless please various of our men.

Elaine had never found out much about Adam's family
history. She knew his father, Mac, got killed. Adam's

brother Thomas got shot—Adam had used the word
murdered—at the same time. There was something about
Mac tracking Thomas down, and Thomas actually trying to
shoot his own father, and someone Adam hated shooting
them both. Elaine could hardly face the thought of a son
shooting at his father, but she was learning that the Indians
of the plains had been living through absurd, awful times,
and absurd, awful things went on.

No one in the family spoke about the killings. Maybe
they would when she was accepted, truly accepted.

     It is touching to see the easy closeness of
mother and son. They do not talk much, but they
sit close together often, touch each other fre-
quently, and especially seem to have a rich com-
munication of looks. The juggler says his mother
talks just enough: she has the gift of knowing
when to add word to something and when to let it
be.

     I will be fascinated to see how he con-
ducts himself with his real mother, Annemarie
Maclean. She is still in Montana Territory, running the family trading post, and he has not seen
her

in thirteen years, but she is literate, and they
correspond. She is also a mixed blood, French-
Canadian and Assininboin, Cheyenne by adop-
tion.

     Back to our feast. We are splurging, using up
most of our food in one grand gesture. The
splurge is wonderful for us, all of us. Of course,
we are skinny, even emaciated. Many of us have
been ill. The principal good feasting does,
though, is not for our bodies but our spirits.
Buffalo! The good times back again!

     I, of course, cannot bear to eat only buffalo—
not after you have educated me to the loveliness
of your vegetarian way. My bread and beans and
canned peaches are grace notes to a primitive

menu. I am very fond of canned peaches, but wish
desperately that we could get fresh fruits and
vegetables.

Another stick of bannack was cooked. She set it aside
on a cloth, and started more.

She picked up one hot twist of bannack and hurried
toward Adam, shifting it from hand to hand. How strange—
her body felt queer, legs wavy and stomach roily. The twist
of bannack burned her fingers. She instructed herself to
keep her foolish mind on the here and now.

"It's hot!" she said to Adam urgently. She sat down by
him and put her arm through his as he ate. The twist didn't
seem too hot for him at all. She supposed that being
without the staff of life his first twenty years made him
appreciate it that much more. How odd, to be without
bread.

She put her head on his shoulder. She would suggest
that they take their blankets away from the others tonight
and make love for the second time in their married life. On
the rough ground. She knew he wanted that, and it was past
time. The Brahmin must become a trollop.

She squeezed his arm. "Go tell people the beans are
ready," she whispered. He nodded and jumped up, mouth
full of hot bread.

Watching him go, she wondered if she would act like a
Brahmin if the soldiers did in fact fight—faint dead away at
the first sound of fire. Or worse, she might vomit or her
bowels explode. She was grateful that her husband was firm
about her staying well back with the other women. She was
afraid, not so much of getting hurt as humiliating herself
with her daintiness.

She looked at Adam, spreading the word at a fire
twenty steps off. He seemed light, cheerful, and big enough
to endure anything. She felt a pang for him. She thought of
him once more, sitting down stumped, not knowing what
he wanted to do, juggling his ivory balls for half an hour,
and coming up with marriage. A fascinating and lovable
man, Adam Smith Maclean.

Adam and I are making the feast even more
special with a gesture that is privately important
to us: we are giving away what food we brought—
beans, flour, and a few cans of vegetables. We've
invited all the people to share in our few luxuries,
and any food is a luxury. I proposed the idea, and
my dear husband understood immediately and
touched his lips to my forehead in a grave way that
gave me a pang.

She got up, sighed loudly, twisted the last stick of
bannack, and put it on the fire.

When we have given away our last food, we
will have no advantage over the other Cheyennes.
We will be not only among the people but *of*
them.

This is not so much of a hardship as you might
think. The men bring in game every day, and the
people always have something to eat—more, in
fact, than they had at the agency, where they were
forced to depend on the government for rations. If
it is still not quite enough, our spirits will be
uplifted to be hungry with the people.

Through this gesture we hope to gain something intangible but immense: until now the
people have treated us—Adam too—as someone
special, someone apart. The reason for this defer-
ence was only in part respect for our positions as
doctor and teacher. It was more an acknowledg-
ment that we could ride away freely from the
people's dilemma, and no one else could. Anywhere we wanted to ride, we would be left alone
by the whites. If we went to the Powder River
country, we could stay. We could ride into one of
the forts sending soldiers against the Cheyennes
and be welcomed. We could even go home to
Brahmin Boston, a mere fairy tale to the Chey-

ennes, and live and thrive. No disease threatens
our bowels. Starvation does not stare us in the
face. Soldier bayonets do not fence our freedom.
Surely our people think that before the time
might come to die, the doctor and teacher would
choose to disappear.

What a color-prejudiced nation ours is!

Elaine Cummings Maclean, though, is determined not to be separate, apart, superior, white.
I have married a Cheyenne, and it means something to me I do not know how to tell even you. I
want to take it into myself fully and truly, whatever it means. Perhaps it means a last taste of the
old, free life. Perhaps it means an opportunity to
inspire an elevation of the people into a new way
of living. Or perhaps it means fleeing soldiers,
fighting, hunger, destruction, and death. I want
my fate, and the fate of my husband and of my
marriage, to be part of the fate of the Cheyenne
people.

That is my decision. Yes, it frightens me.

She closed the ledger book. She couldn't send this
letter—it sounded mad. She did not permit herself the
thought that her life was now mad.

≈ 5 ≈

"Little Wolf says we don't shoot first," Smith told Elaine. Calling Eagle nodded to herself. Little Wolf was a wise man, Calling Eagle thought. In the end it likely wouldn't help, but he was a wise man.

"Maybe the soldiers *won't* shoot," Elaine put in. The scouts were reporting a plain full of U.S. cavalry, but Smith, Elaine, and Calling Eagle were well back, at the top of the gully where most of the women were.

"Morning Star thinks they won't," said Smith without hope. "Since they didn't catch us sooner, he thinks they're not too interested in us. Little Wolf thinks they will."

"What do you think?" asked Elaine. He shrugged his shoulders. He was painting his forehead bright crimson.

My grandson Vekifs is wise, too, Calling Eagle reflected. *Vekifs* was her pet name for him, an affectionate form of *veho*, meaning roughly "Dear Little White Man Who Has Become a Cheyenne." As applied to Smith, *little* was ironic. He is wise, she thought, to decline to try to predict the choice of another man, especially a *veho*. He simply readies himself with his paint. His wife, though, the sign of his foolishness, clings to beliefs about things. She believes the white man is what she calls civilized, so she believes his soldiers will behave in a civilized way. Maybe the blood will make her stop believing. Maybe not.

Smith finished reddening his forehead and started applying three horizontal stripes of verdigris to his nose. Calling Eagle observed wryly the odd expression on his wife's face. Even your husband the doctor is not so civilized, Calling Eagle thought. She wondered what Elaine would say if she knew that the paint medicine was taught to Smith by Owen Mackenzie, the murderer of Smith's father and brother.

The woman had it wrong anyway. She looked at paint and feathers, the great protectors, and saw barbarism. Then she looked at powder and ball, the great destroyers, and saw civilization. Just backward.

Smith finished his face and turned and gave Elaine a mock growl and a big grin. So he could see he was making his young and innocent wife nervous.

Smith's comrades-at-arms were getting ready, too. How strange their medicine objects must seem to the white woman—a little pebble, a dried-up lizard, the skin of a bird, the paw of a badger, the dried heart of an eagle, a piece of fox dung, the feather of a raven. How strange the states of trance, the medicine words crooned over and over. The woman knew the Cheyenne words, but not the Cheyenne soul.

Calling Eagle wished the warriors did not need the white man's weapons. This morning two young men came in with three guns, a few cartridges, and a little powder and some percussion caps. The old-man chiefs had sent them to a renegade trader hidden in the oaks. But for what little they got, they had to give an ancient medicine headdress, two fine-quilled otter skins, their wives' saddle trappings, and lots of beadwork. So much to give for so little, the power of the Tsistsistas-Suhtaio way for the power of the white-man way.

Calling Eagle thought such trades spelled the end of the spirit life of the Tsistsistas and Suhtaio, the life Sweet Medicine taught them. Yet she, too, could see no way to survive without the white-man guns. She and the other medicine people of the tribe could offer no power to compete with the guns. That, she thought, was what was wrong. That was the great regret of her life.

Smith stood up to go to the rocks and do battle. "Go to Lisette," he said gently to his wife. "She's just beyond the spring."

Elaine looked at Calling Eagle expectantly. The old woman shook her head. "I'm going with Vekifs," she said, nodding at Smith. "I go with the men."

Calling Eagle smiled at the puzzlement on Elaine's

face. She did not realize that Calling Eagle was different.
No white people realized. When they were told, they were
outraged.

Well, that would come later. Calling Eagle followed
Smith toward the rocks.

Little Wolf walked in a measured way toward the
soldiers, with Morning Star and other chiefs at his side.
Every man's hands were empty, except that Morning Star
carried the pipe, showing peaceful intentions. An Arapaho
scout came out to meet the Cheyennes. The chiefs did not
like having a man of their friends the Blue Cloud people
come out to them to talk for the enemy, but they said
nothing.

The Arapaho was sent out with the words Little Wolf
expected. Come back voluntarily and the whites will treat
you well. Try to go on and they will drive you back.

Patiently, the Cheyennes said the old words again. We
don't want to fight. We won't shoot unless the whites attack
us. But we won't go back—we're going home to the Powder
River country.

So the Arapaho went back to Captain Rendlebrock,
and the chiefs went back to the Cheyenne soldiers on the
hills. Little Wolf stayed out in front by himself, feeling
ambiguous, easing toward the soldiers, hoping to talk a
little more, or to show something, or do something—just
foolishly hoping.

Watching the soldiers and waiting, he remembered
what he'd said to his warriors a few minutes ago. Don't
shoot first. If the soldiers have to kill someone, let me be
the first one.

And he might be the first one. He wished he was at a
point in his years when he might surrender life gracefully,
but standing out here, waiting uneasily, he knew very well
that he wasn't. He loved being in the swim of things too
much, loved being the Sweet Medicine chief, he whom the

people called their brave man, their dedicated man. He loved taking hold and making even the most terrible decisions of these terrible days. He also loved to fight—how gloriously alive he'd felt that day two years ago on the Powder when he'd been shot seven times. He also loved watching his children becoming full people. Approaching sixty winters, he also felt so much love for one of his wives, Feather on Head.

He had sung many times with the other warriors the great battle words, "It is a good day to die." But he liked his life very much right now, and wanted to keep it. Perhaps that was unworthy of him. Perhaps that was what life had yet to teach him, to ease the fierceness of his grip on it. Teach it to me slowly, he thought—I am in no hurry.

He could imagine feeling less attached to life under only one circumstance: if the Human Beings could not go home to Powder River, if they all must die here in this wretched country, if there was no hope for the Tsistsistas and Suhtaio. In that case he would like to throw his life on the ground in front of the whites in contempt.

With every moment that passed, and the soldiers did not send anyone out to talk to him, Little Wolf became more resigned to his certainty that the whites would shed blood here. That was their nature. He had given up trying to understand it.

He tried to laugh about the whites' dumb ways. It had gotten around camp that the teacher, the wife of Smith, had asked why the soldiers brought Blue Cloud scouts. She did not see that the soldiers like to get Indians so corrupted that they would trade the lives of their friends for a few dollars. But Calling Eagle had answered, so the tale went, that without Indian scouts the cavalry couldn't find dung in a buffalo herd.

Little Wolf liked that. It was good to laugh at white stupidities. But he couldn't find much laughter in his heart.

He was not surprised when the music came across the still, sunny afternoon. The trumpet rang out, "Fire!"

Smoke rose from the barrels into the sky, and then the battle call of the trumpet came across the bright plain. Smith nodded to himself—they're attacking. But it was all distant and abstracted, like a painting of a war instead of a battle itself.

Little Wolf started walking back calmly, without hurrying. Smith watched with breath held, amazed at the chief's courage. Or maybe he had accepted his own death, and that gave him dignity. Or maybe he had made medicine to become invulnerable and was sure he could not be struck.

Smith was well protected in some rocks, walled off from enemy fire. Calling Eagle crouched beside him, her eyes intent on Little Wolf. Smith forced his mind through the odd unreality of it all, forced himself to feel the vulnerability of Little Wolf's flesh moving slowly through the invisible fire, as yet untouched.

Little Wolf walked, measured step after measured step, through the barrage. Cheyenne bullets flew over his head, and soldier bullets plunked all around him. The soldiers were off their horses, every fourth man holding the mounts of his companions, in their way.

Smith heard the Cheyenne women make their high trilling for the chief's bravery from the first little hill to the west. So they had come out from the gullies to watch the fighting, and to hell with the danger. Smith was damn glad—those were *Cheyenne* women. Loudest of the trillers were Pretty Walker, Little Wolf's daughter, and one of his wives, Feather on the Head, and Singing Cloud, the woman Finger Nail hoped for. Smith hoped they'd sneaked off and left Elaine in the gully—surely they did.

Smith rose up on his knees and yelled exultantly *ah-ho*! His voice sounded shrill to himself, so he bellowed again, lower, like the thunder. He grinned sheepishly at Calling Eagle. Getting onto his knees reminded him that he wore pants instead of a breechcloth. Pants below and bare torso and painted face above—half-white and half-Indian. He chuckled at himself.

Little Wolf simply continued to walk. Some bullets kicked up the dust around him, though Smith thought most of them flew into the Cheyenne positions on the hill. This walk was a gesture of greatness—it would be memorialized in the songs and stories of people and wreathed in double glory if Little Wolf came out unharmed. To Smith he seemed to walk even now in an aura of light.

The chief reached the base of the hill and stepped in among its creases. The trillers raised their sound to the skies.

Calling Eagle shook Smith's shoulder, grinning broadly. He knew what she was saying—See, medicine can whip weapons—the spiritual defeats the merely physical.

Smith didn't know. His education was in the physical, but he had grown up witnessing the power of medicine.

Now the soldiers came forward, within easier range for their Springfields. They knew the Indians didn't have many guns, or they wouldn't have dared. So this was the time for Smith to add his lever-action Winchester to the mélée. He held steady on a horse, pulled the trigger, and saw the creature leap about crazily.

After several shots the fighting felt good. He had spent his youth with a rifle in his hands, and the old sense of competence came back. He was still a dead shot, and the lever-action made him fast. The soldiers were too far away for him to hold on men, but Smith made several horses come.

Curiously, it felt fine. It was not hard to shoot at white men. It was as satisfying as shooting at any enemies.

Then Smith saw the thin line of horses bolt out onto the plain and ride hard at the whites—a war charge!

"Hoka hey!" yelled Smith. The warriors were using mostly spears, axes, and bow and arrows to save ammunition. When they neared the soldiers, Smith held his fire. The cavalry line fell back, confused and disorderly. The

young men yelled and shot and dashed forward and back and forward and back again.

The soldiers ran, and the ones at the rear were digging rifle pits. Behind Smith, Calling Eagle made a little trill.

Smith stood up and faced the retreating soldiers. He still felt a little self-conscious about his damned pants. He shook his rifle in the air and at the top of his lungs roared, "*Hoka hey!* You bastards!" He threw an arm around his grandmother and hugged her. He thought, Look at those bastards run.

≈ 6 ≈

Elaine hurried down the hill through the broken rocks and little gravel slides, slipping and half falling. If only her knees would keep steady. She was rushing to join Adam, who was said to be at the foot of the hill checking a man named She Bear. She Bear, they said, was the only man killed in the battle—the other wounds weren't even serious.

Oh, yes, damned lucky, she thought sarcastically. Only one man dead.

She longed to touch Adam, simply to feel his solid arm in her hand, his big back inside her arm.

It had been awful, just awful. From her place in the gully she could hear the guns going off but couldn't see anything. But her imagination had done its nasty work. The whole time it had spewed up images of mayhem and death, and cast them about prodigally. She had simply sat there rigid and refused to pay attention to them, had sat there almost in a trance, knowing nothing, intelligence and understanding and life itself suspended until it was over. She had not let herself scream.

She was not too dissatisfied with herself, really. She had maintained her demeanor. When she got to Adam, when she touched him, she would be all right.

Smith put his arm briefly around Elaine's waist and turned back to his patient. "He's going to be OK," Smith said happily. He felt the route of the big wound around She Bear's head. "It's amazing. It went in here," he said lightly, "and out there."

He felt Elaine touch his shoulder with her cheek and pull away to make room. Calling Eagle and Medicine Wolf had arrived—Smith had sent the old woman for one of the tribe's healers, a practitioner with herbs and incantations. Smith waved the medicine man forward to show him the wounds.

Smith began to feel terrific. She Bear was still groggy as hell, but he would be fine. Elaine looked OK, maybe a little shaky, but Calling Eagle was steadying her. And now he got to do what he had come back west to do—give his people something important by doing what he did best. Smith was grateful to Calling Eagle, who had summoned him to the supposed dead man first instead of getting Medicine Wolf. He laughed to himself. Did his grandmother call Smith first because she thought the man was dead?

"See, the bullet just tiptoed around his skull and didn't penetrate. It made this big gully"—he fingered the bigger wound, which circled toward the ear—"and this little one." He touched the other gully, which angled upward. "The bullet actually split. She Bear has a skull like a grizzly's."

She Bear managed a dizzied grin at this compliment.

Smith picked up She Bear's hat, made out of the skin of a grizzly head, cocked it in the air, and grinned at Elaine. The gesture was silly, but what the hell? Then he got an idea. He felt around inside the hat, and, sure enough—

"I found it!" But he couldn't get it out. He took his knife, picked at the skin of the hat, and brought forth his little prize. "Here's the piece of bullet that went upward. The other one went on through." He stuck his little finger out the hole where the bigger fragment went and wiggled it at everybody.

Smith put the piece of bullet in She Bear's hand. He knew the warrior would want to keep it, perhaps put it in his medicine bundle. "What medicine you made today!" Smith complimented him.

The warrior nodded. He looked more alert now. He'd taken a hell of a lick, though, and Smith meant to keep him lying down as long as possible.

It felt so good to be healing the people. Back at the agency most of them avoided him. More white-man stuff, they said, and they were rejecting all of that. Now, broken and bleeding, his people really needed him.

"Medicine Wolf," Smith said, "don't you think we ought to poultice these? Can you make some poultice?" Smith had confidence enough in folk-medicine poultices— they seemed to work as well as the concoctions he used. The doctor began to rummage in the geometrically painted rawhide box he'd brought, called a parfleche, his improvised version of a Gladstone bag.

"I think I'd better sew this big one up," Smith said. "Would you hold the skin for me?" Medicine Wolf eased in close and pressed the torn edges toward each other. Elaine was good at doing this, but it was important to teach Medicine Wolf, and Elaine would understand that.

When he'd threaded the needle, Smith carefully made his row of neat stitches with silk thread. Medicine Wolf watched keenly. See what happens when you treat him as a colleague? Smith said to himself. "You can sew up the next one," he told Medicine Wolf. "It's easy." See what happens when you treat your people as adult human beings?

He turned back and smiled at Elaine. She didn't look so pale anymore. I'm getting it done, he wanted to cry to her. I'm getting it done.

"*Hou! Hou!*" shouted Twist throatily. Morning Star, the great Morning Star, had also spoken up for the war charge. A real, old-time Cheyenne war charge. Overrun the soldiers—they deserve it. Didn't they attack us, even our women and children? Aren't they dog-manure-eaters?

"*Hou-hou!*" Twist shouted again, his inflection rising with the other men's. All the young men wanted a war charge, and the great Morning Star was on their side. Was

he not one of the two old-man chiefs? The young men
looked at each other with blood lust in their eyes.

Twist wanted to count coup on the soldiers. He wasn't
a member of the society of Dog Soldiers, because he was
without honors. In the last two years, the younger Tsistsistas had had no chance to show their daring at war. No
chance for coups, no chance for glory, no chance to gain the
standing in the tribe that would enable a man to take a wife.
To Twist, that was the worst part of the imprisonment on
the cursed agency. For Twist it was even worse, for he was
small and ill-favored.

Now Twist exulted. Even Morning Star was for the
charge. Twist scowled at the tall white-man doctor known
as Smith—damn the white men!

But Little Wolf, the warrior turned old woman, spoke
up now. He argued that the people should simply accept
the good luck they'd had today. They'd held off the soldiers
without wasting too much of their precious ammunition. No
Human Beings had been killed, and only a few soldiers.
Maybe the officers, even though they were white, would
not feel so humiliated that they would telegraph for the
railroad to bring five times as many fighters and kill a lot of
Indians to get their self-respect back. A very lucky day. So
if the Human Beings just waited, the soldiers would run out
of water down there in their rifle pits and have to go home.

It would be very satisfying, yes, to ride out there and
get personal glory in the only way a warrior could get it. But
the responsibility of the old-man chiefs, both himself and
Morning Star, was the welfare of all the people, not just the
young men. The whites back east had too many soldiers and
too many guns.

Twist felt bile in his throat. This chief would turn all
the Cheyenne warriors into women. Then who would
protect the people?

Little Wolf asked several men to tell the warriors about
the whites' overwhelming numbers—the four men who had
been sent to prison far off in Florida, and the white-man
doctor, who had been all the way to a place called Boston.
Twist didn't care what they had to say. The four had been

broken in spirit by their time in the white man's jail. The
doctor, worse yet, had the whites whitewash his Indian
spirit and paint over it with what they called education.

When Smith began to speak, Twist fixed him with a
malevolent glare. Naturally, the doctor spoke as the coward
Little Wolf told him to, and as the others did. Yes, yes,
more soldiers and guns and ammunition than we could ever
imagine—the doctor parroted his lines perfectly, like the
others halter-broken by the whites.

Now Little Wolf, satisfied with himself, tried to put
even more hobbles on the warriors. When the young men
were out trying to trade for horses and guns, he argued,
they should steal nothing and kill no one. The white people
got more excited by Indians' raiding farmers and ranchers
than their fighting with soldiers. Peace, Little Wolf coun-
seled all of them. Don't shoot, don't steal, only trade.

Twist looked across at Black Coyote, and his friend
sent back a hooded glance. Some of the warriors would
ignore this stupid advice.

Inflicting a bad defeat on the whites, Little Wolf
summed up, would endanger everyone. If the warriors
made the whites mad enough, there might even come a day
when not a single Tsistsistas-Suhtaio of the northern band
would stand between the earth and sky. The only way to get
back to Powder River country was to walk as quietly as
possible.

Twist felt disgust as real in his throat as vomit. When
Little Wolf asked for the sign of assent, and even Morning
Star gave it, Twist found it almost unbearable. But he
noticed that maybe a dozen young men, like himself, gave
no sign at all.

Now the dog soldiers, under their leader Tangle Hair,
were assigned to watch the soldiers during the night and
keep them from going for water, but to avoid killing them.
Since Tangle Hair would charge him with the duty of
staying peaceful, Twist strode away from the council.

The doctor made him mad. That Smith had no business speaking up in a war council—he wasn't a Cheyenne.
His father was a white man, and his mother the offspring of

the old Frenchman Charbonneau and an Assiniboin woman. Besides, his mind had been spoiled by education.

The doctor and his schoolteacher wife were pretending to be on the side of the Tsistsistas-Suhtaio. But at the same time they tried to convert the people to white ways. It was worse than forcing the people to live like whites—these two wanted to take over their minds and make them *want* to live like whites.

Twist's blood was up. He felt like clubbing the doctor's head in. He knew that killing another Cheyenne was the unpardonable sin, always punished by banishment from the tribe. And the old-man chiefs said the doctor was a Cheyenne. But the people—would the people say so?

Twist thought they would see that the doctor was a white man's disease. They would praise the warrior who purged the people of disease.

Some men found her by accident not long before sunset, when a few clouds were gathering for a little rain. She was back in some low rocks, whimpering, a wounded animal seeking a lair. They summoned Medicine Wolf, and this time the man of red medicine sent for the man of white medicine. Smith felt honored by the summons.

"Her name is Leaf," Medicine Wolf muttered. She looked about six years old, and Smith could see she was scared of the strangers hovering over her. He could also see what was wrong—she was shot in the right ankle, the mortis was hit, and it was never again going to work the way it should.

Elaine clambered back among the rocks and reached for Leaf's hand, but the child cried out and rolled away. It was pitiful to see the way she rolled, managing to leave the ankle where it was, unmoving.

Just then one of the warriors came up and spoke to her. Christ, it was the one who glared at Smith back at the council and looked so antagonistic. When the warrior slipped around and put a hand on her head, Leaf didn't pull away. Medicine Wolf whispered that he was Twist, her uncle, not her father—her parents were dead.

Smith felt a rush of compassion for the child. There were too damn many Cheyenne orphans, like the ones coming up from behind now. He looked at the uncle. The man's eyes were bitter and hateful. Well, Smith was ready to overcome bitterness and hatred. Medicine and compassion were his tools. Now was a good time to start.

Smith sent Elaine for more of his tools and medicines. He asked Medicine Wolf to get a piece of green buffalo hide—Medicine Wolf would be able to judge the size and might well be as good at making a splint of it as Smith.

Before leaving, Medicine Wolf whispered some sharp sentences back and forth with Twist. Smith didn't have to hear the words to know that the warrior wanted the white-man doctor away from his niece. The medicine man made a decisive gesture and left. Smith chose not to be angry at Twist for his hostility and to be grateful to Medicine Wolf for his support.

Smith turned his attention to the child. How had she gotten into the area where there was shooting? They would never know. It was what came of having no mother to look after you.

Smith looked at the sky. About an hour to sunset, and the rain clouds were making it dark already. The bullet had to be drawn, the wound poulticed, the bones set in place, and the splint put on. The bones would fuse—the mortis would allow little or no motion again—but if he set them properly, she would be able to gimp around on the ankle, maybe gimp pretty vigorously.

He put his mind on the order of the tasks he had to get done and deliberately did not think of the girl's jerking and writhing and crying out.

He started building a little fire to sterilize his tools, thinking as he went through the motions. He made himself think of his grandfather, Strikes Foot, who had spent his entire life on a prosthetic foot. A buffalo hoof as a prosthesis. Strikes Foot had limped, but had actually turned the hoof into a kicking weapon in combat, making a disadvantage into an advantage. That could be done. A bad ankle didn't mean a ruined life.

With a nice little blaze going, Smith had to quit putting it off—he reached for the ankle. The child grasped her uncle's hand and allowed Smith to pick up the leg with only a little mew. That was a good start. The bullet was still in there—no exit wound. That might be the lead he could feel on the medial side, or it might be a sizable piece of shattered bone. No telling whether it would be hard to get out—might be a bastard. As Smith examined the ankle, Leaf mewled softly, but did not cry out. She was a brave little girl, a Cheyenne, and Cheyennes endured pain without complaint. Her little cries would be the musical accompaniment to Smith's job, and he would hate that.

He set the leg down and looked at Twist. The man was a smoking volcano of antagonism—best just to ignore him.

Smith couldn't get his mind off the one medicine in the bag Elaine was bringing that would help. Chloroform. It would help a lot. Save Leaf a lot of pain. Keep her still, and let Smith cut without damaging a tendon or an artery because she jumped at the wrong instant. Without it, Smith might not get the job done at all. Without it, he could ruin her ankle completely. Without it, he could set her to bleeding and kill her.

Smith knew damn well he wouldn't get to use it.

In his months at the agency, Smith had not been able to get any Indian to take chloroform. He showed them how it worked—he wanted them to make their decisions with open eyes—and they despised it. Pain was not important to them. The little death they saw, the death of the spirit, overawed them. They did not seem impressed that men who passed through the little death came back apparently as good as ever. The idea of surrendering the spirit to unknown forces—that was what horrified them.

Of course, they didn't denounce Smith's medicine. That would have been rude. Tolerantly, they said it was fine for the white man. But when the time came to take it, they shook their heads stubbornly.

Elaine and Medicine Wolf came back together. Elaine set the tools and medicines next to Smith's fire. Medicine Wolf's piece of hide soaked in a bucket, even though it was still green and soft. Smith and Elaine got to heating the scalpels and tweezers in the little flame. The rain held off, but the wind picked up—typical plains rainstorm, plenty to blow the dust around but not enough to wet it.

All right. No more delaying. Talk the bastard into it. "I want to put her to sleep," Smith said boldly to Twist. Twist controlled his face furiously. Medicine Wolf and Twist waited for Smith to finish speaking, as courtesy demanded. Smith spoke of how the little sleep wouldn't hurt the child, would save her a lot of pain, might help her walk

better, might even save her life. Smith spoke the words
smoothly, confident on the outside, on the inside hopeless.

Twist gave Medicine Wolf a sneering look, turned to
Smith, and shook his head.

"No little death," Medicine Wolf added hoarsely.

Smith looked at Elaine. Her eyes were sharp with
disapproval and anger. He and she disagreed about this.
You have to do what you know is right, she argued, whether
they see it or not. You have to treat them like adult human
beings, he answered, and recognize that they're in charge
of their own lives. Otherwise you're as big an ass as the
agents and missionaries who force "improvements" on
them.

Elaine handed Smith the sterilized scalpel without a
word.

Smith looked at Leaf's eyes. She was scared to death of
the scalpel. She would do her damnedest for her uncle, and
she would be goddamn courageous, and if Smith had to look
at her eyes, it would drive him crazy.

Work! he ordered himself.

He propped the lower leg on his lap with the medial
side in. If that was the bullet, he would have to be careful
of that artery. But the lead looked like it lay to the side of
that tendon.

He motioned Medicine Wolf and the uncle close and
got them to hold knee and foot—tight! he told them, as
tight as you can.

Then he made the incision, and the jerk was not too
bad, and his hands were devoted wholly to his task.

Unfortunately, his mind still listened to Elaine and
Medicine Wolf shout back and forth in imagination. Elaine
snapped self-righteously, "Do what's right, for pity's sake!"

"No little death," Medicine Wolf answered implacably.

The world *death* gonged in Smith's mind, and Elaine
shouted over it, "Do what's right!"

* * *

The blood hit him square in the cheek and blinded him in that eye.

Smith grabbed Leaf's leg back. Christ, she'd had a spasm and her foot had moved and obviously he'd cut the goddamn artery and he couldn't see anything and damn blood was everywhere and . . .

The spurt stopped. Instantly he got a compress on the bleeder. The heart pumped and blood sprayed again.

He threw the compress away and pressed on the artery above with both hands and a lot of his weight. The blood still spurted a little. Goddammit.

Elaine was already putting the tourniquet on. Damn, she was good. She started cranking. Smith put more pressure on the artery with both hands and blinked his eye, trying to get the blood out. The bleeder still spurted a little.

As Elaine got the tourniquet tight, the spurts changed to oozes. Smith could see the bleeder, cut transversely, its end poking out rudely. He would have to tie the son of a bitch off.

Elaine gave him a fierce look, but, hell, self-accusations were already clanging through his head. He couldn't knock Leaf out, but he had to. Smith felt like his chest would bust. He wanted to bellow like a gut-shot bull.

He looked frantically at Leaf. She was relaxed now, her body no longer convulsed with pain. Except for her eyes, you could almost believe she was asleep. Her eyes were huge, and transported by pain.

He had to put her out. He couldn't put her out.

Suddenly his mind went blank and calm. At that moment the rain came, big, sparse drops blown hard.

"Thread!" he said in English. Elaine handed the silk to him and he went to work on the bleeder. He tied it off easily—he felt nimble-fingered as an elf. The tie looked like it would hold, for sure.

"Loosen the tourniquet," he said in English. She did. The artery bulged and the tie held.

Smith felt peculiarly lucid. "Give me some alcohol on a compress," he said in English. With that, he wiped blood off the outside of the wound. Antisepsis, he thought serenely.

He was peaceful with it now. So he was an ass. He asked Twist and Medicine Wolf to get the canvas ground cloth from under the girl and hold it over her against the rain. When they were fully occupied, he said to Elaine, "Give me some chloroform on a compress." He spoke without emphasis and again in English. She acted without expression. Twist and Medicine Wolf were unfolding the ground cloth.

When he had the compress in his hand and smelled its familiar, sickly-sweet odor, he leaned forward onto his knees and clamped it hard onto Leaf's mouth and nose.

Twist seized Smith's wrist and elbow and pulled hard. Smith resisted for a moment and then gave in. The child had taken a big breath reflexively when Smith covered her nostrils, and she was already out.

Twist grabbed for Smith's throat, but Medicine Wolf held him back. Smith was sure that if he weren't needed to finish the procedure, the Indian would have killed him in that moment. Instead he cursed the goddamn *veho* vividly, mixing in the white-man word *goddamn* over and over.

Smith met Medicine Wolf's eyes over Twist's shoulder—they brimmed with contempt.

Smith simply pointed to the ground cloth and turned back to his work. In only moments he held the bullet in his hands. He put it on the child's chest—she might want to keep it. She was asleep now, and he felt her peace.

As he started to set the bones, the rain really came, hitting hard. The cloth seemed to cover all of Leaf, but not much of the surgeon. Smith smiled to himself about that.

He set himself and pulled hard on the foot—it came. He eased off and slid the bones together—they went into place with amazing ease. He could feel that they were right. He was profoundly glad. He was proud.

He put Medicine Wolf's poultice on the wound and bound it with white cotton, his hands still sure.

He asked Elaine to trade places with Medicine Wolf. Taking the hide out of the bucket, he asked the medicine man, "Will you help me?"

Without a word Medicine Wolf took the hide and began to splint Leaf's leg. Then he stitched it tight with sinew and cut a hole to give access to the flesh wound. In a few days the hide split would dry rigid, firmer than any wooden splint. In a couple of weeks Leaf would actually be able to walk on it.

It was done. It was done well. Smith touched Medicine Wolf on the shoulder and smiled.

"Thank you," Smith said to Medicine Wolf. He had to resist shaking hands. "Thank you" to Twist without looking at the warrior, then "Thank you" to Elaine. They let the ground cloth down and covered Leaf carefully with it. She wasn't stirring yet.

The medicine man stomped off. So Smith had lost the support of the man of red medicine.

Twist sat down at Leaf's head stiffly, one hand against her cheek. Smith refused to look at his face. Elaine gathered up the tools and medicines and went to put them away.

Smith knelt by his patient. He wanted to move up and hold her head, hold her until she came out of the anesthetic. But he could feel Twist's fury radiating through the storm-blown air.

So Smith just knelt there in the rain. In a few minutes Leaf would come around. He wanted to be there and speak words of reassurance to her.

Already he was drenched. He smiled to himself a little. Drenched with pride. Drenched with humiliation.

What an ass he was.

≈ 8 ≈

Elaine felt Adam stir, and she came awake with a start. Calling Eagle was shaking him. Calling Eagle had found Elaine and Adam where they hid in the rocks, so their lovemaking would not be overheard. Half-awake, half-dreaming, Elaine imagined that the old woman saw everything and knew everything and understood everything— she was omnipresent and omniscient, like some sort of pagan deity. She doubtless would have communicated her knowledge of the future to lesser mortals if it would have helped them, or given them hope.

"The people need you," Calling Eagle said mysteriously. Adam picked up his parfleche of medicines and moved out, still pulling up his pants. Elaine was almost as quick behind him. They walked fast after Calling Eagle through the dark toward the head of the gully.

"*Hoka hey!*" exclaimed Adam, and turned back to Elaine with a big grin. Beyond him Elaine saw Enemy, one of the two women who had led the lost group of women and children.

"*Hoka hey!*" Elaine answered her husband in his language. Her Cheyenne was reasonably good, and she smiled at herself for feeling self-conscious using the phrase.

The lost women and kids must have slipped around the soldiers in the middle of the night. They were crowded around a couple of small fires, eating soup and fresh-roasted meat, half a dozen women and three times that many children. Probably fifty of the people were awake tending to them and talking with them—everyone had been so worried. Though no one said so, they all knew that if those who fell behind didn't come in—if the soldiers turned them back, or they went back out of weariness—their families

68

would have to go back to the agency. And that would make the group weaker.

Elaine looked at the faces of the women, haggard from their nights of travel, but happy and animated now that they were with their families and being fed and would have a little chance to rest. The children looked worse. Some of them were barefoot, the soles of their feet raw and bleeding. Others looked truly exhausted, falling asleep as their relatives ladled soup into their mouths. Elaine supposed they were mostly orphans.

A middle-aged woman clopped stiffly toward them, and Calling Eagle embraced her. "Brave One also led them in," Calling Eagle said in introduction. A brave one for sure, thought Elaine.

Adam stopped to look at the feet of a boy about eight and started to rummage in his bag for an unguent, but Brave One said, "Rain first."

Smith looked askance at Elaine. Then Elaine remembered. The girl named Rain was a relative—the wife of Adam's cousin Red Hand. In fact, Elaine knew her a little. She used to bring her younger brother to the school and sit in the back and do beadwork during his lessons. She was a slight, shy creature, uncomfortable talking to Elaine, but endearing. She had a remarkably lovely oval face. She'd stopped coming to the school months ago, before Adam came to the agency. Elaine never knew why she stopped coming, but Adam did say later that Red Hand had died, and Red Hand's older wife, who was Rain's sister.

The teenage girl named Rain was huddled beneath a blanket. She didn't look so much asleep as half-dead. Elaine supposed she would recover, but her beautiful face was wan and pinched, suggesting fatigue beyond human endurance.

Brave One drew back the blanket. A boy-child a few days old sucked at Rain's left breast. The breast looked so withered the infant must have been starving to death.

"Dehydrated, both of them," said Adam to Elaine in English. "Water and a cup and rag." His bossy mode, but

Elaine didn't mind. In a couple of minutes they had the
child sucking on a teat of wet cloth, and Adam bathed
Rain's face and dribbled water into her mouth.

"She fell behind us to give birth," said Brave One.
"She just caught up this afternoon. We didn't think she
would."

Adam nodded. "A little soup, too," he said to Calling
Eagle. "We thought she'd stayed behind at the agency," he
told Brave One.

Elaine remembered. She'd said she couldn't travel
because the birth was so near.

"What is the child's name?" asked Elaine. She held the
boy, feeding him.

"There's a story behind it," said Brave One, glancing at
the white woman curiously. Elaine knew she wondered
whether a white person would understand.

"Out with it," prompted Adam.

"She will tell you," said Brave One, smiling.

Elaine sat with Rain all night. Adam circulated among
the children and juggled his ivory balls for the ones who
were awake. Elaine felt touched by Rain, a fragile creature.
The girl even had a fancy cloth dress, undoubtedly taken
in a raid, to make her seem more beautiful. Somewhere in
the middle of the vigil Elaine realized that she had a
new . . . sister?

Rain was some kind of family. The last several years
of warring and dying; sickness had killed her parents.
She was wed to Red Hand because her sister was his first
wife. Now they were dead, and Rain had only her dead
husband's family. That's all the child had, too, a child so far
nameless.

Near dawn, after eating a little broth, she was able to
talk. She spoke softly, sometimes hesitantly, often looking
at the infant sleeping in her lap. Though she kept her eyes
down, modestly, Elaine could see how intently she meant

every word. "I was about to give birth in an open place,
afraid the soldiers would find me. Perhaps kill me, and rip
the child out of my belly with the long knives. Like Sand
Creek." Calling Eagle gave Elaine a hard look.

"Just as he . . . came out, a big soldier did come. I
couldn't do anything—couldn't run, couldn't defend
myself." Elaine knew that Cheyenne women were very
modest, and intensely private about childbirth—poor Rain
must have been terrified.

"But I was *not* afraid," Rain went on. "I thought the
birth would kill me anyway, and my child would die from
lack of care. So I had given up on living. I just wanted to
get him out into the air and hold him and lift him to the
four directions, to let him see the earth and feel the
powers while he breathed." She touched her son's head
delicately.

"But the big soldier just watched me. He didn't say
anything, or do anything.

"Then I understood. He was not merely a soldier—he
couldn't be, he would have killed me—he was a spirit in the
form of a soldier.

"Such power frightened me a little. More than a little.
But I knew everything would be all right, everything would
be blessed." Then the words came in a soft, quick rustle. "I
pushed the child out, held him up to the four directions,
the sky, and the earth, and he was alive and made special by
this spirit and I was profoundly happy." She was silent
awhile.

"But I couldn't nurse him. My dress was closed."
She opened the blanket on her shoulders and indicated the
bodice of her fancy dress, which was ripped open to
the waist. She closed the blanket modestly. "So I asked
the spirit to undo the buttons." She used the English
words *buttons*, since Cheyenne had no equivalent. "Instead
the spirit cut open my dress the way you see. It made
me feel . . . shaky"—she shivered just remembering—
"to let the blade come so close. Shaky but grand." She
hesitated, and when she spoke looked transcendent. "Then
I simply exposed my breasts in front of him and all the

world, and nursed my son. I knew the spirit would not hurt me.

"No, he helped me. He cut the dress open for me. And then went away. Without a word. He didn't give me a song, or show me a dance, he just walked away.

"I am awed at this appearance, this power at the birth of my son. A warrior took care of him. He will be a great warrior. I have named him"—she used the English words—"Big Soldier."

By noon the mother and child looked better, much better. Smith and Elaine had taken them to the family fire and were still keeping a close watch on them.

A dog soldier, Calling Eagle reported, had stolen some cavalry horses during the night, and one set of saddlebags held a little ammunition, and another held lots of dollars. Now it would be easier to get horses and guns.

At noon the soldiers were pulling out in the direction of the agency. Cheyenne warriors stood exposed within shooting range, but did not shoot. Elaine stood tremulously between Adam and Calling Eagle and watched them go.

"Maybe the powers were with us here," murmured Adam.

"We are very lucky," said Elaine. "All of us," she said, thinking of Rain and Big Soldier.

Calling Eagle looked at her piteously.

The Tsistsistas-Suhtaio moved out to the north. Though they had escaped the soldiers once, though they were all together again, and though they now had more horses, their mood was caution. Everyone was worried about the Arkansas River, the next big obstacle. This rainy summer it would be high, and likely hard to cross. Worse, the railroad ran along the river, so maybe they would run into soldiers, maybe lots of soldiers.

On Bear Creek they had a little skirmish with soldiers, but drove them off easily. But that night they got bad news—the first Cheyenne had been killed by white men. Black Beaver had gone to a ranch with some dollars to buy horses, but the whites shot him and took the money. The young men wanted to ride out and kill the whites and burn the ranch, but Little Wolf held them back with pointed words.

And a couple of days later, farther up Bear Creek they exchanged a few more shots with soldiers. "They're like goddamn gnats," Smith told Elaine. "They're not serious, but you can't shoo them off." He gave her an imitation of his carefree grin, but she didn't smile back.

That evening Smith saw Twist, Medicine Wolf, Bridge, who was another healer, and Young Eagle hurrying toward the other end of camp. Twist scowled at Smith as they went by. Medicine Wolf kept his eyes on the ground. Young Eagle carried his medicine flute.

Smith's throat clenched. Elaine touched his hand gently. So that was it. Nevertheless, he wanted to see, so he followed the medicine men.

The victim was Sitting Man, brought in by other scouts on a litter, and he was shot on the inside of the thigh. It was bleeding profusely—Sitting Man would bleed to death pretty damn quick.

Without thinking, Smith pushed through the family members around Sitting Man. Before Smith could squat beside the patient, Twist was there. His hand was on Smith's chest, his face in Smith's face, virulently bitter. He pushed Smith backward almost as much with his eyes as his hand.

Medicine Wolf said lightly, "The family wants the

medicine of the Human Beings, not the whites. Bridge is going to stop the bleeding." Bridge nodded.

Smith thought, He's going to die. Then he yelled at himself in his head, It's up to him—he's got a right to decide. For a moment Smith felt like brain cell ground against brain cell while he forced himself to a decision. Then he spoke with a thin edge of control. "I want to watch you do it."

Bridge hesitated, and then nodded.

Bridge gave Sitting Man something red to drink— Smith couldn't guess what it was. While Young Eagle played his flute, Medicine Wolf sang and shook a rattle. Sitting Man was quickly asleep.

Anesthetic, Smith said to himself, taken aback. But the patient could have passed out from loss of blood, too. Smith's hands were quivering with frustration.

Bridge passed a painted gourd across Sitting Man's chest, over and over, more and more slowly. All the while he sang his chanting song, and sometimes snorted or bellowed. Smith's eyes were on the wound. At first the blood still welled out. Gradually, it slowed. Finally, it turned to a trickle.

Everything was hushed except for the flute—it seemed to Smith the world itself was hushed.

Bridge had stopped the bleeding.

Or the bleeding had stopped on its own? Smith asked himself.

To the accompaniment of the soft tones of the flute, Bridge cleaned the wound with silver sage, sprinkled it with tufts from a puffball, and bound it with cloth.

Bridge glanced up at Smith—only a brief glance, but there was pride in it, Smith thought. Justified pride.

Twist stepped around the unconscious Sitting Man and came toward Smith, glaring.

Smith turned and walked away quietly. He wanted to think, and recover. He would juggle for a while.

* * *

The next day they traveled during the daylight—sometimes they chose day, sometimes night, depending on whether they needed to keep the soldiers from actually seeing them.

That night they had a good feed. The young men had run off a few cattle from some ranch, and there was meat for everybody. Elaine was so hungry, she didn't care that they had no vegetables—she wolfed down the beef.

"Meat is good for Big Soldier," Adam told Rain. Elaine knew he worried that the girl didn't eat enough. Big Soldier had been premature, and needed lots of nourishment. He seemed plenty hungry. Even now, while Rain ate, Big Soldier sucked away. Rain had on a Cheyenne-style dress of deerskin now, one that had huge arms that were laced underneath, so she could slip the child in and out without compromising modesty.

"Next summer maybe we will have a brother for Big Soldier," said Calling Eagle.

"That would be good," said Lisette.

Elaine saw Adam start to agree and then back off, eyeing his mother.

"A cousin," said Elaine. Rain put her Big Soldier on her shoulder to burp him, but Elaine rose and picked him up.

"No, a brother," said Calling Eagle. "Or sister."

"I never have gotten the ways of speaking of relationship straight," said Elaine. She began walking back and forth, patting Big Soldier on the back.

"One father, two mothers—brothers," Lisette said cheerfully.

Now Adam had a glint in his eye.

"One father—Adam is considered the father because he has taken Rain and Big Soldier in?" Elaine felt her innocence and began to feel something more. Big Soldier's stomach growled.

"Yes, sort of," said Lisette. She smiled. Elaine had seldom heard Lisette talk so much.

"Mostly because Vekifs is now the husband of Big Soldier's mother," said Calling Eagle. Big Soldier's stomach growled.

Elaine saw Adam look a warning at his grandmother. Was there something going on here she didn't know about? Some sort of conspiracy?

She approached it cautiously but firmly. "Adam is my husband."

Calling Eagle nodded and smiled wickedly. "And Rain's husband now."

Elaine lost her balance for a moment and nearly fell. Adam grabbed her, and she clung fiercely to Big Soldier.

"*What?*" Elaine snapped at Calling Eagle.

The old woman shrugged. "It is our way."

Elaine suddenly felt sure she'd sold herself into barbarism with this marriage.

"That's enough," said Adam.

"Adam Smith Maclean, you haven't—"

Adam cut her off. "They're teasing you." Big Soldier's stomach rumbled again.

"It is our tradition," said Calling Eagle, shrugging. "You are obliged to take Rain in. . . ."

Rain smiled at Elaine, and Elaine hadn't the damnedest idea what that meant.

"Adam Smith Maclean," she started in. . . .

Adam took her by both shoulders and looked her in the eye. "They're teasing you," he repeated. "We have no such custom. I can take her in without taking her as a wife."

Elaine felt she might collapse if Adam weren't holding her up.

"You are all the wife I can handle," he said.

Lisette came and put an arm around Elaine's waist affectionately. "We really were just teasing," Adam's mother said.

"They were unkind to tease you like that," Rain said.

"You better believe I'm all you can handle," Elaine

snapped at Adam. But she wondered if he didn't want more sex than she could offer.

"You are all the wife I want," Adam told her straight in the eye.

Big Soldier emitted a long, raspy burp.

Calling Eagle lay in her blankets before first light, unmoving, looking at the great patterns of stars. She had lain here awake for nearly an hour, accepting. She had seen it clearly in her dream this time—had seen herself dead—and had heard the song the wolf sang for her. It was not being dead that concerned or surprised her. It was that there in the tree, on her scaffold of death, she was dressed like a man. And she was laid out with the weapons of a warrior. She, Calling Eagle.

In the first dream night before last she had not seen it clearly—it had come to her as it might be seen through the white man's glass windows, murky and distorted. It had come in jumbled bits and pieces, shards and splinters. She had not even actually seen herself on her scaffold—at least she could not bring back the picture. She woke up unsure how she got the impression that she was dressed like a man. Perhaps she had heard someone in the dream speak of her breechcloth or leggings. Or heard someone actually speak of herself as *him*.

This time she had seen it all. Not only the breechcloth but the pattern and colors of the quillwork on it. Not only her man's face but the paint on it. Tomahawk and war club laid across her chest. And the song.

It was wonderfully strange. A he-wolf sat below the body on the scaffold, like a mourner, and he sang. He didn't howl—he sang, with a human voice, dark-timbred, reedy, but human. Calling Eagle heard the words of an old victory song, the invitation of the wolflike Cheyenne warrior for his cousins the wolves to feed on the bodies of his enemies:

> Ho! Listen! Come to us! Feast!
> O wolves!
> Feast and make merry,

> *Yo ho! Gather*
> *At the dawn.*

The victory song of a wolf warrior. Now she knew. And she would act accordingly.

With the practiced discipline of seventy years, she put away that matter, which was of the highest importance, and turned her attention to what else disturbed her during the dream.

The white woman. During the dream Calling Eagle had not seen Elaine, but she kept having an urgent feeling that the people had to get the white woman out of camp, get her gone. Sometimes a desperate feeling.

Calling Eagle felt for Elaine. She thought Elaine was giving her life as a gesture of love to Smith and to the Tsistsistas-Suhtaio. But even love could be wrongheaded.

In Elaine's understanding the Cheyennes were child-like people in need of affection and assistance. She and the agent and the missionaries and the doctors were ministers of kindness, wise, benevolent adults tending to ignorant children.

This understanding kept Elaine from seeing the realities before her face. She thought this flight northward was a heroic show of spirit, but misguided. She thought the way to a better life was capitulation. She was waiting for the people to give in to the greater physical force.

Elaine's understanding did not allow her to see that the struggle here was of the spirit. Not barbarism against science, or arrows against bullets, but old, mysterious powers against new, mysterious powers. Powers of honor and beauty against ugliness and falseness. So Elaine could not understand, in her kindly, white way, what the Cheyennes had to live for, or to die for.

Calling Eagle herself did not know much about the great powers. In a long lifetime of study she had learned only how to make certain gestures of obeisance to them. Certainly she could not command the powers. But, unlike the white woman, she did feel their presence.

Calling Eagle thought it was odd, surpassing odd, to

walk the earth and be unaware of the powers. How could
the whites have no sense of the mysterious power in water
that makes it flow downhill, in grass that makes it turn
green in the spring, in a bird that makes it rise on the wind?

After decades of observation, though, Calling Eagle
had come to accept the fact that white people did not see
and hear the powers. They saw the rock, but not the spirit
of the rock that made it hard. She pitied them for their
blindness.

Of course, the white woman understood nothing about
Calling Eagle either. Elaine did not grasp that Calling
Eagle had special powers given only to the *hemaneh*.
Elaine did not even imagine such powers, or imagine
Calling Eagle's true way.

There in the dark Calling Eagle smiled a wrinkled and
distant smile. Elaine would be upset when she learned
Calling Eagle's way. All the whites had been, even the
Cheyennes' friend De Smet, the blackrobe—even Mac
Maclean, Calling Eagle's son, her first Vekifs.

Well, the blind Elaine would soon see more about
Calling Eagle. How would the white woman respond?
Regrettably, it made no difference.

The old woman rolled over. She had brought her quills
and paints. She could get a good piece of cloth from
someone. She would help Lisette and Rain do the
quillwork—Calling Eagle was especially skilled at quillwork. To save the people, it had to get done fast.

The scouts brought bad news that day. The white
people all over the country ahead, which they called
Kansas, were in an uproar about Indian troubles. Their
newspapers talked about little else. Their governor helped
arm the town of Dodge, a ride of a day or two from where
the tribe would cross the Arkansas. Army posts were on
alert. White people everywhere were demanding protection from the marauding savages.

Scouts who had spent time among the whites sneaked into Dodge City and Fort Dodge and got all this news. Everyone agreed they were lucky to know what was going on. Smith read the newspapers the scouts brought back and confirmed that things were at least as bad as the scouts said. They could expect big trouble at the crossing of the Arkansas, if not before.

What no one could understand was why the whites thought so many ranches had been raided, so many people killed. It was true that Little Wolf and Morning Star could not always control the young men, but the newspapers were reporting at least a hundred whites killed. The Tsistsistas-Suhtaio could count six.

A special train would take troops and volunteers from Dodge City to the river crossing the whites called Dull Knife, one of the names of Morning Star, turning two days on horseback into two hours by rail. That was where the Cheyennes were headed. Volunteers meant cowboys and other men who were eager to kill Indians. That was bad. The people had encountered white volunteers before—at Sand Creek, and at the fight against the buffalo hunters on the Sappa Creek, and other places. Volunteers lacked the discipline of troops and went wild. Sappa Creek had horrified these Cheyennes, and they still wouldn't talk about it.

In camp tonight the people were worried. Maybe a big massacre here, another Sand Creek, would end it all.

So they were astounded when the crier came around the camp announcing a great feast to be offered by Lisette two nights from then. A great feast meant a day spent in camp when they needed to be hurrying north every hour. But it also meant powerful medicine, medicine that might change the destiny of the people. They couldn't imagine what.

* * *

Smith and Elaine were as curious as anybody about why his mother would give a feast now. When she asked them to get a horse for the feast, though, they asked no questions, but simply rode out to trade for one. At Elaine's suggestion, they decked themselves out as respectable white folks. Elaine put on her best dress. Smith wore his proper doctor's outfit, his black Prince Albert coat, gray woolen trousers, and Jefferson boots.

Smith felt silly dressed up that way, maybe even dishonest. Could clothes make a giant, long-haired half-breed look respectable? But Elaine looked at him benevolently and said, "You *are* a doctor, you know."

It turned out that Elaine's idea was a good one. Despite her presence the rancher eyed Smith suspiciously. But he got a fat animal in exchange for his revolver. The rancher said he needed the weapon more than a critter the marauding redskins were going to run off anyway. This remark came with more dark looks.

Elaine and Rain spent all the next day cooking. Lisette and Calling Eagle couldn't help because they were busy doing something in private—sewing, Smith gathered. The horse would not make a proper feast—buffalo would have been a better way to set off an auspicious occasion. Smith knew his mother also would have wanted to serve cakes of cornmeal, Jerusalem artichokes, coffee with lots of sugar, and other treats. But she didn't have them, and Calling Eagle wouldn't wait. Though Smith had no idea why, he felt patient. Patience was something he'd learned from his people.

Elaine reflected that evening, as she tasted horse meat for the first time in her life, that she had changed. She didn't quail at tasting this flesh at all. She merely hoped that it would help the people recoup their strength.

The loss of a day's travel worried her—it just gave those soldiers another day to get on the train and out to the

Dull Knife crossing and intercept the Cheyennes. But she saw that the day's rest did the people some good, especially the children. And she saw that everyone was cheered at the prospect of some beneficial medicine. Though she was glad for anything that raised their spirits, she wondered that their minds were not more on the menace of rifles and cannons. They really were children.

During the meal, Adam was a little too attentive to her—too many white smiles in his dark face, too many mischievous looks, too many affectionate touches. She wondered what surprise was coming. Probably Adam wondered, too, she reflected.

Calling Eagle waited until full dark to gather the people in a big circle. Adam and Elaine sat right in front. In silence Calling Eagle started the fires laid by Adam. She laid out on the ground a handsome breechcloth of dark blue trade cloth with a four-directions wheel quilled into its front in gold, light blue, and rose. Beside that she laid a cudgel. Elaine had seen the cudgel before. It was a bighorn ram's horn pulled to three-foot length and ornamented with a brass head—a handsome piece, and heavy. It had belonged to her husband, Strikes Foot, and occupied an honored place in the lodge Calling Eagle and Lisette normally shared. Next to the cudgel Calling Eagle set a parfleche box, but Elaine couldn't see what was in it.

"What's she going to do?" whispered Elaine.

Adam said softly, "I don't know." He didn't sound happy about it.

"I had a dream," Calling Eagle began gently, crooning the words. Elaine got that phrase, and most others, but she had difficulty with some. Calling Eagle spoke in a ceremonial way, an elevated blend of speech, prayer, and song. She faced each cluster of people in turn, so that her back was sometimes to Elaine.

Elaine got the gist of it: Calling Eagle dreamed that she saw herself dead, on a scaffold, dressed as a warrior. Elaine felt a thrill—she had heard of woman warriors among the Indians. Maybe Calling Eagle would claim this rarest of stations.

The people knew that many years before, Calling
Eagle chanted, the child Calling Eagle had seen herself as
a *hemaneh* in a dream. That was a great calling to power.
Calling Eagle repeated once more, and for the last time,
she said, the song she had been given in that dream.

Elaine wished she knew what *hemaneh* meant.

So, the old woman continued in singsong speech, she
had followed the way of the *hemaneh* all her life. She had
lived with Strikes Foot—Elaine wasn't getting all of this—
she had gone on hunts and pony raids, she had sung certain
songs, performed certain ceremonies for the benefit of the
people, had lived in the way her vision showed her.

Now, in this time of trial for the people, the powers
had sent her a new dream. Now she would live in a new
way.

Elaine was fascinated—she felt goose-bumpy. Adam
slipped a comforting arm around her. He seemed tense.

Now Medicine Wolf began to beat softly on his drum,
and Calling Eagle began to sing, a song given her by a wolf
in the dream, a song that spoke of the new way. And as she
sang, turned sideways to Elaine, she walked close to the
people on the west side of the circle and began to pull her
dress up over her head.

The sight of bare flesh was rare among the Cheyennes,
a modest people, and Elaine noticed that almost everyone
sat with eyes averted. Elaine gritted her teeth, but she
supposed all the people were as shocked as she was, and
only religion could compel this behavior.

Soon Calling Eagle stood entirely naked, her ancient
dugs the merest hints of breasts. As she sang, she took
paints from the parfleche box and began to paint her face.

Still singing, her face painted, Calling Eagle turned
her back to Elaine and approached the people on the north
side. Elaine caught most of the words of the song—the
phrases *youthful power* and *untapped power* kept recurring. A hush of awe came over the people.

Calling Eagle now walked toward the people on the
east side of the circle, to Elaine's right. Calling Eagle tied
a wolf's tail into her hair. Still she sang her hymn to *power*.

Elaine strained to see something odd in the area of Calling Eagle's hips, but the firelight was too weak.

At last Calling Eagle approached the south side, directly in front of Elaine and Adam. Elaine felt Adam's arm tighten around her. Elaine saw unmistakably, in the pride of full revelation, that Adam's grandmother Calling Eagle was and always had been a man.

≈ 10 ≈

Elaine held on to Adam's arm, pinching it, and she didn't
care if it hurt. "You better have something to say," she
snapped in English, "and quick." He kept pulling her away
from the circle, where the people were dancing. Calling
Eagle had been given a new name, Sings Wolf, and
everyone seemed disgustingly elated.

Elaine had tried to sit through the rest of the ceremony—Adam had practically held her down—but she saw
and heard almost nothing. Calling Eagle dressed herself—
himself!—as a man, starting with the breechcloth. He took
a new name, Sings Wolf. He held up weapons and promised to use them against the whites. That brought a rousing
chorus of *hous*! from the men and trills from the women.
The whole time Elaine fought against dizziness that came
high, lurching waves.

She tried to swing Adam around and make him talk to
her. He gave her a look of—what?—some maddening
combination of chagrin and amusement—and pulled ahead.
"Down by the creek," he said in English. "We'll talk."

English—good. They usually spoke in Cheyenne, but
now she meant to make herself damned plain.

When they got to the creek, she couldn't sit down
and couldn't think of a thing to say. Humiliated—she had
been savagely humiliated. Deceived, deliberately deceived. Duped, gulled, taken in, cozened, misled, cheated,
taken for a ride, flimflammed, made a fool of—god*dammit*!

She knew she would get furious all over again later.
Furious about degeneracy, and being sucked into living
with degenerates. But now she was apocalyptically angry
about her husband goddamn *deceiving her*!

"I'm sorry," Adam said.

"Sorry about what?" she demanded, glaring.

"Sorry you had to find out this way," he answered mildly. He corrected himself, "Sorry you had to find out at all."

"Why?" she exulted. Her husband was hanging himself.

"Because it doesn't make any difference," he said stubbornly. "When he was a woman, he was still a fine person."

"When he, she, or it was a woman," she enunciated mockingly.

Adam nodded. "When he was," he said, making a point of sounding matter-of-fact. "Now he isn't."

"Degeneracy doesn't make any difference," Elaine said sarcastically. "Pederasty doesn't make any difference."

"He's not a pederast," Adam answered sharply. "He doesn't have sex with children. Never did."

"Oh, you want me to say *so-do-my.*" She punched out the syllables one at a time. "That makes it all right, then."

Now Adam did sound annoyed. "I don't know what will make it all right with you. It's all right with him, it's all right with me, and it's all right with the people."

"Fine. Just fine. Wonderful."

He clasped her wrist gently, but she jerked her arm away and glared at him.

"It's our way," he said pathetically.

"Maybe you better tell me about the rest of *your* way, and his, hers, or its way."

Adam turned on her now. "Ours, is it, and not yours? Sorry you're here? Want to get out?" Now he roared. "Why don't you go, bitch?"

She slapped him. Openhanded, with a full arm swing behind it.

It felt good. Clean. She was done with him and this marriage and these . . . losers.

She burst into tears.

He let her be. Let her cry by herself. Didn't reach out, didn't hold her.

After a few moments she staggered forward and leaned

against him. She sobbed hard now, out of control, chest
heaving up and collapsing like surf crashing on the sand. He
put both arms around her shoulders and stood still and let
her sob.

She lay with her head on his lap, her sobbing eased to
soft, relentless weeping. She was tired and worn down and
frustrated, Smith knew, and living among strangers. He
stroked her hair gently and waited.

He remembered when he first went to St. Louis,
fourteen years old, he and his brother Thomas in tow
behind their father. Mac Maclean had been born and raised
in that frontier town with pretension to Frenchified ele-
gance, and he meant for his sons to get an education
there—and at the Westover Academy, a prestigious school.

Smith and Thomas had never slept in a bed, never
worn a shoe, never eaten in a restaurant. The first few days
the white people drove them crazy. Looked at them baldly,
like trying to crawl through their eyeballs into their brains.
Touched their beaded pouches and tried to buy them.
Asked them prying questions: Who are you? Who are your
parents? Are you an Indian?

It was hard enough getting used to the most ordinary
things. Wagons would nearly run you down in the street.
Everything was crowded, and people jostled and shoved.
You had to eat with knives and forks, and you had pants
with a fly that buttoned. The boys' uncle Hugh, a store-
keeper of philosophic bent, was much amused.

Smith told his father that he damn sure wouldn't stay
in any town like this, damn sure not. But Mac and Hugh
Maclean sweet-talked the boys into staying among the
white folks and learning to get along in civilization. Necessary, said their father. Essential, echoed their uncle.

When their father headed back upriver and the boys
settled in with Uncle Hugh, things got worse instead of
better. Men insulted them on the street. Women and girls

wouldn't talk to them. Clerks who couldn't even read assumed they were stupid and tried to cheat them on their change.

Worst of all, to Smith, he never knew how people would take him. When he spoke, they acted like he was being forward. When he was silent, they called him sullen. Polite was understood as aloof. Friendly was overfamiliar. Smith acted respectful to people, so he had little eye contact with men, none with women. His respect they misunderstood for deviousness.

He had a rotten time with it. Two people got him through—Uncle Hugh with his sly humor and cunning insights into people, and Mr. Highsmith, the science teacher at the school, with his mad, all-absorbing love of plants. Smith's uncle taught him to get along in society, and his teacher took him on marvelous field outings to collect specimens.

Society was the hard part. Smith managed it, and after a while it was as easy as speaking English with his father but Cheyenne with his mother. Still, Smith hated it for a long time. He thought the white people were stinkingly offensive. As Elaine thought now about the Cheyenne people.

She had stopped crying, but didn't want to raise her head.

"Want me to tell you about Calling Eagle?" he asked softly. He apologized in his head to Sings Wolf for using the name of the person who had not yet transformed himself into a warrior.

She nodded. "I may run," she murmured.

"What?"

"I feel like jumping up and running off."

Smith wiped her face with his bandanna. "Calling Eagle was a *hemaneh*," he began. "It means 'wants to be a woman.' My people believe that some men are directed by the powers to live as women. They are told when they are boys, or young teenagers, to follow the female way. So we call them *she*, they walk like women, they talk like women, they dress like women, they dance as women, we treat them entirely as women. They take husbands, as women do. They cook, they sew, they do women's crafts like beadwork and quillwork.

"Still, we keep the awareness that they aren't women—they're something special, *hemaneh*.

"They have their own signs of not having been born women, too. Their dress isn't exactly feminine. They wear little things that men wear. Any Indian would know a *hemaneh*'s dress immediately. But white people don't."

He pulled at her fingers, stretching them the way she liked. "People weren't trying to fool you about Calling Eagle. What she was was there for you to see, in the open. When you were ready to. But we didn't tell you, because we know white people have a violent reaction to that. Even our white friends do. Even my father did.

"I didn't tell you either. I was part of the . . . It must look like a conspiracy. I was afraid to. I should have."

He caressed her earlobe between thumb and forefinger.

"These people are special to us. They alone can dedicate the medicine-lodge ceremony. They build the bonfires for the scalp dances. They create love songs, set up marriages, and help reconcile troubled couples. They do very beautiful work in beads, quills, and other women's crafts—even more beautiful, often, than the women.

"Our men ask them to go on hunts and pony raids. Strangely, because of their male power. Their unused male potency." He hesitated and went on softly, "You see, they aren't like queers"—he lay the word in gently—"in the white world. They don't do the same things. They only have sex one way, like women." He let it sit for a moment, thinking what words would be explicit enough. "They go through life with their virility unexpressed."

He wondered if she would still be repulsed. He asked himself whether she would want to stay with the tribe, and with him. He knew only that he wanted her to.

"I may run," she said.

"That's why the people were so glad at his . . . transformation. Only a vision could have told Calling Eagle to withhold the male expression. Only a vision could have told Sings Wolf to release it. Now he has a lifetime's worth to release. Declare. Explode. He will be very powerful in battle."

He raised her hand to his lips and kissed it lightly.

He waited.

He grew a little tense and waited some more.

At last he spoke. "What are you thinking?"

"I'm afraid, Adam. I'm afraid."

He lifted her to her feet and held her. And you may yet run, he thought. After a while, uncertain, he kissed her. She responded a little, then more than a little.

They went to their bedrolls and carried them into the night, both rolls on Smith's big shoulders, Elaine's arm around his waist. It was awkward, and they staggered like drunks and chuckled at themselves.

Out there in the dark they made love for only the third time in their two weeks of married life. For the first time Smith felt urgency in Elaine.

Urgency, he thought later, looking at the stars while she slept on his shoulder. Good. Something sharp about it, clawing, anxious. Violent, too. Passion. Yes, passion. Good. Unless it was a way of saying good-bye.

Lying there under the stars, in the peace that comes after love, his beloved wife sleeping snuggled close to him, Dr. Adam Smith Maclean felt unreasonably, hopelessly, infinitely forlorn.

The Human Beings obeyed Crier and scurried into the hills as fast as they could. The infantry was behind them, pushing at them, the cowboys dashed in and out on their horses, raising a lot of dust and noise, and the cavalry was trying to cut the tribe off ahead. Quick, into the little breaks of the hills.

Not that it would necessarily make any difference. The people were flabbergasted at how many soldiers there were. If the whites wanted to stay and fight this time, no Human Being would leave these clumpy little hills, ever.

Some of them hoped that the new medicine of Sings Wolf would save them. They thought of his ancient song:

> Ho! Listen! Come to us! Feast!
> O wolves!

They knew, though, that the soldiers wanted to get even for General Custer, and probably would.

The young men found a commanding place. Back a little way was a spring. While the men dug holes for rifle pits, the women dug holes to protect themselves and the children. There was nowhere else to get away from the fire.

Little Finger Nail, the painter and singer, showed his young cousin what to do if Nail was shot. "Hold the rifle high," said Little Finger Nail, "and let the bullet drop on their heads." Nail sounded cheerful. "If we die here," he declared several times, "the people will remember us forever."

A double handful of women came into the men's rifle pits this time. If the men fell, the women would pick up their guns and shoot until they died, too.

The warriors painted themselves. They sang songs over small objects of power revealed to them in visions and dreams. They put on their war gear, whose protection was spiritual as much as physical. They sang their death songs, declaring that they knew they would die today, preparing their spirits for it, accepting death.

Sings Wolf walked among them, ready. Ready to die. He had never gone into battle before. He wore the breechcloth he had seen on the scaffold, plain moccasins, and nothing else. His face was painted the way it was in his dream. It was white from the eyes up, black from the eyes down. The eyes were circled in red, the mouth in ocher. His hair was woven into a single, long braid. Old Black Hand had given him a necklace of grizzly claws, strong medicine, and he wore it around his neck.

He carried in one hand the cudgel of his husband in his former life, Strikes Foot, the brass-headed sheep's horn. In the other he held a lance borrowed from a boy. Strange, slight armament, he was declaring, but enough for Sings Wolf, a man of spiritual strength.

He walked among the warriors, letting them see that he was ready, letting them feel his power. He felt it himself, welling up in his body, seventy years' worth of masculine vitality. His arms felt fluid, his legs more supple and strong than they had since he was young. In his heart and in his mind he was fierce.

Sings Wolf strode with formal dignity among his people. He did not know what he might do today, and he did not wonder. Maybe he would strike a coup. Maybe he would take a scalp, his first. Maybe he would lead the young men in a war charge. Maybe he would live— maybe he would die. But he walked with body and spirit elevated by the powers. Live or die, he stood transfigured.

Elaine could not bear it. She crouched next to Adam in the pit while he fired his lever-action Winchester. When he told her to, she reached up without looking and cooled the barrel with her wet rag. And she thought she would go berserk. Turn into a woman tetched, or *witko*, as the Cheyennes' cousins the Lakotas said.

It was the noise. First the soldiers attacked, infantry and dismounted cavalry running closer and closer while the Cheyennes held their fire. Then, when Little Wolf called for return fire, this mind-numbing, sense-blasting din.

Elaine would have done anything to put an end to the madness. Anything. She thought her mind was fragmented, a rock smashed by sledgehammers of sound.

She felt shorn of her other sensations. She still saw, touched, and smelled, more or less, but it was all a screaming chaos. She felt an urge to hold on to the earth so she wouldn't fall off.

Adam yelled to her something about a charge off the hills behind them, to keep some mounted soldiers away from their rear. Elaine could barely sort out his words. It seemed so stupid that while the tornado sucked her understanding out, Adam would try to say something about the idiot pranks of the men fighting, on either side.

Wasn't it enough that these people, these good-hearted but crazy-minded Human Beings, were throwing their lives away because a queer decided to stop wearing dresses? In front of Adam she called Sings Wolf not *him* but *it*.

Suddenly the shooting around her stopped. An uncanny quiet held the air, a space between realities.

Then the world lurched back into its awful joint. Cheyenne war-horses roared almost right over her—a mad war charge. Sings Wolf rode at the fore. He, she, or it held a frail boy's lance held absurdly high, his, her, its body armored by his, her, its fantasies. He, she, or it was bellowing out its new song about wolves.

In her mind Elaine heard raucous, cackling laughter. A sudden memory swept through her—the stupid laughter of neighbor boys in Massachusetts. She had caught them cutting the legs off frogs one by one and throwing the creatures into the water to see if they would sink. Then the

boys smiled slyly at each other with their eyes, boasting of
their daring.

In eerie inner stillness she watched the warriors gallop
down the hill toward the lines of soldiers, lifting their
screams and their clubs and lances to the sky, while the sky
threw back at them simple, gray, solid, murdering bullets.
In her mind's eye she saw a bullet smack into a rib cage,
sundering flesh, splintering rib, smashing lung to a pulp of
blood, pink meat, and air bubbles. In her mind's eye—this
must be what they mean by a vision, she thought
caustically—she saw a bloody stump of leg whirl end over
end through the air, an arm suddenly show a black cavern
where it met its ribs, a headless body teeter on a horse's
bare back, sway giddily, then catapult into space, end over
slow-turning end, against the sky like a dark sun.

Adam's yell hit her brusquely. He was standing up,
waving his rifle in the air, hallooing. Down on the plain the
warriors rode back from the charge, and the soldiers ran
back toward their mounts and wagons. She saw, sicken-
ingly, that Adam was exhilarated, infected by the madness.
She registered remotely that the soldiers really were falling
back. The warriors regrouped and charged again. The
soldiers faced them raggedly and made smoke puff out of
their rifles. Red men and white men fell into disarray and
retreated.

Adam whooped. Elaine looked at him with a shudder.
He was so stupid. They were so stupid, all these men. And
Adam's man-woman grandmother.

Adam sang a few words—her mind didn't make words
into sense anymore. He grinned at her absurdly. She
buried her face in her hands and tremblers quaked up and
down her nerves.

The soldiers didn't come back. It was unbelievable, it
was too good to be true, it was glorious. Smith watched the

infantry and cavalry and even the cowboys move off to a distance and give up the fighting.

"They can't stand the taste of steel," he shouted out loud, surprising himself. "Not when it's rammed down their throats!" He was exultant, his nerves jumpy with excitement. He looked at Elaine. She seemed sort of traumatized. He'd heard of soldiers in the Civil War getting like that in battle, going blank.

He touched her arm and she jerked it away. She'd be better in a few minutes. A little peace would calm her down. So would knowing that the people had driven the goddamned soldiers off. The people led by Sings Wolf. Smith wanted to sing hallelujah.

Why not? "Hallelujah!" he hollered. He gave forth a few notes of the "Hallelujah Chorus" tune. "Hal-lay-ay-lu-yah!"

That night the Human Beings slipped out of the hills and made their way to the north, once more to the north, toward the crossing of the Arkansas River.

They talked it over, and decided it was the only thing to do—go north, walk toward the next river and across the next railroad track, trudge around the next town, circle the next fort—head north until they catch you and kill you. Or until you get home, home to the Powder River country.

Yes, there might be sentries tonight, and you might not get away. But go. It may be futile. What else is there to do?

Many of them now began to believe that it was not futile. They felt a conviction that they would reach the Powder River country and be permitted to stay there. In the beginning some had felt that conviction, and many had thought this journey inevitable but futile. Of those who believed, some were foolish or naive. Others were simply prideful and bullheaded. But a few thought they had a hazy glimpse of the future. Those few were men and women of vision. Others believed in the vision because they believed in the seers.

Tonight, after the Human Beings had turned back the soldiers again, against absurd odds, more believed. More dared to hope.

They would still take whatever came. But more of them smiled when they thought about it.

Sings Wolf smiled. It was a visionary's faraway smile, yet it was crossbred with irony and wariness. He had hoped at the beginning, barely hoped, and thought he was deluding himself. Now all was changed. He was transformed from a woman into a man. He was endowed with potency. He led a battle charge, and the powers expressed their will through him. Through him the people were more potent.

And the white soldiers seemed less potent. Twice they had come, seeming formidable in their strength, and twice they had gone away. No one knew why they went away—probably even they did not know. The war cries of the strong had turned futile, and the war cries of the weak had gotten strong.

Today Sings Wolf turned the soldiers away. Tonight he still could feel power rising in him. Maybe he wouldn't get home—he was old, and the powers could abandon his old body at any moment—but he still felt hope that the people would get home. What was crazy was, his hope no longer seemed crazy.

The Human Beings went quietly through the night. They found no sentries and headed for the Arkansas contentedly enough. Yes, the soldiers would be waiting for them at the river crossing. But they would venture forth, and the venturing no longer felt hopeless.

≈ 12 ≈

One fugitive, Elaine Cummings Maclean, felt in her bones that it was hopeless. She felt tired, so damn tired, of hopelessness.

They were in a big draw, in the dark, and Elaine could smell the river from here, a sweet, ripe smell. The only sounds were animal sounds, a horse clomping here, another letting out breath there, others fidgeting and creaking.

The Human Beings were fording the Arkansas at night, those who usually walked pulled up onto horses. Scouts were out looking for the white soldiers, who were surely around somewhere. The chiefs' sons Wooden Legs and Bull Hump were shepherding riders across this shallow place, showing them how to stay away from the quicksand.

Elaine couldn't see the river from where she sat her horse, but she saw it in her mind's eye, her gelding breasting the water chest deep, the moonlight reflected on the dark surface ahead, and the little waves breaking the moonlight into shards of shiny, broken glass.

The railroad tracks lay across the river on the north side, a brazen sign of danger. But the railroad brought to mind a world Elaine was no longer part of, a world where men changed life with huge railway engines, steamboats, bridges, and plows, a world where mind transformed the earth. Now Elaine lived in a world of pony drags, rivers to wade, sacred pipes, and enchanted songs, a world where magic transformed men. The white world was remote now, infinitely remote.

Adam leaned out of his own saddle, touched her arm. She knew he was worried about what she might do—run away. Except for her marriage vows, it was true, she would have fled in a moment. The gesture was no longer noble, just stupid.

Adam urged his horse forward with his knees, and she followed close behind. Lisette behind her, Rain next, bearing Big Soldier on her back, and Sings Wolf in the rear. Adam and Elaine rode big American horses, the others small Indian ponies. Without hesitation Elaine's gelding plunged into the river, the liquid making a delicious, soft, shushing sound on its belly. Already she was in almost to her knees and moving implacably across. She felt drawn to the black water. No matter how it roiled around her, it seemed cool, peaceful, enticing.

She couldn't see beyond Adam, but she followed him without thought. At times the water was only fetlock deep. She looked back and saw Lisette, Rain, and Sings Wolf following, but couldn't hear them. She felt oddly isolated, cut off from family ahead and behind, and oddly passive, distant, uninvolved. Though she must look precarious, hanging off the horse sidesaddle, she was not at all frightened of the fording. Suddenly the river rose to her thighs and her bottom and her horse was swimming.

Adam turned in the saddle and said something sharp to her. She didn't understand. He gestured hard upstream. He must mean for her to point the horse up. She did, but it was difficult to make headway against the current, and it didn't seem important. She supposed she had let him drift a little downstream. She turned the horse's head up again, but he took the bit in his teeth and swam straight. Elaine saw Lisette over her shoulder, coming up close on her pony on the upstream side.

They were getting near Adam, but farther below him than she'd thought. Elaine could hear a little turbulence in the water ahead—must be a rock. The horse struck the earth with its forefeet and started clambering into a shallower spot. She urged him up with her quirt, and the horse's hooves slipped on something slick. The big animal floundered for an instant, but lurched forward and found some footing.

Just then Lisette's pony pulled out of the deep water on Elaine's upstream side, also struggling for footing. The pony got its balance and then slipped and fell and banged into Elaine's mount. The horse jumped sideways and . . .

It was all blackness and flailing and thrashing and no air anywhere. She felt the bottom, a big rock beneath her legs and soft, sweet mud under her head. Sharp hooves slammed into her leg. It didn't matter because there was no air and there was something sweet about the water and it's all right Adam and . . .

Something huge rolled over her and for one entire eternity ground her into the river bottom and she rose above the pain, she saw hues, she floated in a world of no air but many iridescent, delicate colors and she would breathe in these utterly lovely colors and . . .

Arms came like gods and ripped her upward into the air.

Elaine sucked. It felt utterly blessed, that air. Her whole body shivered a little with the deliciousness of a breath.

A voice snapped something out—not Adam's voice, she was distantly surprised to hear, but the voice of Sings Wolf, almost in her ear.

Strong arms heaved her. Pain took her breath away. In the first shock she couldn't tell where the pain came from. Then she felt it—her shin, her right shin. She heard herself cry out a little.

Then a long time, a different eternity, of jostling and hurting and sharp mutterings before she was set down and felt the dirt underneath her back and shoulders and hips. She sensed, with a sweet regret, that perhaps she must draw away from that dark, pleasant world under-water.

Someone rolled her over and began pumping at her back. Then she recognized Adam's voice close behind her, urging her, pleading with her. She heard desperation in his voice—he must care for her. She supposed she would come back to him. But for now she must rest.

* * *

Smith crouched over his wife, less agitated now. Lisette, Rain, and Sings Wolf stood behind him, looking at doctor and patient, seeming less worried. The patient was easier—he'd administered some laudanum—so the doctor was easier.

She lay sprawled on the canvas on the riverbank, unconscious, limbs sprawled out, skirt bloody from her leg, body looking tortured but her face at peace. A peace that came out of a bottle.

A rider trotted up in the dark and dismounted. Lisette stood up and held the pony. It was Medicine Wolf. The healer squatted beside Elaine.

"The horse kicked her and rolled on her," Sings Wolf said. "Here." Smith lifted the sleeping woman's dress to show Medicine Wolf the wound, an open fracture high on the shin. The splintered tibia jutted out naked and raw.

Smith felt embarrassed, an odd reaction, he told himself, for a doctor. It wasn't that Elaine's modesty was violated by a display of shin, though she wouldn't have liked it. He felt odd that her mortality should be shown to the world, naked, through a splintered end of bone. That felt desperately intimate.

His mother touched him softly. He put an arm around her waist. Lisette had been close, quiet and steady and helpful, all through it. He always felt so good just to have her nearby. In a rare moment of foolishness she'd said it was all her fault—she'd let her pony bump Elaine's horse when the animal had poor footing. Smith said, "Nonsense." He would reassure her again later.

"Let's go to it," said Medicine Wolf, looking Smith in the eye.

Yes, he'd been stalling.

He'd had a time getting the bleeding stopped. Now they had to try to get the ends of the bone together. Otherwise the tibia would never knit, or would knit with

the ends overlapping, or maybe the wound would never
heal. Then Elaine might have a crooked leg, or a short leg.
Or no leg. Or she might die. Smith made himself use the
word in his head: Die.

He didn't think they could get the ends of bone back
together.

"We should send for Bridge," said Medicine Wolf.
Which meant one of Bridge's healing songs, the monotone
chant with snorts and bellows.

Right now that sounded ridiculous to Smith. He
wondered at himself for his intolerance. But he just shook
his head and said, "White medicine for the white woman."

Medicine Wolf moved down, sat, and put Elaine's foot
in his lap. He looked at the situation for a moment, and
without hesitation braced his moccasined foot in Elaine's
crotch for something to push against. He looked at Smith,
and Smith nodded.

Medicine Wolf began to pull. There would be nothing
delicate about this procedure. Medicine Wolf had to stop
the ends of the bone from overlapping—stretch them
beyond each other. Then Smith had to manipulate them
until they touched, and preferably matched. It was tricky
work under any circumstances, feeling bones through the
musculature of the calf, getting the splintered ends to mesh
perfectly. The dark and the desperation made it worse.

Smith grasped Elaine's ankle with his huge hands and
helped Medicine Wolf pull.

Smith squatted and rested his hands on his knees and
tried to rest his mind from it. He felt like he'd got the bones
to touch—Medicine Wolf had had a hell of a time pulling
the leg out far enough—but the leg didn't look right and
didn't feel right.

Medicine Wolf sewed the splint of green hide onto her
leg now. The splint wouldn't mean anything if the bones
didn't knit square.

Lisette and Rain sat quietly beside Smith, and he felt like holding her and getting teary. He was grateful for the closeness of Rain as well as his mother. Sings Wolf stood, and Smith could not bring himself to look into the old man's face.

"Is she all right?" Sings Wolf asked.

Without looking up, Smith shook his head.

"Can you help her?" the old man insisted. He was deliberately being hard.

"If we could put her in traction," Smith said, using an English word that could mean nothing to Sings Wolf. "She may end up with a crooked leg." Smith mulled over the next words. "Or no leg. And she may be hurt inside."

"She has to go to the white people," said Sings Wolf.

Smith raised his head and looked into his grandfather's eyes. Maybe Sings Wolf meant only that Elaine needed medical attention. But Smith heard hints of other declarations. That Elaine was no good for the tribe. That the Tsistsistas-Suhtaio were moving further into the world of spiritual power, where a white person didn't belong. That Sings Wolf's power might get the Human Beings through, if Elaine wasn't there with her *veho* spirit.

Smith spoke hard. "We'll have another look at the leg in the morning," he said. He refused to grant more than that. Which was stupid.

Hooves clopped, a horse shook audibly, and two riders appeared out of the night, out of the river. In the lead Smith saw a young dog soldier—he couldn't remember the man's name. These men brought up the rear, guarding against the soldiers.

Smith decided to bring the men into it. "We need poles for a litter," he said.

"For the white woman," the dog soldier replied tersely.

"For the woman," Smith said defensively.

The other rider reined his pony in beside the dog soldier. It was Twist. Staring at Smith with contempt, the warrior made a hissing sound, like a snake.

Smith wanted to kill the bastard.

The two riders touched their heels to their ponies and rode on. Refusing to help was a grave and deliberate insult.

Smith started to his feet, murder in his eyes.

A strong hand pushed him back down. "I'll get the poles," said Sings Wolf. Smith thought his glance said, See what I mean?

On a fine morning in late September a couple of days later, Smith stood naked by a little campfire, holding up two pairs of pants. He'd just slipped out of the ones he'd torn up for leggings. He was about to put on the others, a fine worsted pair, suitable for a college graduate and professional man. He looked across the fire at his grandfather, who was relishing Smith's discomfort.

"It feels dishonest," said Smith.

"It's honest," Sings Wolf mumbled, smiling around a piece of antelope meat.

Smith pondered that a moment. It might mean that Smith was really a white man and belonged in those damned things with a fly that buttoned. He looked at Sings Wolf for irony, but saw nothing but his grandfather eating greedily. Sings Wolf tended not to judge, merely to observe with amusement.

Still, Smith felt dishonest.

To hell with it. He pulled the pants on and reached for the shoes, properly short Jefferson boots. He'd ripped up his other pants for use with a breechcloth.

He felt good about something, at least. He was doing what needed to be done. Today he would get Elaine to Dodge City or Fort Dodge and find the best doctor available. He looked at her wrapped in her blankets, still not talking much, sipping on the broth he'd insisted she take. Her face was haggard, which meant she hurt pretty bad. This morning's laudanum wasn't helping her yet. She had to be medicated to travel, because the travois bumped and lurched.

The morning after the ford of the Arkansas, when the Cheyennes stopped to sleep through the daylight, Smith had been able to make the decision comfortably. Elaine might have internal injuries. She surely needed traction for that leg. She had to go to Fort Dodge or to Dodge City, east along the railroad. Had to—everyone agreed.

Smith told them all he would rejoin the Tsistsistas-Suhtaio about a week ahead. Their trail was high, wide, and handsome—as easy for Smith to follow as for the soldiers. Smith could see some of the Cheyennes didn't think he'd come back. They thought he was taking this chance to get his ass safe, away from the shooting. And his wife's ass.

Evidently, though, Smith's grandfather believed he would return. Sings Wolf volunteered to come with Smith to help cover his back.

But Smith wasn't sure that his grandfather's coming along was a vote of confidence. The truth was, Smith himself wasn't sure what he would do. The truth was, he couldn't imagine going off and leaving his wife. The rest of the truth was, he couldn't go off and leave his people in the middle of the worst trouble they'd ever had.

He slipped on his best white-man shirt, the one with a wing collar. Today was the day. It made sense then and it made sense now. His wife was white—she needed white medicine.

He brushed at his pants. He really did prefer a breechcloth.

"I won't wait for you beyond tomorrow," said Sings Wolf without warning.

Smith looked at his grandfather warily.

"I'll leave after sundown. I don't expect you. I think you should stay with your wife until she's well. You can meet us in Powder River country later. No one will blame you for taking care of her."

Smith didn't know what to say. He'd been acting like his decision was made, that he was coming back to the Human Beings. It didn't do to pretend to your wise grandfather. "The people need me, Grandfather. She will be in bed a long time." He was trying the words on for size.

Sings Wolf nodded. "The people need and your wife needs you." He rubbed the side of his nose the way he did when he was considering. "No one will blame you," he repeated.

That was true, Smith reflected. They would not exactly blame him. They might not even think he was a coward. They would just think he was a white man and acting like a white man.

Truth was, he didn't have any idea what he wanted to do.

He stopped beside Elaine. Her face was still drawn, but she managed a little smile now, a vague, lotusland smile that meant she appreciated what he was doing even through her drug haze. She had stayed in that lotusland for two days, and would need it this morning.

And what do you want, Elaine Cummings Maclean? he thought. What do you want, my love? Would you like to give up this noble experiment in red-white relations? What did you mean when you said you feel like running away?

He looked at her splinted leg. He felt guilty for letting her start on this damned trip. How could he have let her get shot at? She'd almost gotten killed. He was confident now that she wouldn't die of internal bleeding—she'd already be dead. At least she wouldn't have to risk her life getting shot at anymore. He was glad of that. Now they only had to worry about whether her leg would heal or mend short and crooked or would get infected and have to be amputated. No worries at all, he told himself mockingly.

Meanwhile should he stay with her? Or should he go back to his people and see if he needed to throw away his life to help them?

He touched her hairline gently. He thought, If I disappeared from your life, would you secretly be relieved?

But she couldn't answer. Not really. She wouldn't be able to give a real answer for days or weeks, and he might not be around to hear it.

"Give me a little more time," Smith said to Sings Wolf, his eyes still on Elaine. "Until first light."

"Until first light." His grandfather said it with that glint of smile that meant, "Isn't it fine, having to decide what it is to be a man?"

13

Dodge City lay three or four miles closer than Fort Dodge. It sat west of the fort, perched right on the river. Smith got all the way to the outskirts of town without trouble. There he got some queer looks from two men on a wagon. Fer Chrissakes, he could almost hear them mutter, a fancy-decked-out man who looks to be a long-haired half-breed dragging a hurt white woman on an Injun travois. Smith smiled to himself as the wagon men rolled by. Life is full of strange doings, fellows.

What he noticed first about Dodge City was the stink, the pungent, acrid smell of manure. He remembered the stockyards at Kansas City smelled like that. He didn't see the cattle pens, so they must be east of town—the wind blew from that way. White people amazed him. They complained about the odor of an Indian village, which was vivid enough in its way, and then lived kissing-cousin close to knee-deep cow shit.

He knew about Dodge City. In 1864 he and his brother Thomas had come south with their grandfather Strikes Foot to visit the southern Cheyennes. Then the Indians had gone to see the way station the soldiers built on the Santa Fe Trail, but it was just some dugouts. The Human Beings couldn't imagine why anyone would live in a dark, dank hole in the ground when he could live in a light, mobile tipi. But white people are crazy, they said, and surely will act like white people.

Later, some whites built a store close to the Fort Dodge property to trade with the buffalo hunters. Pretty quick the Atchison, Topeka & the Santa Fe arrived, and a little town sprang up and called itself the hide capital of the plains. You could see buffalo hides stacked wide as a river, the Cheyennes said, and tall as a tree.

Soon the buffalo were gone, and a new business came rollicking in—Texans drove their cattle to Dodge City for shipment east. That meant a town full of men who had just got paid and wanted to eat, drink, gamble, and whore. Some even got haircuts, or stayed in hotels. That was why the citizens of Dodge didn't mind the stink of manure—it smelled to them like money. Besides, Dodge City was the talk of the Nations. Wide open was what the white men called it, with a wild and wayward roll of their eyes. Sin for sale, they said, drawing a line under each word. The way they told it, the mayor, Dog Kelley, instead of enforcing the laws against prostitution, had a lady of convenience for his own mate when she wasn't working. And the county sheriff, named Bat Masterson, was overfond of card games.

Smith smiled to himself. Time was, he liked such girls himself. He recalled the first one he'd ever used, Chinese girl up in Virginia City. The thought still tickled him. But the time for that was past.

He got off and checked Elaine, as he did every mile or so. She looked comfortable enough, as comfortable as you could be lashed to a travois. In her half-conscious state, she didn't care.

Smith rode right down the middle of the main street, and no one offered to lend a hand or even said howdeedoo. Damn right they noticed. A pony drag carrying an injured white woman was scarce as ice in August, and not one of them would ever have seen a half-breed spiffed up like a banker. Plus, they could see he was looking for a doctor and could use help carrying Elaine. But they ignored him. He wasn't a human being. Even Elaine wasn't, now now.

Smith had seen plenty of this treatment when he went to school in St. Louis. His father and his mothers had gotten it in spades from the gold-rushers who came to the Yellowstone country. He had learned to put up with it, but never stopped hating it.

He saw lots of signs, but no shingles advertising doctors. The town surely led the nation in saloons per square block. The Saratoga must be a fancy one—the sign bragged of a full orchestra for your entertainment. Other watering establishments appeared to be the Alamo, Beatty and Kelley's Alhambra, Mueller and Straeter's Old House, the Opera House Saloon, and the Long Branch. But since whiskey couldn't kill all the germs, there must be a doctor somewhere.

He tied his horse to a hitching post and Elaine's alongside it. He couldn't wander away from her, so he looked around. An old fellow lay propped against the front of Rath & Company General Store, passed out drunk. Smith took a few steps toward some men collected farther down, whittling and spitting, Texas cow-boys from the look of them. "Hey, mister," he said softly.

A cow-boy with his hat brim pinned to the crown in front turned his head, noticed Smith, and gawked. He reeked of trail dust and chewing tobacco.

"Where's the doctor, mister?"

The fellow's mustaches twitched—they hung below his jaw—and his mouth showed a couple of beaver teeth. Seemed like maybe he thought everything in life was comical. He eyed Smith up and down and took his time running his gaze over Elaine and the pony drag as well.

"Right yonder around the corner," the Texan drawled. "I'll help you fetch her down there."

Which goes to show, Smith told himself, that there are more things in heaven and earth, Dr. Redskin Maclean, than are dreamt of in your philosophy.

Dr. Wockerley, M. T. Wockerley, initials but no names, put Elaine on a narrow bed on his back porch—clearly she would have to stay for a while, and couldn't occupy his examining room.

He was a young man who constantly seemed about to speak and never got it out. He moved with self-conscious stiffness around his patient, who was mostly unconscious. He checked her eyes, felt her forehead, cut off the hide splint delicately, and examined her wound minutely—

peered at them, felt them for warmth, sniffed at them.
Smith knew Wockerley wouldn't find any infection, at least
not yet. But he treated the wound with yeast in combination with elm bark and charcoal, a familiar smell to
Smith—he wished he'd had some yeast two nights ago.
Wockerley also gave her yeast by mouth, in some
whiskey—probably he didn't have porter in the house.

Last, Wockerley studied with scrupulous care the
shape of the shin that hid the setting of the bone. His thick
glasses made his eyes look goggled. The man was thorough
and proper, though, even if he did act like a clown. The
torn flesh made it hard for him to tell the normal shape of
the leg and surmise the fit of the bones underneath.

"Feels displaced to me," said Smith. It was a guess on
Smith's part—you judged from the look of the skin and the
feel of the bones under it. If the match of jagged ends wasn't
good, the broken bones would take a long time to heal, and
Elaine might have a crooked leg. Ten years ago, amputation
would have been automatic, because of the danger of
infection. Now the better doctors knew about Lister and his
work in antisepsis. Smith would insist on cleanliness and no
amputation.

Wockerley pulled a thoughtful face and nodded. He
seemed about to blubber something, but it didn't come—
maybe Smith made him nervous.

Smith supposed Wockerley caught on. Smith had told
him where and how it happened and suggested that Elaine
might need traction. That should let the man know why
Smith couldn't take care of her himself, on the move with
the Human Beings.

Wockerley was acting peculiar. Though he was obviously intent on his patient, he kept *not* looking at Smith,
seeming not to hear Smith, not asking questions of Smith,
and conspicuously not turning his back to Smith. Wockerley would even align himself at bizarre angles, standing
over Elaine with his shoulders strangely cocked so he could
see Smith out of the corner of his eye. But he never looked
right at his colleague. His only condescension to profes-

sional mannerliness was that he seemed embarrassed by his behavior.

Maybe Smith should cut his hair. Or be light-complexioned. Or half a foot shorter. It would have been funny had it not been maddening.

Smith used every trick he could think of. He described the break and the wounds and the way he'd treated them with all sorts of medical terms—filled his talk with *tibia*, *antiseptic*, *open fracture*, *displaced*, and *comminuted*. He spoke of his concern about infection. He told Wockerley where he took his training, Boston Medical College. He mentioned one staff member, Abraham Grantly, whom this Wockerley might know of because of his work on disinfectants.

Wockerley didn't have anything to say but "Ahhh" and "Mmmm." When Smith asked where Wockerley had been trained, the man didn't even make one of those sounds. It was weird. It was rude.

Suddenly Wockerley stood erect, beamed awkwardly at Smith, and said, "Yes, well, certainly you wouldn't scalp us all while I'm trying to help your wife, would you?"

Whoo-ee! There's polite parlor conversation for you, thought Smith.

Then Wockerley rang a bell with self-conscious vigor. A pale young woman came in, so stooped and skinny she looked cadaverous. Wockerley addressed her formally as "Mrs. Wockerley," which Smith found bizarre, failed to introduce Smith, and asked her to send for the sheriff.

When Mrs. Wockerley brought the officer with a badge out of the house, the doctor asked him where the sheriff was. "Mr. Masterson sends Dr. Wockerley greetings and salutations," the man said with a twang, making an effort to get the words exactly right, "but he says to tell you he's holding three kings at the moment and taking all his orders from them." The man let it sit a moment. "Truth is, he ain't even setting at poker right this moment, but that's what he said to say."

"I need him to send a man to fetch Dr. Richtarsch,"

said Wockerley, trying to sound imperious. "This woman needs him."

"The sheriff has authorized me to reply to further requests at my own discretion," answered the man with a badge. "Since I'm the feller as would do the fetchin', I can safely say that Sheriff Masterson has no one available for that duty at this time and suggests you do your own fetchin'." The man headed on across the porch and out the door without so much as a fare-thee-well. Smith admired his style.

"He's at the fort," Wockerley said to Smith as he handed Mrs. Wockerley a cotton swab to throw away. "I don't suppose you could . . ." Wockerley pretended to be preoccupied with his examination for a moment. "Being in the military, Dr. Richtarsch has seen a good many affairs of this sort." He cocked an eyebrow officiously at Smith. "It will take you a couple of hours to get out there and back with Dr. Richtarsch. At least two." The man actually kept repeating Richtarsch's title as though Smith should be awed by it.

At last Wockerley risked a joke. "Of course, the good doctor may regard this as aiding and abetting the enemy," and tsk-tsked a dry little imitation of a laugh.

"I'll fetch him," said Smith. Being in the army, the fellow was probably an old hand with trauma. But before he left, Smith couldn't resist having a little fun. "Mrs. Wockerley," he said, "I'll just sleep on the floor next to Elaine. I have my own bedroll."

The poor woman could hardly keep man and wife apart, could she? But she certainly looked like she wanted to. And Wockerley gave Smith the biggest, phoniest smile he'd ever seen. They'd probably lock the porch door and sleep with the shotgun close by the bed. Smith went out chuckling maliciously.

* * *

Two hours later he was back in Dodge City alone—Richtarsch had been out hunting, but an orderly promised the doctor would come to town tomorrow morning. Meanwhile, Smith was ravenous.

The Dodge House Saloon and Restaurant stood right in front of him. Why not?

Why not was, Smith didn't have any money. He'd given his savings to Little Wolf to buy horses and weapons for the Human Beings. He'd traded his revolver for the horse for Sings Wolf's feast. So what was left? He'd better not try to sell Elaine's jewelry—he'd probably get lynched for having killed a white woman. Nor could he sell his own pocket watch, a railroad watch made by Waltham and given to him by a Boston family for his college graduation. So he went to the livery to sell Elaine's gelding. People knew Indians actually owned horses. Her sidesaddle and jewelry he'd leave with Wockerley to help pay for her care.

An hour later Smith drank his third cup of coffee filled half an inch deep with sugar, the way the Cheyennes like it, the way he'd never lost his taste for. He'd finished a platter of pork chops and eggs and buttered toast and potatoes, and he felt like a glutton, and that felt good, damned good. He still remembered fondly the first time he'd eaten a sunny-side-up egg, in St. Louis. It had made him think maybe the white doings weren't so bad after all. Eggs and the thought of women for pay made him more willing to stay in the big town and go to school, but he never did get any of the women, not St. Louie women anyway.

It was pleasant to sit and eat a meal and not think about his situation. Smith never permitted himself to stew about anything while he ate. Eating was a time for enjoying something basic, so you didn't fret while you ate. You gave your whole attention to tastes and smells and your feeling of satisfaction.

So while he ate, he was able to get his mind off his

preoccupations of the ride to the fort and back: the awful idea of going off and leaving Elaine with strangers. The terrible arguments for and against. His notions that he was doing what was best for her, that he had to stick with his people or never go among them again, that she would want him to go. All put up against a single feeling as elemental as blood—you took this woman, you belong to her and she to you, you stay with her.

Stop it, Smith ordered himself. He pushed away from the table and walked irritably into the gaming room. It was crowded, bustling with a kind of sleazy energy. Cow-boys up from Texas were jammed at tables with games of poker, faro, and monte. Professional gamblers sat there coolly in their black-and-white getups and took the boys' money in tense silence. At big tables dice games went on, chuck-a-luck and hazard, and once in a while a rousing shout would go up when someone won some money. The whole operation was arranged to take a cow-boy's money in a genteel way and with a wicked smile that let him know that broke was what he was born to be, and rich was what the proprietor was born to be.

In a corner a man played a hurdy-gurdy, and several bar girls and cow-boys danced to its raucous, lively tunes. The cow-boys danced with a peculiar zest. They cocked their big hats back to forty-five degrees. Their huge spurs jingled at every clop. Their revolvers flapped up and down ridiculously in their holsters. Their sails full of liquor and lust, they hoed it down with a whore, more colorfully known as a soiled dove, sporting woman, frail sister, calico queen, painted cat, or *nymph de la prairie*. A cow-boy had little finesse but great enthusiasm—sometimes he whirled his partner for a whole circle in the air and saluted his feat with an earsplitting whoop.

Before long the cow-boy would get sufficiently full of himself to follow his nymph to the back rooms and invest some of his trail-driving money in a good time. It would be a strange transaction between a blustery lad and a cynical lass, both probably teenagers, one with too little experience and the other with too much. As both a come-on and a guard against intimacy, the girl wouldn't tell the cow-boy her real name, but would give him a nom de guerre. Girls working in Dodge City at that time were called the likes of Timberline, Hambone Jane, Dutch Jake, Wicked Alice, Peg-Leg Annie, Roaring Gimlet, Tit Bit, or Lady Jane Gray.

Lust, thought Smith, good, healthy lust. Something white folks always spoke ill of—they didn't even have a word for it that didn't sound disapproving.

Lust, something Smith was full of and hadn't been able to let out with his wife. Two and a half weeks of marriage but not two and a half weeks of loving. She'd been passionate once, but there was something desperate about that. That was the night she'd spoken of wanting to run away.

What a honeymoon he'd given his wife. If her family knew, they'd have called out the army to get her back, and get Smith hanged. Well, she was out of it now, well out of it.

Came a mocking inner voice, Out of what, redskin?

Smith kicked himself toward the bar. He got whiskey from a black bartender with droopy, all-knowing eyes. He went to the dice table where they played chuck-a-luck and waited until the point was four, a magical number to the Cheyenne, and bet a dollar on it. Four won. He got more whiskey. He bet on four again, and again, every time he saw it come up. He got more whiskey, and bet on four some more. Toward midnight by the railroad watch he had no use for, he kicked himself out the door toward the porch where he would sleep. He'd bet on four seven times (another magical number) at one table and won five times, and seven times at another table and won six times. He'd come out ahead two ten-dollar gold pieces.

Walking down the middle of the street, not entirely sober, he muttered, "Hoorah for the Cheyennes." He nearly stumbled into a rut. He reconsidered his mutter. This time he raised a mock toast to the sky and bellowed, "Hurrah for the goddamn Cheyennes." And repeated it in

Cheyenne for the sake of any Cheyenne gods who might be
listening.

Then he thought of one more toast. He lifted an
imaginary shot glass to the heavens and roared, "Here's to
the gods, goddamn them!"

Chuckling, and weaving a little, he angled toward
Wockerley's house, which was half a block off the main
drag, Front Street. Smith was sober enough not to stumble,
or make any noises that would offend the good doctor and
his wife. Rather, the objectionable doctor and his wife the
cadaver.

The good doctor had a good house, Smith thought,
looking it over. A two-story affair in proper Victorian style,
respectable and good-looking. Since doctoring hardly paid,
he must be profiting in patent medicines. House was plenty
big enough for a home and office both, even a back porch to
take care of convalescents. With a separate porch entrance
in case the convalescent's husband was a man of color. Right
for a respectable but officious doctor and his corpse of a
wife.

Smith went up the path toward the porch, thinking of
Elaine there in her drugged sleep. Then something scuffed
in the road behind him.

He jumped instantly to one side with his knife ready.
It felt good to be fast. It felt lousy not to see anything in the
street.

It hit him in the back and head and knocked him
facedown, hard.

Smith made out that it was a human body on him. He
tried to roll, but he was pinned flat. A hand grabbed his
hair. Then he felt the sharp tip of the knife at his throat. He
decided to lie quiet.

"Very good, *veho*," whispered a voice in his ear. In
Cheyenne. He recognized the voice but couldn't place it.
The bastard had waited on the porch roof and tricked Smith
with a rock thrown into the street.

"I see you are where you belong now," rasped the
voice. "You eat the white man's food, gamble for his gold.
Did you take one of his women-for-pay? Mmm?"

Smith kept his mouth shut and waited.

"While you gamble, *veho*, who watches your *veho* wife? Who but me?"

Smith quivered with fear, and his enemy tightened his grip on Smith's hair. Smith ordered himself to put the fear away.

"You should stay in this town, *veho*. The white people would pay you their money to make their bodies well while their spirits rot. You are good at that. You could get lots of gold. See what a fine, big house this doctor has, the one who takes care of your wife. Your wife could work as a woman-for-pay and get lots of gold, too. You could be rich. That's what you *vehos* want—rich."

Smith just waited. It would come.

"Turn your head, *veho*, and see who has your life to take or give back. *Turn!*"

Smith rotated his head slowly, away from the knife point.

It was Twist, his face full of triumph and malice.

Twist switched to his bad English, except for the one word he kept repeating. "Do you wants your life, *veho*? I gives it to you. Is no honor in kill a *veho*."

Twist took the knife point away, but ground Smith's head into the earth with one arm. "Now Twist gives you your life, he tells you where spend it.

"Stays in Dodge City, *veho*. Stays away from the Human Beings. Your *veho* spirit corrupts the people. Your wife tries turn them into white men. Stays away. If you comes back, Twist cuts your guts out. Then, during you die, he fucks your wife in front of you and cut her head off while he fucks her.

"Thinks of that, *veho*."

Smith flinched when the knife point touched the socket of his right eye.

"Now Little Wolf will give you something to help you remember," the warror said in Cheyenne.

Pain jerked hot through him, and something else felt incredible—Smith couldn't believe it. The knife point ground against bone. It circled the outside of his eye socket—it felt to Smith like it was screeching soundlessly. He felt hot blood run into his eye.

Then Twist's weight lifted off him, and the muzzle of a pistol pressed against the top of his spine.

"Lie still, *veho*," growled Twist. "If you get up while I can see you, I will shoot you." He cackled hideously, but Smith thought it was a stagy cackle, thought out in advance. The pressure of the muzzle disappeared.

So why didn't you kill me, Twist? Smith asked himself. If you really think I'm a *veho*?

"I would enjoy killing you," Twist said softly from a few steps away. "Why don't you move?"

It's because I'm a Cheyenne, Smith thought triumphantly. You don't want to kill me because I'm a Cheyenne. You're afraid of being banished for wasting the blood of one of the Human Beings.

Smith wanted to holler out gladly, and mockingly. But he lay still. Twist was crazy, and a crazy man might do anything.

You're afraid to kill me, Twist, Smith thought gleefully. He rubbed the blood out of his eye.

After a long while, maybe five minutes, Smith got cautiously to his hands and knees. Nothing happened. He stood up. Still nothing. He ran to the porch where his wife lay sleeping.

He lit a candle. Elaine seemed to be asleep, and at peace. He felt for the artery in her neck—she had a steady pulse. She looked very beautiful in sleep, he thought. She lay on her back, her head angled to one side revealing a classic New England profile, the sort of profile that idealists like abolitionists and suffragists showed in magazine pictures. Smith like that. He felt tender toward her, and admired her. But, he noticed, his feelings were as though from afar. He shook his head—how odd.

Then he noticed that something looked wrong—a hump on Elaine's chest. He reached and carefully drew the covers down from her neck. The ribbons of her nightgown had been untied, and it lay open, exposing her pale body. Between her small, delicate breasts reposed a horse turd.

Smith picked it up. Not quite dry.

He felt a spasm of hatred. "You're dead," Smith said softly to Twist. He pictured the Indian riding silently through the night, back toward the Human Beings. "You're dead."

14

Smith endured Richtarsch's needle ironically, but there was something frightening, intimidating, about having stitches done next to your eye. He sucked in his breath quickly, got pierced again, and forced himself to relax and let it out.

No doubt Richtarsch and Wockerley thought Smith had been fighting and fornicating last night. How else would he get cut around the eye? And the neatness of the incision let experienced eyes know it had been done by a knife. A knife fight, how like an Indian. You can paint civilization onto a barbarian, but what you get is a painted barbarian.

Praise be, his colleagues were not going to ask any questions about how he got cut, or let on that it was anything out of the ordinary. They were going to maintain the facade of collegiality.

Richtarsch set down the needle, clipped the ends of the thread, and slapped his hands together as though brushing dust off. "That will do it, I think, Dr. Maclean, and very well."

He handed Smith a hand mirror. The stitches made a black row of tracks around the outside edge of his eye. The effect was piratical.

Richtarsch was the opposite of Wockerley—talkative, dynamic, respectful (overrespectful) to Smith, and cocksure of himself. He was ultra-military, his uniform gleaming, his bearing erect, his movements snappy, even his buttocks, Smith noticed, taut.

Now he moved around Elaine with the air of a man on the stage he was born to. He held up her wrist and declared her pulse normal. He touched her forehead and judged sonorously that she was not feverish. He felt and smelled her shin wound and found it warm. He also observed that it was not inflamed.

"*Gut,*" he said, "no infection." Sometimes Dieter Richtarsch's German birth spoke through his English pronunciations. Wockerley said he'd earned a considerable reputation as a surgeon in the War Between the States and become something of an authority on serious fractures.

Richtarsch inspected the shin minutely where the bones were broken and palpated it firmly. Smith watched Elaine's face for pain, but Wockerley had her deeply medicated, and she looked placid.

"It is displaced," Richtarsch said authoritatively. He gave a formal smile through his red mustache and beard.

He stood and brushed his hands as though to get dust off them. "Well, it is not zo bad, Dr. Maclean. We have seen many of these in the Rebellion. Many plus many. The treatment is straightforward—traction. We got a good result many times, but sometimes not." The surgeon's *w*'s were only halfway to *v*'s, which was not bad.

"Of course it takes weeks. At the fort, fine, she could be there, but it's not so good to move her now. Dr. Wockerley, could you see fit to care for the patient here? I could come in and check her every few days, which would be sufficient."

"Of course, Dr. Richtarsch." Wockerley was all the deferential fool now. "Of course, the fort would be less expensive for Dr. Maclean." Apparently the army would help out a civilian and charge nothing. A white woman, anyway.

Richtarsch waved that consideration off. Evidently Richtarsch judged that money couldn't be a consideration to a doctor, even a redskin doctor. Or if it could be, it would be not mannerly or not collegial to admit the possibility.

Smith wondered if Wockerley agreed to board Elaine because he wanted the pay, or because he would cater to whatever Richtarsch wanted.

"So. Why not today, hmmm? Things are not getting

any better as we wait." The German doctor looked boldy at
his two colleagues, and neither protested. "I will ask
Private Connors to go get the mechanical equipment."
Smith supposed Private Connors was the soldier waiting at
the buggy outside. "In the meantime, let's get some lunch.
Will you join me, gentlemen?"

Wockerley accepted eagerly, but Smith said he wanted
to stay with Elaine.

The two doctors made their way toward the street,
Richtarsch talking enthusiastically. "I like the Saratoga," de-
clared Richtarsch. "That Chalk Beeson sets an excellent table.
Remarkable name, isn't it—Chalk? Very American . . ."

Smith could no longer hear the fellow.

He looked at his wife and sat down next to her. He
took her hand, surrounded it with his oversized ones, and
rested it in his lap. She still felt the effects of the laudanum
now. Richtarsch would be ready to reset the bones in about
three hours, so she would need more anodyne in about two
hours.

Maybe, just before then, she would be better able to
hear and understand him. Maybe he would be able to tell
her. Ask her. Whatever. It was then or not at all.

She heard Adam only now and again. She seemed to
be borne up on a cresting wave of consciousness and
dropped into a trough of oblivion. Though she couldn't
make out all the words or be sure what he was asking, she
knew the music of what he was saying, knew the melody
but not the lyrics. He was uncertain. He hurt. He didn't
know whether she wanted him. He didn't know whether to
go back to the people or stay with her.

She felt washed in regret. She felt for Adam and
wanted to reach out to him. She couldn't—she didn't have
whatever it took to reach out to him or anybody. He was too
far away. Everything was too far away.

She tried once to take his hand, but succeeded only in

flopping her own hand off her lap and onto the bed. He didn't see what she wanted to give him, and didn't grasp her hand.

She wanted to tell him that she wanted to be married to him and to live with him forever. But she couldn't tell him that now—she couldn't have if she'd been all right. It was too momentous, too dangerous, and she was too shattered, too much in need of being put back together. She wanted to want him. She thought she would after she was safe, nurtured, and whole.

Making declarations to him now would be talking of life ashore. She didn't know whether she would get to shore.

She knew what he was going through, what he thought, what he feared. She had known right along, known without admitting to herself that she knew. He felt ashamed that he had brought her into his world, and nearly destroyed her life. He felt ashamed of the barbarous way his people lived, and of himself—and at the same time he felt proud of the beautiful and spiritual way they lived, and of himself. He felt unwanted because she'd been reluctant to make love to him . . . well, in the rocks and the dirt. He felt not good enough for her, and at the same time hated her for thinking him not good enough. Which she didn't. He feared she'd meant it literally when she made that dumb remark about running away.

She regretted it all, but the regret seemed far away. She did not so much love him as she wanted to love him. She would love him when she got back to shore, she knew she would, but that was so far away, perhaps unreachable.

He took her hand, and that made her glad. She opened her eyes and looked up at him. Tears glistened on his broad, flat, manly face. A lovable face. She did love him. She squeezed his hand affectionately and closed her eyes.

It was so hard, it was all so hard.

She had a picture in her head, splinters of timbers covered with foam and floating in the sea, being borne away from the shore by some unseen but all-powerful tide. She wondered whether she and Adam were caught up in such a tide. If so, they had no say in where it would take them.

Suddenly she felt a great urgency. She must say something to him. She must set him free to go to the Tsistsistas-Suhtaio with a good conscience, she must. She began sorting out the words in her mind, like polished pebbles she wanted to give him. Sometimes she lost track, but then she rearranged her pebbles, and at last turned onto her side and tried to raise up on one elbow. Adam grasped her, concerned.

Speak, she shouted at herself. Speak.

Smith held his wife up, wondering what she wanted. Did she want to tell him something? He'd gotten used to talking to himself, talking himself through whatever he had to go through, a solitary passage.

Elaine fell back and lay still. Occasionally her lips worked, but only a whispery rasp came out, far from language. He wondered if she was saying, "Don't go." Or, "Come back."

But he didn't know. Smith could permit himself no illusion or sentimentality, not at a time like this. He would have to go on. He would have to go without feeling sure where their marriage stood.

He would go on with the Cheyennes toward the Powder River. Toward it, and maybe only toward. If all turned out well, he would come back for her—hunt her down if necessary. But he would understand if she wanted to end the marriage. Maybe she hadn't understood the life she was letting herself in for. Truly not.

He loved her. He loved her. He loved her.

Adam Smith Maclean stood up, looked at his sleeping wife, bent and kissed her forehead. He would not wait for the doctors to come back, would not help them set up the traction. She was not infected, and that would have to be enough.

His lot was chosen. He would get his horse from the livery and go back to being what he really was, a poor, desperate Indian.

≈ **BOOK TWO** ≈

BOOK TWO

≈ 1 ≈

Riding was doing for Smith what juggling normally did.
Repetitive, wearying, relaxing, it lulled his head into the
peace of thoughtlessness.

He told himself what he wasn't thinking about was
Twist. What he really wasn't thinking about was Elaine.

Sings Wolf hadn't said a word about Smith's coming
back. He merely asked whether Elaine was OK. Smith said
only, "I think so." Sings Wolf acted like he expected his
grandson's return, but seemed neither pleased nor displeased by it. He made no comment when Smith changed
his white-man clothes for hide shirt, breechcloth, and
moccasins, and no comment on the stitches on the outside
of Smith's eye.

Smith felt embarrassed to tell him about Twist and the
episode in front of the porch. He'd reacted slowly and
carelessly, he admitted, and in a flat, laconic way told about
being pinned down and threatened and cut, not even
hinting at his outrage. He even told the part about the
horse turd between Elaine's breasts dryly.

All Sings Wolf had to say was, "You are a Cheyenne."

"I have to do something about him, Grandfather." But
Smith knew what Sings Wolf meant. The taboo against a
Cheyenne killing another Cheyenne was inviolable. When
it happened, the buffalo hat began to stink like rotting flesh,
and the sacred arrows became speckled with blood. The
powers would turn against the people in lots of ways until
the rottenness among them was purged.

Of course, times were changing. The hat and arrows
were left behind in the south, and they no longer seemed
to have their old power. But Smith couldn't afford to be the
one to show the weakness of the hat and arrows.

And how fitting for a doctor, Smith mocked himself in his head, to seek to bring medicine to a people who shunned him, who would not let him live among them or even speak to him. If he killed Twist, he would be throwing away the life he'd worked for.

If he didn't, Twist might kill him.

Sings Wolf had said, "You are a Cheyenne." Clear enough. Smith knew it made no difference that his father was a white man—when the Tsistsistas-Suhtaio accepted you as one of the people, you were one forever.

Years ago the Cheyennes captured a bunch of Crows and took them into the tribe. Later, the Crow tribe attacked the Cheyennes and killed many. In their grief, the Cheyennes killed some of the former Crow captives. And the buffalo hat stank, and the sacred arrows got bloody. So the people knew that even a person adopted into the tribe was truly a Cheyenne.

Well, Smith told himself, you're going to have to do something about Twist. He fingered the stitches around his eye. He damn well intended to take care of Twist. But he had no idea how.

Smith and Sings Wolf pushed their horses long but no harder than necessary for a night and a day and a night, keeping to a lope as much as they could, getting the most distance from man and beast. They rode generally northwest, hoping to catch the other Human Beings where the people would cross the Smoky Hill River, or at least pick up their trail there.

Sings Wolf knew the country, but it had changed plenty. Where buffalo plains had stretched only five winters ago, farms and ranches claimed the land everywhere. Though the two rode in silence, Sings Wolf made an occasional snort of disgust.

They had to keep an eye out. They were two Indians on the move through a territory crazy with Indian fever.

The newspaper in Dodge said Colonel Lewis and his troops had taken the railroad west from Fort Dodge and would intercept the Cheyennes at the Dull Knife crossing of the Arkansas or pursue them north and punish them. Colonel Lewis, the paper said, considered this campaign against the Indians a travesty. Now he intended to annihilate them. He pledged to come back victorious or dead. The paper also said that if the Indians got as far as the Platte River, where the Union Pacific Railroad ran, thirteen thousand soldiers would be mobilized to corral them.

Thirteen thousand against three hundred! Actually thirteen thousand fighting men outfitted with Springfield rifles against fewer than a hundred men, old men, and boys mostly armed with spears, clubs, and bows and arrows.

It made Smith smile to himself when he told Sings Wolf about the thirteen thousand. There was something grand about making this foolish gesture, and Smith was exhilarated at being part of it.

But Smith and Sings Wolf didn't want to fight with any of the settlers in this country, which might raise the thirteen thousand to thirty thousand. So they rode all night, kneeing the horses to a canter on the wagon roads and easy ground, walking through the more broken country. They rested themselves and the horses for a couple of hours at sunup, noon, sundown, and when the Big Dipper said midnight. Otherwise they stayed on the move, keeping their eyes out for trouble. Smith had no illusions about any white people sparing him. Not after he'd seen the hysteria in Dodge City.

Every time they saw a fence, Sings Wolf turned sour-looking. Even the white ranchers didn't like fences. The farmers were staking out the land. Fences turned the circle of the world into square-mile parcels. Fences spoiled both the life of Indians who followed the buffalo and the lives of the cowboys who herded cattle. Worse, Smith doubted that this dry country would ever work out for farming. Dumb, the whole business.

From time to time they saw buildings at a distance, but stayed behind the hills where they wouldn't likely be seen.

And in any case they pushed the horses along hard enough
to make any pursuers work like hell to catch them.

At first light on the second day, well away from farms,
ranches, roads, or even paths, they cantered toward some
cottonwoods along a little creek a mile off in the bottom,
eyeballing them carefully. They didn't see the damned
preacher until they topped the rise and practically rode
over him.

The Reverend Ecclesiastes Bountiful Ratz, an itinerant
man of God, endowed with beard and belly of apocalyptic
dimensions but only one usable eye, heard the hoof beats
coming. He reached for his side-by-side, eager to do battle
with evil. When he saw a pair of the Lord's vermin loping
up, he cut loose with a blast of hot and holy buckshot and
hollered, "Praise the Lord!"

His daughter Hindy, scrunched into the bottom of the
wagon, figured she and her father were finally dead. And
Hindy no longer had any hope of heaven. If her pa
preached it, she knew it was a figment of a demented
imagination.

Dead. What a relief.

But through the cracks between the wagon boards she
saw the big horse in the lead go down hard, and the Indian
went rolling like a wheel knocked off.

The Indian behind swung to the outside of his horse,
and the shot from Pa's other barrel gutted the space above
an empty saddle.

The Indian rose and let go an arrow toward Pa. The
way Hindy saw it, that arrow sailed slow as a feather falling.
It lofted over one side of the wagon, sang its way through
the air above Pa's supplies, and aimed straight for Pa's head
behind the other wagon side.

The Ratzes' vehicle was a platform spring wagon,
bought as only a tongue, frame, axles, and wheels for a
restoration project. The Reverend Ratz repaired it with the

haphazard attention that he gave to all earthly things. He had tacked on some warped outhouse boards to give the wagon a pretense at sides and didn't care that they came together all jangly, like in-laws.

Ecclesiastes at this moment had his one good eye fixed on the action through one of the gaps in the warped boards. He thought it was a handy gap, too, until that arrow by rarest chance hit the lower board and splintered it.

The arrow would have missed, but the board deflected it into Ecclesiastes's ear, where it plowed a rip-roaring furrow.

Unfortunately, the splinter, thick as a man's thumb and twice as long, pivoted and poked straight into Ecclesiastes' nose next to his good eye. Blood issued forth abundantly, rendering the good reverend entirely blind.

With the world gone out, and his life's blood gushing down his face and neck and chest, and those two unholy vermin no doubt taking aim to dispatch him, Ecclesiastes Ratz felt a single imperative. It erupted inside him like the fateful lightning where the grapes of wrath are stored: he wanted to run like hell.

And run the reverend did. First he howled like a steam whistle. Then, still howling, he lit out like an engine run off the track. He was about the size of a railroad engine, and could see about as well as one, and looked about as graceful going cross-country on the Kansas plains. He spun his wheels. He rolled over sideways and teetered upright again. He plunged into a gully and careened back out. He slithered and spun and churned up dust across another fifty yards of prairie, dived into a bigger gully, and stayed put.

Smith swore later that he emitted a last gasp of steam.

The two Indians and the teenage girl watched engine Ecclesiastes go amuck in awed silence.

Then Smith walked the hundred yards to see if the poor devil was all right. But Ecclesiastes Ratz, who hadn't been all right for years, had taken leave of this world. Strained to support his three hundred pounds even standing still, his boiler had burst.

Smith found no pulse and no heartbeat and no breath. He folded the man's arms over his chest.

He walked back to the wagon where the girl squatted. Before he could get a word out, the girl declared, "I'm yourn now." When the Indians looked puzzled, she made signs: Me. You.

Oh, darn it, Hindy realized, the signs didn't make any sense. "I'm yourn!" she said loudly. She thought about it for a moment. "Squaw belong to braves!"

Hindy Ratz wasn't afraid. The Indians would either kill her or they wouldn't. Would rape her or they wouldn't. Would take her home as a squaw, or they wouldn't. There was no place to run and no place to hide. Hindy was what life had made her, a fourteen-year-old fatalist.

Why not a fatalist? Hindy had lived for more than a year now, ever since her ma died in Topeka, with a crazy man. Ecclesiastes Ratz kept hearing call after call from the Lord, and he followed the calls across the vast and empty plains like vagrant winds that sometimes blow here and sometimes blow yonder but always blow.

From town to town they went, sleeping in the back of the wagon, eating whenever someone would stake them to a meal, talking about the dark meanings of the riper passages in the Book of Revelation. The Reverend Ratz knew the King James Version of the Bible the way the actors of his time and place knew Shakespeare, which is to say in bits and speeches quite unrelated to the larger whole, such as the book the words might have come from or the prophet who might have spoken them. But the reverend had a fecund imagination and could hold forth for hours on the meaning of a single phrase.

Some people cottoned to the Reverend Ratz's style of exegesis and would put something in the hat he passed. An occasional widow was moved to supply him with an entire sack of flour, or similar bounty. But most of the Reverend Ratz's admirers were only the poor, the disenfranchised, the people society had no place for. So Hindy was as likely to find kernels of corn in the hat as small coins. She was grateful for the corn, as a supplement to her irregular meals.

During their year on the road the Reverend Ratz had become more and more spiritual. That meant he forgot to pass the hat half the time. Forgot to clean himself. Forgot to eat—even at three hundred pounds, he'd lost fifty since Hindy's ma died. Forgot, literally, to come in out of the rain. And kept hearing those winds that sent them on cross-country gallivants through territory unspoiled by roads. The reverend didn't believe in taking the round-about route to do the Lord's will. As a result he and Hindy pushed their wagon up the steep sides of many a gully and out of lots of axle-deep sand.

Hindy didn't know how they'd survived a whole year. She'd long since, without telling Pa, taken to begging for food, and even stealing. She would have done anything she could think of to get a little less miserable in this world. In particular, Pa always warned her to beware of lustful men, who only wanted to take her to bed. That became her heart-of-hearts hope—a bed sounded warm and dry. Compared to the back of the wagon, it would surely be soft. She took to letting her bottom sashay a little extra when a man might be looking. But she never got so much as a lecherous whistle.

So, even looking at these verminous Indians, the girl figured her lot couldn't get much lower. In one way it would probably be better. The Indians might be vermin, as Pa said, but they probably weren't crazy.

"Me yourn!" she hollered, as though volume would clear the language hurdle. "Take squaw!" If she thought it would have helped, she would have dropped her drawers.

So she was flabbergasted when the young Indian, the one who'd gone rolling like a wheel, said politely, "Don't be afraid. We'll help you."

His English sure didn't sound broken—it sounded right proper.

"Is that man your father?" the young Indian asked, nodding toward the fallen Reverend Ratz.

"That's Pa," Hindy said meekly.

"I'm sorry," the Indian said. "He's dead. His wounds were nothing, but his heart gave out."

"Could you let me have something to eat?" Hindy asked.

≈ 2 ≈

Smith just reined in his big, clumsy horse and sat and looked disgustedly at Sings Wolf. Now, he said to himself, we're ass-deep in manure.

The three scouts also sat their horses still, there on the rock outcropping, their carbines held steady on Smith, Sings Wolf, and Hindy. Two white men and a breed, from their hands. Since they were silhouetted against the late-afternoon sun, Smith couldn't see their faces.

How had the soldiers seen them and they not seen the soldiers? How had Smith and Sings Wolf gotten so sloppy? Smith felt old and not up to the game.

"Throw your weapons on the ground and dismount," said a metallic voice. "Now!"

Another voice barked the same words in broken Cheyenne. So, thought Smith, one of them knows something. He looked hard at the man on the right, the one who spoke the Cheyenne words. He didn't recognize him. Jesus, but the bastard had an arrogant face.

Smith leaned over and set the butt of his .44 on the ground and let the rifle fall as softly as he could.

So now they would get arrested for kidnapping Hindy and killing her dad. They'd likely be shot.

Sings Wolf didn't make a move to drop his rifle, but Smith went ahead and slid off the horse. At last Sings Wolf did the same.

They had rested for two hours, but in the cottonwoods, not in Ratz's crazy campsite in the open with no water and no shelter from the wind. Hindy had eaten all they'd let her have and begged for more. Smith gathered that she was relieved to be with someone other than her father, anyone else, redskin or white. From what she said about her pa, he understood why. She was a lively little critter, and Smith couldn't help liking her.

But Smith was considerably irked. The reverend had killed Smith's horse. The wagon was useless—where they were headed, it would only slow them up. The reverend's supplies were barely worth taking, some sugar and half a sack of cornmeal. The shotgun would come in handy. So they put Smith's saddle on one of the draft animals for Hindy and Smith rode the other bareback. He wasn't as comfortable on the clumsy beast without stirrups, and Hindy probably couldn't keep up, so they were slowed down.

Sings Wolf said in Cheyenne that they'd get in trouble for taking the girl along.

But what else could they do?

Just to the nearest farm or ranch, Smith said.

And now they would keep breath and body together only if Hindy Ratz vouched for them. Smith felt a little edgy about having his life in the hands of a kid he didn't really know—a white kid who had a crazy father and might have crazy fears about Indians. He felt very, very edgy about having his life in the hands of United States soldiers, any United States soldiers. It wouldn't do to admit that he especially mistrusted the half-breed.

"*Gut* evening, Mrs. Maclean," said Dieter Richtarsch. He strode from the house onto the porch with the air of a confident man, intending to lift the spirits of his patient. And he was confident, but not about this patient.

Elaine Maclean put down her book. "Good evening, Dr. Richtarsch," she replied. "It's good to see you." She'd seen him both days since Adam left, in fact. Though he came from the fort to check on her, she had the impression that the good doctor also liked the nightlife in Dodge City. Well, she told herself, an army mess wasn't much, and

Dodge City was said to provide fancy meals. It also provided women. Fran Wockerly—Elaine had finally found out her first name—said Dr. Richtarsch was fond of the fleshpots.

Richtarsch looked at his mechanism for traction, which seemed to be in perfect order, the weight pulling properly. He drew her nightgown up and removed the splint. Something in the demeanor of this particular woman made him aware of the routine act of compromising her modesty. She had style, this particular New Englander—that was good.

He removed the dressing and palpated the area of the break delicately, trying not to hurt the patient or to reopen her wound. The bones seemed to be in good order. A nasty-looking wound, though, all jagged. Human flesh was really not a very durable commodity. But the wound looked OK. He applied more yeast with elm bark and charcoal and put on a new dressing.

The wound was beginning to hint that it might give trouble. He sniffed at it. He couldn't detect bacteria in this one by sniffing—sometimes he could, but not this time. He noted to himself that the area was inflamed and warm to the touch. He thought it was infected. The question was whether the woman could throw off the infection.

He counted. Six days since she got injured. That was a little long, but possible for infection still to show itself. He felt curious about the infection—how did she get the bacteria? But there was no way to know. Especially when she was handled by savages. Maclean might have gone through medical training, but in Richtarsch's professional opinion you never knew about a savage. Not his fault, of course. Savages were genetically different, as proven by phrenology

"Well, you're coming along nicely," the doctor assured Mrs. Maclean. "Some question of infection in your calf, but you are a strong young woman—you can throw it off."

"I intend to," she said.

"What are you reading?" He spoke to her with deliberate cheerfulness.

"Moore," she said. The Irish poet Thomas Moore was in vogue in the United States those days. "I'm so lucky that Mrs. Wockerly had this book."

"Yes," said Richtarsch sagely. It didn't do to let the Americans think you were a dummkopf, which they usually did if you spoke with an accent. So he sang one line: "Believe me if all those endearing young charms." Everyone knew the song based on Moore's verse.

That seemed to please the patient. She said, "My favorite is,

"At the mid hour of night, when stars are weeping, I fly
To the lone vale we loved, when life shone warm in thine
     eye;
And I think oft, if spirits can steal from the regions of air
To revisit past scenes of delight, thou wilt come to me there,
And tell me our love is remember'd even in the sky."

Richtarsch looked at her approvingly, shaking his head. He noticed the lines had something to do with a lost love, and wondered if she was thinking of her husband. Long gone, that one, Richtarsch thought. A barbarian— what can you expect? Richtarsch was worried about the effect Maclean's abandonment might have on his patient.

She's a whipcracker, though. He'd come across them before, these New England women with determination in their blood. Tough. Unstoppable. Admirable. Too bad they didn't realize this aggressiveness was so unappealing in a woman. And this one was so *schön*. She'll make some man a fine—he chuckled to himself—boss.

He stood up to go. "You're a strong, healthy, and spirited young woman," he said. "You'll do well. I shall return to see you tomorrow. We're keeping a close eye on that little infection." He went to the outside door, apparently done with his visit to Dr. and Mrs. Wockerly.

"Thank you, Dr. Richtarsch. You're good to sit with me. I miss having company."

The German doctor smiled, executed a short, tight bow, and went out.

And when, Elaine thought, will my juggler come to me? She didn't blame him—she understood. She just missed him. It was terrible how much she missed him. And maybe she didn't really understand. She just wanted Adam.

≈ 3 ≈

Smith heard a scraping noise, something on cloth. Heavy cloth—canvas! In Hindy's dog tent.

And then a stifled squeak.

His stomach turned nauseatingly. He knew what it was. Rape. The son of a bitch was raping Hindy. That bastard Nelly Burns.

Smith flopped, hard. He was wrapped in a tarpaulin and bound and gagged and there wasn't a goddamn thing he could do. Except flop around in the dark and kick and make noise and wake somebody up and . . .

Now he knew why that bastard put Hindy in a tent—and Smith had thought stupidly that Burns was acting decent to her.

Smith lurched as hard as he could toward the tent—maybe he could knock the goddamn thing down—and found himself looking into Calling Eagle's eyes.

What remarkable eyes. Calling Eagle heard the sounds, too, and knew what they meant. Her eyes were deep and still and aware, accepting the pain of the world.

Calling Eagle! He meant Sings Wolf. Not his grandmother, his grandfather. But Sings Wolf was unsexed now, wrapped in the heavy tarpaulin from foot to mouth, almost nothing but eyes and hair showing. Smith congratulated himself yesterday for not once failing to call her by her new name, Sings Wolf. Then it occurred to him that he was nonetheless thinking of Sings Wolf as *her*.

But Smith wasn't a damn bit interested in being accepting about this pain or any other. That son of a bitch was violating Hindy!

He gyrated around and kicked and banged his back against the ground—he got into a frenzy of kicking and banging—and it made no difference at all. Until he heard the tent flap move.

What he saw was the half-breed Nelly Burns looking at him down the barrel of a Navy .36. And holding his pants up with one hand. And smiling viciously.

"Lucky you didn't stir anybody, *Doctor*. I'd blow your nose out through the back side of your skull."

Smith lay still. Nelly Burns was a mad dog, and there was no sense getting bit.

Smith could hear Hindy mewling softly now.

Burns pulled his pants up and stuck his revolver into the waist. "I'm looking forward to seeing you die, though, you and Grandpa there. We'll even do it legal, soon as Lieutenant Garber comes up. Don't it make you feel better to die legal?"

The three scouts had made camp here expecting the main column to come up. But for some reason it hadn't, only several more scouts. They'd gone back to find out why, leaving the three captors here with their prisoners.

"I'm looking forward to seeing you beg, *Doctor*, and shit your breechclout, *Doctor*, and seeing the coyotes sniff your guts." Burns cackled, shaking his head at Smith. His left eye opened oddly, giving him a know-it-all look.

Smith supposed it was just as well he was gagged. No sense getting shot for cussing Burns, or spitting on him.

The scout went and sat against a tree, the only tree for miles around on this plain. It was Burns's watch. Soft sobbing came from the dog tent. Yes. Smith was better off gagged. No words, but when the time came, he would kill Nelly Burns.

Smith had picked up some facts from the scouts, and they all pleased him. This Garber was in command because Colonel Lewis was dead. The soldiers had attacked the people in some hills this side of the Smoky Hill River, and the Cheyennes had driven them off. Colonel Lewis, sure enough, had made good on his promise to annihilate the Cheyennes or die trying.

Smith was beginning to believe in a kind of mad

destiny. It seemed to be the Cheyennes' fate to win battles in spite of overwhelming odds. It looked like their destiny to get back home to Powder River country. Unbelievable, but he was coming to believe it.

Not that Smith would necessarily live to get home. This damn Burns was likely enough to kill him. Smith had known men like Burns all his life, border scum, men who felt loyalty to no community, no tribe, no nation, no nothing. Men who were worse than animals because they liked to torture and maim and kill. Men like Owen Mackenzie, who killed Smith's father Mac and brother Thomas, men like Nelly Burns.

Of course, Burns liked to mock Smith with the fact that they were both half-breeds. Burns was half-Pawnee—he said his father had been a trader to the Pawnees. So Smith let himself indulge in the age-old Cheyenne hatred for Pawnees.

The other scouts weren't bad men, the ones headed back to the main column or the two in the other dog tent. None of them was army. The army used old-hand frontiersmen to figure out where it was going on the plains and in the deserts and mountains. None of them had much civilization. But only Burns was a mad dog.

If Burns didn't kill Smith and Sings Wolf, Lieutenant Garber might well have them executed. Smith pondered the old preacher's body back there. Since they hadn't had a shovel, they hadn't buried him, just covered him with rocks. If Hindy told the soldiers where her father was, Smith and Sings Wolf were dead. Hell, she didn't have to tell them—the wagon sat there like a tombstone, marking the spot.

Maybe Garber would judge them guilty on the face of it anyway: Smith and Sings Wolf had stolen the draft animals and kidnapped Hindy. If she claimed she'd gone along willingly, they'd think her horrible experiences had warped her mind.

And maybe they had. Her father, the Reverend Ratz, had made a good start at it—maybe this rape had finished the job. Smith couldn't hear Hindy now. He would have felt better if he could hear her crying, for silence was worse than her sobs. Maybe Hindy was ruined.

Elaine wrote in a slanted, efficient hand, not an ornate one like her sister Dora's. Yet Elaine's handwriting was attractive if the reader saw beauty in polished simplicity.

She was writing to her sister rather than her mother. She knew that Dora would inform Mother right away, and Elaine wanted Mother to know. But Elaine couldn't name all the terms of life in this place to her mother. Now *that*, she realized, is an attitude Mother would not approve of. Nevertheless . . .

She dated her letter the first day of October, 1878, and pitched in. She picked up where her last letter left off—how the fight at Turkey Springs turned out OK, like violence among children, much declamation, little damage. She felt guilty for this misrepresentation, but it was literally true, and she couldn't bring herself to tell Dora how she felt about it.

She voiced eloquently her admiration for the toughness of Rain, who bore a child alone and in desperate circumstances, and now was her sister. She mentioned lightly the superstition that so dominated the girl's mind that she could believe a soldier who watched her bear the child was a spirit.

She told how the Cheyennes were accepting Adam's medical help more. Though they still wouldn't tolerate the little death, they saw that he helped, and they were a practical people. Besides, Adam's grandfather (she wrote grand*mother* and crossed it out) put it well—Indian medicine for Indian illnesses, white-man medicine for white-man diseases. They would let Adam help with white-man hurts, like bullets.

She wrote of miracles—Little Wolf's walking through the hail of bullets untouched, and Bridge's stopping the

arterial bleeding of Sitting Man. She surmised that the God
who reigned over the earth, called by various names as he
was, had room in his heart for poor red men, though white
men did not.

She wrote that sleeping on the ground without a
shelter, riding fifty miles in a day, and going hungry were
hardships she had adjusted to easily. She said nothing about
the hardship of living in perpetual fear, or about how her
circumstances chafed at her fledgling marriage.

She puzzled at length over what to say, if anything,
about Calling Eagle's transformation into Sings Wolf. At
length she wrote,

> One of our women had a dream, and in that
> dream saw herself dead, dressed as a man, outfit-
> ted for war, and being buried with the honor due
> a warrior. She took it as a sign and revolutionized
> her life! She traded her feminine name for a man's
> name and gave up her clothes and adornment and
> all her feminine ways to live as a warrior would.
> Her first day as a man she led a war charge that
> turned back the soldiers, and we won against an
> overwhelming number of bluecoats.
>
> Her conversion is truly a blessing because we
> are so short of men able to fight, and it is taken by
> our people as a great sign that in desperate
> circumstances the Powers will provide in a truly
> miraculous way.
>
> There is more to the story, which I shall tell
> you in person. It illustrates wonderfully with what
> awe our people regard dreams.

But she didn't know whether she could bring herself to
talk even to her sister about the facts of Sings Wolf's
anatomy.

She said nothing about the apparent disloyalty of
fighting United States soldiers. Her family had opposed the
authorities in the Revolution, when they were British, and
opposed the authorities again when they tolerated slavery.

Mother and Dora would understand that one fought for the right.

Finally Elaine got to the night of the crossing of the Arkansas.

> My horse stumbled and fell, and in the dark water stepped on me. I fear that the result is that I have broken my right leg, but am getting excellent care. Adam brought me here to Dodge City, where I am doubly watched over. The surgeon from Fort Dodge attends to me medically while the local doctor gives me room and board. If his wife did not sit with me and talk for long hours—poor creature! no one else seems to talk to her!—I would be parched for company.

She decided to brighten her pages with what she'd learned of Dodge City from Fran Wockerley, a shy but eager gossip. Elaine told how the vast herds of half-wild cattle were herded up from Texas—"aristocratic beeves, descended from the great ranchos chartered by the King of Spain!"—to be jammed into cars and shipped to the hungry East.

> So large numbers of cow-boys (most of them truly *boys*) gasp into Dodge City all through the summer and fall. Thirsty for amenities after their months on the trail, they collect their meager wages and set out to indulge in what they fancy to be the luxuries of civilization (really the depravities which are its regrettable by-products). Straight to the pleasure palace the cow-boy heads, the spot for drinking, dancing, and gambling all in one—Dodge's streets are dust, its saloons gilt! Before long the country fellow has lost his wages to a professional gambler, gotten too inebriated to care, danced with a pretty girl (and maybe stolen a kiss!)

—Dora would understand this euphemism—

> and had a fight with someone who insulted the "great state of Texas." Having gotten what he came for—he has "seen the elephant!"—he heads for a home hundreds of miles away, broke, hung over, banged up, and happy.
>
> It is all in the spirit of fun, of course, and one cannot feel begrudging. It makes me wonder, though, that the people of Dodge should be so certain of the superiority of their "civilization" compared to the style of living of the Indians who just fled past them in pitiable circumstances, poor, hungry, dirty enough, and plenty ignorant, but possessed of dignity and elevated by the strongest spirituality.

She set pen and paper down a moment and rested. She tired easily these days. But she had to get to what she'd been avoiding:

> Now I am in traction—I'm painfully bored not being able to move about—but Dr. Richtarsch says my break is mending "nicely," so I shall no doubt be running races soon. Adam is gone on with the people to the north country, and I will meet him there when I can travel. Meanwhile, think of all the time I shall have to write you letters! And to read your letters. *Please* write me in care of Dr. M. T. Wockerley, Dodge City. Dr. Richtarsch says I shall be here at least a month.
>
> Though my bone is knitting, the cut in my leg is infected, Dr. Richtarsch fears, and today he expressed concern about it.

The good doctor had used the word *concern*, but Elaine knew he was deliberately understating its seriousness. She did the same.

I am confident that I shall throw the infection off quickly—you remember how my colds lasted only a day, and yours a week!

She rested again. She told herself that her anxiety was foolish—"feminine frippery!" she accused herself. She was more than half aware that the frippery was a premonition— a premonition that she would die of this little infection—die in miserable Kansas, die a failure at marriage, die far from her husband, far from her family, die without being held, without being cherished, without being loved. Die a sort of spinster. She had risen above such feminine foolishness since she was a little girl, though, and she wasn't about to regress now.

Lying back, half-exhausted, she thought of Adam. Adam who was riding across the plains with Sings Wolf, trying to catch up with a hapless people. Adam who was running from her. Lord, she ached to tell him she loved him. She wondered when she would get to hold him and tell him.

"I love you," she wrote in the letter to her sister, and signed her name.

She would take a nap. It was amazing how tired she seemed to be from this broken leg. And in the afternoons she was feverish. She would take a nap, and then Dr. Richtarsch would be here, and they would visit a little while.

The flask landed with a clink. It lay across the coals that remained of the fire. It sounds empty, Smith thought, so he's as drunk as he will get. It was an expensive-looking flask of embossed silver. Smith wondered what body Burns had stolen it from.

Burns got up and staggered over to the fire. He was a small man—Smith could have broken him of the know-it-all eye over one knee. Smith cursed himself again for hurrying and getting ambushed.

Burns just stood there, like he'd forgotten why he came. Did he mean to pick up the flask he'd thrown? Or would he not think of it until morning, when he was hung over and needed the hair of the dog and didn't have any?

Smith had worked and worked at his bonds, hands and feet, and thought he might be making some progress. He was afloat in the damn tarpaulin and couldn't chafe at the ropes much. He'd rubbed his back hard on the ground, though, and it felt like he'd moved the hemp up in back. Maybe before dawn he could scooch it up over his shoulders. He wished to hell his shoulders were narrower.

He figured that not long after dawn he and Sings Wolf would be seeing a lot of U.S. soldiers. And not long after that they would be dead.

Sings Wolf was sleeping. Smith had indicated Sings Wolf should look at the ropes on Smith's back, and he had. Then he shook his head gently no and closed his eyes and went to sleep. Smith's grandfather was not one to fret pointlessly or struggle to no effect.

Finally, Burns squatted down by the coals near Smith's head. He held his long Arkansas toothpick into the fire, as he would roast meat, but the end of the knife held no meat. It was a wicked-looking knife, long, sharp-pointed, and double-edged—one of the few knives good for throwing and ripping. He set it on a rock, tip still in the coals, and pulled a glove onto his right hand.

"I been thinking about you, *Doctor*," said Burns in a slur, "and I don't like you."

He let a while go by, a drunk's pause between stupid remarks—he'd probably forget he'd been talking.

"You're a goddamm Cheyenne."

You Pawnees have plenty of reason to fear and hate Cheyennes, Smith wanted to say through his gag. You've stocked horses for us for generations, ready whenever the Tsistsistas-Suhtaio need them. You've provided women for the sport of our warriors. The reason we haven't whupped on you much recently is that it's a doubtful honor to count coup against a mere Pawnee.

"You're a white man, too. You didn't say so, but anybody can see it." Burns studied the end of his knife in the coals for a moment. "Nothing I hate more than Cheyennes and white men."

Burns sat for a while. Was this easing up to it part of the act, Smith wondered, or was Burns really drunk? Both, Smith guessed.

He saw that Sings Wolf was awake now. Smith's grandfather had rolled to face him, looked at him with still, deep eyes.

"What's more," Burns ambled on, "you're a know-it-all. You been to one of them colleges. Can't learn that doctoring without you go to one of them colleges, can you, *Doctor*?"

Burns turned his head sideways and looked at Smith with a big smile. He looked almost amiable. Smith noticed foolishly that Burns had all his teeth, unusual on the frontier. He looked predatory.

"You talk high and mighty. 'As I said,' you said to us. Us ignoramuses. '*As* I said.'" He took the knife out with his gloved hand and inspected the tip closely. It glowed red. "Ain't much anybody likes less than a know-it-all."

Burns cackled, a high, piercing sound that came from nowhere and related to nothing.

"'*As* I said.'" Burns fell into silence again, his eyes fixed on the end of the knife among the coals. He kept still.

Smith could feel little prickles of cold forming in the small of his back.

Finally, Burns brought the knife out and inspected the end again. Smith couldn't see how it could be any more red-hot.

Burns changed tone suddenly. From laconic mockery he switched to a stage whisper. "But you don't know nothing. You don't even know who you are."

Burns let it sit for a moment, holding the knife in the fire again. "How can a *doctor* wear a breechcloth and leggings? How can you do that, *Doctor*? How can a white man go on the warpath with Injuns? Hmmm? Tell this nigger that, now."

Burns took the knife out and inspected it. "How can a white man kidnap a little white girl, pore thing?" He snickered. "How can an Injun be a know-it-all doctor, *Doctor*?"

"So I got me a idea. Hear me, now. What you is, is a big question mark. Didn't think Nelly Burns knew what a question mark is, now, did you? Didn't think Nelly Burns could read." He took the Arkansas toothpick out of the fire. "So I think you ought to die tomorrow with a big question mark on your face. A *big* question mark."

He knelt close to Smith, the knife glowing in his hand. "Now this nigger noticed them stitches on the outside of your left eye." Burns worked the fingers of his off hand into Smith's hair for a good grip. "Shame you need them stitches, ain't it? Did one of my Pawnee *compañeros* get to the doctor before this nigger did? Did his knife hurt? Hmmm?"

Burns jerked Smith's head back hard.

Smith had heard all his life about stepping aside mentally, holding the spirit apart from the body. He wondered if he could.

"Well, I want to finish that question mark. It needs that little dot underneath."

Smith saw the red-hot knife tip come toward his eyes and felt a stab of heat that took his breath away.

It was already over. He felt surprisingly calm. A warm trickle of blood flowed down his cheek, but it didn't seem like much.

"Silent, are you, *Doctor*? What a brave, white-man, red-man doctor. Tell me, *Doctor*, when they breed a Cheyenne mare to a white burro, what do they get? Do they get a mule? Are you sterile, *Doctor*?"

Burns slugged Smith viciously in the groin.

Smith deliberately didn't react. The tarpaulin absorbed most of the force anyway. Now he was determined not to let this scum make him cry out through the gag.

Burns wrenched Smith's head back by the hair. Smith

elt the bastard's hot breath and then Burns's teeth in his
ear. He jumped, but made no sound.

Quickly, in a fury, Burns cut an arc around the outside
of Smith's other eye.

Smith just stared at him. He pretended blood wasn't
running into his eye.

"See, Doctor," Burns purred, "a question mark on
each side of your brain. What is it, a white-man brain or a
red-man brain?" He cackled low.

Now Burns began to slide the Arkansas toothpick up
Smith's face. Smith felt the warm touch of it under his chin,
in the cleft, under his lower lip, on his upper lip. It didn't
seem to be cutting, just touching.

Burns eased the point of the knife deep into Smith's
nostril.

"Burns," drawled a Southern voice, "you cut him again
and this boy will kill you."

The knife stopped.

Smith held his breath. He thought Burns might ram
the knife point home right now.

Burns took the knife out, stuck it in its scabbard, and
stood up over Smith, smiling casually. "What's the matter,
Riley, you think he needs to look pretty to die in the
morning?"

"Burns," said the scout, "you're relieved of this
watch—I'll take over."

Riley looked in the dog tent at Hindy and apparently
saw nothing wrong. He walked over to the fire and studied
the two prisoners. Seeing Smith's face, he said contemptu-
ously, "A knife is a greaser's toy. Down home in San
Antone, I been known to take a knife away from a greaser."

Burns slashed sideways with the knife—Smith thought
he could hear it cut air.

Crack!

Burns yelped, and the knife fell into the dust.

Riley had the muzzle of his Colt Dragoon under
Burns's chin, forcing his head back.

Burns held the wrist of his gun hand. "You broke it,"
Burns whispered.

"I hope so, Burns. I'd like to kill you," Riley said slowly, as though making a casual observation. "But I don't like court-martials." He stared Burns down. "Now get in that tent and make me think you're sleeping."

Burns went.

Riley sat down by the tree.

Smith hoped he was alert. Otherwise Burns would kill him.

≈ 4 ≈

Smith felt a weight set down on his stomach. He took a moment—it was a good idea not to show your enemy right off that you were awake, especially when you were wrapped in a tarpaulin and tied up. Then he cracked his eyes in the direction of his belly.

What he saw in the predawn darkness was a head. Nelly Burns's head. Just the head, severed, and held up by a hand in its dark hair. Looking at Smith from his belly, one eye was gaped and the other still know-it-all.

Twist chuckled maliciously. He guffawed in a stagy way to make his point. Smith took the point: all three scouts were beyond hearing anything.

Twist cut the gag and ropes off Sings Wolf and then came to Smith. He got out his knife and pointed it at Smith's newly injured eye. He emitted that weird cackle again.

"Grandson," snapped Sings Wolf. It was an admonition to behave like a human being.

Twist cut Smith's bonds and put away the knife.

"Grandson," said Sings Wolf, "I saw nothing and heard nothing." He was paying compliment to Twist's skills, and deservedly so.

"Good-bye, Grandfather," said Twist. "Keep the *veho* out of trouble. Tell him to go back to his wife." Twist disappeared into the darkened plains.

Smith stretched out his kinked-up legs and arms, then slipped into the tent and quickly cut the ropes and gag off Hindy, and told her she would be OK. She held on to Smith and said nothing, but she wouldn't let go.

After a few moments Smith disengaged himself. Riley was still against the tree, dead. Smith went to check the other tent. Two bodies, including Burns, still in the bedroll, headless. The other was halfway out, his throat cut. Too slow.

Yes, Smith thought, Twist had brought off a remarkable feat. He'd sneaked into camp, cut Riley's throat without letting him cry out, and crept into the tent and killed both the other scouts before they could do a damn thing. Then he'd brought Smith that gruesome trophy.

Twist had known exactly how many men were in camp and where they were. He must have seen and heard everything—must have been hiding nearby in the dark. He'd plainly been tracking Smith and Sings Wolf all along, tracking them from well back, waiting for whatever opportunity came. By chance the opportunity was to save Smith's life instead of taking it.

So now Smith owed his life to Twist. He didn't like that. Twist would gloat over it. And now that Twist had killed more whites, more soldiers would come after the people.

Twist wouldn't care. He would just strut and preen and brag about his coups. He was a mad dog, just like Burns.

Dr. Richtarsch gazed down on his patient. She slept restlessly. She had mostly slept, said Dr. Wockerley, for two days now, and had been steadily feverish. She tossed and turned a lot. They'd had to wake her to feed her.

The doctor frowned. This one was taking a bad course, quite bad.

"Mrs. Maclean," Richtarsch called cheerfully. She stirred a little. "Mrs. Maclean," he repeated, booming. She stirred again, and he began to shake her by the shoulder.

Richtarsch felt a certain liking for Elaine. Though she had committed the foolishness of marrying a red Indian, he thought, at least she had gotten a decent name out of it. *Schottisch*, the doctor thought—Scottish. A good name for a widow. That's what she should give out, that she was a widow.

He shook her vigorously.

She came to with a little start. Yes, she felt bad. She had all the signs.

"How do you feel today, Mrs. Maclean?"

She shook her head, trying to wake up. "Depleted," she murmured.

This one had a brain. Even when she was sick half to death, she used an expressive word. "All day yesterday and today, depleted?" Richtarsch asked.

"Yes. Don't seem to have any energy. Completely drained. Did anyone mail the letter to my sister?"

Yes, my dear, you have an infection, a bad one. "The letter has been taken care of. Mrs. Maclean"—he spoke urgently now—"we are approaching a critical time. We must make a decision." She closed her eyes, and he wondered if she heard him, and if she was capable of making a decision.

"Your infection is serious. As your physician, I believe it threatens your life. I recommend that we remove your leg above the infected place, in other words just below the knee. You will still be able to walk. What do you say?"

He waited, and for a moment didn't feel sure she'd heard him. When she opened her eyes, though, he saw the pain and grief.

"How long do I have to decide?" Ah—pain, grief, and increased awareness. Good woman.

"I would prefer a decision today. I am prepared to do the procedure this afternoon. Waiting is dangerous. If you insist, we will wait until tomorrow. Given the seriousness of the situation, though, I cannot recommend even that."

"Please give me the facts as you see them, Doctor."

She looked more awake, at least. Richtarsch told her truthfully. "The wound on your calf is infected, and the infection has spread systemically. That means through your entire system. You may overcome the infection through your constitution, but I see no signs of that. To wait for that would be to risk your life. I recommend removal of the leg

below the knee, as soon as possible. You will be able still to
walk, with the help of an artificial limb." He stopped and
waited.

"Does the surgery," she asked softly, "also put my life
at hazard?"

"It is not without risk to life. It can go wrong. The
other course, however, is more dangerous."

She reached and patted his hand lightly, a gesture he
found too familiar.

"Perhaps, Doctor, if you would ask Mrs. Wockerley to
bring me a cup of coffee to help me stay alert, and give me
thirty minutes to think."

He nodded. Yes, good woman. "Naturally," said the
doctor, with the stress on the second syllable, making it
sound like *natürlich*.

How do you say good-bye to a leg?

Elaine dreamed. Not by mistake, or through drowsi-
ness. Knowing necessity for what it was, she let herself go
in a reverie, drifting, floating in and out of time and space.
Strangely, and sweetly, in the reverie what she saw and
heard and smelled and felt seemed not half-real but
ultra-real.

Later she would not be able to remember most of what
she spun from the warp of memory and imagination, and
the weft of something like vision. He saw herself running
behind Dora, just barely behind, on a race to the pond, and
wondering if she had a right leg and being unable to see it
or to feel its foot striking the earth and knowing it must be
there but being eerily sure it wasn't. She dared not look.

She saw herself standing up beside her husband-to-be
in front of the missionary, in her yellow dress and about to
be wed, and seeing her right foot planted solid on the floor
and feeling glad, absurdly glad that it was there, reaching
down to feel it—warm and fleshy it was—and looking up at

Adam and laughing like buddies with him because she was feeling her own leg in front of the preacher.

Afterward—or was it an entirely different time?—Adam lifted her up to help her into her sidesaddle and nipped her playfully on the shoulder with his teeth and let her go, and because she had no right leg to hold on to the horns with, she fell out of the saddle and through his reaching arms and past the earth and into the eternal void, falling endlessly.

She woke up after that one with a start. Lying back down, she reminded herself that self-torture wasn't necessary.

She returned to the scene of her own wedding, and laughing with Adam about feeling her own leg, and the leg turned to squish in her fingers and bled scarlet all over her hands and arms and her wedding dress, and she fainted.

In this reverie, this heightened state, not merely what the whites meant by *dream* but what the Cheyennes meant, the eight-year-old Elaine did a cartwheel in front of her father, daringly exposing her bloomers to her daddy and her whole family. Elaine, though, noticed only her daddy. And he laughed with delight, the top of his beard trembling, and the second time she cartwheeled he grabbed for her legs and got hold of one ankle but she pulled the other, the right one, back at the knee, because it was, most strangely, at once there and not there. And she grabbed his big head to her breasts (yes, she was grown and had breasts) and held him and said how sorry, how very sorry, she was for the awful, missing leg. And he started to weep with her, but she realized she was holding an emptiness to her breast—her father was not there—and she woke again in a fright.

The awakened, alert, adult Elaine Cummings Maclean made a grimace for a smile and got hold of herself. She drank her coffee, which was cold. And she saw Dr. Richtarsch coming up the walk. A soldier followed him bearing what appeared to be a tool kit.

When Dr. Richtarsch opened the door and looked

questioningly at her, she said only, "Yes." He nodded curtly at the soldier.

Dr. Richtarsch went inside to get Dr. Wockerley. The soldier started unpacking the tools, several scalpels, silk thread, needles, scissors, a small saw, and some sort of burner she'd never seen. The soldier set it up, calling it a Bunsen burner. She smelled gas as he touched a match to its top, and it made a steady, blue flame.

Elaine felt a great wrenching heave through her insides, like violent nausea, but she didn't throw up.

Dr. Richtarsch picked up the saw and looked at it for a moment. Dr. Wockerley stepped forward with a folded linen cloth, and the familiar smell of chloroform came over her. As she lost consciousness, the saw rose in her mind's eye, tidily gnawing at her leg bone.

≈ 5 ≈

Sings Wolf sat his horse and waited for Smith to decide. He was well mounted now—all three of them were, riding the dead scouts' big American horses and their light McClellan saddles, with the rest of their gear, U.S. Army issue, packed on Hindy's draft animals. They looked down on a baker's dozen horses in a fenced pasture, and the ranch building beyond.

"The people need them," Sings Wolf said simply, without emphasis.

Yes, but . . . Smith was wanted for kidnapping a white girl, maybe for killing her father, for killing three scouts of the U.S. Army, and stealing army horses and equipment. Fortunately, they could execute him only once.

And fat chance they would mistake his identity. Nothing more common around here than six-and-a-half-foot Indians who speak English like a Dartmouth graduate and are trained in medicine, is there, Doctor?

He wondered whether Elaine would suffer on his account. Would they persecute her somehow for being his wife? Would they mock her for being married to a murderer? Would they hold her to guarantee his surrender?

His wife seemed to him an infinity away. He thought of her in his bedroll at dawn and dusk, when he got a little nap. He hoped she healed rapidly. He hoped she would go to Fort Robinson and wait for him. He feared she would go home, and become a Massachusetts schoolmarm, and eventually make a respectable marriage. Whatever she decided, it was beyond his reach. He had moved into a world with its own gravitational pull, which he could not overcome.

So why didn't he want to steal this rancher's horses?
Why not, indeed?

Smith knew he would do it. It was right for Sings Wolf.
Sings Wolf looked and sounded marvelously martial. He
was full of his own virility. After six decades as a woman, he
glowed manhood.

Smith chuckled. He said to himself, Maybe you can
store up your virility. But wasn't the whole idea to spend it?
And have a good time spending it?

He nodded once at Sings Wolf. The old warrior told
Hindy to wait for them in the ravine north of the ranch
buildings, a couple of miles from here. They would come
immediately after dark, which was only an hour away. The
girl walked her big horse off. Ever since the rape, she'd
been pliable and listless, acting half-dead. Smith was
worried about her.

The old man sat down to paint his face like a veteran of
a thousand raids.

As soon as she felt able, the third day after her surgery,
Elaine dictated a telegram to her mother and sister:

I HAVE SURVIVED STOP RIGHT LEG AMPUTATED BELOW THE
KNEE STOP LONG REHABILITATION MAY MEAN VISIT HOME
STOP SAD BUT BEARING UP STOP YOUR LOVING DAUGHTER
ELAINE

Sings Wolf gazed into the small fire. The dawn light
made it nearly invisible. He was uneasy. Not tired, just
uneasy.

Since he had claimed his manhood, Sings Wolf felt
strong. His body was no longer seventy winters worn, but
new. So he had been able to push the stolen horses hard all

night with Vekifs and the white child, not sleeping at all. Sings Wolf thought this push unnecessary. They had made off with the horses at night and had seen and heard nothing of the white ranch people. He thought maybe the people were gone into town because of the Indian scare. Or else they hadn't been watchful.

If the ranchers followed the horses' trail, thought Sings Wolf, they had not started until the next morning, and so would be too far behind to catch up before the animals were part of the herd of three hundred Tsistsistas-Suhtaio. The people's trail was fresh now—Sings Wolf, Vekifs, and Hindy would catch up with the people tomorrow.

And they would ride to a descant of evil. Sings Wolf was beginning to feel that evil now, no more visible than the wind but just as real. He felt it in the turning of hairs on his arms, in the small turbulence in his chest, in his oppressing sense of blight here, in his held-back despair.

He realized that his two companions did not notice it, not Hindy napping there across the fire, not Vekifs standing watch on the horses. To him it was remarkable that they could look about and see nothing but the usual arid, rolling plains of the country between the Platte and the Arkansas. They did not sense the hints here, and they would not hear the awful melody, thrummed loudly by all the living things, at the hill where the blood ran deep. Sings Wolf shrugged and stood up.

"Let's go," he said, not loudly.

Hindy sat up immediately, rubbing her eyes. A willing girl, that one—she will make a good woman of the Tsistsistas-Suhtaio, he thought. A little food, a little nap, and she is ready to ride all day.

Vekifs came to get his saddle. He picked up a saddle in each hand, his and Hindy's, and headed back toward the rope corral. His strength was wonderful.

But if some of his blood was not white, he would feel what was here. He did not, so Sings Wolf would have to tell him. Last evening the sky had even sifted down a thin snow for a few minutes, the first sign of winter, and a sign that it was time to tell stories.

Sings Wolf gave it a moment's thought. He had best
tell his tale here, before they got to the hill where the
whites had done most of the killing three years ago. There
the spirits acted out the slaughter perpetually. And all
the malignity, the darkness of human beings and of the
universe—it was still there, a palpable evil. If the spirits
heard Sings Wolf speak of the evil, they would be ill-
disposed toward him and his companions.

But if Vekifs was to be truly Cheyenne, he must hear,
feel, know, understand. So when Vekifs started to take
down the rope corral, Sings Wolf stayed his hand.

"Grandson," began Sings Wolf, "you do not know what
happened a little below here, down the Sappa River."
Smith had gathered from the hints, the silences, the turns
away from some conversational directions that the Human
Beings didn't want to talk about it. They avoided speaking
the names of the dead, and they didn't talk about what was
too sad for tears. So people died here, doubtless lots of
people. If Sings Wolf was about to ignore the taboo and tell
him what happened, it was important.

Sings Wolf told it simply, without emphasis, without
elaboration, without pause. Except for the quaver in his
voice and the grief in his face, his telling might have
seemed matter-of-fact.

Some soldiers and volunteers (those bastards again)
chased a band of Human Beings in this direction from Fort
Reno because Black Horse refused to go to jail. He broke
away and fled with the Tsistsistas-Suhtaio. They fled rapidly
to the north, back to Powder River country, just like now.
Many people on this trip were at Sappa Creek, including
Sings Wolf.

Somehow the whites got the Cheyennes pinned down
in a difficult place. The women had to dig holes for
themselves and the children, and the men shot from rifle
pits. But the Human Beings had only a few guns and not

much ammunition, and they were finally overwhelmed. It was one of the few times the whites were willing to fight all the way, and the people couldn't hold them off.

Some people escaped, slipping off to the rear. But lots of warriors were killed. Sings Wolf mentioned slaughtered warriors without using their names—the oldest son of Two Feathers, the brother of Blue Knife, the father of Singing Crane. It was too long a recitation. Smith knew many of the warriors and had fought with some of them.

When the warriors were dead, and the soldiers and volunteers came up, many women and children were still hiding in their pits.

Sings Wolf hesitated now, and went on with audible resolve. The whites clubbed the women and children, even the infants, with the butts of their guns. Sings Wolf listed the dead women and children without naming them. He did it evenly, but his eyes gave him away—he had left the present and was in the past, a past that was nearly unspeakable.

Then the whites burned the people's belongings—tipi covers, poles, buffalo robes, everything. And they threw the bodies of the Indians on the fires, some still alive.

Sings Wolf looked Smith flush in the eyes. His wordless gaze said, Do you see? Do you understand? Then the old man untied the rope and let the horses out.

So. My grandfather has spoken the simple truth, and will say no more about it.

Sings Wolf handed Smith the reins of his mount. Smith was too affected to move yet.

Smith was thinking that to him, it was an evil inflicted on the people three years ago. To Sings Wolf it was more, much more. It was a continuing expression of the malign forces in the universe. As such, it was still happening. Sings Wolf gazed upon the present and the past simultaneously. As he rode into the scene today, what happened there would be happening again. It would always be happening, murder after murder, implacably.

And for Smith to put the event back to three years ago,

to push it away, made no difference. He was stunned, dumbfounded.

Sings Wolf was mounted. He yelled at the horses and moved them down the trail. Smith had to get going.

The day after she sent her telegram, Elaine got a wire back:

BUCK UP STOP OF COURSE YOU SURVIVED STOP YOU ARE A CUMMINGS STOP YOU CAN DO ANYTHING STOP WE LOVE YOU STOP MOTHER AND DORA

Dr. Richtarsch instructed Fran Wockerley to read it to Elaine as soon as she was alert, and to give her the hundred dollars that came with it. Elaine wasn't alert enough until the next day.

≈ 6 ≈

Smith, Sings Wolf, and Hindy caught up with the main band of Human Beings about noon and were received warmly by Lisette and Rain. The people went into camp early in the afternoon—they would rest a day or two to let their weak horses recuperate. Sings Wolf immediately gave the stolen horses away, a genuine boon.

The women quickly fixed Smith, Sings Wolf, and Hindy something to eat. They accepted Hindy into the family without question.

The news was good and not so good. Yes, the Tsistsistas-Suhtaio had whipped Colonel Lewis back at the forks of Punished Woman Creek. They would have whipped him worse, but some young warrior had gotten excited and shot too soon and spoiled the ambush. And they hadn't been bothered by soldiers since that day.

But the people were low in spirit. Their horses were exhausted, and some died every day, or the people killed them for food. And the tribe had limped past the hill on the Sappa River where so many relatives died not long ago. Lisette said no more. Smith knew she implied that the badness of the place, the spirit of evil there, brought everyone low.

So Smith wandered through the camp and found out what was happening in the strangest of ways: Little Finger Nail was drawing in his canvas-covered account book.

Smith had come to like Finger Nail. The young warrior spoke seldom, seemed game for any sort of adventure, and smiled appealingly, the sweet smile of an easygoing, congenial youth. And he was beautiful. His face was striking in a way that was still boyish, his clothes hung on him becomingly, he moved gracefully, and somehow he just

looked like a picture, a romantic version in soft contours
of a plains warrior. He wore a bird in his hair, which
he thought lent him his sweetness of voice. The way
he'd tied the feathers onto his lance was somehow just
right, the painting on his shield was handsome, the way he
sat in his saddle dramatic. All the while with that boyish
smile. Smith supposed that the eye of the artist shaped all
his life.

Finger Nail was depicting yesterday's coups. Some
young men had gone after horses. When they saw the white
rancher had his horses carefully guarded, they knew the
word was out. Finger Nail had crept up on a corral, killed
the guard with his knife, scalped him, and chased the
horses out. Then he had ridden back against the pursuers
and struck one with his war club, a fine coup indeed, facing
rifles to strike a blow by hand.

The fresh scalp hanging from a cottonwood branch told
the rest of the story. Auburn, the scalp was.

Finger Nail talked a little in his soft, youthful voice
while he drew. The young men raided because the Human
Beings needed horses—the people could not walk to
Powder River and carry all their belongings on their backs.
While the warriors raided, they took life and they took hair.
"We remember," he said simply.

Finger Nail looked up from his work when he said
those words. His eyes were large and soft, pretty, but
Smith knew that he was among the most daring of the
young men. "We spoke among ourselves of killing nineteen
whites here." That was the number of Human Beings killed
here three years ago. "We are not finished yet."

Smith left him to his work and talked to others. Before
long he understood: Little Wolf no longer had any control
of his warriors. Morning Star sought no control. Everyone
felt the same way. Stealing horses was necessary for reasons
of practicality. Taking scalps was mandatory for reasons of
the spirit. The policy of walking softly through the white-
man country was dead. It brought no mercy from the white
man anyway.

A hell for them, Smith thought. A hell of the past, a hell of the present.

A hell for us.

Smith was startled when Sings Wolf woke him out of a deep sleep around midnight. After days of hard pushing, Smith needed to sleep, and he was surprised that Sings Wolf didn't. "I'm leading a pony raid," said the old man, "and I would like you to go."

Smith nodded, ready to listen. He knew how it was done. One man felt called to go on a pony raid. It was a weighty responsibility. That man made medicine and listened to what his medicine said—how it should be done, where, in what way it could succeed, and what might cause it to fail. Then he chose companions, and in choosing took responsibility for them. He was saying that his medicine promised success—that the party would get horses and everyone would come back alive. If his medicine failed, he would accept some responsibility for the dead man's family.

The men chosen could accept or refuse. Acceptance indicated confidence in the leader's medicine. Refusal simply indicated that their own medicine told them to stay home or do something else. Embracing the leader's medicine meant embracing the way the raid was to be done.

Sings Wolf said he had heard of a big ranch with many horses to the northeast. They would steal the horses at dawn. The whites would respond slowly, but might follow. The raiders would return without shedding anyone's blood, white man or red man. Nothing would be stolen but horses.

Smith listened to Sings Wolf's revelations carefully. He needed to understand what to do. What he didn't understand was why Sings Wolf was doing this. The old man seemed listless about it, unenthusiastic—he was a warrior now, but it seemed to mean nothing to him. After leading the one war charge, maybe Sings Wolf would have

liked to become Calling Eagle again. Nevertheless, Smith
would not have refused his grandfather.

Smith was glad when he saw Wooden Legs, a son of
the old-man chief Little Wolf and a leader, join them. And
Little Finger Nail, the painter and singer. He nodded at
Raven, a man who'd spoken at councils for killing, but a
longtime friend of Sings Wolf.

Then Smith saw Twist coming. He wanted to speak
irately to his grandfather. He wanted to back out in anger.
But he knew Sings Wolf had considered Smith's feelings
and had strong reasons for ignoring them. He couldn't
refuse to go.

Twist was smirking about the situation, damn him.

Why had Sings Wolf picked out Smith's enemy? Why
had Twist, known for his bloodthirstiness, accepted a raid
that was to be bloodless?

Smith was awake now, and nettled. But it was not for
him to challenge his grandfather's medicine. He wished his
eye wounds didn't hurt, and itch.

Question marks, Nelly Burns had said—question
marks around the brain. Got any questions about yourself,
Smith?

It was no ordinary western-Kansas ranch house. No
soddy, Smith saw in the predawn light, not even a log
cabin. A house framed out of saw timber, and a big house.
The saw timber the homesteaders usually had was the
timber in their wagons. They trundled their wagons out
from the nearest railway stop full of household goods, to the
spot they claimed as home.

Daring imaginations, these homesteaders had, to eye-
ball a vacant, dried-up stretch of prairie and imagine it as
what they meant by home, a place fenced and irrigated and
full of fat cattle and hay and growing kids and a vegetable
garden and even flowers in what they called a yard. Smith
had to admire them, in a way.

When they got to their spot, some place like this on a creek or with a good spring, they unloaded the household goods and stripped the wagons for saw timber to build a house. This house was substantial—this rancher must have hauled more saw timber out from Ogallala. What looked like another home stood across the driveway. Plus half a dozen outbuildings—sheds, barns for stock and feed—all of saw timber. A man of big dreams, this rancher. Smith bet his kids had homesteaded the adjacent sections. That was the way the smart ones did it.

Well, after today, these folks would have to tend their cattle on foot. The Cheyenne nation was about to requisition their horses.

Smith finished his face paint—red forehead, broad band of verdigris on the nose—and walked down behind the ridge to get his mount. A big bunch of white-man horses was in one jingle pasture, just waiting to be requisitioned.

There behind the ridge, before they started the raid, Sings Wolf reminded them again that no one was to be killed.

Twist said softly, and with a bitter smile, "Remember the Sappa River!"

The warriors were taken aback at this rudeness, this defiance.

Sings Wolf looked at Twist somberly. "No blood will be shed," repeated Sings Wolf, "either ours or theirs." It was not an order, but a statement of the right way to do things, the medicine way. It was powerful.

Smith thought his grandfather's medicine must be convincing. Smith had seen the foul mood (the foul spirit, the Tsistsistas-Suhtaio would say, meaning something different) descend on Sings Wolf as they came down the Sappa River. He had seen Sings Wolf congratulate the young men who brought white scalps into camp. He could see murder in Sings Wolf's eyes even now. It was not policy that stayed his grandfather's hand—it could only be medicine.

So Sings Wolf and Twist started down the hill on foot.
It was their job to make sure the horses were unguarded, or
to take care of the guards. If Sings Wolf's medicine was
good, the whites would not be watching their horses. Then
the two would cut the pasture fence and yell and wave their
blankets and stampede the horses into open country. Twist
had a prized pair of wire cutters for the purpose. Stolen,
Smith assumed, and probably from a dead man.

It was the job of the others to bring Sings Wolf and
Twist their mounts and get the stolen horses running back
toward camp, fast. Smith and Sings Wolf would guard the
back trail, to make sure no one followed the stolen horses
too closely. An occasional rifle shot would be plenty to put
the fear of ambush into the hearts of any followers.

The plan came apart, in a roundabout way, because a
teenage girl had to pee.

That dawn was the dawn of a fine Sunday morning in
early October of 1878 in western Kansas. Western Kansas
was then much too sparsely settled for most ranchers and
farmers to be able to go to church. But they did like to use
Sundays for get-togethers. In this case Eric Sunvold had
decided to organize a stockman's association, a group to
register brands, cut down on mavericking and rustling, get
some control of predators and Indians, and advance the
interest of cattle raisers against sodbusters. So he had
invited neighboring cattlemen for miles around to his home
for a big get-together on Saturday night, some talk, a vote
on officers on Sunday morning, dinner, and a lot of long
wagon rides home on Sunday afternoon.

Eric Sunvold was the man to do the organizing—he
was a natural leader, prosperous, ambitious, and he had the
room to accommodate a half-dozen neighbors and their
families, the women and younger kids sleeping in the house
and the men and older kids in the wagons and barns. He
expected to be elected president of the new association.

He was a middle-aged man with a thick, drooping mustache, a roll of hard belly, and a huge, leonine head. He had three surviving children, and was fiercely proud of all of them. Max had built his own house right there on the place, and his wife Kate had a start on a family. Jacob lived at home but would start to work at the bank in Ogallala next month, learning the business. Alene was a pretty, vivacious thing, just fifteen years old.

Eric Sunvold didn't know that his daughter Alene, at the moment of dawn when Sunvold got out of bed, was out by the creek making the beast with two backs with Benjamin Halstead. Ben was just seventeen, and a nearby rancher's only son. He and Alene had discovered this intensely pleasurable activity last summer, without the permission of their parents. Alene was bold at finding opportunities to repeat it—this dawn meeting was the third she'd found since Ben arrived with his folks yesterday noon.

Even though Alene was a romantic, when she completed that vigorous act she felt an unromantic need. She had to pee. Now. Ordinarily, she would have deemed this time and place fitting—she certainly had no secrets from her parents and brothers. But Ben was not family, not yet, and she felt shy. Besides, she'd better gather some eggs pretty quick and get into the kitchen to get breakfast started. So she wrapped the blankets she'd brought around her and headed toward the barnyard and the privy at a trot.

That's when she saw Twist sneaking into the barn, and started screaming bloody murder.

Two days ago Twist had discovered coal oil. White people kept coal oil around their farms and ranches as a fuel. Twist had found some in a barn. Yellow Nose had shown him what it would do. Burn down the barn. And the house. And all the other outbuildings. The ranch people were already dead, so Twist and Yellow Nose took their time and made a thorough job of it. Ordinarily, it was hard to get a building started burning. You had to work at the fire steadily for a while. But with coal oil it was quick. And it looked so fine.

As they crept toward the jingle pasture, Twist told Sings Wolf he was going to create a little diversion with fire. Give the white folks something to think about. So much to think about they wouldn't have time to worry about their horses.

"No," Sings Wolf said simply.

Twist sneered at him, tossed the wire cutters onto the ground, and headed for the barn.

Sings Wolf berated himself for following Twist. He could have gone to the pasture alone, cut the fence, and turned the horses loose. He could have just gone back to his companions. He could have stuck to what he saw with his medicine foresight. But he didn't, and he didn't know why.

He wished he could get out from under the blackness that came on him this morning when he came to the Sappa River. Black memories, black thoughts. Bloody, murderous thoughts. Sings Wolf kept pushing them away, and they kept coming back, like something alien seeping into his mind, body, spirit. But it was not alien, he knew—it was the anger of a man at the killing of his relatives and friends here. It was natural, human. Yet he needed to set that anger aside.

He had seen this pony raid clearly, a glimpse of the future. In his foresight it was bloodless. It included no burning, either. But burning wasn't killing, yet, was it?

The way he saw it had been simple. He saw small pictures of it happening—the approach, the stampede, the triumphant return to camp—in the commonplace way that he foresaw Lisette cooking dinner tonight, the way he remembered his *veho* son Mac, the way he imagined Smith saying good-bye to Elaine in Dodge City. It was clear and simple, as such glimpses usually were. It was medicine foresight.

Sings Wolf fell farther and farther behind Twist. Twist walked quickly, almost openly, making only brief use of obstacles and shadows. He was bold and sure of his medicine, that one. Also bullheaded and stupid as a buffalo.

Sings Wolf moved cautiously, staying hard to see. He crept into a position on a little bench above the yard full of buildings and lay down in the grass with his old flintlock rifle. He got into firing position. He could slow down the whites if they discovered Twist.

At that moment he saw what would happen. A white girl came from the creek wrapped in a blanket. Twenty steps behind her came a young man. Sings Wolf smiled to himself—the whites did not watch after the chastity of their young women carefully. The whites were coming openly into the barnyard, perhaps headed for the house.

Twist was easing around the barn toward the door. When he came around the corner, the three would see each other, right in the open.

Sings Wolf could do nothing. He willed Twist to stop, to peek cautiously around the corner of the barn, to see the girl and the boy following her. Sings Wolf knew his willing would do no good. Something inside him said, It is inevitable.

The girl started screaming.

Twist smiled to himself and said out loud, "It is a good day to die."

He sprinted toward the girl, knife held low and ready. The boy was closer to her but not nearly as quick. It would be a great coup, to kill the woman in front of her man.

The girl screamed crazily, filling the air with the dung of her fear. Twist would cut off her scream and her throat with a single swipe. He felt fiercely happy.

* * *

Matthew Long swung the barrel of his shotgun just like he would follow a duck on the wing, catching up with the red nigger. Just when he was ready to cut loose, he saw Alene, too. At fifteen, Matthew was a poised and laconic youngster, hard to rattle, and a good fowler. He lowered the barrel toward the nigger's legs and pulled the trigger. He knew he'd missed.

Alene went down and clutched at her throat with one hand. Blood ran down her arm.

Matthew ran for the Injun—the bastard was up. If only Matthew's dad had bought him a side-by-side, he could have shot again. But the Injun was all tangled up with Ben Halstead anyway.

Matthew swung his shotgun by the stock. The muzzle bounced off the Indian's shoulder. Bastard swung to face Matthew. The fool grinned like a madman. Out of the corner of his eye Matthew got a glimpse of Ben Halstead— his guts were hanging out. Matthew swung the shotgun again, roundhouse. On his follow-through he saw the Indian thrust forward, and knew he was about to die.

A rifle cracked, and the Injun went tumbling at Matthew's feet.

Eric Sunvold stood on the back porch with his Winchester still held on the Injun. Matthew made a mental note to thank Mr. Sunvold later for saving his life. Meanwhile, he jumped on that goddamn Injun's bloody back.

Another rifle shot sounded, with a different sound— Mr. Sunvold hollered out. Matthew rolled onto his side and held the Injun in front of him for cover. Peering over the Injun's shoulder, Matthew saw black-powder smoke rising from the bench behind the yard. Black powder probably meant an Injun, and an old flintlocker or percussion-cap weapon. One shot. But just in case, Matthew would keep the Injun in front of him. Bastard stank. And he was about half-dead, from the feel of him. Matthew was getting blood all over him from the Injun's back.

Matthew's dad fired twice up toward the bench—Matthew knew the sound of that rifle. He was in the barn loft, a good position.

An Injun on the bench jumped up and ran left, out of the angle Dad had. Dad fired again, but the Injun didn't go down. Matthew wondered if the skunk was alone. Must be, considering that one shot. That redskin would find out that a single-shot, black-powder weapon didn't hold a candle to a Model 1873, center-fire, .44-caliber Winchester with a magazine that held fifteen cartridges. Much less six or eight or ten Winchesters.

That savage needed to catch up with the nineteenth century.

He would also discover that it didn't pay to attack a ranch house with damn near forty white people in it, half a dozen of them men and another half-dozen young men like Matthew, fellas that wouldn't be fooled with.

Damn savage.

Matthew's Injun wriggled, and Matthew held the bastard tighter.

Now Sings Wolf had shed blood. His medicine was gone—he had abandoned it.

He lay behind the thin cover of a sagebrush, ramming a bullet into his old rifle and smiling an ironic smile at his own foolishness. In his mind he told the powers that he was only a human being, that he could not throttle his anger. And he acknowledged that he probably would die like a human being today.

He stretched out and hunted for white flesh with his sights. Twist was still down, still being held by the white boy. He must be alive. The middle-aged man Sings Wolf had shot was hidden behind the back porch and yelling out at people vigorously—he must not be shot bad. The girl and boy lay in the middle of the barnyard, the girl writhing and moaning. The man from the barn loft must be getting into a better position. So must the other two men who'd run out of the barn and darted back in.

Sings Wolf wondered how so many whites could be here, flying out like bees from a hive. He shrugged mentally. That was the way whites were. You couldn't fight them because they were too many. The Human Beings had thought the buffalo beyond counting, but now the whites had killed the buffalo and the whites were beyond counting.

No matter. Though it was getting difficult for a Human Being to live well, it was still possible to die well.

As long as Twist seemed to be alive, Sings Wolf would not leave him. He could have left the warrior. He owed no particular debt to the man who cast away Sings Wolf's medicine like a triviality. But maybe it was the fault of the older men like Sings Wolf that the younger men disregarded medicine. Besides, staying felt like the rightness of the day. Sings Wolf would surely die, and that was right, too.

He chuckled to himself. For this moment it was calm. Sings Wolf enjoyed the calm.

Suddenly four white men dashed out of the barn and around the corner, away from Sings Wolf's line of fire. No sense wasting a bullet on a running target. Two of the men started working their way up the creek through the trees. No point shooting at them. If Sings Wolf let his rifle get unloaded, the whites were organized enough to rush him now. But the whites headed up the creek would get behind Sings Wolf, with a good angle on him.

For a moment Sings Wolf saw one man at the peak of the barn roof. The man didn't have an ideal shot—he wasn't above Sings Wolf—but it would be good enough.

So. It would not be long. Sings Wolf looked about at the white-man buildings and fences and cattle, and thought of the white-man rifles that now surrounded him. He pondered this place, this alien place, for a moment. Then he let anger sweep through his body, mind, and spirit, a flash flood of rage, violent, unstoppable, scourging him, reaming him out like dry, cracking gullies.

Then Sings Wolf began to sing. He lifted to the dawn his death song, a mournful and melismatic farewell to this world, a preparation for his journey on the starry path through the skies:

> *Nothing lives long—*
> *Except the rocks.*

Smith had the uncanny sensation that his fingers had suddenly turned freezing. Then, and only then, did he realize that he was hearing his grandfather sing his death song.

Smith touched his heels to his horse and went charging down the hill.

He knew it was pointless. He, Wooden Legs, Little Finger Nail, and Raven sitting in their saddles on the hill, saw how many white men there were, and how many rifles. They'd seen the three on the barn roof, and even the two circling behind Sings Wolf. The whites had more armed men than places to station them, or Indians to kill. Still, Smith rode like hell toward his grandfather.

The first shot from the creek simply crossed his bow—someone had led him too much. Smith zigged and zagged a little to make their task harder. It's never a good day to die easily.

He was still a hell of a way from Sings Wolf. The old man's voice rose, crooning his death song.

Smith's horse pitched forward and Smith went over its neck and through the sage end over end like a thrown ax handle, bouncing and tumbling.

For a moment he didn't realize he was stopped. Flat on the ground and not in several pieces.

"Grandfather!" Smith yelled.

The old man just kept singing.

"Grandfather!"

Up swam the death song.

Smith knew that Sings Wolf could hear him. He was

yelling louder than the old man was crooning. But Sings Wolf paid him no attention.

Smith looked back at his horse. It was unmoving. It could only have been shot in the head or spine, and was done for.

Smith rose into a crouch. A rifle shot made him flatten out again, fast.

Two more shots fell just short of him. Hell, these came from the top of the barn.

Smith scurried back to his horse and lay down behind it. On the way he picked up his rifle.

Beyond Sings Wolf a woman went running out toward the figures lying in the barnyard, a girl down and squirming, a still boy next to her, and a boy locked together with Twist.

The woman bent over the girl.

Smith knew what would happen. He didn't know how he felt about it.

Sings Wolf raised his old flintlocker and aimed, surely at the woman.

Smith heard pony hooves up the hill.

Sings Wolf fired.

The woman did not fall. No one fell.

Four whites started sprinting up the little bench toward Sings Wolf.

Wooden Legs clattered up next to Smith, leading Sings Wolf's mount. Fire came hard from the creek. Smith expected to get hit every moment as he swung into the saddle. Then he kicked up the hill behind Wooden Legs.

Halfway up, Smith stopped and wheeled around. He wanted to see.

Sings Wolf was standing, one arm raised. The arm must hold his tomahawk, or knife.

The whites closed in. No shot sounded.

The whites got Sings Wolf circled. One of them rushed him from behind, and both went down, and then Smith could see nothing but a pile of men, writhing.

He didn't know if his grandfather was still alive. He didn't know if Twist was still alive.

"Let's go!" snarled Wooden Legs.

≈ 7 ≈

Dear Mother,

You must have found my telegram strange. Please forgive your wayward daughter.

Your reply was inspiring. For you also to send so much money is wonderful generosity. I do not deserve it, but I need it, and I accept it. Thank you.

In fact she couldn't possibly pay her way until Adam came for her without that hundred dollars.

This was the eighth day after her surgery, the first day she'd been able to sit up. She'd been comatose for several days and had slept for several more. Dr. Wockerley still wanted her to stay flat and rest, but he had no idea how bored she was. Lying there helpless made her want to scream.

Dr. Richtarsch judged a week ago that the infection in my calf might sweep me away. I made no quarrel (you will be amazed to hear) but like the Red Queen cried, "Off with her leg!"

I've been mostly asleep in the week since, though Dr. Richtarsch comments often on what a remarkable recovery I'm making. I tell him, with a tear in my eye, that I'm a Cummings, and can do anything.

Of the hundred dollars I've given seventy-five to Dr. Wockerley, who I think was concerned about being taken advantage of, and kept twenty-five back. Dr. Richtarsch has gallantly refused compensation, claiming that I am a casualty of war. He added a half joke about my possibly becoming a prisoner of war, being shipped back east out of the battle zone and being forcibly held away from the action by my family.

Though gallantry usually only amuses me, I am touched by Dr. Richtarsch's generosity and grateful for it. I believe I shall be all right now. Dr. Richtarsch says he will absolutely force the liveryman to give me a hundred dollars for my fancy sidesaddle, which I won't be needing anymore, and a good price for my horse. I fear Adam and I contributed all our ready cash to urgent needs of the people.

You must wonder how it feels to be without half a leg. It is odd beyond the telling. Most of the time I don't notice it at all. It *feels* as it always did. Naturally, I've no chance to try to stand up or walk, you understand! So I notice its absence only when I cast my gaze down in that vicinity and see a sad emptiness there under my nightgown, and below it. A vacancy. A nothingness. Then, sometimes, it seems insupportable, and I gasp for breath. Most of the time, though, I simply imagine myself a pirate, jumping boldly from deck to deck on my peg leg, cutlass cocked for action.

She smiled wearily at the silly picture of herself as a pirate. She was tired now and would nap before she finished the letter.

Eric Sunvold had very definite notions about right and wrong and was strict and stubborn about sticking to them. In this case right was keeping the two damn Injuns alive until the army could kill them.

Sunvold felt irritable and impatient and snarly. Even shot, he didn't feel uncertain. He was shot just under the left armpit—the lead had torn up a little flesh, but he had the blood stanched and could feel that his ribs were intact. He'd been hurt worse and felt perfectly capable of getting done what needed doing.

He would have a hell of a lot easier time making his intentions stick, though, if that old Injun would shut up his caterwauling. Sunvold was trying to get the horses harnessed and get both Injuns into the buck wagon and started to Ogallala, which was a day's journey. The young Injun, Sunvold had shot him up under the rib cage when he was bent over. He was unconscious. If the bullet had got the vitals, he would die. Sunvold checked him more carefully. Hell, he was hit in the spine. Nigger couldn't move his legs. He wasn't going to give no trouble. The old man, though, was putting up a regular ruckus. Singing his death song, Sunvold had heard it called. Well, that Injun's imitation of one of them opera tenors made everybody edgy.

Sunvold knew no one else at his place that day saw things his way. Why would they? Seventeen-year-old Ben Halstead was dead there in the barnyard, his guts spilled in the dust. It would be hard on his dad, Randall, because Ben was the last of Randall's family. The wife and younger son had got taken away by the cholera back in East Texas. Understandably, Randall wanted first to skin that young Injun bit by bit, the little scum that used the knife, and then talk about how to kill him slow and savory.

Max and Jacob Sunvold were in a mood to lynch the Injuns. That would feel better than watching their mother cradle their baby sister, Alene, in her arms. Alene's cut was shallow—Sunvold had checked it himself—and now that the bleeding was stopped, in no way dangerous. But a man couldn't hardly stand to see a knife slice his baby sister's neck. Though Sunvold understood, he meant to do what was right.

Max's wife Kate kept saying to him softly out of the side of the mouth, "You ain't gonna let some softhearted judge turn them Injuns loose, are you?"

Sunvold growled at Max to finish getting those horses hitched and not be all day about it.

The teenage Matthew Long and his father Raymond hemmed and hawed a lot. They didn't have to tell Sunvold they admired Injuns, in a way. The Injuns was right—the country belonged to them. But the white people was gonna take it over, no stopping that. And that was progress, you couldn't argue with it. The way the Lord meant it to be, the higher creature replacing the lower.

Young Matthew wanted to know if Sunvold wasn't mad at the old Injun for shooting him.

Hell, Sunvold would as soon get mad at the wind for blowing in his face. He hardly paid the red nigger any mind at all, except to holler at him to stop that yowling.

Max brought the buck wagon and team around. Jacob had the old Injun tied up hands and feet, and gagged him to shut up that wailing. With Max, Jacob hoisted the Injun into the wagon bed and laid him flat.

The young nigger, hell, his legs were paralyzed.

Jacob asked his father permission to bury the Injun.

"Refused," said Sunvold. The army could bury him, too.

So Jacob and Max threw him into the wagon bed loose.

Jacob climbed up on the seat next to his father, Winchester across his lap, the old man's shotgun on the floorboards.

"Want us to ride along?" asked Raymond. "It's on our way."

He meant, And Injuns might still be around. "Accepted," said Sunvold, "as far as your place." That was eight miles down the creek. Ought to protect them against any Injuns, though Eric Sunvold hadn't seen the day he needed protection.

Sunvold hawed the horses and they moved out. He nodded at his wife, smiled a little at his daughter Alene. A feisty one, that girl. She'd be some upset by Ben getting killed like that—a damn shame—but she'd get over it. He got the horses headed down the rough wagon track at a good pace. Town was a long way.

Sunvold snorted. Her and Ben rutting out along the creek, and everywhere else they could think of for months.

And thinking nobody noticed. He shook his head. He hadn't given a damn. How else did families get started?

Now he just had to hope Alene wasn't with child.

Nothing he could do about that. He was damn glad to have a chance to do a little something about this Injun situation. He meant to shove these critters, one dead and one alive, at the sheriff and rub the son of a bitch's face in what a fine job he was doing. And get the sheriff to rub it in the face of the damned army, and let the government see the results of its damned policies, and make the government do something about it.

It's the way of nature, dammit. Every critter takes what it needs to live, and makes no apologies.

But the government, full of soft hearts, wrung its hands, said how sorry it was, and promised to make up for it by taking care of the Injuns. Then it penned them up and let them get so hungry they'd do anything just to survive. Couldn't blame the Injuns. But the result was innocent white people dead, like Ben Halstead.

So Eric Sunvold would see these Injuns hang, all right—or did the army shoot 'em?

An hour and a half later Sunvold and Jacob said good-bye to the Longs, father and son. Raymond asked if Sunvold didn't want them to ride on into town—the Injuns might still be around. Sunvold thought about the road to Ogallala. It kept pretty much to high, open ground. In a couple of places you could be ambushed. "We'll be fine," said Sunvold, waving.

He'd be careful in those places. He hadn't survived fifty years on the frontier by being careless.

After another hour Sunvold looked back into the wagon bed again to check on the Injuns. His stomach lurched. He had only one Injun—the young one was gone.

How in the hell? Not careless, are you, old man? he

mocked himself. He whoaed the team. "Jacob, how long
since you checked on them Injuns?"

The young man whirled and looked. "Too damn long,"
he said softly.

Sunvold looked back up the primitive wagon track.
"How long since you actually saw him?"

"Ten minutes. Maybe longer."

Sunvold considered. If the Injun could roll himself off
the wagon with just his arms, he could pull himself away
from the track and hide.

"So," Sunvold said to his son, "let him die where the
coyotes will get him."

Jacob snickered nervously, glad of that decision. The
truth was, his scalp didn't feel tight on his head. He kept
thinking that they didn't know how many other Indians had
been back there. But he put a good face on it. "We still got
the other'n," he said with a smile meant to be comradelike,
"trussed up like a mummy."

These red bastards sure are hard to kill, he thought.

Elaine reread her letter to Mother and Dora. She
smiled at the foolish picture of herself with cutlass cocked,
and then frowned. Now she must write from the heart.

> I know I am a disappointment to you, and I
> regret it most deeply. I can say only that once I
> came to the Cheyennes to teach them, once I fell
> in love with a huge, manly, vigorous, intelligent,
> and devoted redskin named Adam Maclean, and
> once the people made the decision they made, no
> other course of action was possible for me.
>
> I do not worry about myself now. I shall be
> fitted with an artificial leg and shall learn to get
> about on it. (I will be fitted with a leg here
> temporarily, but Dr. Richtarsch says he will refer
> me to a "true artist" in Omaha who is particularly

adept at making comfortable and workable legs.)
It may be that my feminine gait will no longer
inspire poets to lyric heights, but I shall do quite
well getting to and from the schoolroom, which is
my calling. I want to be *used*, and I shall be.

I do worry about Adam. He sat beside my
bed here, when both of us thought I would heal
without complications, and told me why he had to
go with his people. I did not need to hear the
words—I knew his heart. He told me that he was
being sucked into a great maelstrom, a whirlwind
of events he could not control, and events might
sweep him far away, so far he feared he could not
find his way back. I could not answer well, for I
was drugged by an anodyne, but I tried to com-
municate to him that I understood, and that I
would wait for him. I shall wait for him, for all of
this lifetime, at least, and want nothing so much as
to live joined with him.

Now life seems so bleak. I have lost a leg, and
somehow nothing is the same. I am *maimed*. Of
course, he does not know.

There are things in that I cannot yet bring
myself to speak of. I cannot imagine letting Adam
see me crippled.

I can say that my dear husband does not
appreciate the difficulty of a New England girl's
living among the Cheyennes. It is not the physical
hardships. Neither you nor I could be dissuaded
by those. It is that they are so *alien*—I cannot
bring myself to put how alien into the naked form
of the written word. To their ancient and barbaric
ways, and strange gods, they are profoundly
attached. To embrace the new way, the light of
civilization, they must come unstuck from what
they are. I doubt that they can do that, and still
retain their wholeness as human beings.

Well, as Father would have said, "On with
it." I must go to Omaha. And Adam must go to

Powder River—if he can live long enough to get
there. I daydream constantly that he will instead
come for me and once more sweep me away. I
long for him.

What's most important, though, is that the
people must find a new way to live. That is
incomparably more important than the fates of
two individuals, and Adam can help with it. I wish
I could.

I shall rest now.

Your loving daughter,
Elaine Cummings Maclean

It was Little Finger Nail who heard it.

He and Smith were trailing well behind the wagon, out
of sight. Wooden Legs and Raven had headed back, with an
inclination to see if they couldn't get some horses on the
way—the Human Beings had to have fresher horseflesh or
they couldn't keep going.

Smith didn't know what to do about the damned
wagon. The four white men must be headed for Ogallala.
Probably meant to turn Sings Wolf and Twist over to the
sheriff, who might turn them over to the military at Sidney
Barracks, or might take the law into his own hands. The
sheriff would give them a couple of weeks in jail, a sort of
trial, and a noose. The commander at Sidney Barracks
would give them the same, but quicker, and ending with a
firing squad. Unless he knew how Indians hated the
thought of hanging—then he'd hang them.

Smith didn't know what to do. These open plains made
it hard to get close to the wagon, and one Winchester
against four rifles and shotguns was poor odds. Nail had
only arrows, lance, and war club. Neither one of them was
any dime-novel hero.

Leading horses for Sings Wolf and Twist, they followed
the wagon and its flankers from a long way back. They could

see it only occasionally, from the top of a rise, and then they stayed behind the rise until the wagon went out of sight. The wagon wouldn't leave the road, and crossroads would be scarcer than Chinamen.

So why were the whites taking Sings Wolf and Twist to town—or to the fort? Why not just kill them right there in the barnyard? Most whites would. Maybe use the hanging rope in order to give themselves a sense of propriety about it.

No telling why. But that made it worse for Sings Wolf and Twist. Both of them were more afraid of being jailed than of dying. So Smith would just have to think of some dime-novel trick and get them loose.

Smith and Nail saw the two riders stop at the ranch on the creek and the wagon go on alone. The white people were awfully damn sure of themselves. Now the odds weren't so long. The two Indians circled a long way around the ranch to stay out of sight and came back close to the creek where the country turned rough for a mile or so. They spotted the wagon far down the road and looked at each other. Time to take a long route around the wagon at a good pace, find the right spot overlooking the road, and set their comrades free.

That was when Nail held up his hand, and Smith stopped his horse. He must have heard something.

After a wait it came again, a soft, throaty cry.

Smith and Finger Nail sat their horses. After a while it came again. The mating call of a sage hen.

Of course, sage hens didn't mate this time of year.

Smith immediately slipped off his horse and hurried around between his two horses. Nail was crouched under his mount. Smith swiveled his head slowly all around the horizon. Well, they hadn't been shot at yet.

The call came once more—a grating musical note like the one made by bowing a saw.

Nail handed Smith the lead rope to Twist's horse, dropped his own reins, and padded off to the north, bent at the waist, moving fast but cautiously through the sagebrush. His mount was evidently well trained.

After a moment Nail stood up in the sage and made the scout's sign for *friends* with his arms. Smith trotted over, leading Nail's horse.

It was Twist, lying spraddle-legged, his back all bloody. Smith dismounted and checked him. Hell, his spine was hit, and his legs paralyzed. A miracle that he'd gotten away from the whites in this condition. He'd lost a lot of blood and was half-conscious. It was a wonder he'd been alert enough to make any kind of call.

The bullet had entered at the bottom of his ribs and traveled upward. A brief examination showed no exit wound. It's nicked something, thought Smith—spleen, pancreas, liver, lung, heart. Twist is dead.

Smith rubbed the stitches on his itchy eye sockets. Every time he'd done that, he'd wished Twist was dead. Maybe he still did. An entrance wound and no exit wound. Paralyzed, even if he does live.

"We need water and we need a fire," he told Nail.

Nail nodded and headed back toward his mount.

Why in hell am I doing this?

Half an hour later Smith started the surgery. He talked to himself under his breath. So now you're going to risk your grandfather's life to save your enemy's life. Crazy goddamn world.

It was the spleen. More than nicked. Clobbered. The wound wasn't bleeding much. He felt for the bullet, and for once found it quickly. Smith had seen this kind of wound before. He had to go after the bullet, and when he took it out, the patient would bleed to death. Exsanguinate, as they called it.

Smith went after the bullet. He got it easily. Then he started sewing up the spleen as fast as he could go. Blood ran over his fingers in rivulets, and into the abdominal cavity. He got the sewing done before Twist stopped breathing.

Smith sat down in the dust. He looked up at Nail. He reached over and closed Twist's eyes.

He wept. He couldn't have said what for.

≈ 8 ≈

He wasn't easy in his mind. Smith was approaching Ogallala
in the predawn light on a good road at a canter. Both the
horses, his and Sings Wolf's on the lead, were well lathered
from hard riding and near exhaustion—if they rode them
hard again without a rest, they'd risk killing them.

He'd sent Nail back to the people. An Indian who
looked like an Indian would be a red flag in this business.

He stopped a half mile outside of town and peered in
at the dusky streets. Ogallala, Nebraska, was another
trail-drive town, this time on the Union Pacific Railroad,
just above the forks of the Platte River. It probably wouldn't
be a damn bit different from Dodge City—cow-boys and
drinking and gambling and whores—and wasn't worth a
glance. Right now the town was probably asleep, like
Dodge City would be, sleeping off the debauch that took
place last night and every night.

He could take the horses to the livery and get them
grained and watered. He had enough beaver to cover that.
But he might need to get out of Ogallala in a big hurry, with
Sings Wolf. He sure couldn't afford the time to be asking a
liveryman kindly to bring the horses out before them there
white people shoot me down.

He walked the animals down to the South Platte,
watered them, and picketed them in some good grass for
half an hour. Rest, beasts, rest, he said to himself teasingly.
But not *requiescat in pace*. We got to hightail it in an hour
or two.

Sings Wolf must be in jail, and nothing was about to
happen to him this early in the morning, surely not. They'd
hold him for trial or telegram Sidney Barracks to come get
him. Either way, a couple of hours wouldn't make any
difference.

So Smith would go in and check things out and decide whether to bring the horses in or hide them here. He set out walking and found that the striding motion felt good after half a night of cantering. Of course, a little sleep would feel good, too.

How the hell was he going to get Sings Wolf away from a sheriff and deputies and hundreds of overwrought white men? That was hairbreadth 'scape stuff like he'd heard about in the East, Deadwood Dick doings.

Smith had no idea what he would do. He'd just go in and do whatever he could figure out. He was going to try something. If he was a little bit clever, and the whites acted a little bit dumb, he or Sings Wolf might even come out of it alive.

That didn't sound too unlikely, and it appealed to him. He wondered if that was the way Deadwood Dick did it.

Yes, it all does damn well sound too cavalier, Elaine, my love, but what can I do? They're going to kill my grandfather.

A tall half-breed shambled down the alley alongside the jail, weaving a little, raucously singing some goddamn song. Goddamn breeds.

At least that's what Smith hoped any whites would think, if they were up early enough to see him. He was supposed to look like a scout, decked out the way those throwback misfits the mountain men got decked out—blanket coat, broad-brimmed hat, moccasins, deerskin pants. Drunk as a skunk. A damn half-breed, sure. People tolerated them because the army needed them.

This one kept leaning against the jailhouse wall every few feet, like he needed it to keep from falling down, he was so drunk, and he wouldn't stop that screeching. That would give the white folks a chance to curse the half-breeds' fondness for booze. Worst parts of both races, they would say. Smith was amused to pretend to be what people thought him anyway.

Smith was mostly concerned about his size. He had tied his long hair up under his hat. The one item that would really make people wonder, his breechcloth, was hidden by his capote, and the bottoms of his leggings looked like pants. People would remember him because of his size, but that couldn't be helped. He'd try not to commit any more crimes punishable by death.

He wondered if there were any wanted notices out on him yet for killing the Reverend Ratz and the three scouts, and kidnapping Hindy. He doubted it. The army wasn't that efficient. But there would be notices. Respectability was getting out of reach.

After another ten feet, Smith leaned his back on the wooden wall again and rapped it smartly with the handle of his knife, twice. He bellowed out one of his favorite songs again, flowing in a minor key.

> *My heart knows what the river knows,*
> *I gotta go where the river goes.*
> *Restless river wild and free,*
> *The lonely ones are you and me.*

This time a song came back, in his grandfather's voice, preparing for death:

> *Nothing lives long—*
> *Except the rocks.*

Smith was gratified to have found Sings Wolf, unreachable as he might be. The wall had no window, of course— the sheriff wasn't dumb enough to invite lynch mobs to shoot prisoners like fish in a barrel. Sings Wolf would be pretty safe in jail. So he'd best scout out the situation.

That would be the good part. First a little hotel coffee—he wished he could spare a dollar for the white man's bacon and eggs, but he couldn't. Then a beer in the saloon. In both places a lot of gossip.

Then, if he was lucky, a visit to the telegraph office.

Smith had an idea. An idea maybe even worthy of the dime-novel hero Deadwood Dick.

Smith headed for the telegraph office. The other white folks accepted him as an army scout—why not the telegraph operator?

The town was grumbling. That damn Injun who killed some folks at the Sunvold place was being handled the way the sissy government did everything—escorted to Sidney Barracks for formal trial. The Sunvolds would have to go all the way to Sidney to testify, a trip of a hundred miles, hang around a couple of days, and then the damn government might not do anything about it. But it was that fool Eric Sunvold's own fault for not taking care of business when he had the chance. Can you imagine the old guy hauling the Injun to town in a wagon when he could have strung him up right there? And he lost one Injun, a young buck, on the way. People shook their heads at Eric Sunvold.

Smith blessed him.

Smith opened the door of the telegraph office and peered down at the man at the desk. His key was ratatat-tating, so Smith held his tongue. The fellow was tiny as a twelve-year-old girl and still had the innocent face of a kid to go with his gray hair. The little man stuck his tongue out of the corner of his mouth as he was concentrating. The key clattered, the clerk wrote in pencil, clattered something in return, and wheeled in his desk chair to face Smith.

"What can we do you for, wayfarer?" His voice was chipper, his eyes bright, and he didn't seem to notice that Smith was a head and a half taller and a hundred pounds heftier than he was. He twitched his nose as though what he'd said had been funny.

"Got orders from Sidney for me?" It was a dumb ploy, and it didn't work.

"What's your name, wayfarer?"

"Cummings. Tom Cummings. I'm out of Sidney. Scout." Elaine's maiden name. He wondered if he could think of a way to send her a telegram. A reach across a chasm wide as death.

The little old man made the gesture of flipping the corners of the telegrams on the spike, though he clearly knew there was nothing. "Not a thing for any Cummings," he said pertly. Smith noticed that his eyeshade had been embroidered with roses. Roses, for heaven's sake. Smith suppressed a smile.

"Supposed to be orders for me here yesterday afternoon," said Smith, trying to put a hint of annoyance into his voice. Seemed to him that anything he did, any false name he used, would still put them on his track if it went to Elaine. Dammit.

"Not a sign, wayfarer," piped the little man. Unfortunately, he didn't go on to say what there probably was a sign of from Sidney, a reply to the sheriff's telegram of yesterday. He got out a pad and started marking with his pencil.

"Good-looking roses," Smith said, feeling like a fool. He was going under a phony name and separated from his wife, and when he needed to be straightening out his life, here he was paying compliments to some idjit on his embroidery. Christ, he wished he could think of a way to send a telegram to Elaine without leaving a trail of evidence.

Whoa, maybe he ought to run—was that fellow drawing a picture of him? Just what he needed, a picture to go with the wanted notice. Smith put his hand in front of his face and fooled with his hat brim.

"Hope you don't mind if I make some notes," said the operator brightly. "I'm doing some little articles for the newspaper back home, and they're keen on how Westerners look. Especially a scout, like you. Care to sit down?" He gestured toward the office's one other chair.

Smith took his hand away and sat. The fellow was setting down words, not lines. Maybe Smith could get him to talking.

"Had any adventures you might care to pass along to our readers? Just a typical bit of Wild West experience?"

Why not? He thought of one of the old stories from his home country. "Come down a funny kind of crick yestiddy," said Smith. He supposed he'd seem more authentic if he talked a little crude. Ridiculous, a man born and raised in the wild territory around the Yellowstone trying to seem authentic to some Easterner. "Named it Alum Crick."

"Why was that?" the operator asked helpfully, scribbling as fast as he could go.

"It was all sticky from alum. So sticky it was twelve miles going out, but only six back. Even the miles puckered up."

"Ha-ha," said the operator, grinning. He actually said "ha-ha" instead of laughing. At least the greenhorn caught on. And he never stopped scribbling.

"Where'd you get that beadwork hatband?"

"It's quillwork," said Smith. "My mother did it." He paused for effect. "One of my two mothers."

The little man did glance up with a gleam in his eye. "Your mother's of what tribe?"

Best to fudge a little here. Cheyenne was surely a trouble word. "One Sioux, one Arapaho. My dad was a trader on the Platte." The little man made with the words. "Say, any telegram at all from Sidney today?"

"Not yet," piped the operator. "Couldn't tell you anyway, 'less it was yours."

Smith nodded in agreement.

"Is that a Hudson Bay Company blanket your coat's made from?"

"Witney blanket," said Smith.

Just then the key clattered. The little man answered back quickly, in his spunky way. For a minute or so the telegraph operators ticked away. Then the little man licked his pencil and wrote carefully on a different pad, his tongue sticking out again. The tongue had a dark, lead-colored stripe.

When he finished, he tore the top sheet and the carbon copy off the pad and whacked the carbon onto the spike. Then he seemed to look up at Smith with a particularly bright eye. "Say," said the little fellow, "would you keep an eye on things for a minute? I've got to run over to the sheriff's office." And out the door he darted.

Smith thought for a moment. Seemed like the little fellow had caught on to him somehow. Maybe the operator was setting Smith up. Or maybe he was giving him a break.

Smith stepped over to the desk, looked around to make sure he wasn't being watched, and looked sideways down at the carbon copy. Origin, Sidney Barracks:

HOLD PRISONER FOR US ARMY STOP DETAIL ARRIVES LATE TODAY ESCORT PRISONER HERE STOP YOUR COOPERATION APPRECIATED STOP COLONEL A W DEYO

Well, there was his answer. So a full afternoon ahead. Too damn full. Maybe Smith should just slip on out now. Still, it would look less suspicious, and more grateful, if he stayed and gave the operator a little yarn for his newspaper stories. Smith settled back down in the chair and tried to find his good humor. What could he spin for a little fellow who didn't know fat cow from pore bull? Oh, sure, one of his father's favorites:

"I ever tell you about the time Old Ephraim run me up a box canyon, shook me out of a tree, and begun to claw at me?"

Breathlessly: "Nawsir, what happened?"

"He killed me and et me, naturally."

Smith eyed the horseback figures in the distance, walking their horses toward Ogallala. Two of them, plus one horse being led. Looked like Kossuth hats on the men, but he couldn't be sure. A couple of minutes would tell. He hoped it wasn't another false alarm. He wriggled himself flat against the rock and got his Winchester into place.

Smith had fussed about it and fussed about it and made

his decision the only way he could. He'd go by how he felt and to hell with the arguments he carried on in his head. He wouldn't kill the soldiers. He'd disarm them and tie them up and take their horses and uniforms and boots and leave them where they couldn't get to the road before dark, much less to town. And if that was taking a dumb chance, he'd just have to take it. And to hell with you, all you bloodthirsty bastards on both sides.

They were Kossuth hats, and yellow-striped uniform pants. These were surely his boys. Well, it would be fun to pull on them what the cavalry scouts pulled on Smith and Sings Wolf and Hindy back there. He couldn't see how it wouldn't work. The road was in the open, with no cover nearby but what Smith had. No one else was coming—he could see five miles and more either way. The point of rocks gave him perfect command of the road. The distance was about sixty yards, potshot distance.

If it was a stupid chance, he'd just have to take a stupid chance.

A sergeant's stripes on one. So they spared a noncommissioned officer for this detail. The rest of the goddamn soldiers were probably readied to go chasing after Cheyennes as soon as the scouts brought word where they were.

The sergeant was a little in the lead. Smith would warn them.

Sergeant Brock was tired and irritable. He'd covered over forty miles on horseback since daybreak, walking and loping the horses alternately, his lower back hurt, and he was sober.

Drunk or sober, he hated horses. Horses were created, in his opinion, to make some men feel goddamn superior and give others back pain. He was condemned to pain. He'd started out in the cavalry to get up off the ground and see and saunter like a lord, but the years had tortured his spine, and now he spent his life on horseback hating horses. He loved to see a Jehu, handling a freight team, giving it to the bastards with bullwhip every few seconds all day long.

He looked back at the horse on lead. He'd picked a critter that was so docile it acted half-dead to lead to Ogallala and back. If the damn Injun tried to make a break for it, he'd feel like he was trying to gallop underwater.

Brock had tapped his flask regularly all day, ignoring the sidelong looks of the lime-juicer kid, but all day was too long for a little flask like that, and he was naked, ugly sober. He pulled the flask out of his jacket where he kept it tied on the pommel, drained the last of the whiskey in one long swig, and wiped his huge mustaches on his forearm pointlessly.

Rawl Cooke kept his eyes front. The big old bastard didn't pass the bottle, and Rawl did resent it. He didn't care about a drink—he didn't need the juice—but he resented the moat the sergeant kept around himself. Pull your head in and hide like a turtle, you old bugger, and sink into the mud of your own sourness.

Rawl wasn't sharing his elixir either. Rawl was in love—in love with life, with youth, with soldiering, with adventuring, and with Cotton. He rocked in the saddle all this day long lulled by memories of the lullaby of Cotton's voice, the warmth of her arms, the teasing roll of her bed.

Rawl was her name for him. His given name was Raleigh. He loved the way Cotton said Rawl, drawling it on her soft, Southern tongue. Like the way she said "gawd," and "dawg." She'd got the other chaps to calling him Rawl, too, smiling teasingly when they did it but making him one of the fellows.

He didn't care for that thought much. Other chaps. He knew she had plenty of those, plying her trade there in the bawdy house at Sidney. God—or rather, Gawd—he wanted to get her to quit. He had fantasies of setting her up in a home, the mistress of his life. Home to East Anglia, and Mum, and the kindliness of a settled country, gently green. Or any civilized place. Certainly it would have to be a good way from Sidney.

Of course, he couldn't blame her for what she did to keep body and soul together. Everybody had to do whatever he had to do. And he knew she did like it sometimes—the two of them had grand romps together. He couldn't help wondering whether she *always* liked her job.

The chaps liked her. They called her, as she asked, Cotton Tail. That was because her hair was so fair, almost white. And the color was, well, it was her true color. Bit of bawdy humor there.

Rawl Cooke drifted back into a fantasy of the naughty things Cotton Tail did with him, and to him, and sometimes all over him. His bottom rocked gently in his saddle and in his mind he rocked raucously between her thighs.

Probably the whore who called herself Cotton Tail would have been pleased, fleetingly, to know that the last fantasy that cute limey soldier ever had was of her own white tail.

"Stop. Stop right there!" came the voice. The sergeant turned toward the rocks. Shit, a slug! Seemed to whine by just in front of the sergeant's hand holding the reins.

Aw, shit! The sergeant's horse shied. Crow-hopped clear off the road. Gawddammit! Lost his feet and went over sideways!

Thumped there onto the ground, the breath knocked out of him and his boot pinned under the damn horse, Sergeant Brock made a field command decision. He was pissed off, and he intended to fight.

Before he got the carbine all the way out of the scabbard, a .44 slug entered Sergeant Brock's chest cavity and pierced all the way to his guts, destroying vital organs and life willy-nilly.

Private Cooke might well have survived. He exercised control of his horse. But he hesitated, coming out of a reverie. When he saw the sergeant go for his rifle, Cooke reached for his sidearm. It was the last movement he made

alive. The slug blew out his heart. He stayed in the saddle
for several long seconds, dead, swaying, before his boots
levered out of the stirrups and his thoughtless body
thumped to the earth.

The horses, well trained, stood still.

Smith stood over the sergeant, angry. Goddammit,
why had they gone for their guns? He'd made up his mind
not to kill anybody. Looking at two slaughtered human
beings, he felt sick. Nauseated.

He got onto his knees, slipped an arm under the
sergeant at the waist. Then he had to back away and wait to
see if he would retch. He didn't.

He made up his mind to it and lifted the sergeant off
the ground at the waist. The big man was amazingly heavy
and cumbersome. But he had to get them away from the
road, where no one would find their bodies for a while.

Fifteen minutes later he was changing clothes. He took
the written orders from Sidney Barracks. Then he collected
their weapons. He felt like a thief, and he hated it. All
right, yes, he would take the sergeant's field glasses. And
naturally the horses.

Goddammit. Goddammit.

Randall Halstead was a little drunk. Not drunk enough
to be happy, nor to be falling down. Just enough to be
mean. More important, to be cunning.

Also drunk enough for his scar to itch. Whenever his
face got flushed, the white scar alongside his nose itched
like the devil. He rubbed it.

"Let's whip the tiger!" he rasped loudly. Diphtheria
had left his voice a permanent rasp. He put a Chinese coin
on seven to lose. He'd bet every card to lose tonight, and

had talked his newfound compañeros into going against the tiger on losing numbers. In faro you could bet any card to come up winning or losing. They called the game the tiger because of the fancy tigers painted on the faro boxes.

Tonight was a night to bet on all cards on the losing side, Randall told his gambling buddies. Losing was in the air. The damn soldiers who came for the Injun were going to lose that nigger, and the Injun was going to lose his wretched life. Randall had been from soda to hock a half-dozen times now, and he was consistently losing. His fellow gamblers felt a little irked at losing at faro, but that was fine and dandy—irked was what Randall needed them.

He just wished those soldiers would show up while everybody was primed. Where the hell were they, anyway? He'd given that towheaded kid four bits to watch and let him know when they came for the prisoner. It was already dark now.

Randall figured his drunkenness was just about right. If he was normally half horse, half alligator, right now he was all alligator, and he meant to bite somebody's ass off. Anybody who got between him and his new compañeros and that Injun.

He'd fixed his mind on the Injun yesterday while he and Ned, his brother, were burying Ben on the bench above the house. Ben, the last of Randall's family. Killed dead by that sneaking, slinking, knife-wielding Injun bastard.

All day yesterday Randall felt numb. He moped around the place and stared at the cattle and didn't give a cow pie and even got into a Texas-sized argument with Ned. He wondered whether he wanted to raise cattle anyway. He and Ned could do it, but when you didn't have a son, what was the point? He sat on his bed and looked at the picture of his wife Moira, his daughter Amy, and Ben in front of the Texas house—all of them gone now—and asked aloud, mournfully, "What's the point?" He was so numb his lips would hardly shape the words.

The truth was, everywhere he looked that day Randall Halstead saw Ben, seventeen years old, lying there in the barnyard, his guts splayed out into the dust. He didn't want to see it, he hated seeing it, but he couldn't stop.

So he decided, this morning, to scourge his mind of that picture. He decided that the way to get rid of the picture forever was simple: he would kill the little Injun with the knife. And the little Indian was in the Ogallala jail, where Eric Sunvold took him. That idiot Sunvold.

Now Randall knew that the little one had got away. He would deal with Sunvold about that later. He thought maybe Sunvold deserved a horsewhipping. The big ass thought he was a hell of a hand, but he couldn't hit the ground with his hat in three throws. But right now the old Injun was in the jailhouse down the street, and the goddamn army was coming after him, and half the town was riled about it, and Randall Halstead knew how to take advantage. Unless the army boys sent half an army. And this fine edge of drunk would only help.

Randall walked to the bar, not even having to navigate carefully, got another bottle, and brought it to the faro table. "Come on, boys," he growled, "let's enjoy ourselves before the tiger eats all our money."

He scratched the scar alongside his nose.

It went slick as an eel on ice for Smith. The sheriff's office was closed, but a towheaded boy lounging around in front told Smith he knew where the deputy'd gone for a drink. The boy disappeared into one saloon, came out with a little man who must be the deputy, and ran across the street into another saloon.

Smith thought he looked fine for the white folks. The uniform jacket he'd taken from the big sergeant covered the .44-caliber hole in the blouse. No part of the uniform fit, but none would have if Smith had really been in the army either. The government just didn't accommodate men six and a half feet tall. Smith's stolen orders looked fine,

too—they just said to turn the prisoner over to Sergeant
Brock. They didn't even mention a second soldier.

The deputy was a small, bent fellow with an oversized
head and a sweetly misshapen smile. He might have been
eighteen or thirty, and Smith wondered if he was retarded.
He offered Smith his hand and introduced himself in
a light, girl's voice, "I'm Ramsel, the deputy." His hand-
shake was squishy. Smith wondered if Ramsel was the
fellow's first name or his last. He took the orders from
Smith, looked at them, and moved his lips as though
reading them, then unlocked the jailhouse door. Though
Smith was prepared with a story about a soldier back there
twenty miles so drunk he couldn't sit a horse, sleeping it off,
Ramsel didn't ask why the sergeant was alone.

"What tribe is this buck?" asked Smith, deliberately
using an offensive word.

"I'm afraid I wouldn't know a Sioux from a Comanche,"
the deputy answered in his high, soft voice.

They strode through the sheriff's office—Smith didn't
glance sideways at the wanted notices—and into the back.
Here was a room with some tack and weapons, off to one
side a room that was probably where the deputy slept, and
off to the other the lockup. The deputy looked through the
little window in the heavy, wooden door, then turned the
key and opened it.

Sings Wolf was stretched out on the bunk, perhaps
asleep. He looked across the room when the door opened,
but showed no particular interest in Smith. He was
wrapped in his blue blanket coat for a cover and wore the
look of tranquillity Smith supposed came with age and
wisdom. The young man felt a pang of love for his
grandfather.

In the Crow language, not Cheyenne, Smith said,
"Pretend you don't understand me." He barked the words
to make them sound harsh.

Sings Wolf didn't move.

"From his moccasins, he's a Cheyenne," Smith told the
deputy, "and this child don't have no Cheyenne words."
Maybe if he left a few false trails, it would take the army a

little longer to catch up with him. "Ramsel, why don't you keep a weapon on him while I get him mounted and headed out?"

The child-man gave Smith a big smile and what may have been a lopsided wink. Evidently he thought a gun was an unnecessary precaution. But he reached for a side-by-side without complaint and broke it at the breech to make sure both barrels were loaded.

Smith got Sings Wolf's hands tied in front of him, for show. Then he pushed his grandfather ahead of him toward the street roughly, like the worst sort of malefactor.

Smith stepped out the door and saw his mistake.

A crowd of men circled the horses with the brand of the army, which were tied at the hitching bar. Several men in front had rifles or shotguns, which meant they were serious. They were half lit by the lamps of the hotel next door. A dark-faced bastard with a very white scar alongside his nose stood in front, rubbing the scar and smiling the most malicious smile Smith had ever seen.

Smith's mistake was that he'd pushed Sings Wolf out ahead. Now Smith and his grandfather were vulnerable, and the deputy was in back of them with the shotgun. Smith reached for the sergeant's revolver. The scar bastard raised a shotgun to his shoulder. Smith eased the pistol out anyway, keeping it at his side. The man behind the scar bastard flipped a heavy knife, maybe an Arkansas toothpick, in his hand, playing with it. That seemed peculiar.

"Back off, *Sergeant*," the scar bastard said in a loud rasp. "We don't have any quarrel with you."

Just then Ramsel came pushing out between Smith and Sings Wolf with the shotgun leveled. Good fellow, thought Smith.

"Sammy, get the sheriff," yelled Ramsel.

The towheaded kid took off down the street running hard as he could go.

"That boy's right handy, ain't he?" growled the scar bastard. So that was how they knew Smith was here for the prisoner. Damned kid. "But that sheriff is surely going to be too late." He smirked at the deputy. "You cain't stop us, Ramsel. Even a defect likes to live, don't he?"

"Men," hollered Smith, "taking a prisoner from the U.S. Army is a crime for the firing squad." He didn't know whether it was or not. "Back off and let us head to Sidney Barracks. This Injun will get a fair trial."

"He will," rasped the scar bastard. "Just like my boy Ben got."

Then Smith understood. And just as he understood, he saw the glint of the knife blade in the half-light. He saw it just as the knife hit him in the head. Falling, he heard a shotgun blast. Losing consciousness, he almost had time to think that it wasn't blasting in his ear, so the shotgun wasn't Ramsel's.

Sings Wolf hung from the hay hook attached to the loading beam jutting out from the livery. He was still tied in his blue blanket coat, and the edges and belt whipped in the gusty wind. Sings Wolf's body rocked in the wind and twisted on the long, thick hemp, rocked and twisted back and forth restlessly.

Smith took the wet rag on his forehead and wiped his whole face. His head felt like it had been stepped on by a horse. He was still stretched out on the boardwalk.

"Got a sad one here, we do now." Irish pranced in the voice. Smith looked at the speaker haunched down beside him. A stalwart man of maybe fifty with gray hair, a mustache of indecently bright red, and eyes that looked like they saw a lifetime's worth of grief right then.

"I'm Sheriff Galway. Ramsel is dead here." He jerked his head to indicate behind him. "The Injun's dead yonder. The bad 'uns are fled away. You'd be a corpse, too, if you

weren't a soldier. They be not afraid of the sheriff, but they
are afraid of the colonel. This mick will make them afraid of
the sheriff in future. Maybe none will testify agin 'em, but
a sheriff with his dander up can make life prickly."

"What did they get me with?"

"A rascally lad name of Lawrence Byrne cracked your
noggin with the handle of his Arkansas toothpick. He's a
handy one with that knife, is Lawrence. Too handy. He can
hurl it to do ye with the blade or the handle. Double-
jointed evil, that lad. Your head's going to hurt mightily for
a day or so, and you'll have a lump you could use for a hat
rack."

Smith sat up. The world made a quarter turn, slowed
down, and stopped. "I'd best take the Indian back," Smith
said. This time he said it in three syllables, *In-dee-un*. "The
colonel will give the body to his people if they want it."

"You want to get started now?" asked the sheriff. "You
want to eat first? Sleep?"

"Ramsel got any family?" asked Smith.

"I'm his family," said the sheriff. That was why the
grief. "Townfolk think he's my son, but he's a foundling. I'll
say any words need saying."

Smith nodded his head, and nodded it again, thinking
and keeping control. He was obliged to keep up the
pretense that Sings Wolf was none of his kin. Seemed like
being around white people was a lot of pretending.

"Well," he said, "let's get the one cut down and the
other one in the ground."

The sheriff stood up and brushed off his hands. "Kind
of you to help," he said.

Smith got to his feet. The world stood still this time,
but lightning flashed in Smith's skull. He wiped his forehead again with the wet rag. A knot had risen smartly, for
sure.

"Where's the boot graveyard?" asked Smith.

* * *

Sheriff Galway reached down into the grave as far as he could without falling in and set Ramsel down gently. The lad was just a lump in canvas now. The Injun was wrapped in canvas, too, and tied onto the extra cavalry horse.

Galway slipped a copy of Mother Goose out of his coat pocket and tossed it onto the lump in a gesture meant to look casual to the sergeant. Ramsel never would have learned to read even a little bit without that book. He loved to say its jingle-jangle poems out loud in his singsong way, grinning all the while.

When they started pitching dirt in, Sheriff Galway couldn't remember which end was Ramsel's head. He was glad, for he didn't think he could stand to shovel earth onto the lad's face.

When the hole was filled, the sheriff held his hat at his belt, looked down at the mound of dirt, and began to chant musically. The sergeant stood at attention. He wouldn't know what the sheriff was saying, but it didn't matter. The words were Gaelic, their meaning a wail of grief and a prayer for safe journey to the other land. Sheriff Galway's grandfather had taught the chant to him, and he was sorry that no one would remember enough Gaelic to speak it over his grave when the time came, to ease his way.

When he finished, the sheriff saw that the sergeant was crying. Tears just streaming down his face.

Funny, a hard man like that, in tears for a man-boy he didn't even know. Well, it must be the conk on the head. Or the music of the Gaelic. Gaelic is a beautiful language, the language of grief, thought the sheriff for the thousandth time, for the Lord God has sent the Irish so much grief over seven centuries. Such a language will make a grown man weep, now, won't it?

≈ 9 ≈

Elaine absolutely hated them. She wanted to throw the cursed things across the lawn. Or the scruffy patch of dirt that the Wockerleys pretended was a lawn. Which she was probably going to fall down on any moment and break her other leg so she couldn't clump about at all.

She banged the crutches out in front of her, leaned forward, swung, and planted her good left leg. She teetered forward and then sideways and nearly fell. The left leg was weak, she was weak, and she had poor balance. Too long in bed. But she was determined to get stronger and get mobile and get out of Dodge City and on with her life. Her life, by God, with Adam. It was fierce in her, a surge, a need not to be struck and stagnating in this house of strangers, this town of gamblers and whores.

She wondered where the people were. She didn't know Dodge City, actually, but she didn't want to. No one came to see her but the fatuous Dr. Richtarsch, the stiff Dr. Wockerley, and the pallid Fran Wockerley. Fran and the doctor were so absorbed in their marital dance, he dominatingly proper, she cringingly lonely, that they had no room for anyone else. At least, though, Elaine could give the poor creature some company.

Elaine did see the town's habits, and she didn't like them. It woke up not at dawn but at midday. Many of the town's businesses didn't open for business until the afternoon. Even Dr. Wockerley had office hours in the afternoon only. And the morals! Wasn't the town's mayor, Dog Kelley, living openly in sin with one of its ladies of the night, a creature called the Great Easton? Wasn't the sheriff himself a notorious gambler? Mocking the laws so flagrantly symbolized something for Elaine, something smart-aleck and crude, something she hated.

She clopped on ahead, making her tight little square on the small plot of earth outside the porch where she slept. This was the third day since Dr. Richtarsch brought her these crutches, and her sixth episode of clumping around in the little yard, all six painful. She had wishes: she wished she could do her practicing in the house, where she would not be seen. But she had never so much as seen its interior, and she was sure Fran was not the one keeping her outside. She wished she felt free to ask Fran to help her into one of her dresses. She was wearing only one of Fran's wraps over her nightdress, which she'd lived in for weeks, and she didn't feel presentable enough for outdoors. The truth was, though, that she'd fallen several times, twice catching herself against the house but once crashing all the way to the ground and making her stump hurt like the dickens. It made no sense to get one of her dresses dirty or torn.

She had dreams of getting showy on her crutches, of doing pivots that would amaze adults and delight small children, of striking a figure that would be the envy of all, supported under each arm or not. And then topping the pivot with a curvet. She wished she were as tall as Adam so she could command everyone's eyes and stun them with the graceful way she comported herself with her handicap. She imagined her full-length skirts swirling and her hair, let out all the way to her waist, waving elegantly in the breeze as she moved.

For now she took one step forward awkwardly, and painfully.

A little head jerked back around the corner of the far house. After a moment two heads poked out, a boy and a girl. They peeked at Elaine from behind the house next door, on the side away from the main street. When they saw her looking back, they giggled. The boy stepped out and gawked openly. Another head, of a younger boy, stuck out from behind the corner.

Elaine bent one arm at the elbow and waved. "Hello, children," she called, trying to sound nice. She wished she felt nice. She waved again.

The older boy sauntered out, hands held behind his

bottom, shoulders held back, in a strut. He was a cherubic-looking child, blond and blue-eyed. The other two stood out from the corner, "Don't, Jake?" said the girl, but she tittered like she hoped he would. The cherub stopped.

"Jake, is that your name? Jake?" tried Elaine.

The cherub waggled his torso and grinned, all shy tomfoolery, but he said nothing. Elaine thought he had a sneaky look on his angelic face.

"You children could visit me sometime," Elaine said. "I live on this porch." The porch which she wanted to move away from as soon as possible. "We could play games together. I'd like that." She adjusted the crutch under her right shoulder. She leaned more heavily on that one, where her leg was truncated, and it got uncomfortable.

The cherub clawed the air aggressively and growled. Elaine didn't understand—was he trying to scare her?

He began weaving toward her in exaggerated play movements, like he was sneaking up on something. "Are you a panther?" she asked. "Am I a deer?" She felt tremulous, but tried not to show it.

Suddenly the boy let out a huge, lionlike roar and charged Elaine.

She flinched.

Near her, the boy clawed at the crutch on her right side. His hand didn't come close.

But Elaine jerked back, tried to pull the crutch out of his way.

She teetered. She lost her balance. She tottered backward, tried to catch herself with a crutch, and failed.

Involuntarily, she stuck out her right leg.

Her stump hit. The pain was excruciating. Her bottom and back slammed in the ground.

Elaine let out a scream—it sounded awful even to Elaine, throttled, unnatural, monstrous.

It took her a minute or two to clear her mind. The children were gone. She supposed she'd scared them off. She shook her head. She trembled all over. She didn't know whether she was laughing or crying.

The children had run off. Frightened, she supposed. But of her? Or themselves?

Smith went about it all in a deliberate way, a way that honored his grandfather, that showed him respect, and especially that gave room for remembering his grandfather.

He built a scaffold in a cottonwood tree along the south fork of the Platte River, which the Cheyennes called Geese River. He cut the poles patiently from dead cottonwood trees. He rushed no motion and did everything as well as he could.

While he cut, he remembered his times with Sings Wolf when Sings Wolf was a *hemaneh*, a half-man, half-woman. He remembered when she taught him to play the hoop-and-stick game. He remembered when she played the hand game with him, a game of betting on being able to guess which hand the bone is in. One day she stopped letting him win and took his pocket knife to teach him that you can lose at gambling, and only let him earn it back the next day by splitting a lot of wood, after a night of agony and hatred.

He remembered when she held him, after the deaths of his father and brother. Though he was grown, she grabbed him and pulled him to her breast, wordless, with only a hint of rocking, and kept him there for a long time, until the tears came.

He remembered how she went, with his mothers, and avenged the murders: the three women caught the killer through a sexual wile, knocked him groggy, cut off his penis and testicles, and then skinned him slowly, while he was alive. When he finally died, they cut off his head.

With all these memories Smith honored his grandfather.

He remembered how Sings Wolf, then Calling Eagle, received a great dream of death, and in that dream saw herself as a fallen warrior. He remembered how Calling

Eagle accepted the call to manhood with dignity, despite her personal inclination and a lifetime of custom. He recalled how she announced her vision in a beautiful ritual, how she transformed herself into a man, how she seemed as fitting and attractive a man as she had been a woman. He remembered how, shortly thereafter, the man-warrior Sings Wolf led a war charge that turned away the soldiers and saved the Human Beings. In these memories he honored his grandfather.

He remembered how his grandfather, sometimes his grandmother, had been the wisest human being he had ever known. He remembered her warmth when he came to her with the problems of growing up. He remembered the depth of her understanding when he spoke to her of the pain of being a white man and a red man at once, how she spoke of herself as among the people but not quite one of them. He remembered what she said—that a human being has one fundamental choice in life, to live joyfully according to his particular nature, or to fight his nature and have no life at all. He remembered her sympathy when he began to want to go to civilization and learn science and maybe— hope beyond hope!—become a scientist himself, even a doctor, and remembered pondering her words about fulfilling his nature then. In these memories he honored his grandfather.

After a couple of hours, he had the scaffold ready. Then he walked along the river and cut some willows. It was surprising to him how fresh the world seemed in the face of death, how sharp the sounds, how keen the colors, how savory the smells, how warm and gentling the wind.

He hoisted Sings Wolf to his shoulder, then heaved him onto the scaffold. It was an awkward effort, and he flushed with its humiliation. He climbed onto the scaffold, wrapped Sings Wolf in his blue blanket coat, and laid his knife, tomahawk, spear, and bow and arrows around him. Then he patiently built a little basketwork of willows over his grandfather, to keep the birds off for a while.

At last it was done as well as it could be done, with no effort spared. His mother would likely want to come back here, in a month or a year, after the flesh was gone, and pay her respects to the bleached bones.

Still, words were needed now, and gestures, and a spirit of awareness of the Powers.

Smith lit his pipe. He offered it, starting in the west and proceeding sunwise to the south, to the Maheyuno, the four sacred persons who dwell at the four corners of the universe. He offered it to Maheo, the All-Father, also called more formally Maxemaheo, and to mother earth. And then he spoke.

"Maheo," he said, "and all the other Powers, Maheyuno, Maiyun," and he named some of the Maiyun— "sun, thunder, moon, morning star, the whirlwind, badger, and you other Powers, my grandfather Sings Wolf has taken the Milky Way trail to the good place, Sehan."

Tears swept his face now, with no holding back.

"I commend his spirit to you."

"I regret that his children and grandchildren and all his other relatives do not stand here beside him. They revere and honor him, as I his grandson honor and revere him. I regret that his horse does not lie here beneath his scaffold, so that he might ride swiftly along the trail. But the Human Beings are in desperate need of horses, Powers. My grandfather would rather walk himself than make the small children and their mothers walk.

"Powers, of few Human Beings, almost no other Human Being, could I say this: He was a good man, and a good woman. As a boy he heard you Powers calling, and took the call to his heart, and set aside the ways of men and of the warpath, and became as a woman, dressing as a woman, speaking in a woman's way, being a woman in the lodge, comporting himself as a woman in every way.

"He made a splendid woman, Powers. He was the sits-beside-him wife to my grandfather Strikes Foot, and for many years they filled the lodge with their love for each other and for their children. Their hearts were big, Powers, and they took many children born to others into their lodge, and called them son and daughter, and reared them with loving kindness. This they did with my mother, Annemarie."

As a mother Sings Wolf cooked well, kept a handsome lodge, made attractive clothes, and worked hard at all a woman's duties. "Yet as *hemaneh* she did more. She made the fires for the scalp dances. She created love songs. She brought man and woman together in marriage. She helped them conquer the troubled waters of living together. She brought power to our men on hunts and pony raids. She came to excel at making beautiful patterns in quillwork and beadwork, and to supersede other women in these crafts that belong to women.

"Most of all, Powers, she dedicated the medicine-lodge ceremony. And she kept untouched her male power, the power she was born with and that you asked her to save, unused."

Smith rested a moment, feeling wrung out by his own tears.

"Therefore, great Powers, she was able to hear your call when it came again, beyond her seventieth winter. You sent a wolf to ask her to take off her dress, set aside her pot and her awl, take up these weapons laid beside Sings Wolf today, and seek the way of the warpath. The Human Beings, you said, needed the maleness of Sings Wolf.

"Against a lifetime of custom, Powers, and I believe against personal preference, Sings Wolf obeyed. And very soon the soldiers came, and on that magnificent day, Sings Wolf led a war charge of Tsistsistas-Suhtaio warriors, of men inspired by his male potency. Strong in their hearts, Powers, they turned the soldiers back and saved the people.

"I believe that this deed was the culmination, the true fulfillment, of the life of my grandfather. Powers, he waited, he listened, and he served. The rightness in his daily way brought him to his fulfillment. And after that, I believe, he was willing to die. Willing to help the Human Beings in their need, too, but willing to die.

"So here, now, you see his body. Here and now, I ask you, accept his spirit. Oh, I implore you, sacred Powers,

accept my grandfather's spirit. Make his every step
blessed."

Smith spent the rest of the day sitting beneath his
grandfather's scaffold, smoking, not thinking but letting his
mind drift in a kind of meditative way.

A little after sundown he grew chill and went to where
he had picketed his horse for his coat.

He knew something now he hadn't known before. He
didn't exactly know the words, but he knew. It was his
calling to live among the Cheyennes, as a Cheyenne. Not to
be like the agent, the missionary, and the other whites sent
to the reservation to help the people, who lived among
them, but remained different from them—and let that
difference be their central teaching. Smith's calling was to
be not only among the people but of them.

He chuckled. Maybe then the missionary would try to
save Smith, too.

He didn't yet know all of it. He didn't know whether he
should keep offering the Cheyennes his medicine, the
white-man medicine. He thought maybe the first step was
to ask not what he could teach them, but what he could
learn from them. And he didn't know whether he must give
up his white-man wife and take a wife, or more than one
wife, from the people.

He was aware of this power today, and he knew he
would be aware of it again, perhaps every day. Whatever it
wanted from him, he would give. For there lay the good
way.

Elaine clopped along, poking the crutch tips out,
rocking forward, planting her left foot firmly, leaning

forward, and jamming the crutch tips out again. It was an awkward motion, and she felt ugly doing it.

She got to the corner at the end of the Wockerleys' street and started across the main street, Front Street, full of brittle ridges and deep ruts.

She didn't care if people looked. At least she felt reasonably confident of not falling now—she was stronger and more skilled. Yes, stronger and more skilled, even hunched over her crutches, hopping about like a one-legged toad, making a racket on the boardwalk. Yes, I'm ugly, damn you, and proud of it.

She was dressed properly for the first time since she broke her leg, and felt better for it. She'd deliberately picked an old dress, but it was an improvement to be out of her nightdress.

She heard a scraping, tinny rattle but couldn't think what it was.

She nearly bumped into a pair of legs sticking most of the way across the boardwalk. The man didn't make way for her. She looked at him, propped against the front wall of the Lady Gay Dance Hall there, thinking he might be asleep or passed out. But he wasn't—he was staring at her, eyes big as a horse's. A sign pinned onto his coat, penciled as though by a child, labeled the man a "VICTIM OF THE REBELLION." The tinny scraping sounded again—he was shaking coins in a tin cup.

Then she saw that his right arm was missing—missing entirely, from the shoulder. By his left hand rested a cup.

"Life's a bitch if you're short a limb, pardoning my language, missy."

He still didn't move his legs. More than thirteen years since the war, Elaine thought, and this man was still begging. She eyed him. He looked old, and dissolute, but her serious guess was that he was only in his early thirties. She felt a clot of contempt for him in her throat.

"People ain't considerate of a man's handicap, missy." He smiled with indifferent malice. "Or a woman's either." Another man looked on from a bench, smirking.

She didn't want to speak to him, and certainly not to

ask for anything. She had two choices: She could go outside
his feet. That would take her perilously close to the edge of
the boardwalk, but she could lean against a post there, or
grab it if necessary. Or she could plunge straight across the
man's legs. The main risk there was that he would move
suddenly, or that she would bang his legs.

She considered. Then she jammed one crutch down
right next to his crotch, closer even than she intended. His
left hand jerked toward his testicles and stopped. She
hopped on across.

As she hurried away, she heard him cussing her vilely.

She spotted the striped barber pole. Fran had told her
the barber opened at ten o'clock, and she intended to avoid
embarrassment by being the first customer, perhaps the
lone customer. She was in fact about five minutes early.

But she wasn't first. Pushing clumsily through the
door, she saw a man stretched back in a barber chair, fully
lathered. He appeared to be asleep. The barber stropped
his razor.

Elaine got straight to it. "I want my hair cut." The
barber stopped in mid-strop and gawked at her.

She poled across, took hold of the arm of the other
barber chair, laid her crutches on the footrest, and labori-
ously lifted and legged her body into the chair.

"I don' yet cut ladies' hair, madam," the barber
ventured. He spoke in some soft Spanish accent and
dressed like a bit of a dandy, with a lovingly cared-for
mustache and pretty eyes.

The lathered-up man cracked his lids and looked
sideways at Elaine. He was a young fellow, but she wasn't
sure she'd be able to recognize him again, covered as he
was from cheeks to Adam's apple with foam. If she had to
guess, she would have said his eyes were amused. Which
was better than she feared in this bastion of maleness.

"I'll give you five dollars," she said. It was ten times
the usual price.

The barber hesitated. "Don' know how to do it," he
averred. But this was cupidity.

"I'll tell you," she said in a tone of finality.

The barber started his shave. Elaine noticed, across the room, that the coat on the hat rack had a tinned-steel star pinned to it. Oh, my, the sheriff, or the marshal, or some such. Still, she supposed it wasn't against the law for a woman to come into a barbershop. The crime was cutting hair you'd let grow for twenty-seven years.

It was not just a whim—it was a need, a compulsion, a . . . She didn't know what. She'd been mostly in bed for four weeks. She hadn't wanted to take care of it, to brush it, to pin it up. She didn't like the way it got into everything, into her food, onto her books, got pinned under her elbows, got caught in the bedspring. She resented its tangles, its snarls, and the unkempt, disreputable appearance it gave her. She'd come to hate it.

Amazing, she knew, when she thought how she'd treasured it, and Adam had loved it. She'd brushed it out a little this morning, to make it straight for the cutting, and felt a moment of sadness about it.

She'd given thought to how it should be cut, and that was a problem. No women's hairstyles permitted anything but full-length hair, none at all. The only women she'd ever seen cut their hair were Cheyennes, who hacked it straight at shoulder length when they wanted to express grief. Elaine was feeling plenty of grief, at the loss of her leg, at the absence of her husband—a temporary absence, by the Lord!—so hacked off straight at shoulder length it would be.

The barber finished the shave and covered his customer's face with hot towels again. Elaine wondered if the lawman wanted to hang around to see the crazy lady get shorn. Well, take a gander, Mac.

The barber came toward Elaine with scissors snicking, smiling obsequiously.

She flipped her hair behind the headrest and shook her head to get it to hang right. "Just straight across, nothing fancy," she said, "at the shoulders."

The scissors snicked. She saw the lawman looking out from under his towels at her and wondered idly what he was thinking. She pictured the long hanks of brown hair floating to the floor behind her.

No, she wouldn't look when she was finished. She wouldn't ask the barber for the fallen hair. He'd sell it for good money, thinking he was tricky. Which was fine. To hell with the hair. God damn the hair.

Weary and discouraged, Smith rode into the canyon of White Tail Creek and into the Cheyenne camp just at dark. He had worn himself out catching up with the Human Beings, just as they had worn themselves out getting here. He'd read the tracks all day long and had figured out most of it.

From the two forks of the Geese River, which the whites called the Platte, it was the old story. The Human Beings were being chased hard by soldiers, two separate, large groups of soldiers from behind. The Indians were desperately short of horses. The men took turns—riding awhile, then sending the horse back to a partner so he could ride, meanwhile running in the all-day-long warrior's lope. So the double-used ponies covered the ground three times.

Smith found the result of that tactic along the way— horse carcasses. He was glad he had his own horse and the three cavalry mounts to help out. But he knew that with the army constantly putting in new troops and horseflesh, such a flight was doomed.

He needed to sit in his own lodge behind his own fire, with his wife at his side, eat and listen to his children playing, smoke a pipe, and talk about something simple and domestic with his wife, perhaps what goods they would trade for at the post. Except that he had no wife, no lodge, no children, no tobacco, and nothing to trade. The post was still there. He thought of his mother Annemarie at the trading post on the Yellowstone. It was a post he had never seen, for his mothers had moved it from the Yellowstone after he left home. Yet it was in the heart of Cheyenne country, and it would be home. Certainly home if the Human Beings were there. Certainly home if his family was there. And the sights, the sounds, the smells of the first two decades of his life, his memories, his sense of the earth under his feet in the right way.

As he looked about the camp, he saw that not only the horses were worn out. The people were like old cloth, tattered at the edges and rubbed thin in the middle. They wouldn't last long at this pace.

Lisette did have a small fire among some rocks. When he dismounted, she held him for a long moment, for she knew what it meant when he came alone, leading three riderless horses. "He is riding the Milky Way Trail to Sehan," Smith told his mother formally. He felt tears well in his eyes again and roll down his cheeks. "A mob lynched him in Ogallala," he murmured softly in her ear. "Hanged him. Killed a deputy getting him." Smith felt his slender mother was comforting him, not he comforting her. Yet she was the one who called Sings Wolf father. "I couldn't. . . ." His voice clotted, and he stopped trying to speak.

His mother led him to the fire. Hindy stopped eating and started cutting Smith some meat, doubtless horse meat. Rain nursed Big Soldier. He did have a family, of sorts. He smiled at them wearily and, before he sat, touched Rain gently on the cheek and tousled Hindy's hair, like she was a boy. He took the meat gladly and sat by the fire, legs crossed. He was grateful for his family, his women. He wished he had Elaine among them.

Smith felt his mother's hand, gentle, insistent. He wondered how long he'd napped here by the fire. An hour, perhaps. He looked into Lisette's eyes. "Two men have come in from Little Chief," she said. Her eyes were troubled.

He raised his long frame off the ground and shook himself. His thought was, What now?

Little Chief and those who camped with him had been left behind on the march to the south. Now these two men had run away from Little Chief's people while they were being escorted to the Cheyenne and Arapaho Agency by the army.

The people shook their heads. Even as they risked their lives, and lost lives, to escape to their home country, their relatives were being forced south. Is'siwun, the sacred buffalo hat, and Mahuts, the four sacred arrows, were in the south. It seemed that the Cheyennes were fated to live far from Nowah'wus, the sacred mountain, their power perhaps broken. Unless the will of fewer than three hundred fleeing Cheyennes was stronger than fate.

Smith stood with Lisette in the crowd to hear whatever the runaways from Little Chief had to say.

Little Wolf asked, with an unexplained tone of significance in his voice, whether the country around Red Cloud Agency was full of soldiers. The runaways nodded. Soldiers everywhere, they said.

Morning Star stood to speak. "We are almost in our own country, my friends," he said. Smith supposed the handsome chief had been terribly stricken by the death of one of his wives, Short Woman, about a week ago. Now he seemed a weak, old man. "The soldiers up there with our friends the Sioux have always been good men."

Little Wolf leaped in, "They are up there to catch us and kill us."

"We have a right to be with Red Cloud," said Morning Star as though to a child. The Human Beings had been with Red Cloud when they agreed to go look at the agency in the south.

"With the whites you have a right to nothing that you do not already hold in the palm," asserted Little Wolf plainly.

Now Morning Star lost his temper. He turned on the Sweet Medicine chief and ordered him to shut up. He said they would never make it to the Powder River country.

Winter was coming. The people were exhausted—some babies had died, just today, from banging around in the hide sacks hanging from their mothers' saddles as the Human Beings ran from the soldiers. Little Wolf was a fool not to see that the Human Beings were forced to go in to Red Cloud, a fool.

This was fighting talk, and right away men of the Dog Soldiers began to step in close behind Morning Star, men of the Elk Society behind their leader, Little Wolf. Faces mottled with anger, and hands tightened on weapons. Smith and Lisette didn't move.

Little Wolf got up slowly and made his declaration. "We cannot divide now. We *cannot.*" He paused. He repeated his motto: "An Indian never caught is an Indian never killed. Together we can get away."

But Dog Soldiers and others still stood behind Morning Star looking angry. Little Wolf waited, but their faces didn't soften. He understood. They were tired, tired unto death. They thought going to Red Cloud, even if a slender chance, was the only chance they had.

So the Sweet Medicine chief relented. He said he would move his camp a little apart. Those who wanted to go on to the north, to the Powder River country, could camp with him tonight.

In the morning, Morning Star and his followers were gone. The division of the Tsistsistas-Suhtaio was about even. The men of the Elk Society and their families and some others elected to try for the northern land. The Dog Soldiers and their families and many of the young men went toward the Red Cloud Agency. Little Wolf supposed the young men anticipated that there would be more young women to choose from among the Sioux.

Smith's women moved their few belongings to Little Wolf's camp, and Smith staked his horses there in a little grass. Powder River, he thought. Home.

No one had energy for more than lying about in blankets and occasionally putting a small log on the fire. They ate from the soup Rain had made of the horse meat, without vegetables and without salt. Smith couldn't get enough of the hot liquid.

He looked around at his family. What family he had left. His father dead, one mother several hundred miles away, his brother dead before the age of twenty, one sister moved to the settlement at Helena, the other, the palsied one, dead in her youth, his grandfather lying on a scaffold back near Ogallala. Here with him, those who would be of his lodge, if he had a lodge, his mother, his cousin's widow, the infant Big Soldier, and an adopted white girl. Quite the motley crew, Smith, he told himself.

"What will happen to us?" asked Hindy.

He liked her. She hadn't been cared for, she'd been abused, she'd seen more of the brutal side of life than a teenage kid should have to see. She didn't know what to do with herself. Didn't see a way to make a life, present or future. She was afraid. But it seemed to Smith that she might endure it all. She wore her pain right out in front, on her face. Lisette said she'd even started doing some wisecracking. She might come through.

After too much thought, Smith said quietly, "I don't know what will happen to us."

"What will happen to me?" Her catawampus face was courage and fear, both rampant.

Smith looked fondly at her. "You are my daughter. You are a Cheyenne. You may do whatever you want in the world." He chuckled. "If we're alive tomorrow."

The next morning before dawn the Morning Star people were gone. They had left a buffalo robe with hair on it. On the robe were ammunition and powder, a gift for those who would continue fighting. Little Wolf would go on with one hundred and twenty-six people, including forty men of fighting age. Five hundred miles to Powder River.

Elaine sat on the steps of her porch, getting a little sun and making herself do some work. The Kansas sun was

warm on this Indian-summer day in late October, so she
wore only the wrap borrowed from Fran over her nightdress. It wasn't polite, sitting outdoors in a nightdress, but
she didn't feel polite. She knew she'd never looked worse.
Her hacked-off hair was unflattering. Her fingernails were
bitten for the first time since she was a teenager. She'd
developed the strangest nervous habit the last week—she
would bite on the knuckles of her fingers until it hurt. She
didn't know why she did it, but she couldn't stop herself.

The work she'd started was an article about the flight of
the Cheyennes toward their Powder River homeland, for
the *Atlantic*. She and her sister had published poems in
that magazine when they were teenagers, and one of the
editors professed himself an admirer of theirs. Maybe her
welcome would still be good. And maybe a few words in the
Eastern press would make a difference, would mitigate the
punishment the Cheyennes were headed for. So it was
worthwhile.

She was also reading everything about the Cheyennes
in the local newspapers, the Dodge City *Times* and Ford
County *Globe*, which were as informative as a fit of
apoplexy. She had written Dora for whatever she saw in the
Boston paper, or other Eastern papers, and had even
written the editor of the Kansas City *Journal* in the faint
hope of getting some of the coverage done in that newspaper. Kansas City was near the turmoil, but not in the midst
of it, and possibly not so bloodthirsty.

"Mizz Maclean?" came a voice.

The man stood in the street, for Dodge City mostly
hadn't the graces of sidewalks yet. He was an interesting-
looking man, only medium-sized but powerful-looking and
with a certain aura of . . . something.

"Yes?" said Elaine.

The man held a telegram. He came forward gently,
with a smile that was mere politeness. His eyes were gray
and had a glint of devilment about them. Something was
familiar about this man, something in the eyes.

"I'm Bat Masterson, Mizz Maclean. The sheriff here.
Thought you ought to see this."

The telegram was from the provost marshal of some division of the army in Fort Leavenworth. It described two Cheyenne Indians, companions, a young man estimated to be six and a half feet tall, and an old one. It said they were wanted for the murder of the Reverend Somebody Ratz, the kidnapping of his daughter Hindy, a juvenile, and the murder of three scouts of a brigade of the cavalry, U.S. Army, these crimes committed near Dodge City, Kansas. The younger man was suspected to be a half-breed, Adam Smith Maclean, formerly a physician at the Cheyenne and Arapaho Agency in Indian territory, well educated and able to pass for a white man. No guess was ventured about the identity of the older man. County sheriffs located in Dodge City, Wallace, and Hays, Kansas, and Ogallala and Sidney, Nebraska, were asked to be on the lookout for these fugitives.

Well. They army had done its work well enough in figuring out who Adam was. That's what happens when you're outstanding, she thought. The old man must be Sings Wolf. She snorted a little. It was still hard to think of her as a man—*him* as a man.

She realized the sheriff was waiting, his eyes sharp on her. "Yes, Sheriff . . . I'm sorry I've forgotten your name."

"Masterson, Mizz Maclean, Bat Masterson." He just stood there, eyeing her. Now she wished she didn't look such a fright, in this half-decent wrap and her hair ugly. "Is Adam Smith Maclean your husband, Mizz Maclean?"

"Certainly, Sheriff . . . Masterson. But my husband hasn't killed anyone unless he was attacked. He's a physician—he *saves* lives."

The sheriff smiled a little, as though he'd expected her to say that.

She expected him to say that decision of who was a murderer and who was not was made by a court of law, not by him, and not by her. Instead he said, "These are strange times, Mizz Maclean. Strange times."

He kept looking and smiling a little, perhaps with a hint of . . . what? A hint of menace, she thought. Now she knew him. The man getting a shave in the barbershop. She knew him, too, for what he was, a masher, a seducer, what men called a ladies' man. Well, he had an attractive devil-may-care air. She was a little shocked at herself for thinking so.

"Where is Mr. Maclean now, Mizz Maclean?"

"I don't know where *Dr.* Maclean is," she answered.

"*Dr.* Maclean," Masterson repeated. He waited a couple of beats. "It's a crime to protect a fugitive from the law," he said.

"I wish I could protect him," she said. "I fear that he's in grave danger. He's trying to help his people return to their homeland at Powder River, and the army is treating them like criminals. I don't know where they are, or where he is. I'm confident he's done nothing wrong."

Masterson nodded a couple of times again, an odd mannerism, perhaps confirming something to himself. "How long do you plan to be in Dodge City, Mizz Maclean?"

"Sheriff, my right leg has been amputated below the knee. I'm sure I'll be in Dodge City for some weeks. Dr. Richtarsch hopes I'll be able to start walking with a wooden leg in perhaps two more months. I may move into a boardinghouse in the meantime, if you need to ask other questions."

Sheriff Masterson didn't appear inclined to take the hint. "Yes, ma'am." His eyes twinkled wickedly, the rogue. "I knew a lady once lost her leg like that," he said. "She learned to ride with a sidesaddle, it being her right leg that was short some. Dr. Richtarsch tells me it's your right leg."

Elaine said, "I sold my sidesaddle, Sheriff."

He nodded. "That's what I heard. Over to Ham, at the livery." Cheeky fellow, and certainly not Elaine's sort. "That lady learned it," said the sheriff, giving all his phrases an extra pause. "'Course, she was a sporting lady." Only his cool, gray eyes smiled at that.

Well, Mr. Masterson, she thought, saying such a thing to a lady. All right, if you want to play that game.

He touched his hand to his hat brim. "Mizz Maclean,

you let me know if you hear from your husband now, will you? Be sure. Army looking for him—that's not too serious, because they don't look too hard. Too busy fighting Injuns. But it's best to get things like this straightened out."

"Of course, Sheriff Masterson." *Of course if I knew Adam was headed into hell, I'd point you toward heaven.*

The sheriff touched his hat again and walked off, the walk of a man who supposed he was being watched by an attractive woman, and liked it. Elaine gave a quiet *hummpf.*

An hour later the liveryman brought her sidesaddle. The note read simply, "Compliments of Bat Masterson."

Little Wolf told his people to scatter into the Sand Hills. He said they'd leave many trails, like birds scattering through the brush. The soldiers would not follow any trail so small, he said. Let the soldiers follow Morning Star, who was going in to surrender anyway, and who said he trusted the soldiers of this country.

Little Wolf named a place on the north side of the Sand Hills and west of the head of the Snake River where they would meet. Not far from there Little Wolf knew a place to make a winter camp. It was time to stop running, and time to hide.

The camping place they reached two weeks later was Lost Chokecherry Valley, a small, cupped formation with a lake. It promised some warmth and lots of ducks and geese. Some of the men said it was too close to the Black Hills Road, that they would be discovered, but Little Wolf said it was the best choice, and that was enough for everyone. The people were tired, desperately in need of rest.

The next morning Wooden Legs and some of the other young men brought in a few cattle for food. Luckily, they were even unbranded cattle, so the cowboys of the ranches would not come looking.

No one knew whether the Human Beings could hide here all winter. But the Elk Society men would keep a diligent watch. When army scouts came, the people would hide in the bushes, and if spotted, they would scatter into the little hills and come together again somewhere else. It was the best they could do. For now the people must rest and eat.

Smith thought it would be a damn rough winter. No buffalo-hide lodges, the pride of every Cheyenne family.

No canvas tents, not even any blankets to speak of. They would have to live in brush huts and in holes in the hillsides. He wondered if they could get enough food. It would be dangerous to shoot the guns so near the road, and they didn't have much ammunition anyway. So they would have to live on what they could get with the bow and arrow, and then be careful not to leave a moccasin trail back into Lost Chokecherry Valley. Smith had not hunted with a bow and arrow in fifteen years, but he could do it, and he would get his skill back this winter.

Smith kept his mind off Elaine, three weeks along toward a mended leg now. She would survive there at the Wockerleys' house. She would still be stuck in her bed, in traction, surely lonely and bored, but safe. He couldn't help her except by giving her some company. And right now his family and his people needed his company, his support, his protection, and whatever else he could offer.

Elaine had her mind made up to try to ride by Thanksgiving day, and she did. The day before the pilgrims of her native state gave thanks for a bountiful harvest, Sheriff Masterson led a mare around opposite the porch door for her, with the sidesaddle already cinched on, and the mare tied to the back of a surrey.

Of course, she'd refused the sheriff's gift of the side-saddle. But Sheriff Masterson had prevailed upon the liveryman he called Ham to loan it back to her without charge. The man had done some repairs, too. It looked smart.

She simply clumsied to the bottom of the little steps—what choice did she have? Standing there getting her composure back, she saw a shadowy figure behind the curtains in the window next door. Well, she was probably a neighborhood curiosity. Strange that she'd never seen the children playing out near her porch again.

She poked her way to the road on her crutches, now

rather proud of the way she maneuvered. She was swift to heal, Dr. Richtarsch said, and remarkable at rehabilitation—"amazingly dedicated," in his words.

The sheriff stayed in the road by the surrey while she crutched her way across the little patch of lawn, its grasses browned by the late-autumn cold. The surrey had been his idea. When she tired, she could sit in the little carriage and be driven back. She knew she might tire in a block, but suspected she would be good for a mile, perhaps farther. She thought she was sneaky strong.

When she got to the carriage, she beamed at Sheriff Masterson. Why not beam? She felt like a child on a lark. Her hair was ugly at shoulder length, but it was nicely brushed out. She was going out on the town, sort of. She wished her escort were Adam, but at least the sheriff was a good-looking man.

She nudged the thought of Adam out of her head—she was angry at him. Why had he been out of touch for nearly eight weeks? If he still wanted her, he'd have been in touch somehow, by telegraph, at least. She wondered whether Cheyenne culture taught casualness about marriage. When you can have three or four wives, how much difference can one make?

But she had no intention of doing what everyone hinted at—consider the facts available, and face them. As they put it. She would have her husband back. When she found a way to bear letting him see her crippled.

She grasped the saddle horn, handed Sheriff Masterson her crutches, and he set them in the surrey. She was grateful that he had been thoughtful enough to let her gimp her own way across, not supported by a man. Evidently he wasn't going to fuss over her, and that would be splendid.

She reached out and gripped the sheriff by his shoulders. He gave her a mischievous grin, took her firmly by the waist, and—here came the dicey part—gave her a good hoist into the saddle.

First pleasant surprise: It didn't hurt yet, or not more than a twinge. She held to the saddle horn. She got her left foot into the stirrup and her knee braced against the leaping

horn. That was easy. Then she laid her stump over the
higher horn, which supported her leg just above the knee.

She put some pressure against the horn—that would
be her cross to bear. Whoa! It was going to hurt. She
pushed away the sad memory of learning to ride under
Adam's tutelage and thought of exactly what exertions
would be needed to ride the horse. Yes, she recalled, the
pressure on the horns fluctuated with the motion of the
horse's back. It peaked when . . . Ow! She wouldn't be
able to do that today.

"Sheriff," she said, "perhaps today if you'd just lead
her. We could stay right in this street." So much for a mile.
So much for sneaky strong.

The sheriff nodded and smiled. Elaine noticed that he
liked to look a lot and say little, and constantly made his
own quiet judgments.

She took in her breath and gave a fair squeeze against
the horns.

God! She nearly blacked out. She damn near fell off.

Sheriff Masterson quickly supported her by the waist
with both hands. She used his forearms, forearms as thick
as Smith's on a much shorter man, and got her seat back.

She really thought she couldn't do it.

She got her breath. So, if she couldn't, she would just
fall. She'd fallen off a horse before. She refused to be
stymied by something as simple as pain.

She noticed Masterson's face. He just watched her, his
cool, gray eyes taking in everything, curious, interested,
but without compassion. What an odd man, she thought,
admirable in his way, but quite cold.

Of course, she supposed his interest in her was
seduction. Certainly not passion. No, a detached and
amused wondering if he could seduce her. She imagined
this sort of man made some gesture in the direction of every
half-suitable woman he met. Perhaps in her case he was
also curious about her . . . handicap. She refused to
contemplate the ugliness of that sort of interest.

In any case, she thought, he would make his effort, and
with a certain style. It would do him no good. Right now

she didn't want warmth or even real friendship from a man, and certainly not morbid curiosity about her stump.

Fran had told her that Sheriff Masterson had shot and killed a man over a dance-hall girl. Elaine thought he could. He also had a reputation as an avid gambler, not calculating, but daring, full of bluffs and high spirits.

"If you'll lead, please."

He untied the reins from the surrey, looked back to her to check, and started slowly down the road.

She lurched and had to grip with her legs—Oh! She gasped for breath through the pain and choked back a cry. After a moment she wiped the tears from her eyes and forced herself to look ahead. She abandoned all pretense about sitting with style, and held on to the cantle and the saddle horn with all her might. The sheriff appeared not to have noticed her little upset, but she thought that was just his politeness, for he noticed everything. She was grateful.

They got to the intersection at Front Street. Sheriff Masterson looked out sharply for traffic, circled the horse slowly in the larger street, and headed back toward the Wockerley house. Elaine noticed that heads on Front Street turned toward the lady being led around by the sheriff.

No doubt most of those heads wondered who the lady was. No doubt some of them knew—the fool who went to the Injuns and paid a leg for her trouble. No doubt tongues would wag.

Well, considering that right now she felt as though she couldn't attract flies, that was not unflattering. The tongues could do all the scandal-mongering they liked.

The sheriff stopped the horse by the surrey, tied the reins without a word, and lifted his hands to help her down. She slid to him gratefully. She'd have to be careful of this getting off the horse, or she would end up in his arms in a suggestive way. She preferred to be careful.

He handed her the crutches, she pegged across the lawn, and at the stoop he held the door for her. "Thank you for your courtesy, Sheriff," she said with a smile, which took some effort.

Bat Masterson gave her that devil-may-care grin back, wheeled, and was off. To your gambling dens, Sheriff? To your sporting women? Too bad. He wasn't an unattractive man.

In the hard-face moon, which the white men called November, the Human Beings hidden in Lost Chokecherry Valley got bad news, and then a great stroke of luck.

The bad news came by messenger from Morning Star. During the big blizzard near the end of October, his people were captured by soldiers and herded to Fort Robinson. Instead of joining Red Cloud's people, they had become prisoners at the fort. No one knew what would happen. The soldiers talked of escorting them back south to Indian territory, but were waiting for instructions from Washington City. The people would not go back, said the messengers, no matter what the whites said or did. They preferred to fight and die at Fort Robinson, if necessary.

Little Wolf smoked his pipe in silence over this news. Smith guessed the Sweet Medicine chief found it too sad for comment. If the soldiers were adamant, and the people were adamant, the snow would turn red, and the earth beneath would be thawed by warm blood.

Smith thought how glad he was that his family was here, in Nebraska. True, they were not yet home—home to Powder River, home where he was raised, home to both his mothers. True, they were hungry and cold. But they weren't penned up in some fort, waiting for some soldiers to tell them whether they could live.

The stroke of luck came shortly after the bad news. The scouts spotted a great, dark line coming from the north. Once they would have thought, buffalo. Now they thought, soldiers. The women began packing their few belongings. But then Raven saw the advancing line for what it was—elk. A huge, migrating herd of elk.

Raven directed everyone to the sand pass where the

elk always used to cross. They waited until the leaders got down into the gully and began to fire—arrows and spears only, no guns. Soon elk fell over the bodies of the beasts in front of them.

Little Wolf and other older men kept a close watch, for the situation was very dangerous. Maybe soldiers were chasing the herd. Maybe soldiers would spot the scavenger birds over the carrion. Little Wolf directed the women with packs of meat to go back toward the Lost Chokecherry Valley by a roundabout route to the north, misleading any trackers.

Though no longer a first-rate shot with an arrow, Smith downed two cows and a bull. His women hurried out to skin them, grinning irrepressibly. Bloodthirsty bitches, ain't they? Smith commented teasingly to himself. Then he acted like a *veho*—he went to help them get the meat packed and get out of here. This place was likely to be trouble, one way or another. The soldiers would either come on them here or spot the carrion birds above the leavings and follow the people's tracks back to the valley.

He was as glad as his women were for the elk. The meat would get them through the winter. Just as important for their spirits, he thought, were the elk teeth. Cheyenne women decorated their fancy dresses with elk teeth, but for a long time now his mother had been poor as a white woman. Smith would give the teeth from one animal to Lisette, from one to Rain, the poor creature, and from one to Hindy, her first elk teeth. And you'll make a fine savage yet, girl, Smith thought.

Then came another miracle. As the people hurried off with the meat, snow began to fall, first gently, then thickly.

Damn, thought Smith profanely, Maheo is with us.

The snow would cover their tracks. Better yet, it would cover the carcasses and entrails and keep the carrion-eaters away. There would be no high-circling buzzards for the soldiers to see.

That night the Tsistsistas-Suhtaio feasted. Every fire had meat aplenty. Not buffalo, true, but the elk was fat for the coming winter, and some of the people wondered aloud

if even buffalo was so good. Smith's women roasted the guts
first on sticks over the open fire, and then the ribs, the
tongues cooking for later. Smith loved ribs—he liked the
feeling of gnawing straight off a bone, stripping the last,
clinging fragments with his teeth. It made him want to
grunt mockingly, "I am animal. Good."

After supper, and after Smith smoked a little kinnikin-
nick, Lisette came and sat beside him and put an arm
around his waist and nuzzled his shoulder with her head.
She could act familiar—she was his mother, and he didn't
have a sits-beside-him wife, not here. Besides, Lisette had
always done what she wanted. He had heard tales about her
sexual explorations when she was a young woman. He
looked into her face. She was still damned attractive, fifty
years old or not.

"You need a wife," she said in English.

Smith laughed and put his arm around her teasingly.

She chuckled and said softly, "Rain needs a husband."
He was glad she'd chosen English. He didn't want Rain to
hear.

It had occurred to him. Rain was the widow of his
mother Annemarie's brother Red Hand, she had no family
living, the union would be suitable in every way, and he
had a responsibility to her. Besides, she was lovely.

He had also made up his mind about it. "I have
considered," he said to his mother, "and decided against it."

That was enough. Even Cheyenne mothers listened
when their grown sons spoke like that. She stayed leaning
against him, though. Smith luxuriated in his full belly and
the closeness of his mother.

The next morning he took Lisette aside and said, "My
family is now fed for the winter. All the people are fed."
Since they didn't have to hunt, he went on, but could stay
hidden in the valley, the danger from soldiers would be
slight.

He thought with a sneaky smile of what he had decided
to do. A couple of hundred miles' ride, or more, but so
what? It was crazy, but he loved it. He said, "I am going to
Dodge City." He didn't add, "To see Elaine."

* * *

Early in the big hard-face moon, which the whites called December, and which Dr. Adam Smith Maclean called by either name, according to circumstance and mood, a scout rode down Front Street leading an extra mount, both cavalry horses. Past the Alamo he came, a saloon popular with Texas cow-boys, past the Opera House Saloon, and past the Lady Gay Dance Hall. All three entertainment palaces were empty now that the cattle-drive season was over. He turned onto a side street and tied his horses opposite the porch of a self-consciously proper house. He went up to the porch door and rapped firmly. He appeared to be looking in the big windows that fronted the porch.

The plump young woman in the house next door, Sue Loveday, eyed the scout with raging curiosity—her life was knowing what went on in the neighborhood—and quickly made a shrewd guess about who this immensely tall scout was. She smiled to herself. Had her children been home to see, they would have seen on their mother's face, with the emotional perceptiveness children have, a fluid wash of delight and malice.

Sue reached for her shawl. There was no time to lose. The poor man.

Through the front door she waddled hurriedly, but once outside she affected the air of a woman out for a stroll on a delightful Indian-summer afternoon. She saw out of the corner of her eye that the scout now had his nose to a window, his hands blinkering his eyes. The poor man.

She slowed her walk carelessly. When he turned away from the window, she started, as though she hadn't seen him until that moment. Then she stopped and spread the look of the uninvolved but sincerely concerned across her round face. "Oh!" she cried. "Dr. Maclean?"

"Yes, madam," Smith said politely. He wondered where in hell Elaine's belongings were. Certainly not on that bare porch. He had no attention to spare to wonder what sort of creature he faced.

"Oh, Dr. Maclean, you must be looking for your wife."

"Yes, madam."

"I think you'd best ask Sheriff Masterson. Two days ago I saw him help her move her things. I can't think where she might be living." In fact, the woman knew very well that she was at Mrs. Yancey's boardinghouse, but Sue Loveday didn't hand out information freely—she traded it in a delicious little game of sharp glances, vocal nuances, and expressively bitten lips.

Smith nodded gravely. Ask the sheriff. Smith was badly scared. Maybe Elaine had finished her traction and was gone back east in her splint. Gone back east for good.

Now he looked at the woman before him, her face a vivid melange of feelings he couldn't add up. What was he to her that her eyes should be so bright, her face so florid? What was Elaine to her? Had she gotten to know Elaine— they were next-door neighbors—and come to care about her? What was she not saying? He had a strong notion that the truth was not in this woman, and he acted on that notion.

"Thank you, mad*am*," he said, giving the word a hoity-toity stress on the second syllable. He touched his hat brim and turned away to untie his mount.

Sue gaped at him. The man certainly didn't show any curiosity! And about his own wife! If they were really married! A white woman to an Indian!

Sue stood there for a moment, miffed, trying to think of something more to say, something to keep the exchange going. But she was trapped by her desire to appear simply helpful, and of course not really involved.

Smith rode off toward the sheriff's office.

"Sheriff," said Elaine, "I'm afraid I have to stop."

This ride was the first when they'd ventured beyond

the town streets. She'd felt up to more effort, and she intended to miss no opportunity.

But now she was tired. Maybe to herself she could even say "exhausted."

She reached out to Bat Masterson, who had come around to help her dismount. She slid off the sidesaddle half into his arms, and instead of lowering her to the road, he slid one arm behind her legs and carried her to the surrey. A little embarrassing, but very convenient, and they weren't in public. She appreciated Bat Masterson, he of the thick, strong arms, good looks, and attentive politeness. He lifted her straight in the seat.

Dr. Richtarsch had given her the peg leg the coffin maker had fashioned for her, from a good piece of hardwood shipped all the way from Missouri. She could start trying the leg a little each day in a couple of weeks, he said. A fine Christmas present, then—her first steps without crutches.

The sheriff clucked to the horses, turned them in a wide arc off the road, and pointed them back toward town. The motion of the surrey jolted her, and she realized how exhausted she was—she'd exerted herself with her legs today, and now they were trembling from the effort.

She looked around at the woolen blanket the sheriff had laid on the back seat, in case it got cold, he said. But the afternoon was sunny and warm, a lovely day to be out riding.

She was tired beyond tired. Maybe she could take a little nap on the way back to town. She shouldn't, but then she was doing so much she shouldn't. She shouldn't have moved into a boardinghouse where she was the lone woman. But what was she to do when she couldn't afford to stay with the Wockerleys, and Dr. Wockerley wanted to be rid of her anyway? She shouldn't be spending time alone with the sheriff. But he was the only friend she had, and she was very lonely. Besides, she needed to get started riding, and no woman would be strong enough to help her get mounted and dismounted.

Of course, the hens of Dodge City would say what they

wanted about her consorting with a man like the sheriff. But she was married, and meant to stay that way.

She reached into the back for the folded blanket and laid it on the sheriff's shoulder. The shoulder would make what she was going to do seem less intimate. With one shy glance up at the sheriff's face, she laid her head on the blanket.

In two or three minutes her fatigue, the warm sun, and the motion of the buggy carried her off to sleep.

"You the sheriff?"

"Unnershuriff."

"I'm Adam Maclean," said Smith. "I'm looking for my wife."

The fellow was taking his ease leaning against the front wall of the office. It was that nice a day, for December.

He gave Smith a flat look. Smith supposed he didn't like Smith's tone much, or the fact that he stayed on his mount. If a white man spoke to the undersheriff from horseback, he was powerful and got the bended knee. If an Indian did it, scout or not, he was insolent.

The fellow started rolling a cigarette with one hand alone, a cow-boy's trick. Took his time with it, too. "Might look out along the road toward the fort," the fellow said. He took a deep draw. "She's out riding with Sheriff Masterson." He blew the smoke toward Smith. His expression was unreadable.

Out riding? In her splint? With Masterson? As Smith recalled, Masterson had some name as a fellow ready to mix it up, and as a ladies' man.

Smith said, like the cow-boys, "Obliged," giving away no more than the fellow did. He reined his horse in that direction.

*　*　*

Smith saw the buggy in the distance, crawling like a spider back toward town. He stopped and focused the field glasses he'd stolen from the sergeant he killed. And couldn't believe what he saw.

A surrey with a driver, and a horse tied behind. And a woman next to the driver, her head resting on his shoulder.

If the driver was Masterson, and the passenger was Elaine . . .

He flushed. He had an impulse to gallop off, to get out of Elaine's life, to go back to . . .

Humiliated. He felt humiliated, bitterly.

He was just a goddamned red nigger. Red nigger cuckold.

He had to know. And by God he would let her feel the whip of his anger. He gouged his horse with his spurs.

Elaine swam one stroke toward consciousness. Then she felt Sheriff Masterson's hand shaking her arm gently, and she rose to the surface.

She opened her eyes. The surrey had stopped. A mounted man leading an extra horse stood in front of them, a tall mam. He . . .

Adam!

Elaine jerked her head up off the sheriff's shoulder.

Adam spoke slowly and clearly in the soft and melodic Cheyenne language. He must be speaking so distinctly because he wanted her to remember the words forever. His face was dark, mottled. His words were, "A moose has wet on my lodge." Meaning, something has happened that's beneath my contempt. "I send you back to your relatives."

She couldn't respond for a moment. Then she screamed, "Wa-a-i-it!"

At that moment Adam put the spurs to his horse and was gone in a clatter of hooves.

My God, she said to herself, disbelieving.

She watched the rider get smaller, galloping toward the fort, galloping out of her life.

"What did he say?" asked Bat Masterson.

She looked at the sheriff soberly. "My husband says he divorces me," she murmured.

The sheriff got down from the buggy and looked down at the road, maybe at Adam's tracks. Then he looked after the two horses, already getting smaller in the distance.

"We can't catch him in this surrey, can we?" Elaine said hopelessly.

"No," said Bat Masterson, drawling it out. He got back into the surrey. "We can catch him with a posse, though. And we will. Remember, he's a wanted man." The sheriff lashed at the horses, and they broke into a run.

Divorced. My good God, divorced.

≈ **BOOK THREE** ≈

≈   1   ≈

On the second day she roused herself enough to go to the sheriff's office.

She'd spent the days in a crazy state of mind. That first afternoon she'd lain about, apathetic. She threw herself about her room, actually pounding on the walls and falling on the floor. She wept, hopelessly, self-indulgently, extravagantly. She screamed. She bellowed and moaned.

At some point early on she passed beyond being nervous about what the other lodgers must think. Probably they thought she'd gone mad. They'd send men for her and lock her up. Maybe they'd put her in the cell next to Adam, and at least she could see him and be near him until they hanged him.

She fingered her shoulder-length hair. So now, bitch, you really have something to grieve about.

The next day, in what seemed a fever of rage or despair or . . . something, she crutched all the way to the telegraph office. There she wrote a telegram to her mother and sister in Massachusetts:

ADAM HAS ORDERED ME BACK TO MY RELATIVES STOP THAT
MEANS HE HAS DIVORCED ME STOP I ASK IN SHAME IF YOU
CAN SEND ME TRAIN FARE TO COME HOME STOP YOUR
DAUGHTER ELAINE

Then she started to edit it down, to get the point into as few words as possible to save money. Suddenly, for no reason, she wadded the form up, slammed it into the wastebasket, glared at the operator nastily, and stomped out. She felt ridiculous trying to stomp without two feet to stomp with.

The day after that she managed to hie herself to the sheriff's office. The man behind the desk looked like he couldn't be roused to care about anything on earth. He didn't get up. She wondered if he could talk around the huge chaw in his mouth.

"Are you a deputy, sir?"

"Unnershuriff."

"May I speak to the sheriff?"

"He ain't here."

"Will he be in today?"

The undersheriff shrugged. "No telling. Out with a posse." So the fellow didn't intend to let on that he knew who Elaine was.

"Would you send word to Mrs. Maclean at Mrs. Yancey's boardinghouse when he gets back? Whenever he gets back, day or night?"

The undersheriff made a shrug that meant, "I guess," or, "Why not?"

"It's important," Elaine said.

The man nodded vaguely.

"Thank you, Unnershuriff," Elaine said with a maliciously formal smile.

She crutched away with all the dignity she could muster and did not glance back. She thought in thunder to herself: I will get good on that peg leg, I will get graceful with it, I will wear skirts to the ground so people won't be able to tell, I will be slender and beautiful. Meanwhile she thought how hideous she must look, at the moment, to the undersheriff.

And I will show them that I can teach and be *useful*.

For despite her tempests, her rampages, her demonstrations, she supposed she had accepted Adam's decision. Yes, it was unfair. Yes, Adam had made a mistake. Yes, she was misunderstood. But that was just his excuse to get what he wanted anyway. What he wanted, for whatever reason, was an end to the marriage. He'd wanted that all long. She didn't know why, but she accepted.

She would have done anything for him. But she

wouldn't beg. She never would have done that. Now that she was crippled it was unthinkable.

Not that she believed the excuses he must be giving himself. That everything was against it—the times, the cultures, the barrier of race, the tides of history—everything. It wasn't their fault, he would say. The circumstances made it impossible.

Meanwhile only one circumstance made their marriage out of the question: Elaine could never again be a whole woman. She couldn't go to him crippled. And a cripple couldn't make a wife to an Indian.

So there it was. But the son of a bitch didn't even know it.

Around midday on the second day Smith cut the old main trail of the Cheyennes moving north and followed it. Now the tracks of his stolen cavalry horses would be mixed with lots of other tracks. Since his were shod, and fresh, the posse could still track him. But he had an idea.

It was an idea that would keep him from shooting at county sheriffs any more, or the deputized agents of sheriffs. Yesterday he'd had to slow them up by letting them know he was watching his back trail. As a result they had to leave one horse for the vultures.

He kicked his horses up to a gallop. They were tired, but they'd run for a while yet. A well-trained horse would run as long as its rider asked, until it died. These horses just needed to put a little distance between Smith and his trackers. It wouldn't do to be seen working his wiles.

He hurried right along for twenty minutes, then stopped with some rock underfoot. He'd have to work fast. He tied the reins of the two horses together. Then he got his big knife from his belt, lifted the front right hoof of the saddled horse, worked the tip in beneath the shoe, then pushed the knife down to the hilt. A little twisting and the shoe came right off—it wasn't as hard as he'd feared.

Seven patient repetitions. Being deliberate brought his pulse up nicely, but it saved time, and it was something he needed. He had to concentrate to keep his emotions calmed. He couldn't afford to think about the life he was riding away from, or he wouldn't end up getting away from it—he'd end up in the hoosegow.

There, he was finished. He put the shoes in his saddlebags, mounted, and got up to a gallop again. He needed a little distance, and then the horses could rest the whole afternoon and night. His shod tracks disappeared, and his horses became two of several hundred Indian ponies.

After two or three miles, he saw what he needed, one set of unshod tracks forking away from the main trail to the northwest. Over that way was a long hilltop. He could set himself there and watch. Mixing fresh tracks with old ones was a risk. A first-rate tracker might guess what he'd done. But Smith thought none of these white men would be as good as a Cheyenne tracker. If they were, Smith would just have to shoot him some deputies. And why not a sheriff, a goddamned sheriff who would steal your wife and make sure of her by hanging you?

He picketed his horses beyond the ridge line, hoofed back up to where he could see the main trail, and got prone with a good shooting angle. Ten minutes later Bat Masterson's posse came to where Smith had left the main trail and rode on north without even a close look.

Bye-bye, Sheriff Masterson. You ass.

Anguish raged through Smith. After slipping away from the sheriff's posse, Smith walked the horses away from the trail, his head down, his steps despairing. Now his memories swirled around Elaine, his mind aflame with jealousy.

He did manage to take the routine precautions—waited until past the early sunset and doubled back into some rocks to make a fireless bivouac in the dark. There he sank into a kind of stupor, a miasma of memories of Elaine, fragments of conversations, odd bits of music they'd heard together, tastes of meals they'd shared, often quite ordinary meals, all of it made piquant by intermittent touches, and made absurd by great globs of sticky desire that entangled him, mocked him, and infuriated him.

In the middle of the night it began to rain, a thin, chill drizzle that suited his misery perfectly.

When he woke wet in the morning, he honestly wasn't sure he'd slept, whether all those throes had been fantasy or dream. He let the horses rest on some fair grass for half a day while he fretted and tried to watch his back trail, and then set out toward Ogallala. He was shaking like leaves in the wind of his own rage.

He found them stuck where the crude road crossed a wash running an inch or so of water, a teenage boy and his father, heaving at their wagon to get it out. They were headed out from town and probably could have gotten through that wash easily except for the rain and whatever their load was. Smith sat his horse and watched them from the top of a little rise for a moment, making sure they were alone, and what they seemed to be, and wondering why they were so inattentive in rough country.

The man had his hair shaved back from his forehead in the manner of devotees of the Chautauqua circuit, of all things. Well, Smith supposed intellectuals came to Nebraska, too. Even awkward-looking intellectuals like this one. The boy seemed sullen. Smith wondered whether he blamed his father for letting them get stuck in a cold drizzle.

Smith rode down close and saw that the faded lettering on the wagon said "DANA DIDEROT, MARBLE MONU-MENTS." Three big gravestones lay in the back of the wagon. Smith wondered what rich family could have been unlucky enough to have three deaths at once. He noted that Diderot didn't have sense enough to unload the wagon so it would come out.

"Trembul-ling titties, we've got company," said the

gangling man. He affected an exaggerated drollness, as though he'd seen Smith coming, which he hadn't. The kid jumped like he'd been bit. Diderot grinned madly at him, pretending they shared some secret joke. He signed a greeting of friendship to Smith.

Chuckling inside, his face somber, Smith signed friendship back.

"Tottering testicles, a *friendly* savage," said Diderot with clownish merriment. "I wonder if he's a helpful savage." The man abandoned the expressive sign language of the plains for kids' gestures: You. Us. Wagon.

Smith put on his best silent, stoic, noble face. If you're going to be a stereotype, you may as well be a thundering one. He swung out of the saddle, led his horses to the front of the wagon, and picketed them.

He was trying to sort out the queerest impulse he had. He didn't want to speak English with these people. He didn't want to be Dr. Adam Smith Maclean. He wanted to give them what they saw, a dirty, stinking, ignorant savage.

He said in mellifluous Cheyenne, "I see you have troubles. I will help you," and he repeated that promise with his hands.

"Jesus hallelujah," Diderot went on, pronouncing Jesus in the Spanish was, "Hay-soos." "I wish I knew what tribe he belongs to," said Diderot. His son had nothing to say. The kid just stood there looking pissed off, like an engine building up steam. "His skull looks like the Cro-Magnon type. I'm sure there are tribal patterns. The intellectual capacity may be limited." He played the scientist amused at a specimen.

Smith considered for a long moment. No, he wouldn't speak English. It was the oddest feeling. He walked to the wagon, climbed in via a wheel, noting that the wheels were dug in deep. He lifted one of the gravestones and dumped it into the wash. One by one, wordless, conscious of the eyes on him, he dumped the others. The carved stones each weighed as much as a sizable man, and sank deep into the sand. Lifting them took a huge effort—for someone of

ordinary size it would have been impossible. Smith made a
point of seeming to do it easily.

He watched the rivulet of water run around the big
stones and deliberately did not look at Diderot.

"Tottering testicles," said Diderot, with an idiot smile
at his son.

Smith jumped out of the wagon, taking Diderot's
length of hemp with him. He tied the hemp to the axle and
to his saddle horn. Then he motioned to Diderot to lead the
team, and lisped, "Plis, plis," as though he were unsure of
the English word. He went forward to lead his own horse.
The horses strained, and the wagon came out with a gritty
suck!

"*Parlez-vous français?*" he asked Diderot as he pulled
the picket on his second horse. When Diderot shook his
head, Smith said in French, "May it always burn when you
piss."

Diderot held out his arms in a gesture of helplessness.
Smith switched his saddle from the tired mount to the
rested one and pulled the cinch tight.

He said to Diderot in the Crow language, which he
had spoken from childhood, "May your family put you out
to starve." The man smiled stupidly at his son and muttered, "Moronic maunderings."

Smith swung into his saddle. "May your grandchildren
all be idiots," he said in Lakota, with a big grin and a
friendly wave of the hand.

He touched his spurs to his horse's flanks and was off.
Before long, he was sure, the intellectual would recall that
the gravestones were in the wash, and start considering
how to hoist them back into the wagon, and not like the
answer.

It was a damn nuisance. Every time she stepped, the
peg banged, or clopped like a hoof on a boardwalk. Just
what a lady wants, to sound like a horse when she walks.

And the thing didn't seem to give her decent balance. When she put her weight straight on it, she was balanced. But when she put part of her weight on her good leg, the peg seemed to want to scrape around and act like the deck of a pitching boat. And when she stepped forward on it, it seemed to throw her forward onto her good leg too quickly, making her feel as though she was lurching.

Oh, hell, she *was* lurching. That was what she would have to overcome. She certainly wasn't going to be seen around town constantly saving herself with her left leg, like the strap on a swaying train. She was going to be seen walking gracefully, making people admire her carriage, and even fooling those who didn't know. And to hell with Adam.

She sat and took the damn thing off. It was a simple device, a hardwood peg screwed into a flat, round top, then a piece of rawhide that laced tight onto her leg, with a pad of buffalo hair to act as cushion for the stump. Dr. Richtarsch had feared she didn't have enough leg left below the knee for the rawhide to lace onto, requiring a peg leg that reached up to her thigh, but this one seemed to work.

Lord, her stump felt raw. Maybe she *was* hurrying the process. But she couldn't stand being on crutches a day longer than she had to. She would leave Dodge City looking good. Though she was through with the West— through with it! through with it!—she wouldn't leave until she could look like a lady, not a cripple.

All right, one more circuit of the walls of her room and she would quit. The pain was, well, all that Dr. Richtarsch had predicted it would be. She kept her mind off it by talking to herself about Sheriff Masterson.

Really, she thought some brazenness in the flirtation might solve the problem. Bat Masterson had come back from the chase disgruntled. Adam had given him the slip somehow, and that displeased him. "Pissed him off," as he kept saying earthily. Until Adam showed up and threw her over, Bat seemed not to take the wanted notices to heart. Now he acted like the lover who was thwarted.

She'd gotten a little news from the sheriff. The Cheyennes had been captured and taken to Fort Robinson—

they'd probably be returned to Indian territory immediately. God, she felt for them. She supposed Adam would go with them. Or they would all fight, Adam included, and all would end up dead.

She came to a wall and turned. She hated that infernal clumping noise she made.

Bat should have been thinking of it the other way: it must seem to people that if there was a rivalry, he'd bested his rival. Not that Bat Masterson did think of it that way. He wasn't that interested in her, except as a curiosity. Possibly a one-legged sexual curiosity, morbid thought.

But instead of reveling in his victory, he kept talking about how Adam had kidnapped the Ratz girl and murdered her father right here in Ford County, and he wasn't paid to let people commit mayhem and walk away. He sent telegrams to other sheriffs, and went on and on about putting together another posse, and seemed to be slowed in the chase only by the unnershurriff's reminders that the voters of Ford County wouldn't favor spending a lot of money to chase one single, scruffy Indian. Really, Bat was being immature about it.

She hurt badly now. Another length of wall and she could collapse onto her chair and get the damn thing off.

So maybe she could distract Bat. A little flirtation certainly wouldn't hurt, especially now that she was a divorced woman. She wouldn't let that little morbid thought affect her.

It was damned queer. First Smith felt as though he couldn't speak English. As he rode the last miles toward the Lost Chokecherry camp, he felt peaceful, somehow. Now he was free of the torments. Now he had said good-bye to Elaine. Now he had an answer. But the queer part was, he'd never had a question.

The answer was, See Raven and ask for help in making the sacrifice.

The answer was, Give your flesh and your blood to the sun.

He knew, somehow, deep inside himself, not to question why that was the answer. He knew he must simply do it.

≈   2   ≈

Bat Masterson knocked apart some packing-crate material
in a hurry to build a fire in the potbellied stove.

Really, they were very lucky. The weather had been
pretty this Christmas morning. Elaine and Bat Masterson,
both far from their families, had planned a ride to celebrate
the festive day, and a picnic to cap it off, though she made
him promise no gifts, from either of them. When they were
ready to leave, it looked a little gray, but nothing to fret
about. A couple of slow miles out, the wind had come up
and the snow began to come down with a gritty determination.

They took shelter in this empty house. According to
Bat Masterson, the man of the house came alone in late
summer and built it for his family, not just a cabin but a real
post-and-beam house. Two months ago he went back to
Kansas City on the train to get them and hadn't been seen
since. Domestic strife, maybe. "I'm not going to give up
Kansas City for horizons filled with cow manure, Henry."

The house had no furniture except for packing crates to
sit on, but it was new, and did have windows to keep the
wind and snow out, and the stove. She had gotten badly
chilled in the last few minutes outside, so the fire would
help a lot. And they would eat their picnic inside, that's all.

She was overtired again, and her stump hurt like hell.
But she had to learn to ride—she refused to be a shut-in.

"Here," said Bat, "warm up with this," and held out a
flask.

"No, thanks," she said.

"Medicinal," he insisted, shaking it at her. "You need
it."

She shrugged, took the flask, tilted it, and swigged.

Acchh! She didn't know how men could stand the taste of whiskey. But the burn felt kind of good in her throat.

She pegged painfully over to the window and gazed into the snowstorm. It had become a full-scale plains blizzard. She wondered if they could get the wagon back to town, or if the drifts would stop them. If so, she would make Bat Masterson ride the draft horse and they would force their way through the two miles of drifts. Elaine wasn't going to stay out overnight and let Mrs. Yancey, at the boardinghouse, make her out to be a slut.

Ironic. She'd enticed Bat Masterson into promising her a Christmas-day picnic partly to control him. A courting sheriff couldn't be chasing after an ex-husband. Now Smith's trail was covered with snow, anyway, and she was very much in Bat Masterson's control.

The fire was crackling now. Bat spread out the blankets from the surrey next to the stove, and she laid out the picnic lunch she'd gotten from the hotel.

She had to get off her peg—it was killing her. She used a crate to lower herself to the floor, and then leaned back against it.

Bat Masterson ate avidly, as she'd expected, in an almost predatory way. Though he seemed to think he maintained decorum, he attacked the food like a trencher-man, ripping meat off a drumstick with his teeth, scooping up potato salad, gobbling buttered rolls whole. And all the while gulping it down with a kind of grim concentration, without a word.

Underneath your gentle manner, thought Elaine, you are no gentleman, Bat Masterson. She would have to be careful of him.

"Sheriff," she said in a carefully modulated voice, "would you turn your back? My peg is hurting and I must remove it."

The way his eyes glinted, she really must be careful of him. Right now. He turned away. She lifted her skirt, unlaced the rawhide strap, slipped the peg off—what a relief!—and set it on the crate.

She had to admit she thrived on his attention these

days. She saw no one else in Dodge except Dr. Richtarsch. And a lady could enjoy the warmth of the flame without getting burned.

"Thank you, Sheriff," she said formally. And Bat Masterson turned back and looked at her with his hunter's eyes.

She must be careful. Outside the snow swirled down thickly and the wind howled and they really might not be able to get to town tonight.

The first words of out Lisette's mouth were, "Do you want to eat?" Smith smiled to himself. They had rigged a lean-to with some brush and covered it with his paulic, which Lisette called by its proper name, tarpaulin. He sat behind the fire pit in the position of the man of the lodge, poor as the lodge was, and she handed him elk stew.

His other women kept shy eyes on him to see whether he needed anything. When he had eaten, Hindy brought him his pipe, with a little real tobacco, Navy plug. He had no idea where she'd gotten such a luxury, but simply accepted it with a smile.

As his smoke filled the little lean-to, he contemplated his family situation. He felt good about Hindy. She was getting rounder, more a woman and less a pubescent girl, and she had steadily gotten more and more comfortable with the Human Beings. He wasn't surprised. She had been deprived of family, really, for a couple of years, and had never had the experience of community. Now, abruptly, she had both, and she embraced them thirstily. Before long, though he had just acquired his first daughter, he would have to marry her off. To a Cheyenne, of course. He smiled at that idea.

Rain was beautiful. Though still thin, she no longer looked haggard. She now had a certain maternal radiance to enhance her ethereal innocence. At the moment she was feeding Big Soldier, a lusty-looking little boy—he'd gotten past his low birth weight just fine.

Smith eyed Rain in a new way. Maybe his mother was right. Maybe he should take Rain as a wife. He'd rejected the idea once, but that was before he divorced Elaine. Not that Rain, or Lisette, would care that Smith already had one wife. He did care for Rain. He didn't love her, not in what the white man thought of as a romantic way. He didn't lust after her either, but he knew he could feel desire for her in other circumstances. Anyway, there would be no need for sex between them for some time, even forever. Not with a marriage that was essentially a gesture of being his family's keeper. Maybe it was a good idea. He had in his lodge a mother and a daughter, but no wife and no son. Yet here were wife and son, waiting for him, beckoning to him. Maybe life was telling him something.

He tapped the ashes from his pipe into the fire. Whatever he decided about that, first he needed to get his spirit righted. He stood and walked through the camp, a damn poor camp, he noticed again, to the wickiup of Raven.

They sat and smoked—Smith made a gift of the real tobacco. They spoke politely of matters other than Smith's reason for coming. At last, pipes finished, Smith began. "Grandfather, will you help me make the sacrifice of the piercing? I want to thank Maheo for bringing me back to my people. And for bringing the people back almost to home, the Powder River country."

Raven sat silent. He understood. He understood that Smith asked him because he and Sings Wolf had been friends, and Raven would know Sings Wolf's respect for Smith. He may have understood that Smith wanted to commit himself to being Cheyenne. He did understand that Smith wanted to bring back to the people a sacred gesture that had been missing for several years, one generally made during the medicine-lodge ceremony and possibly at other times. And Raven thought this reminder would be good for the people.

Smith watched Raven ponder. It was strange to Smith

how clearly and simply he felt the need to make this sacrifice. It was the answer to the question he had not asked. It was his statement to his people, and to the white world: I am a man of the Tsistsistas-Suhtaio. Somehow it was his way of laying down his old life and beginning a new one.

Ironic, then, or maybe suitable, that the winter solstice would be in the next day or two, and Christmas a few days later.

What disturbed Smith was how confused and fearful he felt as he came to Raven. He might have described himself as a man suspended between the worlds of white and red man, a physician not accepted by his people, an employee condemned by the Indian Bureau, a man without a home, a man recently divorced. He would have said he had no future: he could not truly become an Indian who went back to the blanket, for that would be a pretense. He could not go to, say, Kansas City and become an affluent physician, a pointless existence. But all these difficulties were not the entire point. In himself he felt more than could be explained by circumstances, a mysterious and pervasive uneasiness of spirit. He was bewildered. He was in pain.

Raven nodded and said, "We will go tomorrow. Four days. Say nothing of it to the people."

Raven didn't need to tell Smith not to talk. Later, Smith thought, everyone will see the scars, and rejoice.

Four days. A sacred number. And a number longer than many guides would have chosen. Maybe Raven wanted Smith to prove something to him. Maybe Raven wanted Smith to prove something to himself. Yes, thought Smith. Yes, I will.

He didn't know whether he was worthy to pass the test. He didn't know what he wanted from the sacrifice, what sort of man he wanted to become. He only knew that his old life caused him pain. That he must pass through it and into a new life.

He was scared.

* * *

"Tell me about your stump," said Bat Masterson. They were sitting together up on the crate now, and her stump lay between them, a lump under her skirt.

Elaine looked at him, and she supposed he must find the expression on her face very odd. His word *stump* seemed so brutal, yet mentioning it was kind. Among other things, she knew that she did want to tell someone about it. Dr. Richtarsch answered her questions, which wasn't the same at all.

So after one very deep breath, and then one more, Elaine began to talk to Bat Masterson about her stump. She told him how it didn't feel like a stump—it felt like a leg. Her missing foot still got hot and cold. She could almost wiggle its toes. She told him how it constantly fooled her for balance. Simple heft was missing, and that could easily make her fall over when she got into or out of a chair without her crutches, or on or off her bed.

She told him how terribly it hurt when she walked on her peg. That's why she didn't walk on the peg in public yet, she just practiced in her room, and wore it when she rode.

She even surprised herself: she told him how it leaked fluids, thin stuff with traces of blood in it, and dirtied her bandages and sometimes her skirts. She went further: she told him how she worried about its smelling.

She recovered by saying, quakingly, that she intended to be the most graceful woman—person!—ever with one leg.

Bat Masterson reached out and took one of her hands in both his big paws. She let him take it. Then he switched and held each of her hands. Meanwhile he looked at her in the most extraordinary way, his gray-blue eyes now tender and full of understanding.

"I want to touch your stump," he said.

She meant to say no, but her eyes flooded with tears, and the words caught in her throat.

He lifted her skirt a couple of inches and exposed the awful nub end of her leg. He looked at it for a long moment. She thought of the coarse, reddened, folded skin he was looking at, and shuddered. He glanced up at her gently. And he put his hand softly on the stump.

Elaine wept without a sound, tears flooding down her cheeks.

Raven chose a dead cottonwood half a day's walk from camp. It stood by the creek, blighted, its trunk broken off halfway up, its limbs leafless and brittle, its bark gone except for patches that looked like scabs.

Four days, Raven had said. Four days Smith would go without food, water, and sleep. Four days he would dance facing the sun, tied to this tree, the flesh of his chest skewered. At the end of the fourth day he would lean back against the rawhide and jerk the wooden pegs out through his skin. Then his sacrifice would be complete, and Raven would bury Smith's torn flesh at the base of the tree, and he could sleep there.

They said a man making the sacrifice of the piercing sometimes got a vision at the end of the ceremony while he slept. He wondered whether his unworthiness would deprive him of the vision. He wondered if his white-man blood would deprive him. He wondered if dancing during the shortest days of the year, the darkness nearly twice as long as the sunlight, would diminish the sacrifice.

He looked at the sun, low in the south. Though today or tomorrow must be the turning of the winter sun, when it got as low in the sky as it could and the earth moved into winter and toward spring, today was a day of what the whites called Indian summer, warm and mild. It was as though it kept its strength to watch his sacrifice.

Raven drew his knife and motioned for Smith to lie

down. He stretched out on the ground and closed his eyes.
He felt Raven's shadow block out the winter sun as his
guide knelt over him. Smith took a deep breath. "Cut
deep," Smith asked. He knew that many men made that
request as a sign of courage, and that it was seldom granted.
He felt the skin above his left nipple pinched up and he
began to let the breath out.

Raven's knife pierced his chest, and the world was
pain. While he was in the eruption of pain, the piercing was
repeated above his right nipple. Then the wooden skewers
were inserted, left and right.

"All right," said Raven. Smith knew that meant he
must open his eyes and begin. He felt too shaken to stand,
too weak to speak in protest.

Smith got to his knees and then his feet, shakily. He
stared at the sun and let his eyes go out of focus. He knew
he didn't have a chance under the skies of lasting four days.
Nevertheless he began to shuffle his feet in the eternal
dance to the sun.

Now Bat Masterson sat close to her, one arm around
her shoulders in support. Her stump was still exposed, and
she couldn't stop talking, rambling half coherently. The
content didn't feel important. To be leaning against him, to
be held a little, to be telling him the truth, that was
important.

She spoke of her family and her future. She would go
back to the Hampton Institute, she said, where she could
teach Indian children again. Probably she would even go on
a fund-raising lecture tour and speak of her experiences
among the Cheyennes and their need of education. On the
tour, she claimed, she would use her peg leg to excellent
advantage. And maybe she would write a book, an appeal
for help for the Western Indians.

She realized she was being silly, talking on and on, but
it felt good, and evidently Bat Masterson liked listening. If

he thought her a sentimental fool, he was considerate enough not to say so.

She was waiting, she said, for the dreams about her leg to cease. Almost every night she dreamed that she was walking, walking normally, on two legs, and her right foot was suddenly missing below the knee—or clear up to the hip!—and she came suddenly crashing down. She always woke up with a horrible start, in her bed.

He reached out again and laid his hand gently on her stump. It felt like a healing touch, a blessing with a hint of miracle, and she accepted it gratefully. She laid her head on his shoulder. She told him softly that she also had dreams— she'd never have thought she'd tell anybody this—where worms crawled into the end of her leg and up little blood vessels toward her heart.

He kissed her forehead gently. She didn't stop him, and she knew that was a mistake, but she liked the kiss some, and she very much liked everything else.

She put a hand up to touch her mouth and ease it away a little, but he took her hand in his and held it to his chest. He lifted her chin. He kissed her on the lips. She waited, paid attention, explored to discover whether she wanted to kiss him back.

He touched her right nipple through her dress. The sensation was incredibly intense. He circled it lightly, teasingly, and she gasped. She circled his neck with one arm and began to kiss him back.

He unbuttoned her bodice and touched delicately the skin where her breasts began to rise. She lay back in his arm and kissed him. Elaine realized that she was weeping with gratitude.

Adam Smith Maclean, born to Robert Burns Maclean, a Scots fur trader, and named for a great Scots political philosopher—Adam Smith Maclean, son of Annemarie Charbonneau Maclean, a Cheyenne woman sired by the

French-Canadian fur man Toussaint Charbonneau and out
of an Assiniboin woman; son also of Lisette Genet Maclean,
of Sioux and French-Canadian blood—Adam Smith Maclean, an Indian trader, a Cheyenne warrior, a college
graduate, a doctor of medicine—Adam Smith Maclean
danced naked before the sun.

He danced for the sun. He danced into the sun. He
danced to become the sun.

His eyes swam in its light. They were red, unfocused,
drooped, blinded by the weak, amber light of the pale sun
from its winter-solstice low. They were exhausted, glazed,
seeing nothing.

Smith's body was attached to the dead cottonwood by
strips of rawhide. The strips were tied to the skewers that
penetrated his chest, and to the tree. The blood on his
chest, belly, and legs was dried and scaly. Occasionally
fresh blood seeped downward from his wounds, forming on
the old blood a red goo.

He was exhausted and was mired in his exhaustion. He
was wake-dreaming of pistons, the huge pistons of the
engine of a steamship that he had once toured in Boston
Harbor. His legs felt as those pistons had looked, astonish-
ingly massive and heavy, geared to rotate up with patience-
straining slowness, to change direction invisibly at the
apex, and by the tiniest degrees to descend. His legs were
approaching immobility. There in front of the tree, in front
of Maheo, Smith would soon lift his legs and set them down
more and more slowly, until he changed only at the rate
flesh rots, and the wind turns rocks to dust.

Time moved by just as slowly—even more slowly—
and he had given up hope of this day's ever reaching noon,
much less sundown.

And then he saw: he was covered with blood, deluged
in it, not only his chest but his hair, his face and neck, his
belly and groin and legs. He was inundated with his own
blood. And standing in it. His feet squished feebly in what
felt like muck, but it was blood, his vital force mixed with
the dirt. Every moment it was deeper, every moment it
sucked his legs deeper, and soon he would be swallowed, to

his waist, to his neck, to his nostrils, until he drowned in his own blood.

On this third day of his sacrifice, exhausted, starved, desperate with thirst and fatigue, Smith danced through the strangest and most exotic lands of consciousness. Sometimes he had vivid dreams while fully awake: Once he nearly got trampled by horses in Boston. He lay in the road and the horses pounded toward him, pulling their carriage, but they never arrived—they started toward him again, and again, rampaging endlessly toward him, trying timelessly to stomp him into the dust, and never arriving.

Another time he went on a long trip with his mother Annemarie up into the Yellowstone country. They were looking for something, he wasn't sure what, though sometimes he wondered if it was his father's body. The landscape turned crazy on them—not merely hot springs that killed the nearby trees and wrapped them with winding sheets of minerals, and queer geysers, but a mountain where everything was dead—grasses, trees, elk, even the birds had turned to stone. It was a place of sorrow, worse than death, because truly lifeless.

Sometimes he heard music, cosmic music from no instruments that ever existed, ethereal, unimaginably beautiful, and utterly indescribable.

Sometimes he fell ceaselessly through freezing clouds, his hands and feet turned blue, his breath turned to rime all over his body, and he felt himself suffocating.

Occasionally, as now, he felt light-footed, and charged with a buoyant and infinite energy. Dancing, he could feel time pass magically, minutes singing by in a simple lifting and descent of one foot. The foot would rise as gently as fog lifts, stay in the air as long as a leaf takes to unfurl in spring, and fall to earth as lightly as midsummer sunbeams alight.

Sometimes not merely his foot but his entire body rose delicately into the air, and his feet trod softly through space, like milkweed floating. When these moments came, he would take deep rest, and refresh himself for his eternal dance into the sun, his dance that would end when he melded into his life-giving father.

They were beautiful to Smith, these infinitely nuanced movements that allowed time to sing by. By this miraculous power given by his sun father, he might dance from the sun's midpoint to its setting in half a dozen steps.

Not that he had the strength to last a single step of this dancing—his strength, though he was tall and well muscled, his strength had failed. Now he continued through the energy brought him by the all-giving sun, and during the night by the sun's daughter, the moon.

The Tsistsistas-Suhtaio said that all life and strength came from the sun. Smith was a scientist—he was many things, too many, but scientist was one of them—so he knew in more secular terms that all life and power on earth came from the sun. Now he knew it in a new way, resoundingly personal, infinitely precious, and for the first time the knowledge was truly his.

He had given up his own power. His legs and arms and body had wearied and fallen. Without food, without water, with only an occasional brief rest, he was dancing, dancing the sun and moon around the sky. He had surrendered to the sun, and it had entered his flesh and his bones and energized them endlessly in this gentle, lovely, lilting dance. Sometimes, his eyes closed, he felt that he rose directly into a shaft of the sun's light and danced there weightless, suspended, a mote of dust in the air. Sometimes he felt that he traveled immense distances on one of the beams, off the earth and past the clouds and beyond the atmosphere, toward the sun father itself. Always something would bring him back to the world, perhaps the gentle reminder of his guide Raven to open his eyes and gaze into the sun. And for that reminder and his return to earth, Smith was grateful.

With pristine inner eyes, Smith saw the earth as bountiful, as nourishing, as his beloved mother. Perhaps earth was not the only world to live in—Sehan, the trail of the Milky Way that lay beyond death, was said to be a good place—but he loved the earth, loved its grasses and its trees, its various beasts, its vast seas, its overarching skies, and particularly its flowing streams, fecund with life, ceaseless in motion, brilliant with reflections of the sky and the sun. Most of all he loved its people. For the first time he saw their trials, their struggles, their enmities, their pain and confusion for the mere thrashings of the spirit they were, unnecessary, futile, to be shed like a cocoon so a human being could take to the air and then look back on his struggling self with pity and affection.

Now Smith loved everyone, his father especially, both his mothers, his sister who had become a town wife, his brother and sister who walked the Milky Way trail, his grandfather Sings Wolf, recently lost, his deceased uncle-friend Jim Sykes, called the Man Who Doesn't Stir Air When He Walks, his other uncle-friend, the Jew known as Peddler, his favorite teachers at college, his comrades there. He loved also those he had hated, Nelly Burns, Twist, and the man who killed his father and his brother, Owen Mackenzie. He loved even the one who had hurt him most, Elaine Cummings Maclean. He pronounced in his mind his infinite benediction on them all and wished they could hear it. It is well, he said to them, it is well.

When my eyes ceased to see, he thought, I began to see.

The time came at the end of the fourth day. It was the day Smith thought was Christmas Day, the fourth day of the new winter, the winter the whites would call 1879. He danced all day, as he had the three days before—a cosmic dance not on the earth, or toward the majestic sun, that king of kings, that lord of hosts, but in and out of manifold and unimaginable worlds of the spirit. Long ago his body had surrendered. But his spirit, energized by the sun, danced the body onward, and the spirit mounted on wings.

But now the sun was setting for the fourth time of his sacrifice, setting not in a flaming eruption of glory, but in a quiet glow of amber light on scudding clouds, a wan light, like the sun on wet river rocks. Straight to the south and on east, heavy, dark clouds blocked the sky, and Smith thought that the cattle towns of western Kansas must be getting a snowstorm. It was truly winter.

He directed his mind back to the matter at hand. A couple of minutes ago, Raven had said, "It is time to break loose from the pole."

That meant he must do what he had dreaded for all four days—lean back against the rawhide thongs that attached his chest to the sacred cottonwood. He must hurl himself backward. He must rip the skewers from his breast.

He feared that fear might keep him from using his full strength to tear the skewers out. He feared fainting from the pain. He feared even more that he might faint before the skewers tore through, and then he would have to throw his weight against the crazy, stretching strength of his skin over and over, the flesh pulling away from the muscle beneath but not breaking. He had seen that happen at the sun dance.

Therefore, coward that he was, Smith walked forward slowly toward the bare cottonwood, and then ran backward a few steps, testing. Yes, his legs would carry him backward at a run a little. He tested a few backward steps again and decided that he could summon more strength—that father sun would grant him more strength—than he thought he had.

He stepped backward until the rawhide strips were nearly taut. He reached down and aligned three stones leading to that spot so he could anticipate the moment of tautness accurately.

He walked forward all the way to the cottonwood. Then, at first slowly, he began trotting backward. Then faster. Then desperately fast. For an instant the thought shot through him that his strength was failing. Then he saw the first of the stones. He took two decisive steps backward, the most vigorous he could manage, threw his arms backward, hurled his entire body into the air. From mid-air he knew nothing more but pain.

Smith woke up to find Raven cutting the ripped flesh from his chest. Smith knew Raven would bury it at the base of the naked tree. He let himself drift into unconsciousness again.

He woke once more when he felt water pouring into his mouth. Smith drank the sweet liquid, the milk of the breast of his mother the earth. Raven bathed Smith's face a little in it, and laid his head down, and covered him with a blanket.

"Take just this for now," Raven said. He spooned a little broth of some kind into Smith's mouth. "Sleep," he said. "Sleep." The word seemed indescribably seductive.

He slept. He dreamed. He dreamed of the substance he loved most on the earth, water, flowing water.

Elaine watched Bat Masterson's lips as he sucked her nipple and played with it lightly with his tongue. His was a well-formed head, and she liked the sight of it. And he was making a sensual tide flood through her body.

She lay on the blankets from the carriage, the top half of her dress pushed down to her stomach and the bottom half, she feared, pulled up to her belly. Why not? she said to herself wildly. Why not? She had never felt so mad before.

He kissed her belly, kissed it over and over again. Then he slowly, teasingly pulled out the bow knot that kept her bloomers up—it felt incredibly sensual—and gently pulled them down. If she felt a little like an animal being field-dressed, she had not known how delectable it could be to be maneuvered and subjected to a man's will, a mere thing of his pleasure. He touched her between her legs and sent an electric rage through her.

He knelt between her legs—now she was lost. He lowered his trousers, and came onto her, and kissed her, and she kissed him back, and crazily a voice that belonged to her said into his dark mustache, "No."

She stiffened.

"No," she said again. It just came out. "Please no." She knew she'd thought of her juggler.

Bat Masterson wriggled on her, and she yearned for him to be in her. It wasn't fair.

"No!" she said, louder. Thank you, juggler.

He wriggled, and it was almost too late.

She rocked to one side. He held on and locked his eyes fiercely on hers. She rocked again and got a little breathing room. "Sheriff, I've decided to say no. Please."

Something murky moved through his predatory eyes. For a moment she was afraid, sharply afraid. Then he rose onto his knees and stood, half-naked and tumescent, over her.

In a few moments she made herself decent. She rolled onto her one fit knee and looked at the window. She held out her hand to Bat Masterson and said softly, "Would you help me to the window, please?" He supported her in a gentlemanly way.

This Christmas evening was terrible—at least she supposed it was evening. She could see nothing but the snow slanting horizontal in the wind, no earth, no sky, no light. The snow was an indeterminate gray white, and she couldn't even tell if the sun was still up. The surrey, parked just a few steps away, was invisible. Snow was drifted high against the front steps.

Elaine shook violently.

Suddenly she felt weary beyond weary. She wanted to sleep and knew there was no hope of getting back to town tonight. Well, to hell with her reputation. She and Bat Masterson would need each other to stay warm.

She turned to him and searched his face. How was he responding to being refused? Would he resort to force? She could only wonder.

"Sheriff," she said, "would you build the fire up? Then lie next to me and hold me? *Just* hold me?"

Miraculously, he did. She snuggled against him and wept quietly.

After dawn Smith awoke. Raven sat beside him, patient, watchful, waiting. Smith kept his head still and looked around. The mundane earth surrounded him, the simple hills and rocks he had seen here four days ago. That seemed reassuring. He wasn't dreaming. He was glad to see the world again, and sorry to leave the world of his dreams.

He took the canteen from Raven, a stolen army canteen, he noticed, and drank long and deep. Water, he thought with satisfaction. He had dreamed and dreamed of flowing water.

It was time to go back to the tribe now. He had made his sacrifice. He had seen his dreams. He did feel in a way new, aware of something emergent in himself, like a pupa becoming a new creature. He smiled strangely. He was pregnant, and about to give birth to himself. The idea made him laugh a little. It also made him feel quivery, sometimes exhilarated, sometimes downright afraid.

Elaine fought slumping in the hard chair in Vernon May's office. She was tired—she forbade herself to use the word *exhausted*. She had traveled two days on the train to get to Omaha from Dodge City. At least she was through with that stockyard town and the attentions, all too persistent and all too pleasant, of Sheriff Bat Masterson. Dear Sheriff Masterson. He had never stopped trying, in his amiable way. She did not resent it, but she did not want carnal knowledge of him. To her carnal knowledge meant Adam. Maybe that would change someday.

For now she was alone, and it was darned hard. She had to go to bed and get up alone. Eat alone. Manage her valise and change trains and get to a boardinghouse alone, and get to this office today. All the while her damned stump hurt mercilessly, a stern forecast of what the half century of the rest of her life was going to be like.

A few days here, only three, she hoped, and she could go home. Home sounded wonderful right now.

A woman about her age sat across from Elaine, pale and drawn and clutching her arms as though she was freezing. Elaine could hear the muffled voices of a child and a man in the next room, presumably this woman's child and Mr. Vernon May. She wondered what sort of ghoul Vernon May must be, to choose a life of working with mangled limbs. Not as strange as being an undertaker, but ghoulish, still.

Then the little boy came out in Vernon May's arms, laughing and whomping Mr. May on the head with his new wooden arm. Amazing. The child's mother went to take the boy into her arms, and the kid posed the arm for her—he was proud of it, at least for the moment. So maybe Vernon

May was a pied piper. How had he persuaded a child of
about seven, facing a tragedy, to look at it so cheerfully? A
wonderful, man surely.

When the boy and his mother left the waiting room,
Elaine stood with difficulty, shook the man's hand, and
introduced herself. "Elaine Cummings." She had decided
to use her maiden name, like the proud suffragist she was.
She went on, "You must be a miracle worker."

Mr. May looked at her with compassionate eyes. "No
miracles, I'm afraid. We *can* make many of you more
comfortable." He held out his hand for her to go through
into the examining room before him. He had a cute bald
spot reddened by the plains sun. Stumping forward in some
pain, Elaine wondered how anyone could spend his life
facing people who'd lost their arms or legs and stay as
cheerful as Mr. May. Working with cripples, substituting
wooden arms and legs for the limbs God gave them—Ugh!

He put her onto a table and began to unstrap her peg.
She knew only a little about him from Dr. Richtarsch.
During the Rebellion Richtarsch had amputated limbs with
compound fractures routinely, as was the custom at that
time, since infection otherwise killed the patients. He had
an orderly with a knack for making the soldiers' wooden
pegs a lot more comfortable—Vernon May. Mr. May made
wax impressions of the stumps, with all their quirky
irregularities, and then carved, filed, and sanded a block of
wood to sit atop the peg and fit the stump most elegantly,
said Dr. Richtarsch. "Quite a skill that chap has." After the
war, Richtarsch and other army surgeons encouraged him
to set up a private practice and told other physicians about
him. In the end Mr. May relocated to Omaha, which
amused Elaine, because he spoke the sharp accent of the
street kids of New York City.

He inspected her peg and told her that he would make
the wax impression now, and she could keep using the
buffalo-hide padding if she wanted. For the moment she
should just relax.

But Elaine couldn't relax. Every touch on her stump
seemed irritating as the shock she'd felt in the electric

machine at school. So she finally asked for something to read while he worked, anything, as a distraction. Mr. May handed her the *Omaha Herald*. And there—she jumped when she saw it.

Smith sat stripped to his breechcloth before the fire in his brush lodge, smoking and staring into the flames. He touched the big scabs on his chest, which itched. He didn't care if his women thought him strange, half-naked in the middle of winter. He was bothered. He had been fretting all day about what his sacrifice meant, whether his dreams had been a vision, what he had brought back from his days in the wilderness of spirit, what he had learned that might inform the inner circle that represented his life, the outer circle of the life of his family, and the outermost circle, the life of his people. So far he could see nothing.

He chuckled bitterly to himself. His people's life was utterly blighted—half of them here hiding from the soldiers, poor, hungry, and half-naked, the other half captured and imprisoned at Fort Robinson until they could be herded back, like livestock, to a country they hated.

His own life, if anything, seemed to him more blighted. He had no wife, no proper family, no true people, no culture he belonged to, no country. He was a man of many parts, too many, too various, and ill-fitted. He was equally spattered with the blood of the battlefield and of the hospital ward—his fingers had peeled off the scalp and had tied off the bleeding vein. His ears and feet loved the music of the song of the scalp dance, and of the Frenchie's fiddle, and of waltzes he had heard in Boston drawing rooms. He liked his Prince Albert coat, and liked as well his reddish black hair worn long to his shoulders with the deerskin pouch braided into it. He was a mess.

He was cursing himself, too. He had pondered something truly stupid—trying to kill his white-man self, becoming a true blanket Indian. It was stupid because he couldn't change the way his very mind worked. Every flow of water, every rolling pebble brought gravity to consciousness. Every sunrise and sunset reminded him of Copernicus. A compass suggested magnetism. A watch was to him not a mystic revelator but a tool ingeniously constructed of springs and weight and counterbalances—and he loved the ingenuity that so constructed it.

Stupid. Father, he said inside himself, I apologize.

Mother, he thought, picturing Annemarie in the trading post at the mouth of the Little Powder River, I will see you in the spring. Right now he took no joy in this prospect.

God, if he could only stop his mind from churning. What did his women think? Why had he failed at the sacrifice? Had he actually failed at his sacrifice—or was he looking for the wrong result, looking to get instead of give? Why did he feel so confused?

He stood up abruptly. He had an idea. He would stop his damned mind from rolling over and over restlessly. He went outside.

It was dark. Most people probably were eating now. He wouldn't be seen.

He walked down to the small lake. It wasn't quite frozen—the ice was thin and patchy. He walked a quarter of the way around the lake and clambered out onto a big rock that extended a dozen feet into the lake. Quickly he threw off his breechcloth and leggings and leaped into the lake.

He reeled. He yearned for something hard to hold on to, lest he fall off the circling earth. He thought he was bellowing, but then realized nothing was coming from his mouth but the hiss of his own breath.

He got the use of some of his limbs back and scrambled out.

God*damn*, he was cold. He chafed his chest and arms with his big hands. He'd never done the plunge except after a sweat bath. Until now. What a difference.

He started walking back toward his hut. He would warm up in his blankets, then eat a little, and then juggle. The thought of the ceaseless motion of the round balls pleased him.

It worked, he thought. I intimidated my mind into switching off for a while.

CHEYENNE OUTBREAK AT FORT ROBINSON

Elaine's fingers clawed at the edge of the paper unconsciously as she read.

The Cheyennes had broken out of a barracks they'd been imprisoned in at Camp Robinson, Nebraska, in a hopeless situation, and many were dead. Trying to give their families a chance to get away, twenty-one men were killed in the first ten minutes of the outbreak. Nine women and children also died in the first minutes.

The newspaper ripped down the middle on one page. Elaine hadn't known she was gripping it so hard. She held the torn edges together and skimmed the article for a list of the dead, and Adam's name. Nothing.

More than a hundred escapees—why not more than two hundred? Had half of them died? She forced herself to push away the thought of the ones she cared for individually, didn't permit herself to wonder whether the dead were Lisette, Rain and Big Soldier, Sings Wolf, and Adam.

They fled, the *Herald* said, without winter clothing, blankets, or food, and almost unarmed, through an unusually bitter Nebraska winter. It was assumed they would try to get to the Sioux reservation at Pine Ridge, South Dakota, and ask Red Cloud for shelter. They were judged by people who knew the country to have no chance at all of defying the elements and escaping the army long enough to reach Red Cloud.

Elaine let a wave of dizziness pass.

The Cheyennes had broken out of the barracks where they'd been held because the commanding officer, Captain Wessells, known as "the Little Flying Dutchman," had deprived all of them, men, women, and children, of food for four days, and of water for another.

"Bastard," snapped Elaine, and Vernon May shot her the oddest look over the wax he was molding.

Wessells said his intention was to make the Cheyennes agree to go back to Indian territory, as ordered by the Interior Department.

These Indians, though, had run away from their reservation there in September and astounded the civilized world by fighting their way against overwhelming odds all the way to the country where they wanted their reservation, near their Sioux relatives.

Despite this proof, Wessells evidently underestimated their resolve. They chose to die rather than to leave their home country.

Here was a speech by Morning Star. Why the hell was there no mention of Little Wolf? Was Adam among the escapees or not? Among the dead or the living?

"We bowed to the will of the Great Father," Morning Star said, "and we went far into the south where he told us to go. There we found that a Cheyenne cannot live. We belong here. Many times you promised us an agency, but you only took us far to the south country, saying, 'Go and see. You can come back.' Then when we were dying there, and sick for our home, you said that was a mistake, that we must stay because everything was changed. You are now the many and we are the few, but we know that it is better to die fighting on the way to our old home than to perish of the sicknesses."

Elaine was surprised that the newspaper printed this speech. Hadn't Morning Star and Little Wolf told the whites the same thing all last summer in Indian territory? Hadn't they demonstrated it beyond doubt by striking out for home? Old news.

Where in the hell was Adam?

One straw to grasp: Dr. Moseley, caring for the wounded in the post hospital, said, "The will to live runs strong in these people."

Elaine finally realized the *Herald* Mr. May gave her was a week old. She would have the livery service take her to the office of the *Herald,* wherever it was, and read

everything. God, when would Mr. May finish with this
damn mold?

Smith juggled. Then he slept a few hours, ate a little
more, and juggled again in the dark. He could sense the
dawn coming.

He loved the feel of the ivory balls in his hands,
smooth, hard, unforgivingly round, in their way sensual.
And he loved the eternal motion of his hands. He wondered
if he could juggle forever and never drop a ball. He wanted
to go on forever.

And as Smith juggled toward his forever, an awareness
came to him, stealthily yet fully, like a person who did not
enter a room but is just suddenly there, standing palpable
by a window.

He became aware that he heard new inner music. That
was odd, because he had never known that he heard inner
music. Yet it was clear. He heard an inner music that was,
well . . . He couldn't say. Whatever it was, it was him. He
was different.

He wondered idly where this new inner music would
lead him, whether he should dare to follow it. And at that
he laughed at himself out loud. He couldn't choose to follow
it or not to follow it anywhere. It was within him. He might
be able to turn it off—turn it off with that damned dialogue
in his head!—but then he would simply be not listening.
There was no other music to hear.

It was so important, and yet natural and commonplace,
that he kept his mind on his juggling, his eyes a little
glazed. Perhaps some other awareness would come to him,
full-blown as from the head of Zeus.

It didn't. But he got an idea to do something. The
predawn light gave him the urge.

He went outside, looked around the valley lit lilac by
the coming sun, drew the cold of a winter dawn into his
lungs. And then he began to sing. It was a song he'd first

heard sitting beside his father twenty years ago, a song sung then by an old man, a way of saying thank you, Maheo, for a long and fruitful life. He had wondered at the song then, not understanding. He had heard it on dozens of dawns in his life—it was a common song. For the first time he wanted to sing out its blessing.

> He, our father,
> He has shown his mercy unto me.
> I walk the straight road.

He sang it slowly, lingeringly, with feeling. And for the first time since his wedding day, he felt light-hearted.

George Miller, the editor of the Omaha *Herald*, a rakish-looking young fellow, was gracious to Elaine. He not only showed her what had appeared in his newspaper about the Cheyenne outbreak at Fort Robinson, he handed her a file folder of telegraph sheets and clippings from other papers. "The death dance of the Cheyennes," he said with glinting eyes and ironic smile, "is big news."

She read for nearly an hour, in tears the entire time. The Cheyennes had broken out at night. Aside from the thirty dead, thirty-five had been recaptured that first night, mostly women and children. (Almost no names—how maddening!) A leader named Wild Hog had been held apart, and so was "in captivity," like an animal in a zoological garden. Tangle Hair, the Dog Soldier leader, was wounded and recaptured. The army was tracking a large group, three dozen or more said to be led by Little Finger Nail, westward along the bluffs of the White River, where they were hard to ferret out. The whereabouts of Morning Star and his family were unknown. (Why was Nail mentioned and not Little Wolf? Why never a mention of Adam? Wasn't a half-breed doctor newsworthy?)

The rest of the Cheyennes were presumed scattered,

and likely wounded or dead. Scouts were able to find no trace of anyone getting to Red Cloud's camp, sixty miles to the northwest. Without food, clothing, and blankets, the Indians wouldn't be able to hold out long, the news dispatches agreed.

Some of the news stories spoke of the Cheyennes as an inhuman problem, like beasts enduring a hard winter. A few struck a tone of romantic nostalgia for these "last of the free-roaming Redmen of the Plains." Most seemed more interested in chuckling at the ineptitude of the government than in the human predicament of the Indians. Imagine letting a few starving Indians outwit the U.S. Army! they hooted. Imagine having mismanaged the poor creatures into this embarrassing dilemma!

Mr. Miller had written a ringing editorial about the matter that seemed really to understand the Cheyennes. "They will never return to Indian territory unless tied hand and foot and dragged there like so many dead cattle. It means starvation to them. I implore you for justice and humanity to those wronged red men. Let them stay in their own country."

When Elaine got up to stump to the front door, she thanked Mr. Miller for his editorial. She had to resist touching him on the arm in gratitude.

"Yes," he said in his rapid-fire speech, "this business shows the bankruptcy of Grant's Indian policy. I think the administration will retire next year in humiliation." He smiled wolfishly. "Are you a Democrat?" he asked.

Taken aback, she could think of nothing to say and started for the door. She made a point of walking as gracefully as she could.

"Say," Mr. Miller called after her, "what's your interest in this?"

She spoke simply, without turning around. "My husband is one of the Cheyennes."

He pounced. "Can we talk? Do an interview? Will you make a statement?" He rummaged on a desktop for paper and lead pencil. "Were you there? Did you"—he fumbled for words—"get your injury in the fighting?"

She pegged painfully away from him. She resisted saying, "Human blood and bones to you are just a way to sell newspapers." She shook her head emphatically. "I have nothing to say."

"Then come back tomorrow, will you? There'll be more news tomorrow. It may be over tomorrow."

Elaine tried to incline her head toward him in a way that was polite, and even thankful.

Smith pondered. Raven sat silent, the pipe gone out now, resting on its beaded skin bag in front of the fire.

Though he did not understand, he had the strong feeling that telling Raven his dream was part of his way, part of laying down his old life and taking up the new. And part of his new life was that he was trusting such feelings.

He looked at Raven, the older man's face patient, neutral, leaving the decision entirely to Smith. Yes, he wanted Raven to know what they had wrought together. He wanted what he saw and whatever it meant to be shared, to become part of the power of the Human Beings.

"Yes, I dreamed," he said. "I dreamed of water."

Smith considered for a while and decided to skip over the images that had come to him that night in passing, fragmented, incomplete. "I think water was in all my dreams," he said. "I want to tell you of two episodes that seem like one large one.

"I was in a day of tribulation. I was walking in Bighorn Canyon," which Raven knew was the deep, walled canyon of the Bighorn River above the trading house where Smith grew up. "I had walked along the river for a while, clambering over the boulders on the steep sides, laboring over the various difficulties, never able to move fast, or freely. Then I had to start walking up, up toward the walls. I walked up and up the talus, up further than there was to go, up forever, struggling, slipping back, getting nowhere, and I would never get anywhere. Yet I was doomed to this walk. I knew the doom, felt the hopelessness in every step, and knew I would ever claw my way upward, pointlessly, stupidly.

"Suddenly I came to the rock wall." Raven would know these yellow walls, hundreds of feet high. "The end. Nowhere to go. I had not the courage and energy to cry out. I gave up. I fell to my knees. I put my head down where the gravel met the rock wall, and lay my body down flat on the hard, dry gravel, and wept. Wept and wept.

"And then noticed. At last noticed. Water. I raised my face out of the dirt and looked. Water. Water had sprung forth from where I had laid my head, the barren point where the gravel joined the rock. Water, real, live water.

"I turned and looked. It trickled down toward the river. It made its way around rocks and cactus and across patches of dry sand, and into swales of grass, and past and around and through every sort of obstacle, toward the river. I couldn't see where it flowed into the river.

"I laid down in the water, facedown, full length, tried to get every inch of myself into this little, gorgeous trickle. Facedown, I knew I would suck in the water in a moment, and I would drown. And that was OK, that was even lovely, to drown in this gift of water. And after a few moments, I did suck it in, deeply and confidently, and the miracle took place. I breathed it. It was water, and it gave life, like the air.

"I breathed into that miracle, drew it into my body, wanting to be alive now, truly alive, and the water came into me and over me and washed me completely. It even picked me up and rocked me like a baby. I lolled in it, luxuriated in it, I may even have fallen asleep there, rocking in that water like a great, warm bed.

"When I felt like I was waking up, I was an otter. Not an otter of the river, an otter of the sea, which is similar but bigger. Delicious, so delicious, to be sleek and slender, and agile as the wind. I played. I played. For hours, I cavorted in the water. My mate and cubs came out of our den in the earth and we played together, we darted and did loops and nuzzled against one another and dived through the waves and . . . We were acrobats of the sea.

"I dived down and got something to eat, a creature off the ocean sand with a spiny back called a sea urchin. I brought several up for the cubs and my mate, and one for myself—they were orange, as orange as the yolk of the duck egg. At the same time we plopped them whole into our mouths and got the taste. It was the best taste imaginable. I savored it and closed my eyes and rolled over and over in the water, and over and over again, flying high in the sea, until I had sucked all the taste away.

"And then I looked at my mate with a gigantic eye and whistled raucously at her." Smith smiled at Raven. An otter's whistle was a mating call. "Horny old otter. Horny *young* otter, full of the seed of life and wanting to hump the world full of it." He chuckled at himself, his mind back there feeling horny in the water.

"I have no idea why I was an otter. I had no inkling that there was a message in it. And still have none. I *was* the otter. It felt like . . . just for the crazy, wild-hair, blue-sky joy of being an otter." He looked up at Raven, met his eye, spoke directly. "I felt like that otter feeling was what life . . ." He shook his head firmly. Wrong way.

He thought, and said at last, "Those moments were the most pleasurable of my life. Praise be to Maheo for granting them to me."

The newspapers indicated two days later that it was over, or at least over as a hot news event. Elaine went back to the *Herald* office and pointedly ignored Mr. Miller as she read the stories. Now the accounts were full, dwelling on the bloody details.

The main group of escaped Cheyennes crossed a divide one bitter night and took refuge in some bluffs along Hat Creek. They were led, it said again, by Little Finger Nail, who seemed to Elaine too young for such responsibility. Captain Wessells pounded their position with cannon all the next day, getting no response other than two or three random shots. When he went to inspect the site, expecting to find nothing but tattered corpses, Wessells found nothing. Before the barrage the Cheyennes under Nail had slipped away to the next ridge, unseen.

But the next day the soldiers caught up with them again, this time in a dry gulch known as Warbonnet Creek, in a hole in the cutbank, where the Indians threw up a little breastworks. Since the Cheyennes had no chance, and knew it, Wessells went out front and called to them several times to give up. No answer.

Finally the shooting began, and Little Finger Nail cried out, "If we die, our names will be remembered. They will tell the story and say, 'This is the place.'"

The soldiers fired for about an hour with only a few answering shots—the Cheyennes had almost no ammunition—then went up close to the breastworks and fired through. When no one inside could be living, they jumped on top of the breastworks, but one more shot came, grazing Wessells' head.

The soldiers fell back. From the hole in the cutbank came the high beautiful voice of Finger Nail, singing his death song. Then a few other thin voices joined it.

The soldiers charged the breastworks and cut loose a withering fire. When they fell back, waiting for the smoke to clear, the last three Cheyenne warriors leapt forth brandishing their weapons—Finger Nail, Roman Nose, and Bear. The soldiers dutifully shot them down.

The dead were eighteen men, five women, and two children. Among the bodies lay six other women and children, hurt but alive. Blood stood pooled on the frozen earth.

A soldier looked into the hole and muttered, "God, these people die hard."

The remnant of Cheyennes, the wounded and frozen who had lived when they wanted to die, named that miserable piece of cutbank the Last Hole.

* * *

Elaine Cummings wiped the tears from her eyes and cheeks, gave the spying Mr. Miller a volcanic look, and stumped out.

She had made up her mind.

In the new year, 1879, a couple of weeks after Smith's piercing sacrifice, Raven and Lisette walked through the Cheyenne camp in Lost Chokecherry Valley, speaking quietly to each family in the various brush huts. They walked around about dusk, because people would be assembled at their homes preparing the evening meal, or eating, and the two could find nearly everyone. They didn't walk together, but a little separately, Lisette behind. Raven would come into camp, and the man of the house would offer him the honored seat of the visitor behind the fire. Raven would decline the offer, speak a few more words, and move on. Lisette would step close a few moments later, and likewise speak a few words, and move on.

Raven said to each group of people, "Vekifs has become Whistling Otter." They nodded, and accepted this news with a calm that belied its magnitude. The words meant, the man we knew as Vekifs, the son of Dancer and Annemarie who turned into a white man, has learned by his sacrifice, and the powers have granted him a vision. He has laid down his old life and taken up a new one, a life right for a Human Being. I, Raven, declare him a new Human Being, Whistling Otter.

Lisette said to each group of people, "Whistling Otter will take Rain as his wife."

These pieces of news quickened the people with hope. Though Whistling Otter kept his chest covered, they had all heard about his sacrifice and dared to hope that it went well. Perhaps it was a sign that the old powers moved among the people again. Even the name Raven had chosen, an otter calling lustily to his mate, suggested renewal.

The Sweet Medicine chief, Little Wolf, said nothing, but he thought maybe this one, schooled in the ways of the white man but deeply a man of the Tsistsistas-Suhtaio, this Whistling Otter might be cut out for leadership. In the transition to a new time, a time dominated by white men, Whistling Otter might be the best guide.

After dark, though, three of Red Cloud's Lakotas came in from Fort Robinson. They went straight to talk to Little Wolf, and their demeanor told everyone the news was bad. Whistling Otter stood in the circle with the others and listened to the horrors. Half of Morning Star's people were killed or wounded, the other half scattered across the plains and fleeing for their lives. No one needed to be told what this cold spell was doing to people who didn't have adequate clothing, much less enough blankets.

Whistling Otter, known to the whites as Smith, gathered his family and told them simply and regretfully. He had to go to Fort Robinson to minister to the wounded and the frostbitten. He promised not to let the soldiers lock him up and keep him. His marriage to Rain would have to wait until he got back.

Then Whistling Otter borrowed a horse (he had given his mounts to Raven in return for guiding him through the sacrifice) and set out through the night alone. He did not even wait for the three Lakotas, who might go back tomorrow. He must get where he was needed. Later, he promised himself, he would ask the Powers to let him do his helping not all over the Great Plains but at home, at the post on Powder River at the mouth of the Little Powder. He said in his head, I'll be home in the spring, Mother.

≈ 4 ≈

Elaine held the account book. Her hand felt the texture of the canvas cover, but her mind was out on the frozen plains, beside a gully known as Warbonnet Creek. She was seeing the wounds and hearing the blood-choked cries of the Cheyennes who died there a few days ago.

She kept her fingers away from the tattered edges of the two bullet holes that ripped through the book front to back. They cried out too eloquently what had happened to the man who created the book, Little Finger Nail. Nail had been wearing this book strapped to his back when he was shot. Shot from the front, they said.

These items were his, the account book filled with his beautiful drawings done with colored pencils, the shell-core necklace, the bird he had worn in his hair. She picked up the bird. It had looked so alive on his head, alert and watchful, and possibly capable of endowing Nail with that sweet voice, as he thought it did. Now it was just a dead thing.

Captain Wessells had permitted her to look over the belongings the soldiers had taken from the dead. Nail's book was going back to Washington City with Wessells' report, as a document that spoke for the Cheyennes. The other items would be returned to relatives, if the dead owners could be identified.

Elaine set the bird down. She tried not to picture what had happened. Since they refused to go back to Indian territory, Wessells decided to force them into submission. He locked them up. Then he deprived them of food. Then of water. And when they broke out in desperation, headed into the January night without even decent clothing and blankets, he ordered them shot down. And then tracked down.

A man as stupid as Wessells didn't deserve to live.

Elaine shook with rage.

She had to get out before Wessells came back.

She pegged out of post headquarters without even a word to the orderly. Vernon May's new leg or not, it hurt. She imagined the orderly watching her walk from behind, laughing at the cripple.

She went down a few buildings, to where Lieutenant Hancock and his wife Ruth had their quarters. The door stuck. She grabbed the door jamb, balanced on her peg, and whammed the door with her good foot. Still stuck. She kicked it furiously again. It banged open, and she burst into tears.

Luckily, no one was home. She stumped over to a chair by the wood stove, half fell into the chair, and held her palms flat to the heat, bawling.

People here had been kind to her. They had understood that she was exhausted from her long trip, by train from Omaha to Sidney and then by stage to Fort Robinson. James Hancock and Ruth had been superb, offering her a place to stay. The post surgeon, Dr. Moseley, had been gracious and considerate. Even Wessells had been respectful. No one had asked her how in hell she could go so crazy as to marry an Indian, especially an Indian who was about to make war on the entire U.S. government. And unarmed.

But it was all so awful. About half of Morning Star's Cheyennes were dead, half of one hundred and thirty human beings, and most of the others wounded or frostbitten. The post hospital was full, and more would die. The bodies of the dead were stacked outdoors, frozen, like cordwood. Hideous.

She had asked the living who was dead. Many she knew—Morning Star's son and daughter, for instance, Nail, and the woman Nail loved, Singing Cloud. Many, she was sad to acknowledge, were only names to her. How could she have lived with them, traveled with them, fought the soldiers with them, slept beside them, and never learned their names? Never once touched them when they were alive, and warm?

She believed now that Adam was not among the dead. The living Cheyennes all said that he had gone with Little Wolf, who had made a hidden camp somewhere, no one knew where, because the soldiers couldn't find it. Little Wolf's band intended to go on north when they'd recuperated, to Powder River. So Adam was not exactly safe, but he was probably alive.

A great comfort, she thought bitterly, to be a divorcée, not a widow. She supposed she would have to make herself a divorcée in the white man's legalities soon. Gay, brittle, awful word, *divorcée*.

She took control of herself. She must begin to write her report for Captain Wessells. She got up and fetched the pen and paper James Hancock was loaning her from the kitchen table. Wessells had asked her to write down her experiences with the fleeing Cheyennes, including whatever plea on their behalf she might want to put in. He would send it to Washington City with his reports, he said. She sat at the little kitchen table, reminding herself not to make a mess with the ink.

Good, she thought. Splendid. She intended to beat Wessells, the army, the Indian Service, and the entire Interior Department over the head with their own stupidity until they bled from their eyes and ears.

"Who's asking?" challenged the orderly.

Whistling Otter resisted smiling to himself. "Dr. Adam Smith Maclean."

The orderly nodded suspiciously. He surely didn't know his mouth was hanging open. And he surely thought he was being mocked by the big Indian. Doctor, indeed. "I don't know if Captain Wessells is here." The orderly wheeled and disappeared into another room with a semblance of military snap.

Well, Whistling Otter didn't look much like a doctor. He'd left his Prince Albert coat, gray trousers, and Jefferson boots at home. He was wearing a breechcloth, leggings, and moccasins, and his hair was greased. Breechcloth and leggings incensed the white folks because they showed a half-moon of ass cheek on either side. If you wore one, you were sure to get treated like a dirty savage.

The orderly held the door open and jerked his head at Whistling Otter.

"Yes," said the man behind the desk. Captain Wessells, who ordered all the butchery, was a little man, and had the bland face of an anonymous functionary.

Whistling Otter stepped close, so he could tower over the officer. "I am Dr. Adam Smith Maclean," said Whistling Otter in his best enunciation. Look at me, soldier, and you'll see what I am. But Wessells kept his head down, like he was looking at his papers. "I am a Cheyenne. I was the physician at the Cheyenne-Arapaho Agency." Now Wessells looked up at him suddenly. "I came north with the people of Little Wolf and Morning Star. I have heard that I'm wanted by the law. I didn't do it, and I want to face whatever charges are out against me."

"The Cheyenne doctor?" Wessells asked.

"Yes."

"Your father was a white-man trader on the Yellowstone?"

"Yes."

"Just a moment." Wessells jumped out and scurried into the outer room. Whistling Otter heard his voice but couldn't make out the words through the closed door.

Wessells came back into the room and stood behind his desk, awkward and uncertain. "I did have some papers on you," he said, "but not anymore. What were the charges?"

Whistling Otter shrugged. "I heard kidnapping and murder. But the girl I'm supposed to have kidnapped is my daughter, and her father died of a heart attack."

"In Kansas, is that right?"

Whistling Otter nodded.

Wessells got some papers out of a drawer and rummaged through them. He took a lot of time and didn't seem to find anything. Either he was disorganized or he was stalling. Why would he be stalling? Whistling Otter wasn't avoiding arrest.

At last the captain found a document he could read from. Eight names, he sounded off. Whistling Otter recognized Wild Hog, Tangle Hair, Left Hand, Porcupine, and Blacksmith. "Those men are being extradited to Kansas at the request of the governor. They will be tried for various crimes, including murder. They're leaving tomorrow."

Wessells looked Whistling Otter in the eye for a change. "Your name's not here. These are the only men the governor thinks there's enough evidence to get an indictment on."

So. Whistling Otter took a deep breath and let it out. So. What else he saw was that little Wessells had no more appetite for blood. Too late, little man, too late.

"May I go? I want to examine the people in the hospital, and talk with them, and bring them some comfort."

Wessells nodded slowly. Nodded again. He's going to ask me where Little Wolf is, thought Whistling Otter. And I'm going to lie baldly.

Captain Wessells said, "Of course, Doctor. Would you wait in front of headquarters first, please? Someone wants to see you."

"Ready to go now?" Ruth Hancock said from the front door. She was a bright, pert woman in her middle twenties, the sort of woman who lights up a room with her vivacity and is unaware of it. "Shangreau is ready, and I've brought the horses around."

Elaine pushed her writing materials away and nodded yes. She wasn't eager to go, her mood was too somber, but her mood wouldn't change as long as she was at Fort Robinson. Ruth had suggested that Elaine might like to see where Crazy Horse, the great Lakota leader, had been bayoneted, and later died, and hear the story of how it

happened. Elaine did want to see it before she left the
Western country for good.

Elaine accepted a boost into the saddle from the
half-breed scout who held the horses, the fellow named
Shangreau. Elaine studied his face a little. She would never
again look at a half-breed, or an Indian or a Negro, as
though he were furniture, or livestock, or landscape, as she
regrettably had done in her youth. At least Adam had given
her that. Amazing, she thought, how much you put into a
marriage, and how little you may take away from it.

They clucked to the horses and were off. It was Ruth's
idea that since Elaine was self-conscious about how she
looked walking, she should ride everywhere, even a couple
of hundred yards from quarters to the guardhouse and the
adjutant's office. "A lady's got to make 'em look," Ruth said
saucily. Ruth did make 'em look. With her wooden leg and
her hair hacked off at the shoulders, Elaine felt far past that
point, and was painfully amused that Ruth would say it.

In front of the adjutant's office, Shangreau recounted
the affair. The winter after the Greasy Grass fight, where
the Sioux and Cheyennes wiped out Custer's men two and
a half years ago, Crazy Horse had kept his people away from
the soldiers. But it had been a hungry winter, the hungriest
any but the old could remember, and in the spring Crazy
Horse had felt he had no choice but to bring his band to
Fort Robinson and surrender their arms in exchange for
rations. His people were the last of all the wild Lakotas to
surrender, except for Sitting Bull, who went to Canada
rather than capitulate.

The following September, Shangreau said, the army
asked Crazy Horse to help scout against the Nez Percés,
who were then fleeing through Montana Territory toward
Canada. Crazy Horse answered that he would fight the Nez
Percés until the last one was dead. But the interpreter,
Frank Grouard, mistranslated his words, reporting that he
threatened to fight the white troops until the last soldier
was dead. Some people thought Grouard made this mistake
intentionally because he was afraid of Crazy Horse.

General Crook then ordered Crazy Horse arrested.

When the chieftain came to Fort Robinson under assurances of his personal safety, the commanding officer, Colonel Bradley, ordered him put into the guardhouse, the little building Shangreau now nodded to. Crazy Horse was escorted toward the building under heavy guard, both soldiers and Indian police. Many other Indians were crowded around. The Indians were excitable. Crazy Horse had become a symbol among the Sioux. The young reservation Indians idolized him as the last representative of the romantic idea of the old life, of the buffalo days. To others he was a dangerous throwback, and still others were jealous of his influence. All groups were afraid something bad might happen now.

As they walked toward the jail, Crazy Horse's arms were held fast by Indian police, and the troopers had their bayonets bared and pointed at him. When Crazy Horse saw the jail cells, he made a quick motion, grabbing for a concealed knife. Alarmed, the Indian police held him tight, and one of the soldiers ran him through from behind. He died that night, and his parents took his body into the nearby hills.

"I think he wanted to die," said Shangreau simply. "I think he chose to die rather than live the new way, on the reservation."

Elaine sat her horse with her head down. For the Plains Indians, these days, nothing but tragedy. Intentions, plans, good will, effort—everything came somehow, perversely, guided by a malignant fate, to tragedy.

Then she realized someone was calling her. "Mrs. Maclean," shouted a voice. "Mrs. Maclean." It was one of the orderlies from the hospital, trotting toward them and waving. "Captain Wessells says for you to come quick."

Wessells? What for? Was he getting in a hurry for her report? Maybe she'd finally rouse the courage to spit in his face. Elaine kicked her horse to a lope—she rode much better now—and cantered back toward headquarters.

In front of the building stood Adam Smith Maclean, her husband. Former husband. Good Christ.

The first thought she was aware of was that this time

she was glad she looked down at him, because looking up at him would shake her control. Her second thought was that he couldn't see, beneath her skirt, that she'd lost a leg. She reined her horse to a stop with her legs on the side away from him so he wouldn't get any idea. She wasn't ready for this.

My God, Adam.

He wished desperately she would speak.

They stared at each other.

"Elaine," he said. Feelings roiled in him, uncertain and contradictory—they surged, out of control. That little son of a bitch Wessells, not telling him, setting him up. I could have come and gone without her knowing.

"I love you," he did not say. But it occurred to him. She looked magnificent, erect in her saddle, manifestly well healed, radiant, beautiful. She had cut her hair off to her shoulders in the traditional sign of mourning of Cheyenne women. With the hurt and dying in the hospital, and the dead stacked nearby, that gesture reached him, touched him nearly beyond his control.

Goose pimples ran down his arms.

He also did not say, "How is Sheriff Masterson?" He noticed the temptation to utter those mockingly bitter words and thought, The old Vekifs is still within Whistling Otter. And Vekifs is strong. Observe the humiliation you feel. Observe the gall. Observe that you do want to know where Masterson is, and why.

"Adam," she said belatedly.

"Why?" was the question he did not ask—why anything. He smiled a little at himself. He was in heavy surf of thought and feeling, and he chose to hide it behind the mask of his face. It was inexpressible anyway. Yet he felt a tiny calm in the violent waters, an inclination for Whistling Otter to think how terrible life truly is, and accept that.

"You look grand," he admitted.

She inclined her head graciously and smiled a little. That small smile wilted him.

He doesn't know, she thought, amazed, outraged, bitterly glad. He doesn't know or he would speak his regrets. She clung to that notion, her axis in crazy turmoil.

God, I'm humiliated. She composed her face deliberately—he must never know. He thinks I look grand—how delicious.

Adam looked more . . . Indian. Perhaps it was the breechcloth and leggings. Or perhaps it was a new maturity in his face, a gravity. Her mind flicked over what had happened to Adam in the last four and a half months, and she thought, Adam has finished growing up. Life will do that to you. She nodded to herself. It will.

"I have a new name," he said. "Whistling Otter."

"Whistling Otter," she repeated. She knew that would mean a good deal to him, a new name given by his people. Whistling Otter. She liked it. Otters were playful, and playfulness was part of what she loved in Adam. Whistling Otter. The new name felt good to her. It buried her husband, Adam Smith Maclean. Whistling Otter.

"I will take Rain as my wife," he said.

She squeezed the saddle horn. Her mind turned over once and came back to equilibrium. She stared at Adam. If he'd seen that she nearly fell off, it didn't show in his face.

"I wish you the greatest happiness," she murmured, and by an utter miracle the words came quickly, without a break in her voice. She nodded affirmatively. She thought of telling him she would grant the divorce he wanted, but dared not speak again.

Elaine looked full-eyed at the man who once was Adam, her husband, her face composed. She touched her heel to her horse and moved onward. Reeled onward.

*   *   *

Adam Smith Maclean, newly Whistling Otter, stood on the headquarters steps, weeping.

Elaine Maclean, newly Elaine Cummings, sat her horse as it walked back toward the cabin of Crazy Horse's death, weeping.

≈ 5 ≈

The rest of that day and most of the night, Elaine buried
herself in her report to Captain Wessells. She told herself
that she had done it as gracefully and beautifully as
possible. Amputated her marriage.

It seemed supremely important to let it go that way.
She assumed—hoped—that the man now known as Whistling Otter saw it the same way, and was gone. Ruth had
told her this morning the word around the fort was that he
had checked each of the patients in the hospital, spoken in
a kind way with each of them, and left the fort. She hoped
he was gone back to his people. It couldn't be truly over as
long as she feared she might see him again here at the fort.

Beautiful and noble and tragic. Yes, that felt right, the
true course of her life, profoundly . . . suitable.

At noon she had a horse brought round and carried her
report a few buildings down to headquarters—she couldn't
be seen gimping around the fort until she was sure Adam
had gone. Gone back to the Cheyennes who were hiding.
Who had hidden for three months, the entire U.S. Army
unable to find them. Gone into a distant world, his world.

An orderly tied her horse. After a look around, she
permitted the man to help her quickly up the steps and into
headquarters.

She put the report on Wessells' desk and sat to rest. It
was a dumb report. Too long, too fragmented, too full of
detail that didn't count, too barren of the impassioned
language that might count. But nothing would count. This
drama of the Cheyennes, she felt in her deepest self, must
play itself out to the awful end, and no man could alter its
course.

Perhaps the sacrifice that Morning Star's people had

made was the end. Perhaps their hot blood had cauterized the wound. She didn't know. She only knew that neither she nor anyone else could change the destiny that was working itself out.

At that moment the scout Shangreau walked into headquarters. He would know. "Has Dr. Maclean, Whistling Otter, left the fort?"

Shangreau looked at her funny. "Yes, *madame*," he said in his French way. Yes, certainly, everyone at the fort knew about the foolish white woman and Cheyenne man who had tried to make a marriage in an impossible time and been torn asunder.

"Do you know where he went?"

"Yes, *madame*. To Red Cloud."

Where the living remnant of Morning Star's people were.

She stood her full height. She was as tall as Shangreau. She felt calm, and had the wisdom not to think.

"Will you take me to him?"

Shangreau hesitated. Then, "Yes, *madame*."

Shangreau got the wagon more than halfway. Elaine wondered later whether she would have survived the trip if she had had to ride all the way. But the snow was mostly blown off the road, and not until after dark that day did Shangreau come upon a drift he couldn't drive through.

They slept there, Elaine in the wagon and Shangreau underneath it. He treated her curiously, with great delicacy, as a superstitious Frenchman would treat a virgin, or a saint. Elaine felt not a bit like either. In the morning the scout still couldn't find a way to get the wagon around the drift, so they untied the saddle horses from the back and left the wagon where it sat.

She wasn't worried, at first, about whether she could ride that last twenty-some-odd miles. She was terrified that Adam might go on today, that he might greet his people and

minister to them briefly and go back to the hidden camp of
Little Wolf. If all the army scouts couldn't find that camp,
she and Shangreau certainly had no chance. And not to see
him now would be . . . beyond contemplation.

She didn't think about whether he would take her
back. She didn't imagine what words, loving or cruel, he
might say to her. She did not ask herself whether she might
even have to share Adam with Rain as one of two wives. She
did not ask herself whether she could bear to live as a
Cheyenne, and endure whatever was theirs to endure. She
simply went, bearing a gift unconditionally.

She sat her horse in the middle of the circle of Red
Cloud's lodges. "Go find Dr. Maclean, please," she said to
Shangreau. The little guide dismounted with a word, only
a kind of pungent look, picketed his horse, and walked off.

They had ridden into the middle of the circle of lodges,
open on the east, in the traditional manner. Lodges not of
buffalo hides but tattered canvas, she noticed. The people
here wouldn't get their meat by hunting buffalo but by
going to the agency on issue day. The children around her,
trying not to look curious about a white woman, were
gaunt.

Yes, she would have to walk soon. She couldn't say the
words to Adam from this height. But she didn't have to let
these children see her limp on her wooden leg yet. After
most of a day in the saddle, her stump felt like a boil in need
of lancing. She would walk terribly, gimping her worst.

Walk she meant to do, regardless. But she could rest a
moment first.

Whistling Otter stepped out slowly, tentatively,
among the lodges, which were circled as always, the sign of

community. Shangreau followed, he of the unbelievable message, followed like a dog, friendly and curious.

Yes, it was Elaine, sitting a sidesaddle. Elaine. He walked toward her, hurrying but hesitating, half stumbling, uncertain. She held up a hand to stop him from coming closer. She stood up on her stirrup with her left leg and dismounted awkwardly but with a determined air onto a . . . peg? Immediately she strode toward him with a show of vigor, limping conspicuously on, by Christ, a wooden leg.

Dumbstruck, he let her come.

Several steps away his wife stopped and looked at him, in what state of feeling he could not say. She wobbled a tad on her peg. "Adam, I love you," she said distinctly. "I was cowardly yesterday, and could not tell you. I was afraid for you to see me . . . as I am."

She took a deep breath and plunged ahead. "Whistling Otter, I love you. I am yours. Wherever you go, I will go."

Adam was stock still one moment and running full tilt at her the next. He swept her up in his arms and lifted her high, eye-high, and looked at her face. He looked at her peg, and back at her face, agony in his eyes and salt tears on his brown cheeks.

Elaine leaned forward and kissed his tears away.

≈ 6 ≈

The Human Beings under the Sweet Medicine chief, Little Wolf, broke camp during the thaw in late January and headed for Powder River.

Among these people were Whistling Otter, his wife Elaine, his mother Lisette, his daughter Hindy, his cousin Rain, and her infant son Big Soldier.

They moved slowly, for they had not much strength. After some days they passed near the sacred mountain, Nowah'wus, which the whites called Bear Butte. Little Wolf asked them to wait three days while he fasted and meditated on the mountain. When he came back, he sang a song:

> Great Powers, hear me,
> The people are broken and scattered.
> Let the winds bring the few seeds together,
> To grow strong again, in a good new place.

One day, not quite yet the time Whistling Otter figured must be the vernal equinox, they saw geese arrowing north, and they came onto Powder River. The ice was breaking up on the river already. A few days, thought Whistling Otter, and home. These mornings the ache to see his mother Annmarie raged through him like a fever.

But the people were still in jeopardy, and sign of soldiers was everywhere.

One day the Human Beings captured some scouts from Lieutenant White Hat Clark from Keogh, the fort at the mouth of Powder River. They knew White Hat as a good man, and their friend. Little Wolf told the scouts to have White Hat bring the soldiers up. Then he found some naturally fortified high ground, where a fight would cost the soldiers dearly.

When White Hat arrived, Little Wolf went out to meet with him alone, wearing a blue blanket that was almost new, and his peace medal, and as always carrying the bundle of sweet medicine under his arm. He told the people that he did not know whether he would come back, or what they should do if he did not.

White Hat said he would recommend that the Cheyennes be sent to the Arapaho and Shoshone reservation in Wyoming Territory, but could promise nothing. For now he would feed the people well and guarantee that no one would be hurt. Probably he could hire some of the men as scouts. In return he asked the people to give up their guns and horses.

It seemed not enough. The people talked about it among themselves. They believed the words Little Wolf had spoken so often, "The only Indian never killed is the Indian never caught." But they ate well.

Then they asked White Hat to recommend that the Cheyennes get a reservation of their own, here in their home country. He said he could promise nothing, but would work hard for such a reservation. The people talked some more. Little Wolf still felt reluctant, but surely he had to trust some white man, somewhere, sometime. The people left their high ground and rode downstream with White Hat.

The flight of the Cheyennes from Indian territory to the Powder River country had ended. Of nearly three hundred who started, here one hundred and fourteen still walked the earth. On the Pine Ridge Reservation of the Sioux, a few dozen more lived.

The man known to some as Whistling Otter, to others as Smith, and to his wife as Adam, walked out of Maclean's trading post and went down to the river.

It was the first morning he had awakened at the post. He had hugged his mother and inspected the post where he would probably spend most of the rest of his life. It seemed good, a stout structure of logs, like his father would have wanted. It would have enough trade, now that the Cheyennes were back home.

Smith and his two mothers and his wife stayed up half the night trading news and reminiscing. Annemarie told everyone that their friend Peddler was alive and well, still walking all over Indian country peddling his sewing goods at nearly eighty years old—he would surely be here again this summer. They were obliged to tell her that her lifelong friend Jim Sykes, the Man Who Didn't Stir Air When He Walked, had died of the shaking sickness in the south.

Smith sat down on the bank of Powder River, below the mouth of the Little Powder. He loved rivers. He had been raised beside a river, the Yellowstone, a little to the northwest of here. He had spent the summers and autumns of his youth near this river. He loved them both. He wanted to live in a country rich in great, throbbing rivers, this country. Soon he would make a pilgrimage up the Yellowstone and visit once more the enchanted kingdom of his youth, the Yellowstone country, which others had recently discovered and nominated the first national park. A country grand with flowing waters.

Powder River was now in its spring flood, cold, its banks full. He sat down on the bank and stripped off his clothes. Naked, he dived into the river.

The cold shocked him at first, but he was used to it from many years of this springtime ritual. He stroked out toward the current, and felt it gather him up and sweep him along, and being to roll him, turn him over . . .

Smith kicked like hell and got into the eddy. He'd nearly forgotten how powerful these spring-flood rivers were in the north country. He got out, spread his blanket, and lay down to feel the warm spring sun on his body.

Lying there, basking in the sun, a little sleepy, perhaps he began to dream, or perhaps merely to imagine. In his imagination he stroked along in the river, underwater, his eyes closed, and felt himself change. He wasn't clear on how he changed. It was as though his body had melted into the river, the way the spring ice melts, and becomes part of the river. Part not only of the river, this time, but part of everything in the river, part of the fishes and crabs and snakes and turtles, and even the watercress and the algae, and even the microscopic particles of life that are in the water, and are the water. It was as though the cells of his body intermingled with the very cells of the river beings, and all became one huge creature, breathing as one, resoundingly alive, resoundingly fecund, infinitely virile and strong. He felt the water flowing through him, making him move, flow, undulate, the river bringing motion and rhythm to him, everything together, everything the same life, fathered by the sun, mothered by the river, all of the same, flesh of one flesh, soul of one soul.

He abided with these things, and was of them, and they of him, one single, grand dance.

Smith smiled at himself in his daydream. When he was done napping, he would go find Elaine and take her to their bedroom and make love with her heatedly, as they had done last night. Right now he was sleepy.

He dreamed once more. This time he was an otter. He felt so lucky, to dream of being an otter. He played in the water. He splashed. He whirled. He swam in loops. He danced. He jumped into the air and felt the sun on his skin. He whistled. He laughed. He played forever.

≈ Historical Note ≈

The Unites States government, perhaps in shame, gave the Cheyenne people the reservation they asked for, in their home country. They live there today, many of them in the way taught them by Sweet Medicine and Buffalo Calf Woman, honoring Maheo.

≈   Afterword   ≈

The story of the flight of the northern Cheyennes from the agency in Indian territory to their homeland in 1878 and 1879 is well known to the world. I have tried here to recreate the flight, its events, and principal personages like Little Wolf, Morning Star, and Little Finger Nail, with scrupulous fidelity.

Likewise I have presented the culture and history of the Cheyenne people, whom I admire, as faithfully as I can.

The story of my imaginary characters, Smith, Elaine, Sings Wolf, and the others, takes place within this historical and cultural framework. They did not exist, but people like them did.

Powder River is the sequel to my novel *The Yellowstone*, the first book of the RIVERS WEST series. Readers can find there the story of Smith's father, the Scots trader Mac Maclean, and his attempt to create a fur empire for his half-breed wives and children.

—Winfred Blevins,
Jackson, Wyoming
May, 1989

If you enjoyed Win Blevins's epic tale THE POW-
DER RIVER, be sure to look for the next installment
of the RIVERS WEST saga at your local bookstore.
Each new volume sweeps you along on a voyage of
exploration along one of the great rivers of North
America with the courageous pioneers who chal-
leneged the unknown.

*Here's an exciting preview of the next
book in Bantam's unique new historical series*

RIVERS WEST: BOOK 6
THE RUSSIAN RIVER
By Gary McCarthy
Author of THE COLORADO

---

*On sale February 1991
wherever Bantam Books are sold.*

PROLOGUE

Anton Rostov wiped the stinging salt spray from his eyes. He stared out across the choppy and frigid Gulf of Alaska and felt the hardening westerly wind cut at his sealskin parka. It was almost sunset and the light was dying, barely sufficient to penetrate the gray Alaskan fog. All of his attention was fixed on the Aleuts and their two-man skin kayaks called baidarkas.

There were only five boats remaining in the water but they had been hunting since daybreak and had managed to harpoon only twelve sea otters, not enough yet to be allowed to return to the big two-masted Russian schooner, not even in the face of the weather front that was sweeping in from the storm-tossed Pacific.

Anton glanced to the foredeck where his captain, Vasilii Tarakanov, stood as rooted as the mast. Tarakanov was in his early fifties, stout, double-chinned and single-minded. His heavy beard was flattened against his face by the wind and his gloved hands clenched the oaken wheel. His expression revealed a hardness born of the many years he had sailed these treacherous, stormy waters for the Russian American Company out of Sitka, Alaska. Years before, when the otter had been plentiful off the Aleutian Islands to the north, he had been shipwrecked one winter and survived six months of bone-numbing darkness. His hair had turned white and his teeth had fallen out but he had survived, and the company had rewarded him with a Russian medal and a ship of his own to command.

He will not call the Aleuts in, Anton told himself, not

even when the sleet comes and the ocean spray freezes their faces and blinds them. Not even when they are like little bobbing blocks of ice. No, not even then will he call them in.

One of the harpoon wielding hunters suddenly motioned toward the south and the Aleuts churned their double-bladed paddles silently across the dark, roiling waters.

"Captain," Anton shouted, "I see otter to the south!"

Tarakanov purposely, stubbornly, chose to ignore him and the Aleut who were flying across the water toward their quarry. Anton felt his frozen cheeks warm with embarrassment and anger. He forced himself to pivot toward the rail and grip it with his gloved hands. Of course the captain would not recognize him! The ignorant old fool was too proud to acknowledge that a man half his age might have better eyes.

A full two minutes ticked by and the Aleuts almost disappeared into the heaving sea that was threatening to swallow them whole. Anton seethed. He and Tarakanov had disliked each other from the first moment. It was a matter of class distinction—Tarakanov lacked it from birth, Anton possessed it from birth. Their mutual dislike was that simple and that insurmountable.

Just when the Aleuts were disappearing into the face of the storm, Tarakanov turned the wheel and the sloop sluggishly rolled about to port. Its sails caught the wind and the vessel yawed hugely then drove its bow deep into the water and began to race after the Aleuts until the baidarkas were finally sighted about a mile ahead.

Anton moved to the bow as the Aleuts fought to bring themselves into the killing formation just downwind of what appeared to be a large group of sea otter. It was all the Aleuts could do to keep from capsizing. They were clothed in the waterproof skin of the sea lion and each one had lashed his jacket to a ring around the small opening in which he sat so that not a single drop of water could enter his baidarka. It had never ceased to amaze Anton how these men could sit motionlessly for ten to fifteen hours, waiting for a kill.

But nothing was motionless now. The howling wind grew louder and stronger by the minute until it was blowing the baidarkas around like leaves on a pond. Despite their best efforts, the rear paddlers were having an impossible time attempting to bring their little skin boats close to the otter so that the harpoon men could strike with their long bone spears. The otter had dived but they would soon be forced to the surface.

"Look at the spear throwers!" a sailor shouted into the wind. "See how they hover like a dog at the first scent of game."

Anton said nothing. He stared, fascinated by the drama, even though he knew the inevitable outcome. The hunters, raised from small children to survive and kill on the water, almost never missed their throws. And now they forged into position, spears held motionless until, suddenly, the otter popped to the surface, just their heads and shoulders pushing above the water.

Anton did not hear the Aleut imitate the distressed cry of a baby sea otter but he did see the adult animals turn with alarm. In that instant, the spears were hurled from their throwing sticks and Anton almost felt the pain of the otter as the bone spears sank deep into their bodies. Two of the otters died instantly but the other three dove again, pulling the thin harpoon cord behind them so that a skin air bladder traced their futile efforts to escape as they swam in dying confusion. The Aleut paddlers followed the skin bags across the stormy ocean as the hunters pulled their kills back to the baidarkas where the otter would be pelted in minutes and their stripped corpses thrown back into the sea.

"Sir," the sailor asked Anton, "will the captain pull for Sitka?"

"He'd better," Anton shouted. "And we'd better get those hunters off the water in a hurry!"

"Going to be a bad one before nightfall," the sailor yelled as the vessel wallowed in the heavy sea. They were being pushed farther from the Aleuts who were still reeling in their kills. The storm intensified with demented fury until the Aleut were in deadly peril. Three of the baidarka paddlers were attempting to chase the ship but two were still reeling in their catch, in spite of the fact that they were being driven farther out to sea.

"He has to move in closer to them!" Anton shouted. Forgetting himself, he stumbled across the sea-washed deck to the captian and shouted. "You're to far from them!"

In answer, Tarakanov cursed his name and ordered him to lower the two lifeboats. Anton shook his head. They were still too far away for that. In these heavy seas, the lifeboats would be smashed against the hull and crack like broken eggs against a skillet before they could be used to bring the Aleuts back on board with their baidarkas.

"Damn you, more sail!" Anton shouted. "We have to have more sail!"

In answer, Tarakanov's gloved fist lashed out and struck Anton across the face. "Rostov, go below!" he commanded.

"No! We must move closer!"

Anton fought his way back to the rail. Three baidarkas had somehow closed the distance, though getting them on board was going to be almost impossible because the Russian sloop was crashing in and out of the sea and sending up huge geysers of water.

But the other two baidarkas were disappearing into the ocean. They still had not gotten their kills reeled in, kills which were acting like a sea anchor.

Anton saw one of those baidarkas suddenly flip and, though he had seen that happen many times before, this was different. The power of the sea tore the Aleut's parkas from the rings of their craft and water flooded into the little vessel which disappeared like a knife dropped in water.

"They're gone!" he shouted in despair and, before he could turn toward the captain, the second baidarka also was breeched by an immense wave and it never reappeared.

Even in the face of the raging storm, everyone was

stunned for an instant. The Aleuts that were still afloat had stopped pelting their kill and were now paddling for their lives.

"Lower the life boats!" Anton shouted, struggling forward across the watery deck and directing the sailors who moved with skill and grim determination. Four Aleut hunters gone in just minutes! More had been lost during the entire winter! There would be hell to pay in Sitka and, if the remaining six were also drowned, every man on this ship would be held accountable.

Anton twisted in the wind and shouted, "Closer! Bring the ship around into the wind!"

But in answer, Tarakanov raised his gloved fist and shook it as one of the sails was ripped free and began to snap like shot in the wind and the schooner seemed to stagger and tremble with each crashing wave.

There were two lifeboats, one on the port and one on the starboard side. They were solid and seaworthy and, normally, the light skin baidarkas would be loaded into these lifeboats and then hauled up on deck. But now Anton knew the baidarkas were lost. All that mattered was to try to get the six Aleuts topside so that the captain could make toward the nearest sheltered harbor.

"Slow the ropes!" Anton shouted, noting how recklessly the lifeboats were being lowered.

In their panic and because the deck was rolling so badly, the ropes were in danger of becoming hopelessly tangled as the heavy portside lifeboat began to slam against the ship's hull.

Anton knew the lifeboat could not possibly survive more than three or four minutes of such brutal pounding. It hung about eight feet below the deck and, even as he watched, the bow and stern ropes tangled.

The sailors he commanded stood in fixed horror and the Aleuts below stared upward with the look of dead men. Anton tore off his gloves, grabbed the bow line and leapt over the railing to slide down a rope that felt like an icicle. He struck the lifeboat, swung out over the angry water and nearly tumbled into the sea before a foaming mountain of water spun him back against the hull of the ship, then raked him along the barnacle-crusted side. Gagging, he was torn back out to sea, then found himself suddenly bobbing in the water as another monstrous wave gathered off the ocean floor.

Anton was amazed to see the lifeboat, filled with sea water and missing its oars, still dangling just below his feet. He dimly heard the cries of the Aleuts as he dropped into the boat, drew his knife and slashed at the tangled stern and bow ropes. When they severed, the lifeboat dropped into the ocean and the Aleuts paddled furiously toward him while the sailors up on deck hurled clear lines downward. They knew as well as Anton that, if the lifeboat was not linked to the ship, it would be swept out to sea and swamped.

Another wall of water sent Anton and his lifeboat soaring upward. The lifeboat spun crazily, nearly tipped over and then balanced delicately on the crest of the swell before it was dropped with such speed that Anton felt his stomach flop. He saw one of the baidarkas splinter against the ship and spill Aleuts into the water.

Anton twisted around to see the other two baidarkas spinning in a maelstrom of white foam and then he felt the sea again gather itself to strike. He shoved his legs under the bench of the lifeboat, took a deep breath and held on for his life as the wall of water flung the lifeboat back against the hull. The boat shook itself like a wet dog and struggled to stay afloat. Anton felt the mighty pull of sea all around him and his right leg seemed to snap below the knee. He roared in pain, his words were torn from his lips by the wind and when he opened his eyes, he was amazed to see two Aleuts floundering in the boat beside him, calling for their companions to abandon their baidarkas and jump for the lifeboat.

Anton shouted, "Come on!"

Two of the four jumped but missed and were swept out to sea. In their heavy parkas, they were visible for only an instant before they sank. The other pair drove their baidarka's straight for the hull and threw themselves at the lifeboat. Anton, with his leg still twisted peculiarly beneath the seat, blindly caught one of the Aleuts just as another wave struck. His fingernails bit into the Aleut's parka as the bones of his leg splintered.

While he lay drowning in pain and water, the Aleuts, men born to the sea, somehow found and tied new ropes to the lifeboat fore and aft so that its broken remains could be drawn up to the rail, then swung onto the deck.

Anton was upended and dropped unceremoniously to the deck as another wave struck and sent him skidding into a deck stanchion. He hung onto it until his fingers were pried away and he was dragged to a hatch, then shoved downward into the galley below where he lay in two inches of sloshing water and heard the ship inwardly moaning and groaning like an old man forced into hard labor.

He tried to get to his feet but the ship rolled so violently that a barrel broke free of its lashing and was hurled through the darkness to pin him against a bulkhead. Anton felt the weight of the barrel crushing his chest. He struggled then slipped into unconsciousness as the barrel rolled away and then spun crazily to the motion of the ship and the sea.

Anton awoke in Sitka and he lay in the hospital for two days while the doctors argued about cutting off his right leg. As soon as he understood the discussion, he asked the patient next to him for a knife and when the doctors returned to cut off the leg, he told them that, if they tried, he would cut off their balls.

Six weeks later, he had carved his own crutches and stood before Governor Alexander Baranov, the crusty old Lord of the Pacific, who almost single-handledly had won Alaska and made the Russian American Company the most successful fur-hunting enterprise in the North Pacific. Baranov had himself been shipwrecked and had fought savagely to claim this land. He dreamed of wresting Northern California from the weak Spaniards who had not the Russian heart or determination to win the vast wealth in fur and timber that ran unbroken from the wild Aleutian Islands all the way south to Yerba Buena and the great harbor of San Francisco.

Anton had seen Baranov the empire builder before, but never in his castle that overlooked Sitka and the bay. The governor was in his early sixties and, because he was physically unimposing, it was difficult to believe all the legends that were associated with his name. But they were legends built on facts and results. Anton did not doubt for a single instant that Baranov was still indomitable even in his old age.

Anton nervously shifted his weight. His broken leg still ached but he took comfort in knowing that his lieutenant's uniform was neatly pressed and his black boots polished to a lustrous sheen. His dark, heavy beard made his face appear older than his twenty-one years.

"My dear, young man," Alexander Baranov began, dipping his bald head ever so slightly so that the Russian medallion that signified his lofty position bobbed against his chest, "I am sure you know Captain Ivan Kuskov?"

"I do." Anton bowed with respect toward a peg legged man twenty years his senior. "We met when I arrived last year."

"Yes," Baranov said, "then you must be aware of the immense regard I hold for Ivan. He is my most trusted lieutenant. A man bold, courageous and . . . of course . . . loyal to me . . . and Mother Russia."

"As *I* will prove to be," Anton said, gazing at both men.

"Sit down," Baranov said. "Ivan, would you be kind enough to pour us refreshments."

Despite his wooden leg, Kuskov moved with surprising agility and grace toward the small wooden cabinet from which he produced crystal glasses and vodka. He poured generously and when he, Anton and the governor had their drinks in their hands, their glasses were raised in toast. "To California," Baranov said.

"To California," Anton repeated even as he wondered at the strange toast.

Glasses were refilled and Anton swallowed feeling the

heat of the white liquor warm his extremities and nibble away the pain in his mending leg.

"My dear lieutenant," Baranov began, "are you aware that Captain Tarakanov has filed charges of insubordination and attempted mutiny against you?"

Anton almost dropped his glass. "No, sir," he managed to say. "I have not been apprised of that fact. I was discharged from the hospital just this morning."

"On my orders," Baranov said with a beneficent smile. "You see, young man, I have a special interest in you because of your father. He was one of our great heroes, was he not?"

"He was," Anton said quickly. "But. . . ."

"And he was also a friend of a very close friend." Baranov drained his vodka and Kuskov was quick to keep his glass full. The governor's assistant was himself a respected man and, even though he was acting as a subordinate, Anton was sharply aware that the man somehow retained an immense dignity.

"I want," Baranov was saying, "to help you out of this unfortunate misunderstanding you have had with Captain Tarakanov. I am sure I can do this if you wish."

Anton found himself nodding rapidly. "Of course, Governor. But I beg you to understand that I was not mutinous. I was only attempting to save the Aleut hunters. You see. . . ."

"The governor has heard all about it," Kuskov interrupted, cutting Anton into silence. "The sailors have been interrogated. Testimony has been taken."

There was a long silence.

"And?" Anton whispered when he could no longer be still.

"And," Kuskov said, "if the governor wished, you could be shot this very day."

Anton's glass slipped and almost spilled to the floor. He blinked and wondered if he had heard correctly. "The sailors," he stammered, "they spoke against me?"

"No," Kuskov said. "Quite the contrary. And the hunters

said that you saved them from a sure death. But their loyalties are of no interest in the case. You defied Captain Tarakanov's orders to go below deck. You went overboard without permission and you risked your life—a Russian officer's life—for that of Indians."

Anton did not fail to notice that the governor was watching him with great interest. "Sir, as you have said, my father was a military hero. A man of honor. I came here to do him honor and I would never disgrace my family name."

Baranov nodded and steepled his short, chubby fingers. "Anton, you have in your veins the blood of fighting soldiers—not sailors. There is a difference. Did you know that I was raised the son of a shopkeeper in a village near Finland? And that before I was sent here, I was a glass-maker and then a fur trader?"

"No sir."

"I come from very humble beginnings." Baranov blinked. He had a large, protruding forehead and a long, hooked nose that made him look somehow scholarly. "Yes," he mused aloud, "very humble. Unlike yourself. But unlike Captain Tarakanov, I do not envy or fear those born higher than myself. And unlike the captain, I appreciate men of action and courage."

Anton hoped he was receiving a compliment but was not sure so he did not even dare to relax.

"You were," Baranov continued, "both mutinous and foolish with your life, but you are the kind of man that is not easily found. I have, if you are interested, a way out of the unfortunate situation in which you now find yourself."

"I would like to know of it," Anton said with a gulp. "I would rather die than disgrace my family or country."

"I know that," Baranov told him, leaning his chin on his steepled fingers and looking very pensive. "And it seems obvious to Ivan and me that the Aleut hunters are now ready to die for you. Have you not found many small gifts from them each morning beside your hospital bed?"

"Yes," Anton admitted. "But the gifts . . . well, they

embarrass me. You see, Governor, the Aleuts would have saved my life had the circumstances been different."

"No," Kuskov said, sitting up erect, "not before the storm when you went overboard to save them. But now they would. And I am told you speak their language and Spanish very well."

"I studied Spanish, also Aleut and other languages, but. . . ."

"Then," Baranov said with a beatific smile, "we have a proposition for you."

Anton pushed himself to his feet where he stood straight and balanced as he waited, listening to his heart beat as loudly and frighteningly as the drums of the hostile Tlingits Indians who lived nearby. "Command me to do whatever you will."

"Of course," Baranov said, himself standing. "But I ask, never command. And now I ask that you be placed in charge of the Aleut hunters that Captain Kuskov will be taking south with him into Alta California where he will establish a fort, a foothold in Spanish America which will be held against all enemies of Russia." Baranov's voice shook with the passion of his conviction. "A foothold that will prove to be our anchor in America and which will not only feed Sitka and Kodiak but also yield the greatest kill of sea otter that the Russian American Company has ever harvested."

"My leg," Anton stammered. "I am afraid that I might be found wanting."

Kuskov shook his head. "You will heal soon. You are the man that I want to assist me."

Anton felt his cheeks warm with pride. "You will not regret the trust you place in me. Either of you."

Baranov chuckled and signaled for more vodka to be poured. "Of course we will not. It is the ability to judge the mettle of men that determines who will succeed in authority and who will fail. I judge you have the steel of your father. You have won the undying loyalty of the Aleut. Without them, there could be no harvest of otter. You will command them, reward them . . . and yes, punish those who slack from their work."

Anton nodded. "When will we sail?"

"In one week."

Anton swayed. "And how long will I be in California?"

"Until," the governor said in a flat, uncompromising voice, "your life or the need for your services ends."

"Yes sir!"

The governor and the captain relaxed and both smiled, satisfied that they had made the right choice.

Baranov's pale blue eyes seemed to glitter as he pushed back from his desk, raised another glass of vodka and said fervently, "To the conquest of Northern America for Russia!"

Anton repeated the toast and threw the vodka down his gullet to discover that the anticipation of what lay ahead was even more heady than Russian vodka.

In The Tradition of *Wagons West* and *The Spanish Bit Saga* Comes:

RIVERS WEST

TERRY C. JOHNSTON

Winner of the prestigious Western Writer's award, Terry C. Johnston brings you his award-winning saga of mountain men Josiah Paddock and Titus Bass who strive together to meet the challenges of the western wilderness in the 1830's.

☐ 25572 **CARRY THE WIND–Vol. I** $4.95

☐ 26224 **BORDERLORDS–Vol. II** $4.95

☐ 28139 **ONE-EYED DREAM–Vol. III** $4.95

The final volume in the trilogy begun with *Carry the Wind* and *Borderlords*, ONE-EYED DREAM is a rich, textured tale of an 1830's trapper and his protegé, told at the height of the American fur trade.

Following a harrowing pursuit by vengeful Arapaho warriors, mountain man Titus "Scratch" Bass and his apprentice Josiah Paddock must travel south to old Taos. But their journey is cut short when they learn they must return to St. Louis...and old enemies.

Look for these books wherever Bantam books are sold, or use this handy coupon for ordering:

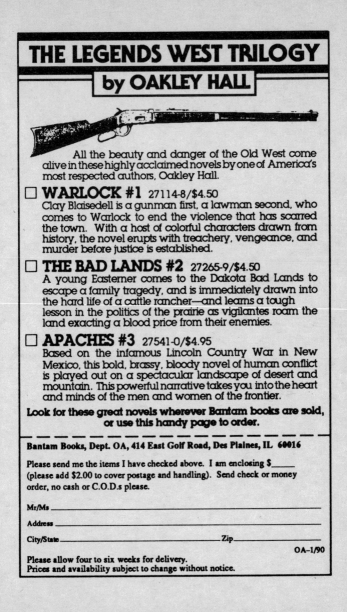